In the Midst

ജ്ര

Debra Jenkins

This book is a work of fiction. Names, characters, places, and incidents are the product of the author's imagination or are used fictitiously. Any resemblance to actual events, locales, or persons, living or dead, is coincidental.

ISBN: 9781516829934

Library of Congress Control Number: 2015913068
CreateSpace Independent Pub Platform, North Charleston, SC

www.debrajenkins.net

Acknowledgments

I would like to thank:

God – for the inspiration to write and share this story.

My parents *Earl & Mildred Woods* –
for making Gabby Mountain a part of our lives.

Friends and family for allowing me to reflect your courage, strength, and humor to bring these fictional characters to life.

My fellow teachers and students for encouraging words.

Mohan – for showing the loyalty of a canine.

Kristie Coggins – for helping me get started.

Judy Haun – for providing feedback and encouragement.

Althea Spineeta with Curls in Her Hair (America Star Books (December 7, 2010) Dicie Kimsey Headrick

Highland Piano Studios mentioned with permission of Patrick Lee Hebert, Alcoa, Tennessee.

Trinity Chiropractic mentioned with permission of Dr. Evan Butcher, Maryville, Tennessee.

Happy Hair Fashions mentioned with permission of Sarah Woods, Franklin, North Carolina.

Cover photos used with permission of Garrett Woods and Ashley Harper Fontenot. Photography by Emily Crisp.

***In the Midst
of life's storms…***

***The Lord your God is with you,
He is mighty to save.
He will take great delight in you,
He will quiet you with His love,
He will rejoice over you with
singing.***

Zephaniah 3:17

Music

Each chapter is named for a song reflecting the emotion of the chapter. Instrumentals, by Highland Piano Studios Artists, have been compiled into an album.

www.debrajenkins.net

All music produced by Patrick Lee Hebert –
Highland Piano Studios ℗, Alcoa, Tennessee (2016.)

Living with a Broken Heart 2016

1. *Living with A Broken Heart* © 2014 Patrick Lee Hebert
2. *Waterfalls Within* © 2014 Jodi Thiele
3. *Secluded Glade* © 2016 Patrick Lee Hebert II
4. *Teary* © 2012 Sierra Hanson Arr. Patrick Lee Hebert © 2016
5. *Tattered Memories* © 2016 Patrick Lee Hebert II
6. *Yesterday's Gone* © 2016 Patrick Lee Hebert
7. *Blue Skies* © 2008 Patrick Lee Hebert
8. *Looking Through the* Rain © 2016 Patrick Lee Hebert II
9. *Simple Notions* © 1998 Patrick Lee Hebert & Chris Lonsberry
10. *Restless Days* © 2008 Patrick Lee Hebert
11. *For Susan* © 2016 Patrick Lee Hebert
12. *Then* © 2016 Patrick Lee Hebert
13. *Through a Child's Eyes* © 1994 Patrick Lee Hebert
14. *For Emily* © 2016 Patrick Lee Hebert II
15. *Escape* © 2014 Jodi Thiele
16. *Without You* © 2016 Patrick Lee Hebert II
17. *Insignificance*© 1994 Patrick Lee Hebert
18. *Peace*© 2001 Patrick Lee Hebert
19. *Soul Search*© 2001 Patrick Lee Hebert
20. *Changes* © 2014 Jodi Thiele
21. *Yesterday's Gone (Orchestral)* © 2016 Patrick Lee Hebert

For

My husband ~ David

***Jonathan, Abi, Misty, Michael,
Morgan, Breyer, John Michael,
Briley, Rachel***

~my family~

Prologue

"**W**alton, *please* slow down," Dalaina Evan urged her husband.

"You said you were anxious to get Eloree home." His tone told her he had drunk too much at the governor's mansion.

"Let me drive for a while," she offered.

"Nothing's wrong with my driving." His jaw tightened.

"Dear, please understand. Tomorrow's Easter Sunday." She placed her hand on his arm. "Eloree'll be singing in the children's choir at church--she's counting on you being there."

He glanced at their sleeping daughter in the backseat. "Eloree should be honored she was invited to an egg hunt on the lawn of the governor's mansion. Not many seven-year-olds get that opportunity."

"Surely your political agenda can wait until Monday."

"Political agenda," he sneered. "There you go again. If you'd show support for me, Eloree could be rolling Easter eggs on the White House lawn."

"Walton Andrew Evan, I've always supported you." She crossed her arms--fed-up with his overbearing tirades.

'When I run for president, you'll probably vote against me."

Dalaina willed her voice to sound calm. "Did you forget how pleased I was when you won the senate seat?"

"Then agree for Eloree to go to boarding school. Come with me on the campaign trail."

"Walton, I *do not* want our daughter raised by someone else."

"You're being irrational about Eloree. You had no qualms about Terrance attending boarding school."

"That was all your idea. I didn't want our son to leave home at twelve years old." Dalaina felt heat rising in her cheeks.

"Look at him now--graduating in a few weeks and going on to serve his country—like *I* did."

"And it's *you* who insists he go into the military. He's only eighteen and trying to earn *your* approval."

"One day you'll see I was right all along."

"Why can't you be a supportive father, and stop pushing our children to do what *you* want?" She pushed back a strand of wavy auburn hair.

"This is ridiculous." Walton bore down on the horn and swerved around a slower car.

"Enough, Walton. You'll wake Eloree, and you're scaring me."

Dalaina heard the child rousing in the back seat. "Mama, are we home yet?"

"No, Sweetie." She shifted and turned to face her daughter.

"Mommy, I'm cold."

Dalaina unbuckled and leaned over the seat to drape her sweater over Eloree. "Go back to sleep."

"I want my bunny with the purple bow."

Dalaina leaned farther and placed the bunny in Eloree's outstretched hands. "I love you, precious Eloree Elise."

"I love you, too, Mama. Sing *Fur Elise* to me."

Dalaina started to hum the familiar tune.

Walton nudged her shoulder. "Turn around and buckle up, Dalaina."

"In a minute," she whispered. "Eloree is so beautiful when she's --"

Dalaina's words were cut short by the screeching sounds of metal on metal and an impact which hurled her through the windshield.

The last words she heard were, "Mama--Mama."

Living with a Broken Heart

꧁ 1 ꧂

Thirteen Years Later

Franklin, North Carolina

Hello," Eloree's voice echoed through the entryway of Gabby Mountain Stables.

"Sorry I didn't hear you drive up." A tall girl with a long, dark ponytail stepped from a corner stall.

Tension rose in Eloree's chest. She knew she shouldn't be here, but the girl smiled down at her and went on, "You must be Pepper's owner. Jesse said you might come today. By the way, I'm Jenna, his sister."

"I've never been here before."

"Was Jesse expecting you?"

"No, but I'd like to ride."

"Okay—well." Jenna hesitated. "Jesse will be back in about an hour. You're welcome to wait."

"I don't have much time." Eloree raked strands of wavy auburn hair over the side of her face.

"Have much riding experience?" Jenna's tone sounded doubtful.

"I've trained with the U.S. Equestrian Team." Eloree tugged at the sleeve of her jacket.

"Sounds like you've done some serious riding." Jenna's eyes widened.

"Some would say so." Eloree focused on the toe of her boot—aware of Jenna's questioning stare. "Do you have a horse for me?"

She held her breath and dug her heel into the loose sawdust.

Jenna sighed and reached for a clipboard. "You can take a short ride on my mare, Nantahala."

"Thank you." Eloree reached for the clipboard, glad to have something in her hands.

"Basically, this form states when riding on Gabby Mountain, you're riding at your own risk with no monetary amount being charged. You're simply our guest."

"So, I don't pay?"

Jenna pointed to a rough-hewn wooden box, nailed to the wall. "If folks are blessed and want to be a blessing, they can leave a donation."

Eloree scrawled her signature and handed the clipboard to Jenna, hoping she wouldn't recognize her as the daughter of despised Senator Walton Evan. She held her breath as Jenna stared at the form.

"How do you pronounce your name?"

"El will be fine. I'll grab my wallet and put a donation in your box."

"Better get your ride in first." Jenna shrugged. "It may rain."

"Sure." Eloree's face tightened and her pulse rose, knowing she was going to finally do something--spur of the moment--not planned by her father or his staff.

"Let's go get Nanta." Jenna grabbed a bridle from a peg, and Eloree followed her to the fence. Jenna gave a resounding whistle. Nanta lifted her head, slung her long, flowing mane and trotted to the gate.

Eloree stroked Nanta's mane. "What breed is she?" "Palomino and Quarter Horse." Jenna slid the bridle over the horse's head. "Of all the horses we've ever had, she's my favorite."

"She's gorgeous."

"Thanks. I'll get her over to the tack room. Grab an apple for her out of my Navè--the woven bag hanging by the halters."

Eloree shrugged with a laugh that barely made its way out of her throat. "I feel awkward getting into someone else's purse."

"Hey, it's okay. I carry everything in my Navè." Jenna took the apple from Eloree's hand and broke it in half with her thumbs. "If you'd like to change or freshen up before the ride, there's a bathroom in the office."

Eloree felt Jenna's gaze as she started toward her black Range Rover. She liked Jenna's easy-going manner, but girls like her made Eloree unsure of herself–though she longed to have self-assurance and freedom. For that reason, she was sure she wanted to take this horseback ride. Feel freedom-be on her own. And she tried to stand a little taller when she strode back to the barn with a Navè of her own over her shoulder.

"Love your bag—that's a new one, huh? Can you believe some politician's teenager daughter designed these?" Jenna giggled, raking a brush along Nanta's flank.

Not commenting on Jenna's remark, Eloree's lips stretched into a forced smile. She wasn't going to reveal *she* was the politician's daughter.

Jenna showed Eloree to a small office with a couch, several folding chairs, and a sparse kitchen. Eloree's gaze fell on the newspaper spread across a small wooden table--her father's picture on the front page. She turned her back to the newspaper—the same way she wished she could turn her back on her father.

"Do you rescue people?" Eloree struggled for something to say and pointed to Jesse's rescue squad jacket, hung on the back of a chair.

"Me?" Jenna giggled. "No, I go to UNC. Home on spring break."

"What's your major?"

"Finishing up pre-med."

"*Pre-med?* How did *you* get to UNC-Chapel Hill?" Eloree felt her cheeks turning crimson.

"Drove a Ford pickup truck down Interstate 40." Jenna laughed.

But Eloree cringed. How she hated the times her inner turmoil overruled. She stared at her feet—unsure what to say next.

"Meet me in the entry. The bathroom's to the right." Jenna shrugged and turned to go.

Eloree stepped into the bathroom and stared hard in the mirror. "I hate you, red hair. I hate you, green eyes. I hate you, pale skin." She pulled a tube of concealer from her bag and smoothed it over the scar on the left side of her face. "I hate you, scar. I can cover you up, but I can never cover up all the terrible things you remind me of."

She ran her fingers through her hair. "Well, should I take a horseback ride or not? Father would forbid it," she whispered and waved to her reflection. She could back out, but something inside drew her--so she made her way to the entry.

Jenna's back was turned, but Eloree sensed uneasiness and racked her brain for something to say. "Do your horses have meaningful names?" She forced a smile.

Jenna turned and swatted at a horsefly. "Yes. Saja, the mare that's getting ready to foal – is named Cullasaja. Cherokee for honey locust place. We call her Saja for short."

"Why do you call this one Nantahala?" Eloree hoisted

herself onto the saddle.

"There's quite a story behind how we got her. You see, I went with Daddy to Nantahala to buy a mare named Sunshine. Sunshine had a little filly, but the man didn't want to sell her with the mare. I petted the filly the whole time we were there. When we got ready to leave and loaded up Sunshine, she cried for her baby, and the baby cried for its mama. I cried for both of them--all the way home. I couldn't stand taking a mama away from her baby."

"What happened to the baby?"

"It's Nanta." Jenna laid her cheek against Nanta's neck. "Daddy stayed up all night holding me while I cried. We both finally fell asleep after he promised we'd call the man in the morning to trade for Sunshine's baby."

"Well, did your father call?" Eloree swallowed hard. She knew her father would never react this way.

"The next morning before breakfast, Dad got the man on the phone and traded a four-wheeler and a truckload of hay to boot. Said we might have to buy hay to make it through the winter, but his baby girl would be happy." Jenna concluded with a broad grin as she fastened the last strap.

"Where's Sunshine?"

"Oh, that's a sad story. About a year after we got her, she got the colic and died - right here in this entry, with little Nanta standing beside her. A sad day for all of us. Nanta's even more special since she's Sunshine's baby."

Eloree gripped the reins. "Am I ready to go?"

"Yes, you're ready, my friend." Jenna stepped back, her hands on her hips. "Stay on Fish Hawk Trail. The signs are well marked and don't get off the horse no matter what happens. Nanta knows the way home from anywhere on Gabby Mountain, so there's no way to get lost."

"How long should this ride take?"

"No more than an hour. It looks like it's going to rain later--maybe even storm, but you should have plenty of time."

Eloree nudged Nantahala and headed out of the barn toward the old dirt road—without a wave or simple goodbye--and she didn't look back until she reached the top of the ridge. She wished Jenna hadn't told the story of Nanta losing her mother. This wasn't a story for her to dwell on, for it touched a place in her heart where she didn't want to go. For now, she wanted to get away and take this ride before her father found out where she was. Was she the only girl in the world whose father protected her from everything and everyone?

The voices in her head wouldn't go away, and she wished she could be like Jenna—tall, with straight, dark hair, and sky-blue eyes.

Finally, she shouted to herself, "Stop it, Eloree Elise. You're riding this girl's horse, and you're on her mountain."

But her heart raced as Nanta continued up the mountain trail. She didn't notice the budding trees and wildflowers. She didn't hear the birds singing or feel the breeze whisking through the trees, and she didn't notice the gray tinted clouds blocking the sun. She was only aware of the way Nanta's hooves echoed on the rocks, almost in time with her heartbeat.

"So Nanta, you're an orphan? Oh, what we have in common. Are you living with a broken heart, the way I am?"

Nanta continued up the familiar path, and the arrows pointed the way to Fish Hawk Trail at each fork. Moments later, Eloree saw another sign--Bridal Veil Falls straight ahead. She pulled on the reins, but Nanta resisted taking the new path. The horse balked and snorted. But Eloree nudged her, and Nanta continued toward the falls--leaving the main trail behind.

A part of Eloree knew this wasn't wise, but she only wanted to get close enough to the falls to snap a picture with her phone. She'd be back on the horse in no time, and no one would ever know. "I like being independent and making decisions on my own. Father would be furious if he knew where I am right now. No bodyguards--all alone in a backwoods wilderness."

As the trail narrowed and the incline got steeper, Nanta's gait slowed. Eloree leaned forward, lowering her head to avoid low hanging boughs. The roar of the river grew louder, and through the pines, she saw the falls. The river poured over a cliff, cascading onto the rocks below.

Nanta stopped and Eloree dismounted. She placed the reins over around a low-hanging branch and climbed down the embankment. Her phone in one hand, she grabbed a bush to steady herself with the other. But the bush gave way, and Eloree hurled down the side of the bluff. She plummeted over rocks and limbs—until her head slammed into the rocks at the top of the falls.

༄ 2 ༄

Waterfalls Within

Jesse stepped out of his pickup truck. "Hey, whose rig is that?"

"A girl came to ride, and I let her take Nanta up Fish Hawk Trail."

"Who is she?"

Jenna shrugged. "I couldn't make out what she scribbled on the form, but she trains with the U.S. Equestrian team."

Jesse hoisted a sack of horse feed from the back of the truck. "Olympics to Gabby Mountain. How long she been gone?"

"About an hour." Jenna reached for her Navè. "Have to be at the beauty shop by 4:00. Trust me, the girl will be back any time."

"Weather man's calling for storms."

"Then, you have nothing to worry about. First clap of thunder--Nanta will high tail back." Jenna waved and strode to her truck.

Jesse called after her. "Next time, don't let some stranger take off while I'm not here."

"You got it, little brother."

"Come on girl." Jesse took Saja's halter. "Let's go out to the corral and walk around a while. You need fresh air and sunshine before your babies get here."

But before Jesse got Saja to the corral, Nanta trotted through the entry—with no sight of the girl. He squinted as the sun came from behind a dark cloud. The wind picked up, more black clouds loomed, and the air smelled of rain.

His heart sank with dread, and his ears burned with fury as he saddled, Tauga, his black quarter-horse and strapped on a saddlebag packed with basic rescue provisions.

"What do you think, Tauga? Reckon the girl's walking down the trail right now? I'll bet she got off Nanta, couldn't remount, and Nanta rushed home without her. Now, you wouldn't leave a girl up on a mountain, would you, old boy?"

He slipped a lead line through Nanta's halter and swung onto Tauga's back. "Come on, Nanta. Why'd you run off and leave a girl in a storm?"

Jesse let out a resounding whistle and Mohan, the black wolf-dog, ran to catch up. Whether he was part wolf, as some thought, or not, he'd performed some remarkable feats. Could finding this girl be one more?

Jesse leaned forward in the saddle. His eyes searched the dirt road ahead, and he peered through the trees and underbrush for any sign of the girl. He pulled Tauga to a halt and called out. No answer. He cupped his hands over his mouth, and blew a long, loud whistle, followed by a loud deep, "*Hello*".

Mohan halted and stood at attention--his eyes fixed in the distance. "What is it, boy?"

The dog jumped and let out a sharp bark.

"Go get her, Mohan. Find the girl." Jesse waved him on, and Mohan disappeared through the underbrush.

Mounting frustration threatened to cloud his thinking. But he cleared his mind long enough to pray, "Heavenly Father, You alone know the situation I'm in. Protect this girl and me from harm and help me find her."

His eyes followed the fresh hoof prints Nanta had left earlier, obviously with the girl on her back. Then the hoof prints left the trail and headed toward Bridal Veil Falls.

"Oh no--surely Jenna told her to stay on Fish Hawk Trail."

He held onto a shred of hope the girl could be making her way from Bridal Veil Falls, but Tauga seemed to sense the urgency of the mission and increased his gait. Jesse felt the horse's strong muscles under his black coat. Even though Tauga was big and his strength matchless, this incline was a test of his endurance. He was breathing hard and beginning to sweat.

Jesse forced Tauga to stop. Up ahead he heard Mohan's proverbial *gr-howl* – somewhat between a bark and a howl. Without command, Tauga sprang ahead. As they reached the embankment leading to the rocky face above Bridal Veil Falls, Jesse peered through the laurel bushes and undergrowth. Then, his heart leaped into his throat.

The girl lay face down several feet below, with Mohan standing over her. With no time to consider the danger, Jesse tied Nanta's lead line to a sapling and urged Tauga down the steep, rocky embankment. He leaned back in the saddle as the horse wove around underbrush, rocks, and trees.

The girl came to and screamed for help, though the sound

of the river going over the falls below all but drowned out her cry. From the looks of things, if the big rocks hadn't been there, she would've gone over the falls.

Jesse bounded to her side. "Thank the Lord, you're alive!"

"I was attacked by a wild animal." she shrieked, and blood from a gash on her forehead spilled onto her shirt.

"I'm here to help you."

Cold raindrops hit his face. "Can you stand up? Is anything broken?" He put his arm around her shoulders and helped her to her feet.

"I don't know," she winced. "I'm dizzy and that wild animal attacked me."

"He's not a wild animal, Miss. He's my dog."

Jesse grabbed a rain poncho from his saddlebag, and took off his own tattered, brown coat and wrapped her in it--then shrouded her with the poncho. Then he cleaned the cut on her head and wrapped it with gauze before hoisting her onto Tauga's back.

The wind grew stronger and torrents of rain soaked the ground as if it had been raining for hours. Jesse grabbed Tauga's reins and started up the steep incline. But they had gone no more than a few feet when the girl screamed and slid off the horse onto the mud.

Again, Jesse scooped her up like a toddler and lifted her onto Tauga's back. He helped her throw her leg over the saddle.

It was risky trying to keep the girl on Tauga, but he couldn't put her on Nanta; she was too skittish in storms, pulling against the lead line and rearing with each crash of thunder.

He wrapped the reins around Tauga's saddle horn and gripped the girl's waist as he walked alongside. This time he'd have to trust Tauga to lead the way.

The storm bore down with lightning and deafening thunder. The ground shook with each rumble--limbs cracked and trees hit the ground. Once they were back to the trail, Jesse decided to start up the mountain to the old cabin instead of heading back to the barn.

"My name's Jesse. What's yours?"

"*El---ee.*" The wind whipped her words away.

"Do you think you can walk?"

"I don't know. My foot hurts," she wailed as he lifted her off Tauga.

"How do you feel? Are you still dizzy?"

"Yes," she moaned, grabbing at Tauga's saddle as she vomited before resting her head on the horse's side.

"Now Ellie, don't worry. We'll take shelter until the storm passes." Jesse cupped his hands to form a makeshift stirrup and hoisted her onto the saddle. He was even more concerned now that she might have a concussion--vomiting and dizziness were two sure signs.

Jesse watched for falling limbs as he led Tauga with Ellie half-slumped over the saddle. The pace was slow as they trudged up the mountain path through sheets of rain and streams of muddy water pouring over jutting rocks.

Hail filled the sky in an unmerciful rampage, and Jesse grabbed Ellie off Tauga like she was a rag doll and stood her on the ground. "Huddle up here between the horses. Keep your head down."

He pulled off his new cowboy hat and placed it on her head--now he felt the marble-sized hailstones sting the back of his neck.

Once the hail stopped, Jesse tied Nanta's lead line to Tauga's saddle and helped Ellie onto Tauga's back "Just a little further to the cabin."

Mohan ran on ahead, tail curled over his back and bounded into the entry of the old log barn which stood a few hundred feet down the hill from the cabin. Jesse led Tauga into the barn with Nanta at his heels--then he reached to help Ellie out of the saddle.

"Look, I'm not getting off this horse. I'm going back to my car." She gripped the saddle horn.

A clap of thunder boomed and Nanta reared, almost jerking the lead line from Jesse's hand. "Calm down Nanta. We're home now."

"*Home*? I want---" Deafening hail hit the tin roof.

Jesse left her on Tauga's back and led both horses into the stable. Without a word, he swooped her out of the saddle, plopped her down on a bale of hay, and went about tending to the horses.

Jesse finished tending the horses. "Let's go, I'll carry you." He gestured toward the cabin up ahead.

"*You* will not be carrying me." She pulled off his blood-stained cowboy hat and flung it onto a bale of hay. "I need to go back to *my* car."

"Listen, I need to put on dry clothes and so do you."

"My dry clothes are in my car. Take me there, I'll pay you well and be done with this escapade. Furthermore, get that beast you call a dog away from me. He tried to attack me." She slung her bag over her shoulder.

Jesse looked at Mohan, then back at her. "Say what you want about Mohan, but Ma'am, he rescued you. Hadn't been for him, I doubt I'd have found you."

"Nonetheless, keep him away from me. I'm allergic to dogs." She put her hands on her hips.

"Shouldn't be a problem there, Ma'am, since he's not a dog." Jesse let his slow, Southern drawl linger. "He's a wolf. Folks allergic to dogs aren't allergic to wolves."

"I have to go." She raised her voice.

"It'll slack soon." Jesse picked up a pitchfork and rearranged the hay.

A long, black racer writhed from under the hay, headed straight for her feet. She let out a blood-curdling scream and climbed to the top of the stack of bales where she screamed with all her might until Jesse scooped the racer onto the pitchfork and tossed it outside.

"He's gone now. Let me help you down."

"Get away from me." She drew back.

He tossed the pitchfork aside. "Then how are you going to get down?"

"I'll get down by myself."

Ellie stretched out her leg, and as she started to fall, he reached for her hand and guided her to the ground.

"Let's get in the cabin where I can re-bandage your head. It's still raining hard so hop on my back and I'll carry you."

She wiped blood from her brow with the back of her hand. "No, I told you I *do not* want to be touched again. Who lives there anyway?"

"Nobody lives there anymore. My family has owned this old home place since the 1800's. But you really need to come to the cabin with me. I'll build a fire where we can dry off and get warm."

"You don't understand. It's imperative I get off this mountain."

"Ma'am, I want to get off this mountain, too. Only problem is, I want to get off this mountain *alive*. It's too dangerous to ride these horses off here, and we can't walk."

"Then how do you propose we get back?"

"It's like this." Jesse looked at his watch. "I was supposed to be at a Rescue Squad meeting about thirty minutes ago. When my buddies realize I'm not going to show up, they'll come looking for me. More than likely in a warm, dry, four-wheel drive rig."

"Will they know where to look?" She crossed her arms and hugged the bag to her chest.

"Yes, they will. So--either let me carry you or give you a ride in this old wheelbarrow. I've pushed Jenna in it lots of times."

She put her hands on her hips and glared first at him, then toward the cabin.

"Well, what'll it be? You can stay here if you want, but I can't guarantee that black snake won't be back."

She shot a glance at Mohan as if he might make a difference in the situation.

"Mohan's going with me. He's hungry, too. You do what you want, Ma'am."

Without saying a word, she hobbled toward the old wooden wheelbarrow. She steadied herself on it, and Jesse pushed the rickety cart into the blinding rain and up the knoll to the cabin.

Once inside, Jesse helped her to a ladder-backed, wooden chair by the kitchen table.

"Turn the lights on," she demanded.

"Well Ellie, it's like this--we don't have electricity up here on Gabby Mountain."

"Why's that?" She glared at him.

"It's doubtful we'll ever get electricity up here if Senator Evan's legislation gets passed." He handed her a towel and went on. "I read an article about him in the paper today. Seems he's bought a vacation home up on Buck Creek and will be spending Easter here."

Jesse lit an oil lamp and placed it on the table in front of her. "Here's some light, Ellie."

"Why do you keep calling me *Ellie*?" she scolded.

"When I found you back down the mountain, I asked you what your name was. Thought you said, *Ellie*. If that's not right, then what would you like to be called, Ma'am?"

"Then *Ellie* is fine. But don't call me Ma'am. Besides, when are your so-called buddies?" She mocked.

"Don't worry, they'll be here. In the meantime, I need to get dried off--then I'll change the bandage on your--"

Mohan bolted through the door, and water from his soaked fur flailed on Ellie.

"Get that creature away from me," she shrieked and kicked at Mohan.

"You just broke a cardinal rule, Ma'am." Jesse's piercing brown eyes stared hard at her. "Never kick at a man's dog. And, Mohan stays. He's not going anywhere unless I go. Don't forget, if it hadn't been for him, I might not have found you."

"Sorry," she muttered and looked away.

Jesse nodded, then lit two more oil lamps and built a fire in the wood cook stove before stepping into the back room to change clothes. He rummaged through the drawers and found a pair of jeans and a red and black flannel shirt, along with more gauze, tape, and antiseptic ointment.

"Let's take a look at your noggin." He said as he arranged the supplies on the table in front of her.

"You must mean my *forehead.* I'll bandage it myself. Where's a mirror?"

"I don't think you should see this. You're probably going to need a few stitches. It'd be better if you let me do it."

"What makes you an expert?"

Jesse cleared his throat. "I've been trained in first aid. Remember, I'm with the volunteer search and rescue squad."

Ellie looked to the side, then back at him again. "I'm a grown woman and I'll do it myself." He watched as she stood precariously on her injured leg and held onto the edge of the table.

"Okay then." He took a small step toward her. "Thought I'd make the offer. I'll carry these things for you. There's a bathroom in the backroom."

He put the supplies on a small wooden table by the sink. "There's no hot water, but I heated some on the stove. I'll bring the kettle and pour it into the washbasin for you."

After several minutes, Jesse called out, "Everything all right in there?"

"Yes." Her reply sounded weak.

"Okay, then. I'm here if you need me. After you finish up in the bathroom, get yourself some dry clothes out of the chest of drawers - there by the bed."

Jesse knew she must be cold and wet--her clothes and boots were coated in half-dry mud and her hair was matted with blood.

After several more minutes, Ellie stepped from behind the blue floral curtain which separated the front room from the backroom and started toward the couch. The precarious bandage slipping over her eye.

"Whoa. You can't sit on the couch until you put on something dry."

Ellie propped against the piano. "I will not wear anyone else's clothes. Besides, we're going back to my car *very soon.*"

Jesse stared down at all five feet of Ellie. He wanted to laugh, but this was no laughing matter. Like a bad movie, it would soon be over--then he could laugh.

"Where are your buddies? When are they coming?" she asked again.

Jesse brought a wooden chair from the table for her. "I'm sure they're on their way. I'll go out on the porch and listen for them." He noticed blood already seeping through the makeshift bandage. "Here's a towel for your head."

As soon as he stepped outside, he heard Nanta squeal, and Mohan followed him closer than usual. Again, the hair on the dog's neck stood up, and a low growl rumbled deep in his throat, followed by a whine. "What is it, boy? Do you see something I don't? Or do you hear what I hear?"

Jesse stood still, filled with dread as the ground rumbled. A tornado roared up Gabby Mountain with the speed and intensity of a freight train. As he ran back into the cabin, he saw treetops swaying and heard the loud, sickening sound as trees twisted beneath the force of the wind.

"Oh God, let this storm go another way. Don't let it hit this cabin or the barn."

As quickly as it had come, the twister went over the ridge, leaving the cabin and barn intact. It hadn't touched down, at least not on this side of the mountain.

꘏3꘏

Escape

"Well, did you hear someone coming or not?" Ellie huffed.

"No, not yet. A tree probably fell across the old road, and they've had to turn back to get a chainsaw to cut it out of the way."

"Sure you don't want to change clothes? Got plenty. All shapes and sizes--here for emergencies."

She crossed her arms over her chest and looked away.

"I want you to be comfortable, so how about you at least wrap up in a quilt. It'll keep the couch dry and keep you warm."

Again, Ellie didn't answer but allowed him to slip a well-worn patchwork quilt around her shoulders and support her as she hobbled toward the couch.

"Are you comfortable now?"

"As comfortable as I possibly could be under these circumstances," she retorted and watched Jesse start a fire in the fireplace.

"Why are you blowing on it? Doesn't that put out a fire?"

"A little wind gets it going. That's how wildfire spreads."

"Have you ever had a wildfire on this mountain?"

"No, not in my lifetime. Some early settlers' cabin burned down once. Funny thing is, it wasn't the Cherokee who set it on fire. They got the settlers out and kept them in their house until the white men could build another cabin."

"That doesn't make sense. I thought the Indians killed the settlers."

"Not up here on Gabby Mountain. My Cherokee fathers and English fathers lived together as brothers. Helped each other out. Raised crops. Hunted. Fished. Wasn't until the federal government got involved that trouble broke out."

"Trouble?"

"The soldiers forced the Cherokee off their lands during The Trail of Tears. Do you remember reading about it in history books?"

"I've heard of it, but I don't like history."

"I say we have to look back to gain knowledge for the future. Like right now. If Senator Evan gets legislation passed to limit landowners' rights, we'll be like the Cherokee, except maybe we won't be forced to walk all the way to Oklahoma in the dead of winter."

"Why are you so passionate about this mountain land that's of no use to anyone?"

Jesse straightened and stared down at her. "No use to anyone? Where did you get that idea? Have you been keeping up with what this dude wants to do with restrictions on private land? I make my living on this mountain. It has plenty of use for my family and me."

"Do you make a living from the free horseback rides?"

"Now that wouldn't be possible, would it?" She caught the irritation in his tone.

She threw her hands out. "What do you do?"

"Grow Christmas trees," he answered, then offered a towel to her. "Your head's bleeding again. Don't want to get blood on that Navè. Those things are pricey. I gave over $100 for Jenna's when they first came out four years ago."

Ellie pursed her lips. "Why did you pay for it?"

"Long story, but a funny one." Jesse straddled the ladder-back chair backward and wrapped his arms around the rungs. "Jenna was getting ready for college and really wanted one. I sold some calves at the Asheville cattle auction--got top dollar for them, so I decided to stop by the Navè store and get her one. I had a wad of $100 bills, just burning a hole in my pocket." He chuckled.

"Well, I had bought some sheep at the auction, and they were in the cattle trailer I was pulling. If you've ever been around sheep, you know they don't hush when they're not happy, and they weren't happy in the hot trailer. When we pulled up in front of the Navè Boutique, we looked like Old McDonald's farm—hot, dirty, the truck smelling like cow manure."

"Interesting." Ellie drew in her bottom lip. Now--she knew she had seen Jesse before. This was the hillbilly boy who had traipsed into the shop the first week it opened—and she had been in another area—watching the scene from security monitors.

"We stomped our boots off, best we could, and put on

clean shirts. When we walked in, the prissy little woman behind the counter didn't know whether to run or hide. You should've seen the look on her face."

Ellie remembered the ladies in the back laughing as the shop manager dealt with this situation. "Was anyone else in the shop besides the woman?"

"I don't think so. I wanted to get the pocketbook and go. The critters in the parking lot weren't patient--the ruckus carried all the way into the store."

"Was another man with you?" Ellie cut her eyes at him.

"Funny you should ask," Jesse scratched his head and went on, "Yes, my uncle Ben and he likes to have fun in a place where people high-hat you. That woman wanted us to hurry up and get out of there."

"What did the clerk do?"

"Asked us if we'd like to come back another day. We took it to mean – don't come back. But Uncle Ben told her we'd have to get cleaned up again. Anyway, we saw the bags on the walls. We weren't going to walk all over the store, but she didn't know that. We already knew which one Jenna wanted. Just to razz the old gal for being so rude to us, Uncle Ben asked her if she had any more in the back." Jesse slapped his knee and laughed harder. "She *pert near* fainted."

"Did she get more from the back?"

"Nope. Uncle Ben told her he was kidding--we'd take one on the shelf. She told us it would be $107.77."

"Did you have that much money?"

"Of course. I knew how much it cost before I went in." He rocked back in the chair. "Listen to this. Uncle Ben started pulling stuff out of his pockets like he was hunting for seventy-seven cents. I could tell she wanted us out of there, so I handed her a $110 and told her to keep the change."

"What happened then?" Ellie gathered he hadn't seen her.

"Oh, it gets funnier." Jesse went on. "We couldn't hold it any longer, and we guffawed back to the truck. Well, the joke was on us--we had a flat tire. Had to change it right there in her parking lot."

"I believe she called the police on us. Before we got the spare on, here came an officer. He was a nice guy--even offered to help us.

"Interesting." Ellie's head pounded like the roar of a helicopter. She closed her eyes and massaged her temples. How had she wound up stranded with the hillbilly boy—who hated her father?

When she looked up, Jesse stared down at her. "Are you alright?"

"No, my ankle hurts—I need an ice pack."

She watched as he grabbed a coat and hat hanging by the door and told her he was going outside for an ice pack.

"Look at this." He showed her the ice crystals he held in a clean sock. "I don't think I've ever seen hail this big. Must be big as quarters."

"Did you see my ride?" She grimaced, as he placed the makeshift cold pack on her ankle.

"No, not yet. Is anybody missing you?"

"Yes, and I can't wait any longer." Her face tightened.

"We don't have a choice. Do you hear that wind out there? Trees are snapping like matchsticks and lightning's flashing like crazy. We'd be insane to get out in this."

"I have to go *now*."

"Better stay a while longer. I'll fix something to eat." He stepped toward the kitchen, and Ellie felt a hard lump rise in her throat.

"Where am I supposed to go, besides this couch? You're not giving me a choice in the matter."

He stopped and turned to her. "You could change into dry clothes. Not many people like sitting around in damp, muddy clothes."

"Why are you so determined for me to take off my clothes?" She watched his face turn a deep scarlet.

"Well, I'm thinking of what's best for you and treating you the way I'd want your brother to treat *my* sister."

"*My* brother would simply dial 911," she retaliated, a smug look on her face.

"I'd call 911 too, that is, if Senator Evan would pass legislation allowing electricity and cell phone towers up here."

"Don't blame my--" Ellie cut herself off. She almost said, *father*.

~~~~~

Jesse carried in more dry wood. He knew no one would come until the storm let up, and he'd have to figure out how to deal with Ellie. Since she likely had a concussion, he couldn't let her fall asleep—even if it meant arguing to keep her alert.

His eyes fell on a little plaque beside the kitchen window that read *God supplies all my needs. His riches are in glory. Philippians 4:19*. "God, supply my need to get off this mountain
~~~~~

and out of this storm, according to Your riches in glory. I have to trust You for I can't figure this one out by myself. There's no other way. I praise You for meeting this need. In Jesus' name."

He glanced around the corner and saw Ellie with her foot propped up, staring blankly into space.

She looked up at him. "Where's my ride?"

"Sorry, I didn't mean to startle you. I'll check your ice pack. Since it's melted, we need to apply cold compresses."

"Enough small talk." She pointed toward the door. "I have to go."

Jesse ignored her as he examined her ankle. "Does it still hurt? Do you think you can walk?"

"Yes, it still hurts, but I'll crawl back to my car. Let's go before it gets any later." She pulled herself to the edge of the couch and stood, propping herself on her good foot. "Let's make a deal, okay? I'll pay you the equivalent of one week's wages to escort me to my car *immediately*."

Jesse found the comment somewhat amusing. "That could be a problem. I don't get paid weekly wages."

She raised her voice. "I will pay you a *month's* salary. Any amount of money you want."

Jesse scratched his head. "Got a problem there, too. I don't get paid a salary either. Trust me--it's not about money. Common sense tells me this weather's too harsh to go now. If you'll be patient, I promise we'll go soon as it's safe. After all, we want to get off here alive."

"You don't understand. Father'll be furious with me for being so late."

Jesse could hear the desperation in her voice. "I'm sure he'll understand when you explain what happened."

"No, he won't. He'll be infuriated." Ellie jabbed a finger toward him.

"Look here, Miss Ellie, he'll be pleased you're alright. If it was Jenna in your place, our dad would be tickled pink she was safe and sound. He'd forget all about being late."

Ellie pulled strands of hair over the side of her face. "My father isn't like that. He never accepts excuses."

Jesse searched for the right words, trying to figure out why she was so fearful of her own dad.

"Please, help me."

"We'll leave the minute it's safe. But for now, I'm going to cook some supper." He took a stack of books from a hand-hewn wooden bookshelf and placed them on the couch. "You can look at these."

"I don't *look* at books. I *read* them."

"Well, I'm getting hungry. What would you like for supper? I'm a pretty good cook, but we don't have a lot to choose from. Canned vegetables and fruit, some canned deer meat. Do you like hominy or sauerkraut?"

"Don't worry about me. I'm vegan, and I only eat a gluten-free diet."

"Wouldn't want you to go hungry. Hominy's made from corn-- sauerkraut is pickled cabbage. Both gluten-free."

"Wait a wretched minute. Did you say *deer* meat? Are you one of those repulsive hunters who kill and eat *Bambi*?"

He was speechless, not surprised at her reaction, but regretted he'd mentioned the meat.

"I won't be staying for dinner or supper, whatever you call your disgusting evening meal." She grabbed a book from the top of the pile.

Jesse busied himself opening jars of green beans, hominy, and spiced apples. He filled cast iron pots with vegetables and deer meat--then placed them on the wood cook stove. Then, he mixed cornbread in a Dutch oven and carried it to the fireplace.

As he scooped hot coals over the Dutch oven, Jesse noticed Ellie stuff a book under the quilt. It was one of Jenna's old children's books, *Althea Spinetta with Curls in Her Hair*--the story of a young girl who didn't like her red curly hair until she learned God made each child different. He assumed Ellie liked it because of her red, curly hair. Whatever the reason, he was glad she was quiet for a change.

"What are you doing? We could be leaving by now," she blurted.

"This is the best way to bake cornbread. Comes out golden brown. It'll be done in no time."

He attempted to smile at her, but she mumbled something he didn't make out and turned away.

He fried hominy in shortening and seasoned green beans with meat drippings. The meal was meager, but it would 'stick to your ribs,' as mountain men would say. And he hoped Ellie would eat something. When he came back to check the cornbread, he noticed Ellie hugging the book to her chest with her eyes closed, underneath a furrowed brow.

Mohan strolled to the couch and lay down in front of Ellie.

"Want me to make him move?" Jesse motioned toward Mohan.

"Doesn't matter. I'll be leaving soon."

Jesse set the plate with green beans, hominy, and deer

meat on the red and white checked oilcloth that covered the eating table. As he stepped back to the sink to fill a Mason jar with water, he offered again, "Sure you don't want some supper? Got plenty."

She ignored him.

"Would you at least like a glass of cold, spring water? Comes straight up out of the ground."

"No. I don't want *anything* you have to offer."

"I hate to eat in front of you, but I'm starved. Been a long time since dinner." He sliced the hot cornbread and closed his eyes, not uttering a word - only moving his lips.

The ground shook as thunder clapped and trees crashed. Wind screeched through the trees. Rain beat the windows and roof. Jesse knew this could last all night, but he prayed there wouldn't be another tornado.

Jesse switched on the heavy-duty flashlight and opened the Bible, which stayed on the kitchen table--content to read the first verse his eyes fell on - Jeremiah 29:11. Well Lord, if You have plans to prosper me and not harm me, what am I doing on Gabby Mountain in this storm, with this girl? He thought about the words as he finished his meal. He had plans for his life; plans that were usually simple and short-term. He trusted they were the same plans God had for him and saw no reason to change them.

Jesse ate in silence, cleaned up the kitchen, and heated more water in the tea kettle. All the while, he noticed the ghastly look on Ellie's face. He looked around the corner to see she had brought *Althea Spineeta* back out and was holding the book to her chest.

He chose a dainty china cup and saucer and decided to fix tea for Ellie—another attempt to start a conversation. Maybe she'd appreciate the treasured pieces.

"Here, Ellie, I fixed hot tea. Would you like sugar?"

"No, thank you. I'll be leaving as soon as my ride arrives."

"I'll set it on the table in case you decide to try it before your ride comes."

"Very well." She pointed nonchalantly toward the table and stack of books.

"I see you like *Althea Spineeta*. The lady who wrote it rides horses up here sometimes."

"Take your stupid book." Ellie hurled the book into the fireplace and knocked the teacup and saucer across the room.

Jesse's jaw dropped. The book went up in flames and porcelain shards lay on the floor. "Why did you do that?"

"It was an accident. I'll pay for it." She leaped to her feet.

Jesse folded his arms across his chest. “You can’t just *pay* for things to replace them. Grow up, little girl. Learn respect.”

She bolted for the door. “I’m leaving *now*.”

Jesse stepped between her and the outside door. “You can’t go out in this storm.”

“Yes, I can. My father will be irate.” She grabbed the flashlight on the table.

“It’s too dangerous.” Jesse planted his feet wide apart.

“You can’t hold me here against my will.”

“I’m not holding you against your will.”

“Get out of my way,” she screamed and smashed his nose with the heel of her hand, then shoved past him out the door.

Jesse tasted blood, and his eyes filled with water. He grabbed a dish towel and rushed onto the porch. He watched Ellie limp to the barn—Mohan in front of her. Jagged flashes of lightning illuminated their shadows through the sheets of rain. He didn’t go after her but watched her disappear into the entry of the old barn.

He heard Nanta and Tauga squealing—then Nanta reared as thunder shook the ground and ran from the barn—Tauga by her side. His eyes followed the flashlight beam as Ellie came into view—but nothing could have prepared him for what would happen next.

A boom, louder than thunder shook the ground, and a ball of fire shot from the big cherry tree beside the barn. Shards of wood splintered in all directions as the tree crashed through the roof of the barn, flattening the stalls where Nanta and Tauga had been.

“Ellie—” Jesse leaped off the porch.

She lay on the ground—mere feet from where a huge chunk of trunk landed. And she was still. Too still.

❧4☙

Changes

Jesse thrust himself into the fury of the storm. The short distance to Ellie seemed like miles. Kneeling in the mud, he lifted her, bracing her limp head against his chest—her arms and legs dangled lifelessly, and her hair clung to her face and neck. He charged back toward the cabin through mud, over fallen branches. Was she dead or alive?

Her eyes twitched for an instant as he laid her drenched body on the couch. "Talk to me, Ellie. Say something. Anything."

Placing his cheek next to her face, he detected quick shallow breaths.

"Ellie...Ellie... come on Ellie..." In his heart, he cried *Jesus, Jesus* and prayed she'd survive and not lose consciousness.

Finally, she trembled and released a shallow breath.

"Squeeze my hand if you can hear me."

She wrapped her fingers around his hand.

"Keep squeezing my hand. You're going to be all right. Don't go to sleep—no matter how sleepy you are."

Her eyes opened with a blank stare. "Cold," she shuddered.

Jesse grabbed another quilt, and as he tucked it around Ellie, she reminded him of one of Jenna's old rag dolls that had been dragged through the mud. But he would see to it she was taken care of--even if it meant arguing with her.

He stoked the fire and added more logs to drive out the chill—then pulled up a chair to keep a close watch on her. As she moved, her hair fell from the side of her face revealing a reddish mark. Jesse almost gasped, but as he peered closer, he could tell it was a scar--not a fresh wound. She had covered it with makeup, which had long since worn off, and now he knew why she wanted to bandage her own head.

She struggled to speak, "Mohan ... animal ... barn."

"Don't worry about Mohan. He ran off with the horses, but

he'll be back."

She took a gulp of air. "Animal...big...black...animal."

"Was it a bear? Sometimes they sneak into the barn trying to get in the horses' sweet feed. I have to keep it in a box they can't open. They're tricky rascals."

"No, long tail," she completed in one breath.

"Tell me exactly what you saw."

"Not a bear." She rubbed her temples. "Mohan ran into the barn ahead of me."

"Okay. Tell me more."

"The horses reared." She struggled to clear her throat.

"Do you need a drink of water?"

She nodded, and he returned with a glass of cold water. He helped her hold the glass as she took a sip.

"Mohan chased the animal out of the barn." She paused. "The horses were scared. They nearly trampled me trying to get out when I opened the stall door..." her voice trailed as if there was more to tell.

"Don't fret over Mohan. He's protective of Nanta and Tauga--but looks like he wants to take care of you, too. He's a pretty good fellow to have around, wouldn't you say?"

He continued to lean toward her, watching her every move. For what seemed an eternity, he stared at her, not knowing how she was going to react.

"I need to be alone," she said.

Jesse stood, getting a strong whiff of horse manure. "Sure, I need to get cleaned up and find some dry clothes. I'll be in the back room if you need me. Just holler."

Not wanting to leave her for very long, Jesse scrounged in the old chest of drawers for a pair of faded Wrangler jeans. As he dug through the assortment of clothes, he considered how he would look in front of Ellie. Then he pushed the thoughts out of his head. Once she got off the mountain, he'd never see or hear from her again. And it was his place to take care of her—and nothing more.

"Jesse—come quick. Someone's at the door."

He rushed from the backroom wearing only jeans. But when he opened the door, Mohan bolted into the cabin. His tail wagged as he shook water in all directions.

"Where have you been--and what have you been chasing? Miss Ellie says you ran an animal out of the barn. Must have been an ole' she-bear-- huh?"

Mohan responded with a *gr---howl,* then trotted to Ellie's side.

Ellie mumbled, "It wasn't a bear. It had a long tail." Jesse didn't argue with her, for he knew she was disappointed the noise at the door hadn't been the arrival of help. He pulled on a faded flannel shirt and propped his boots by the fire, hoping they'd be dry by morning.

He sat on the old piano stool and lifted his guitar from its case, then began to pick the melody, *Fur Elise*. He couldn't tell if she was annoyed or trying to make out the song, but he continued to maneuver his fingers along the frets, picking the strategic strings in unison, filling the room with the magnificent tune.

"That was *Fur Elise*." She seemed surprised.

"Well, thanks to Mr. Ludwig Van Beethoven, we have this masterpiece. It was lost for years, you know. Glad somebody found it. Poor ole' Ludwig. He didn't live long enough to know what a masterpiece he created. Besides, it's one of Mama's favorites. She plays the piano, and I pick along."

"I'm surprised you know so much about Beethoven." She threw out her hands.

"Classicals are like horses. They never lose their beauty, no matter how old they are."

"I'm sorry I turned your horses out."

"Well, Ellie, if you hadn't gone into the barn and let the horses out, the big cherry tree would've fallen on them."

She shook her head. "I'm confused. A loud noise knocked me to the ground."

"What you heard was lightning. It hit the barn and the big cherry tree, just seconds after Tauga and Nanta ran off--and you came out of the barn. The old cherry tree landed on the barn, smack dab, where Nanta and Tauga had been. They would've been killed."

Her face was pale and sullen. "What about the old barn?"

"It's been here for nearly two centuries. If we can't fix it, we'll build another one."

"Will the horses come back?"

"Maybe they'll be back by morning." Jesse rubbed the back of his neck. He knew they wouldn't be back, and he looked long and hard at Ellie, wondering how he would get her off the mountain by himself. "How do you feel?"

"My ears are ringing, but I can hear okay. I feel weak and cold." Her voice sounded stronger.

"We need to get your head to stop bleeding. Will you let me change the bandage and clean it up?"

"Yes. Go ahead. The bandage I put on didn't work very well, did it?"

Jesse didn't know what to make of her change in attitude. Maybe she realized how close to death she had come. One thing was for sure—it was a miracle from God she was still alive.

Jesse found a white cotton pillowcase and ripped it into strips for bandages. It wasn't sterile, but it would have to do. He poured hot water into a metal dishpan and set it on the small table beside the couch. Armed with a washcloth and clean towel, he prepared to cleanse the wound.

She covered her cheek with her hand. "Don't touch this part of my face."

"Okay. Tell me if I hurt you." He looked into her pale green eyes, but she looked away.

As he cleaned the gash on her forehead, he knew it needed stitches, but he chose not to tell her.

"Do you live around here?" he asked.

"Not really." She closed her eyes.

Gathering she didn't want to talk about it, he tried again. "Do you go to school?"

"Sometimes." She grimaced as he rubbed strands of her hair with a washcloth to remove the blood and caked mud.

"How old are you?"

"Twenty. How old are you?"

"Funny you should ask. For two more days, I'll be twenty-one. My birthday falls on Easter Sunday. Our family's got a big Easter dinner planned. How do you celebrate Easter?"

She didn't respond, so he kept going. "Well, there are a few rules up here on Gabby Mountain. One is you don't have to talk if you don't want to, and you don't have to answer any questions you don't want to. Everyone's entitled to their privacy."

"How did you come up with that rule?"

"Let me tell you a story--a true one that happened a long, long time ago," he started, continuing to clean her hair, one lock at a time. "You see, my great-great-great grandpa, Jesse Woods, went out to the old barn one stormy winter night. He heard his hound dogs barking and thought they might have a bear or a panther bayed."

"Here on this mountain?"

"Sure was, at the same old barn down yonder, where we had Nanta and Tauga. Anyway, when he got down there, it wasn't an animal. No siree. He found a Cherokee woman and her daughter huddled in the hay trying to keep warm and out of the storm. The girl must have been about twelve years old, and she was really sick. The story goes she was about dead with pneumonia. No telling how long they'd been out in the elements with no food--wet and cold. The Cherokee weren't treated very well back then. Actually, this was during the time of their ungodly removal from these mountains." He looked into her eyes and was surprised she was showing interest.

"Anyway, he wrapped the girl up in his own coat and carried her through the snow drifts into the cabin - this very cabin where we are now."

"This cabin?"

"Yes. It was a one-room log cabin with a dirt floor back then. It's been built onto and changed through the years, but it's still the same cabin."

Ellie glanced around.

Jesse continued wrapping the bandage around her head. "Well, the rest of the story goes like this. Neither the Cherokee woman nor her daughter ever told anybody who they were, where they came from or where they were going. They didn't even tell their names. Jesse told them they didn't have to talk if they didn't want to. He named them Naomi and Ruth from the story of the two women in the Bible who traveled back to Naomi's homeland, and God provided for them."

Ellie shook her head and shrugged as if she didn't know.

Jesse went on. "The two became Aunt Naomi and Cousin Ruth. Anyway, Jesse and his grandma stayed up all night taking care of the sick girl."

"Why do you call them Aunt Naomi and Cousin Ruth if they really weren't your relatives?" She seemed puzzled.

"Oh, that's how country folks show respect. It doesn't matter if you're related or not. By calling somebody Aunt, Uncle, Cousin it means they'll be treated like family."

"Did the girl live?"

"Sure did. Aunt Naomi helped make herb poultices, and they sang *Amazing Grace* in Cherokee. Aunt Naomi never did speak English, but she understood it. Ruth spoke perfect English from the day they got here. Folks thought her daddy must have been a white man."

"How did Aunt Naomi communicate?"

"Ahh. Jesse and some of the other settlers here on the mountain spoke Cherokee. See, they lived here with the Cherokee and got along. That is until the federal government got involved and the soldiers came, forcing the Cherokee off their own land."

He paused to collect his thoughts. Even though this story had been a part of his family's heritage for over 150 years, he still felt a rush of emotion each time he told it.

"What happened then?"

"Jesse went to fight in the Civil War. Ruth and Naomi stayed here on Gabby Mountain to take care of his grandma while he was gone. When he came home from the war, he couldn't believe his eyes. Ruth was now sixteen and the prettiest girl he'd ever laid eyes on."

Ellie let a trace of a smile escape from her sullen face, followed by what sounded like a shallow laugh, caught in her throat, and Jesse felt his face turn red.

"They fell in love, got married, and had six children. They're my great-great-great-grandparents. I'm named after him, and Jenna's named after her. Thing is, even after all these generations, folks say I favor him, and Jenna looks like her."

"You're saying if Naomi and Ruth didn't have to say who they were or where they were from, then no one else has to, right?" Ellie raised her brows.

"Right," Jesse answered. "Even if you don't want to talk, you need to get out of those wet clothes, or you're going to be sick."

"I suppose I should take you up on it. I have more than just mud on me." She lowered her voice to a whisper. "Don't you smell the barn dirt?"

"Barn dirt? Do you mean horse manure?"

She pinched her nose. "Yes. The stench is more than I can handle. I'm sorry to impose on you, and I'm sure it's on these quilts as well. I'll pay to have them cleaned or replaced."

Jesse shook his head. "No worries about the quilts. Let's get you taken care of."

~~~~~

Ellie slung the Navè over her shoulder and followed Jesse through the curtained doorway into the back room.

He brought in a chair and placed a glass kerosene lamp on top of the dresser. The light flickered in the mirror, dimly illuminating the room. Taking in her surroundings, Ellie noticed the white lace curtains over the window where sheets of rain pelted outside on the panes. A white, cotton bedspread covered an old iron bed in the corner, and the walls were covered with rose-print wallpaper. The room reminded her of a cottage in Wales where she and her mother had visited not long before the accident.

The musty smell of antiques hung in the air. There were shelves filled with books, along with old portraits in oval wooden frames. The lingering scent of aged wood coupled with the earthy
~~~~~

dampness brought back memories Ellie thought she had tucked away forever. Another unwelcome reminder.

"See what's in the chest of drawers to suit your fancy. I'll get some hot water and pour it into the washbasin for you."

"Where did you get all these clothes? Why are they up here if no one lives here?" she called as he disappeared through the curtained doorway.

"We bring them up here and sometimes other people leave them rather than pack them up and take them back home. Seems like somebody's always falling in the creek or getting dirty. We've got a little bit of everything," he called back.

Rummaging through the drawers, she could hear Jesse in the next room, talking to Mohan while picking a lively tune. The moment seemed surreal, and she felt like someone else. This couldn't be happening to her. There wasn't even a door, only a curtain. She was so desperate, she was putting on someone else's clothes. Old, worn out clothes at that. And memories that wouldn't go away dug into her heart.

Ellie washed off with the clean washcloth and hot water. Meager as it was, she welcomed the chance to freshen up. Jesse had even been thoughtful enough to provide a bar of Ivory soap, still in the paper wrapper. The smell of the soap reminded her of visits to her own grandmother's house before the accident.

Her fingers trembled as she fumbled with the buttons on a red and green plaid flannel shirt. It didn't fit, but it would have to do, and she settled for a pair of overalls—two sizes too big. None of the jeans were even close to her size, and she couldn't find a belt in any of the drawers. She pulled on a pair of thick cotton socks and thought of how incredibly ridiculous she must look.

She searched in her Navè for a tube of concealer, but there was none. All she could do was readjust the bandage, so her hair would cover the side of her face. She hated her red curls now more than ever, and her hairbrush was useless in trying to smooth out the frizzy mess.

If she looked more like other girls, Jesse might like her--but why should she care? Even in the dim light, she could tell her makeup had completely worn off. Her heart sank. Jesse had seen the scar on her face, and he didn't stare or say one word about it.

℘5☙

Through a Child's Eyes

From the time she'd arrived at the stable and met Jenna, it had been one memory after another. Nanta, the orphan horse whose mama had died, and *Althea Spineetta with Curls in Her Hair* had brought back more hurt than she could bear.

Jesse had played *Fur Elise*, but he couldn't have known Elise was her middle name or this was her mother's favorite classical piece. And if things weren't bad enough, all this was happening on Easter weekend--the one holiday she hated, dreaded, struggled through from beginning to end. The time of the accident. The day she lost her mother.

She could still see the Easter basket with the broken chocolate bunny, the shattered eggs, and crumpled purple bow. "If I never see another Easter basket or purple bow, it'll be too soon," she mumbled to herself. Here she stood in the midst of a storm in her heart as well as the one outside.

Opening her eyes, she reassured herself Dr. Shanks would be there for her and make her father understand. But could Dr. Shanks help her chase away the memories being here had brought up?

The music coming from the other side of the curtain brought her back to reality. "I'm all alone with someone I don't even know. But I like him. I've been horrible, but he's still kind. And he's not even someone my father is paying. Father--what recourse will he take for what I've done?" she whispered as she braided the lower portion of her hair--took it down. The braid corralled the frizz but did little to cover the scar. What did it matter? Jesse had already seen it.

Sliding the hairbrush back into the Navè, her hand nudged a small leather journal. Dr. Shanks laughed when she gave it to her. "You have more than enough medications, my dear," her doctor and friend said. "Your prescription from me is to write down your thoughts. Things you want to talk over with me and things you only want to keep to yourself. It'll help you sort things out."

At the time, Ellie had no intention of writing in the journal. But now, it seemed like a promising idea. Despite her best efforts, the memories weren't going anywhere. And truthfully, she didn't want them to. She didn't want to forget her mother, and the painful memories would always be there.

Ellie walked into the front room, arms laden with soiled clothing, damp quilts, and the kerosene lamp. Jesse noticed the flame from the burning lamp beginning to singe the fabric. He ran toward her.

She dropped the lamp, and it shattered on the floor, as burning oil engulfed the rug between them. Jesse stood, frozen in place as the flames licked toward his bare feet.

"Throw the quilts on it!" he yelled, motioning with both hands.

Ellie flung the heavy bundle onto the flames. She stood spellbound, her heart pounding, fighting for breath as the sickening kerosene fumes filled the air. Oh no. She'd broken something else.

Jesse jerked on his wet boots, and stomped the steaming pile, snuffing out what was left of the fire. He turned to her. "Are you okay? Were you cut? Did you get burned?"

She stared at him without answering. Here he was again, only concerned about her, not at all angry. What about the quilts? The old lamp?

"Ellie." He took her hands in his--a move that jolted her back to reality.

"I'm sorry. Honestly, I didn't mean to break the lamp," her voice quivered.

"It's okay as long as you're all right. Don't move or you'll cut your feet."

As she watched him cleaning up the mess, she couldn't help wondering if he had a girlfriend and what he thought of her. Would her father ever allow her to go on real dates with a guy like Jesse—instead of arranged companions to his political events?

~~~~~

The stifling odor of kerosene and singed cloth filled the cabin. Jesse propped the door open, letting fresh air in as he carried the mess of quilts and dirty clothes to the porch. Welcoming the cool, damp air into his lungs he stood on the
~~~~~

porch, Mohan by his side.

The rain and wind died down to an eerie calm, and he strained to see into the darkness. Flashes of lightning reminded him the storm wasn't over. The air felt heavy and clammy with the temperature at least ten degrees higher than when he'd last been outside. Perfect conditions for another tornado. With no signs of Tauga, Nanta, or anyone coming to rescue them, they were stranded here until daylight.

He glanced toward Mohan. The dog's ears were raised and the hair on his back stood up. Jesse rubbed his ears, but his only response was a deep-throated growl.

"Are you jumpy about this storm? Come on. Let's check on Miss Ellie. I think she's beginning to like us, especially you." He picked up more logs for the fireplace.

As he raked the burning coals and stacked the logs on top of each other, he was keenly aware Ellie was watching his every move. He wondered what was on her mind and what she thought of him.

But he didn't even know who she was. And why did he want to know? A girl like her would only be interested in a college guy. Only hours ago, he wouldn't have cared one way or the other.

Ellie seemed defenseless since she wasn't arguing with him, and seemed to be letting her guard down, proving to be stronger than she appeared at first. He realized she hadn't cried at all through the entire ordeal. Even Jenna would've been bawling by now.

"How's your head? Let's see if it's stopped bleeding." He reached to adjust the makeshift bandage. She brought her hand to the side of her face. The auburn waves falling over her shoulders did little to camouflage the scar.

"It still hurts, but I'm only a little dizzy now."

"We need to keep it wrapped tight, so it won't bleed again. How about your foot?"

"It hurts some. I can't get my boot back on, but I can walk on it."

She grimaced as he rubbed her ankle, pressing the swollen joint. "I don't think it's broken. Probably just a sprain--keep it propped up." He placed a pillow under her foot. He was sure that come daylight, they'd be walking off Gabby Mountain. From what he could tell, there were too many trees down for a rescue vehicle to get through, and he doubted the horses would be coming back tonight.

Jesse picked up the guitar and began to play, hoping a cheerful tune might lift Ellie's spirits, too.

The glow of the fire illuminated the room, casting shadows each time he shifted his arm. His neck crooked as he watched his own fingers create the melody.

Glancing up, Jesse grinned. "Am I making too much racket?"

"No, not at all." Ellie tapped the beat on the arm of the couch. That's the same tune you played earlier. What's the name of that song?"

"*In the Midst.*"

"Does it have lyrics?"

"Sure does. Mama came up with it when I was a baby. She sang it to me in the hospital--been a special song in our family ever since."

"Sing it for me."

Jesse tapped his foot and began.

Show me who I am Lord, oh be with me
In the midst of it all, I can hear You call...

"You play very well. That's a nice song and a catchy tune. What are the words talking about?"

"Zephaniah 3:17 says God is in the midst of all of our circumstances, and He rejoices over us with singing." Jesse's voice was sincere. "Life's full of storms and hard times, but God wants us to know we're never alone. He's always right beside us, no matter what predicament we get into, and the Bible says there are angels camping around us."

"Angels?"

"Sure, like with Paul and Silas. They were thrown in prison for preaching the gospel. Even though they were chained and beaten, they never lost hope. They prayed and sang hymns every day. One night around midnight, there was an earthquake. An angel of the Lord appeared. The walls shook, and the cell doors flew open. The chains fell off all the prisoners."

"Do you believe all that?"

"I sure do. God always makes a way for His people, even if He has to use a calamity to do it."

Ellie shrugged. "I don't know much about God, Jesus, or church. It's never been important in my family."

Jesse wanted to tell her how wrong she was, but he didn't have the right words, so instead, he leaned the guitar against a chair. "Would you like some hot tea?"

"Yes, please."

"It's okay if you want to stay on the couch. I'll bring it to you."

She hobbled to the table, Mohan at her heels. "You don't

have to be my servant." She half-joked as she sat down at the kitchen table.

"Being a servant's not a bad thing." Jesse lit a candle and placed it on the table. "The Bible tells us that's what God expects us to do. Wouldn't the world be a better place if everybody was looking out for his fellow man? Take Mohan here. He seems to be determined to serve you in every way he can, and he's sticking to you like glue."

Jesse saw her eyes grow wide, when he set another hand-painted, bone china cup and saucer in front of her, along with a sugar bowl and matching spoon. He poured himself a cup of hot tea and sat across from her. The glow from the fireplace met the light from the candle, casting shadows that danced between them.

"Sorry, we don't have any crumpets or cucumber sandwiches. And this isn't exactly the hour for high tea." He teased.

"Have *you* ever had high tea?"

"Lots of times. Been drinking tea out of fancy tea cups with pretty girls all my life." He blushed, realizing Ellie smiled at the word *pretty*.

"Is that so?" He noticed the way her eyes lit up.

"When we were kids, Jenna and her friends always liked to play dress-up and tea party. Made me play with them."

"Did you eat cucumber sandwiches?"

"No, but Jenna and Mama did when they went to England a few years back."

"Did you go, too?"

"No, it was our last year of high school, and the class went there for the senior trip. Jenna and Mama got all excited about tracing our English roots. I didn't want to go, so Daddy and I went backcountry trail riding."

"Don't you think traveling abroad is a better way to expand your horizons?"

"For some people. But I like to trace my Cherokee roots. We went to places few white men have ever gone." Jesse propped his elbow on the table. "It changed my way of looking at things. Gave me the idea to start the riding stables and bring people up here on Gabby Mountain to find a place of *Peniel*."

"What does *Peniel* mean?"

"It's in the Bible. *Peniel* is the place where Jacob wrestled with God. He hung on and wouldn't let go until God blessed him."

"Why would someone want to come up here? Why don't they go to church?" She took a long sip of tea.

"Well, there's a lot more to having a relationship with God

than going to a building. All through the Bible, God speaks of going to the mountain. You know, to get away from everything -- find direction for your life. Even Moses went to the mountain and God gave him the Ten Commandments."

"You know your Bible stories." She leaned to rub Mohan's head.

"Would you like more tea? Are you hungry by now?"

"Yes, please. It's past my dinner time," she stammered.

"Let's see what we can come up with that you might like. How about green beans? Maybe potatoes? Do you like your taters stewed or fried?" He flashed a playful grin. "Got some cornbread and hominy left over. Any of that sound good to you?"

"It all sounds fine. Whatever you have is okay." Her voice could hardly be heard over the sound of the rain coming down in full force.

"Wish I had *fancy fixings* to offer you," Jesse rambled. "On Gabby Mountain, generations of folks have always grown vegetables and fruit. Along with fresh game and fish, they had plenty, such as it was-" He was interrupted by a loud clap of thunder that shook the dishes and rattled the windowpanes.

As Jesse returned to the table with another cup of tea, Ellie commented, "This is quite an elegant tea service. Why do you have something so exquisite up here in this cabin?"

Jesse wiped his hands on a clean towel. "Mama and Jenna bought this tea set in England. If we keep it at home, we'll never take time to sit down and use it. It'll be stuck up on a shelf out of sight. Up here, time slows down--nothing to do but enjoy life. You have time to think and talk. But if we're home, the television's on or we're on the phone."

He could feel Ellie's eyes as he peeled potatoes and onions and dumped jars of vegetables into iron pots.

"Will you eat bread?"

"Yes--my doctors say a gluten-free diet is healthier. And I'm not supposed to have meat or dairy either." Ellie shrugged.

"That's good to know since we don't have much to choose from except canned vegetables and fruit. I'll make us a cake of biscuit bread. In the morning, we can eat it with jelly and honey. Even give some to Mohan."

"You sure do look like a wolf, Mr. Mohan. We must re-write all the fairy tales. You're not trying to eat me. Instead, you keep rescuing me. You're a good doggy, and I like your soft ears."

Jesse laughed. "Yeah, when Mohan likes somebody, he stays right with them."

"Earlier you said he was a wolf. Is that true?"

"I don't know. Your guess is as good as mine is. He's smarter than any ordinary dog, and he does cut loose to howling sometimes. Come on, Wahya. Howl for Miss Ellie." Jesse stopped what he was doing in the kitchen and turned to face Mohan. "*Wahoo*," he began.

Mohan threw his head back, "*Wahoo*."

"Amazing--you *talk* to your dog or wolf. Why do you call him Wahya?"

"Cherokee for wolf."

"How long have you had him?"

"I got him about two years ago from my cousin Jonathan. He got him when he was a pup. Thought he could make a city dog out of him."

"Why can't he live in the city?"

"You can't coop up an animal like Mohan. He's like me. He doesn't like to be in town. He needs plenty of fresh air and room to roam. Jonathan housebroke him, but Mohan needs a place to run. He kept digging out of their yard and even learned to climb the fence. Then he'd run off. Could've been hit by a car." Jesse put a jar of pickles on the table.

"Don't you like the city?"

"It's all right, but I don't like to stay long."

"Did you go to college--like your sister?"

"No, college was a sore subject around our house for a few years. I always said I didn't want to go. But I took all the college prep classes in high school--make Mama happy."

"Your ... mama?" Ellie's voice trailed.

"Mama's a teacher, and she's high on getting an education. Said I might change my mind someday and I needed to be prepared. We always knew Jenna was going to college to be a doctor. I always said I wanted to stay on Gabby Mountain and raise horses." Jesse opened the oven door.

"Have you been happy with that decision?"

"I have. You see, I got a second chance on life, and I reckon life's too short to spend it doing something you don't want to do."

"A second chance?"

"I had ALL, childhood leukemia when I was three. They nearly lost me several times. God wasn't through with me, and He gave me a second chance. Had some smart doctors and my family can't say enough good things about Children's Hospital."

"You must have a lot of bad memories from such an ordeal.'"

"I remember some stuff. I guess kids tune out bad things.

Mostly, I remember what my parents tell me. It's really odd though--I'll remember some random thing. When I ask Mama and Daddy, they say it really happened."

"That must have been quite an ordeal for your family."

"I was in and out of the hospital for almost two years, and that's when Mama wrote the song *In the Midst*. She sang it to calm me down when I was restless."

"Are you okay now?"

"Been cancer-free since I was five. By the grace of God and all those believers who prayed for me, I have to say I'm fit as a fiddle."

"Why do you think God makes bad things happen to good people--even little kids?"

"That's an age-old question. I have an opinion." He stirred the vegetables on the wood stove.

"And your opinion is?"

"God allowed this to happen to me, so others could see Him. The doctors gave up on me, more than once. Other people saw how my family reacted. They prayed, believed, and didn't give up hope. God answered by sparing my life, which gave others the opportunity to see His strength."

"But you were a little kid. It doesn't make sense."

"Right, but Mama and Daddy had to trust God--to let Him give them the grace to stand in the midst of the storm."

"I don't understand."

"People aren't meant to figure everything out. God wants to be the hero in our story. That's why we pray. Call on Jesus—He'll hear you." Jesse's voice had become serious.

"I can't imagine God or Jesus taking care of all *my* problems," she murmured.

"I don't know what your problems are, but God does. No matter what, He's greater than any obstacle you'll ever face."

"How can that be?"

"People try to make God complicated, but He makes it fairly simple. Give your heart to Him. Ask Him to forgive your sins, and by faith, you'll receive His grace and mercy. He'll empower you with hope to live in victory—not be defeated."

Ellie didn't ask any more questions as Jesse finished preparing the meal. And he didn't know if she understood, but in his heart, these were the truths he was supposed to share with her.

௵6௸

Looking Through the Rain

B*on appétit, Mademoiselle.* Here is your *pomme de terre.*"

"What did you just say? Do you speak *French*?" Eloree shrieked with astonishment.

"*Bien sur*, of course, I do. Do you?" Jesse placed a bowl of steaming potatoes and onions on the table.

"Yes, I mean *ah oui,*" she said, not sure what to make of his antics. "Why do you speak French?"

"Jenna talked me into taking French when we were in high school. Said if we had to take a foreign language for college, we might as well take the same one, so we could talk to each other."

"Are you fluent?"

"Used to be--before Jenna went off to college." He brought the rest of the meal to the table.

Along with potatoes, he'd warmed the leftover hominy and heated fresh green beans. The golden cake of biscuit lay steaming on a platter. Ellie's mouth watered.

"Thank you," she smiled--not sure if the queasiness in the pit of her stomach was from hunger or the need to apologize for her earlier antics. Her afternoon medications had worn off, leaving her with an insatiable appetite.

She breathed a deep sigh as Jesse set a place for himself at the table. Was he hungry or wanting to dine with her?

"Well, let's ask the blessing." He took his place across from her.

Ellie bowed her head as he prayed. "God, thank You for this food--we ask You to bless it to the nourishment of our bodies and our bodies to Your service. We ask You for divine protection and angels camping around us. One more thing, God. Keep Your hand on Saja and the babies. In Jesus' name, Amen." He looked up and passed the bowl of fried potatoes to her. "Dig, in. Nobody's supposed to go hungry up here on Gabby Mountain."

Ellie placed a worn linen towel in her lap. "These potatoes look delicious. I don't think I've ever had them prepared this way."

"Have some biscuit bread. This would be better with *Jersey juice.*"

"I'm not familiar with that kind of juice."

Jesse leaned back in the chair, laughing so hard he turned scarlet.

"What's so hilarious?"

"The look on your face." He guffawed again. "*Jersey juice* is milk from a Jersey cow."

"You like to tease, don't you?" Ellie smiled and threw up her hands.

He nodded, and she watched as the glow of the candle revealed a smile on his face that hadn't gone away. Was he still laughing inside at his own cleverness? Or could it be he was pleased to be having a candlelight dinner—with her?

Jesse broke the silence. "How is everything? Better eat plenty while it's still hot."

"Thank you for dinner. Everything's quite tasty."

"You're mighty welcome. Have some more taters and green beans. Care for some fried cinnamon apples? I'll just wind up having to throw out what we don't eat. No need to be wasteful."

"In that case, my compliments to you, Chef Jesse." Ellie filled her plate again.

Jesse tipped his head with a mock salute. "Try some hominy. The Cherokee taught the settlers how to make it."

"Then, I'll be glad to try it."

"It's one of Jenna's favorites. She only likes to eat it when she comes up here, and she only eats it with Ma's bread and butter pickles."

"This is the first time I've ever had hominy, but I'll agree with Jenna," she said between bites of the chewy puffy morsels.

Jesse reached for another slice of bread. "Jenna's quite a girl. I admit, I still miss her and Cindi. They've been gone from home for four years."

"Cindi? Is she your other sister?"

"No, she's Jenna's best friend. Since preschool, those two have stuck together. Cindi was there for Jenna while I was in the hospital. When I was little, I said that if she was going to be Jenna's best friend, she had to be my best friend, too." He chuckled at his own comment.

"How old is Cindi?"

"Twenty-one, same as we are. She stayed at our house a lot when we were growing up. Then, our senior year of high school, she moved in with us."

"That must have been awkward. I mean having your sister's best friend living in your house." Ellie gathered Cindi might be Jesse's girlfriend.

"Not for us. Cindi's like family. The summer before our senior year, her daddy took her to Skagway, Alaska. Told her they were going on vacation, but when they got there, he'd already rented a house and didn't intend to bring her back to North Carolina. She and Jenna were on the phone every day for weeks--bawling their eyes out."

"Couldn't her father do as he pleased?"

"Well, you could say that, but he hadn't been a part of her life until then. Not a good family situation. My family won't stand by and watch somebody get run over. If we have to we'll step in." Jesse's dark eyes told her he was serious.

"Did he let her come back?"

"Not until we flew to Alaska. Daddy tried to talk sense into him. Told him how it was unfair for Cindi to be forced to leave Franklin her senior year."

"Did her father listen?"

"Not at first. Was worried about having to pay child support. My daddy said he'd support Cindi and not ask him for one dime. Then he told Cindi's dad that Jenna would send her a one-way ticket home to North Carolina. And it was up to him. He could let her come back with us, or she'd come back on her own quick as she turned eighteen."

"What did her father choose?"

"He let her come on back with us."

"Where's Cindi now?" she asked.

"UNC with Jenna." Jesse stood and began clearing the table.

Ellie stared at the melting candle wax spilling onto the rim of the candleholder. The emotions rearing up inside her felt like jealousy, yet a part of her was pleased someone else's dreams were coming true. She wished she had dreams of her own. Would that day ever come?

The mantel clock struck nine as she made her way back to the couch, thinking about the situation Jesse had shared with her.

She still wasn't sure if Cindi was Jesse's girlfriend, but she liked the fact his family had gone out of their way for Cindi. Would someone be there for her when she had to face her father? Would she make him understand she had needs?

Pushing the menacing thoughts aside, she searched through her Navè for the medications to be taken after each meal, but they weren't there. Maybe she'd lost them on the way up the mountain or left them in the car.

For an instant, she thought about telling Jesse. Watching his shadow move across the wall as he finished cleaning up, she decided against it, thinking he might see the situation as her ploy to leave the cabin.

She watched Jesse in the candlelight and wondered how he could be so happy at a time like this--whistling as he bustled about, with a red and white checked towel slung over his shoulder. She imagined his family would be so pleased to see him, he wouldn't have to explain anything—unlike her father. What if she'd been killed at the waterfall or by the lightning strike at the barn?

She'd never met anyone like Jesse. She admired the way he took pride in his family and this mountain and vowed to speak with her father about changing his proposed legislation for private mountain landowners. It was the least she could do to repay Jesse.

Her thoughts were interrupted as Mohan returned to her side. The fur around his head and ears was velvety soft and she loved the feel of it as she ran her fingers along his face. Stroking his back, she was again reminded of the dog's unrest, as the hair covering his undercoat became coarse and stood on end.

How could a wild rugged creature be so tame, peaceful and beautiful? Like Jesse--a rugged man with a soft demeanor, whose hands were big and calloused, strong yet gentle, when he held the dainty teacup. She saw his kindness and patience. He wasn't at all the stereotypical country boy she envisioned. He knew about Beethoven and appreciated fine china. He didn't swear, and he spoke French. And above all--he'd used the word *pretty*. And she knew in her heart he meant it toward her.

Jesse carried in more dry wood and stacked it by the fireplace. "We may need this before morning, and I don't want it to get wet. Rain's coming down like pouring out of a bucket."

Then, he picked up the guitar and began plucking the strings as if he was searching for a tune. "What kind of music do you like?"

"I love all genres, but I especially like the song you played before dinner. Care to play it again?"

"Sure." Jesse began to pick the tune.

"If you sing it to me again, I can follow along. Let's try."

He began to play and belt out the familiar verses. Ellie joined him on each line of the chorus.

Jesse tilted his head toward her. "You sound good."

"Thank you. I enjoy singing, and I like to play the piano. May I play your piano?"

"Go ahead. It's got some sticky keys and is a little out of tune. My grandpa hauled that piano up here on the back of a log truck, many years ago."

"I'm honored to play it." She perched on the round stool. "Do you always play that song in C?"

"I play by ear. You lead--I'll follow you."

After no more than two bars, Jesse stopped, but Ellie's hands glided over the keys with ease. She knew his eyes were on her, and she finished the piece--then turned on the stool to face him. She folded her hands in her lap and looked up at him from the corner of her eye, hoping he'd praise her playing.

He shook his head. "You're the best piano player I've *ever* heard. Where on earth did you learn to play like that?"

"Thank you." She blushed. "I studied at Highland Piano with Patrick Lee Hebert," she added, assuming Jesse had never heard of Highland Piano or Patrick Lee Hebert.

"Wow. Mama's got every one of his albums. She says he's a real master talent in the music world."

"It was quite an honor to be chosen to study under him."

"Well, play something else," he requested, but before she could begin, the wind blew down the chimney, filling the cabin with smoke.

Coughing and choking, their eyes burned, and Jesse grabbed her arm, guiding her to the door.

Once on the porch, Jesse draped his old corduroy coat around her shoulders and lifted the hood over her head. She could hardly see, but at least she could breathe.

Mohan reared up on Jesse's shoulders. "What's wrong with--" Before he could get the words out, Ellie heard what sounded like a massive train roaring up the mountain.

"Get back in the house." Jesse grabbed Ellie's arm and half dragged her into the house. "Get under the bed."

She knew Jesse was scared, and it terrified her. *Something* horrible was happening. *Something* much more than just the thunder, lightning, fierce wind, and torrents of rain.

"Stay here under the bed. Do you hear me, Ellie?"

"I hear you." Her voice quivered as she struggled to breathe. Cobwebs clung to her face, and dust fell in her eyes. She couldn't move even if she wanted to, wedged between Mohan and Jesse in the tight space.

The cabin shook as if a giant ferocious hand had control over it. The windowpanes rattled, and she felt the earth tremble beneath the cabin floor. She squeezed her eyes shut--every part of her being trembled.

She heard Jesse talking and was sure he was saying another prayer, but she couldn't make out his words. She wanted to pray too, but the only prayer she knew was the Lord's Prayer. She struggled to remember the words between gulps of air. Were these mere words, or was there a God who listened? Her heart pounded as she gasped for breath, and the tightness of being jammed under the old bed, with the smell of Mohan's wet fur, added to her terror.

The storm raged on, and the rain pounded like an angry giant on the other side of the cabin wall. Trees crashed as if attacked by an army of axes. The wind bore down against the cabin walls with such force Ellie covered her ears to drown out the noise.

After what seemed an eternity, she heard Jesse, "*Jesus, Jesus, Jesus.*" She tried to whisper, "*Jesus*", but a force inside her drove her to shout louder—as though the volume of her voice made a difference.

Jesse reached for her, his powerful grip closed around her hand, and she clung to his hand. Would she make it out alive? Was this God's way of punishing her for not believing in Him?

She whispered, "God, I've been so bad. Forgive me. If you are real, please save me. I don't want to die like this."

Fright faded, and she felt a reassuring peace she'd never known, as though everything would be alright. The violence outside became an eerie calm as if nothing had happened. She was keenly aware of Jesse's heavy breathing and Mohan's whine.

Crash--something hit the side of the cabin with an intensity that shook the bed and the mirror on the dresser.

"Get to the porch," Jesse yelled.

Ellie stood behind Jesse as he leaned over the porch rail. Her heart pounded in the pit of her stomach. Using the scant light from his cell phone, she watched as Jesse peered into the darkness. The rain had stopped, but water poured off the roof. And the smell of fresh mud filled the air. She closed her eyes, half expecting Jesse to grab her arm and flee off the porch.

But instead, he pointed. "Look what a big rock. It's the size of a pickup truck," he said.

"Did it hit the cabin?" Ellie's voice quivered.

"It must have grazed the corner. If it had hit just right, the rascal would have *pert near* taken down the whole cabin. A few more feet and it would've leveled this porch."

"What happened?"

"Must have been a tornado. The old folks used to talk about cloudbursts and hundred-year storms. This had to be one or else it was an earthquake."

She turned and faced him, still wrapped in his old corduroy coat. He rested his hands on her shoulders. She wanted to ask him what was going to happen next. If the monster storm was coming back. If they would be alive come morning. Instead, she pushed back the hood and looked into his dark eyes, in a way she'd never looked at another human being. She was alive, and he was here with her. She wanted to say something—tell him how grateful she was for him—for God—to be alive. But no words came, and he slipped his arm around her shoulders and guided her back into the cabin.

~~~~~

"Stay here. I'm going in the backroom to see if there's any damage." Jesse disappeared behind the floral print curtain.

With only the light from his cell phone, he gazed around the room--then slid an old tin trunk away from the wall, and rubbed his hands along the floor. Much to his dismay, the floor was wet and sticky mud clung to his hand. He hoisted the trunk into his arms and carried it into the front room.

Catching his breath, Jesse made his way into the kitchen for a fresh supply of candles. "We need more light." He placed them on a nearby table. "I'm glad I got to this old trunk. Hope nothing in here's ruined, but the floor's getting wet in there."

He dug to the bottom of the trunk, removing the items and laying them out. He knew Ellie was watching his every move, and each time he glanced at her, she looked down at Mohan, who was enjoying getting his ears rubbed.

Once everything was out of the trunk, Jesse pulled up a chair and sat down across from her. "Thank goodness nothing got wet. This old trunk will have to be cleaned up before I pack all this back in. Sorry for the mess, but I'm going to let it all air out for a day or two."

"Who does all this stuff belong to?"

"There are several old trunks and cedar chests up here,
~~~~~

but this particular one belonged to Daisy Marie." Jesse pointed toward the heap of clothes, antique picture frames, books, and knick-knacks.

"Did she live in this cabin at one time?"

"Yeah, she was born in this cabin. The youngest daughter of my great-great-great grandparents, Jesse and Ruth Woods. Here's a portrait of her."

"She's beautiful. It looks like she had blonde hair and blue eyes. Where did she ever get such a nice colored portrait? It must be hand painted."

"Daisy Marie lived a different life than all the others. Of Jesse and Ruth's children, she's the only one who left Gabby Mountain to go to college. Back then, it was hard for anybody to go to college, but they say Grandpa Jesse wanted at least one of his kids to get an education, and Daisy Marie was the only one who wasn't married. He took her to Mars Hill College, over near Asheville."

"That's a long way from here. How did they get there?"

"In those days, it took two days to get to Dillsboro with a horse and wagon. There they caught the train."

"Why did he want her to go to college?"

"Grandpa Jesse loved books. He taught all his kids to read and write. Daisy Marie was going to come back to Gabby Mountain and be a schoolteacher."

"Did that happen?" Ellie seemed genuinely interested.

"No. Once she got to Mars Hill, she met a rich young man from Savannah. He was from *old money* if you know what I mean. She wound up marrying and moving to Savannah. She finished college and became a part of the rich people's society."

"Did she ever come back to Gabby Mountain to visit?"

"Now that, she did do. When they got married, her daddy told her husband not to ever take her off so far, she couldn't come back home if she wanted to. Her husband kept his word. She came back almost every summer and brought her young'uns. She said she wanted them to grow up knowing what life here on Gabby Mountain was like. And she wanted them to know who their people were. Funny thing is, some of the cousins from that side of the family still stay in touch and come to visit."

"What does your family think about having rich cousins from Savannah?"

"Don't think much about it at all. It's not money that makes a person. The Bible says the love of money is the root of all evil. Not the money itself, just the love of it."

"She had some rather nice things for that day and time."

"Yeah, she used to send things back home. That's where a lot of this antique stuff came from. Her children and grandchildren would send things. She even sent a photographer all the way from Savannah to Gabby Mountain to take pictures of all the family members. There weren't many cameras back then, so our family's blessed to have all these pictures of the old folks."

Ellie ran her finger along the edge of another portrait. "And this is?"

"Grandpa Jesse and Grandma Ruth."

"And you're his namesake. See, I paid attention to your history lesson." Ellie tilted her head at him.

"Are you named after anybody in particular, Ellie?"

She didn't look at him but dropped her head. "No, I'm like Naomi and Ruth. I just showed up on Gabby Mountain, and now I'm *Ellie*."

Jesse gathered from her tone she wasn't going to tell him anything more. He turned to the mantle above the fireplace and retrieved a whet rock--then pulled out his pocketknife and sharpened it with slow methodical strokes.

He thought about home and all the people who must be worried sick. Then his mind wandered to the stable and Saja. Who would tend her if she foaled tonight, and he wasn't there? Did Nanta and Tauga make it back before the brunt of the storm? How much timber must be downed? Was the Christmas tree patch spared?

He turned his attention back to Ellie, propped on the end of the couch with her swollen ankle on a pillow. "How's that ankle doing?" he asked, settling into an old wooden rocking chair by the fireplace.

"It's okay. Hurts some, but I can walk on it," she answered dryly, and he knew she avoided his glance.

So what if she didn't want to tell him about herself? Should it matter anyway? Tomorrow, at this time, they'd be off this mountain, and everything that had happened would be history. Ellie would be history, too.

The thought of never seeing her again after tonight made him study her. She looked up and his eyes met hers. But he looked down and whittled a piece of wood he kept on the mantle. He felt her eyes on him, but he focused on the piece of wood.

"What are you making?".

"Dogwood blossom. I'd say it's finished. If I keep whittling, there won't be much left. Want to see it?" He placed the wooden blossom in her outstretched right hand.

She rested her fingers on his. "Pretty. Did it take you long to carve?"

Stunned by her lingering touch, he swallowed hard before he spoke. "Been working on it on and off since last spring. I wanted to have it finished by this Easter, so I'm going to call it done."

"Why by Easter?"

"Do you know the Legend of the Dogwood?"

She shook her head, and Jesse began, "It shows the story of the crucifixion. In the center of the outer edge of each petal is the print of the nails. In the center of the flower, stained with blood, you see the crown of thorns. Every time we look at the beauty of a dogwood blossom, we're to be reminded of the death of Jesus."

"There's nothing beautiful about death, and I don't like to think about it." Her voice trailed.

"I see what you mean, but if Jesus hadn't died on the cross and rose again the third day, we wouldn't have eternal life."

"You must mean heaven. Well, don't all *good* people go to heaven?"

"That's what some people think, but I'm afraid they're going to come up short on the judgment day. God requires His children to accept Jesus as their personal Savior to be able to go to heaven."

She stared at him, and he felt compelled to share more with her, even though he knew she might try to argue. "The first Bible verse I ever remember learning was John 3:16 – it tells us that God loved the world enough to send His only son, to die on the cross for us, so we can have eternal life if we believe in Him."

"I really don't know what all that means, but something happened to me when we were under the bed. May I share it with you?"

This wasn't the response Jesse expected.

She blinked hard several times--then looked up at him. "I was really scared and didn't know what to do. As the storm raged on, I thought we were going to die. Then I told God if He really is real, to save me because I didn't want to die like that."

"And then what happened?"

"I was still scared, but when we were screaming *Jesus*, I felt at peace--like everything was going to be okay. I know now, God is real," she replied with certainty, looking at the dogwood again before closing her fingers around it.

Jesse took a deep breath. "If you died right now, would you go to heaven or hell?"

"Heaven." She nodded.

"That's the answer we all need to have. Keep the dogwood."

"Thank you." She smiled up at him. "I suppose Gabby Mountain is my place of *penial* now."

"That's right. This was your time and your place." Jesse reached for her hand. "The peace you feel is God's presence. Even the angels in heaven rejoice when you give your life to Christ."

Ellie squeezed his hand, leaving him to wonder why she wouldn't tell him about herself.

➷7☙

Insignificance

Ellie opened her Navè and brought out the journal Dr. Shanks gave her. The blank page stared back at her as she decided where to begin--her mind a flurry of recollections of the past twelve hours.

She fixed her eyes on Jesse as he slept in the wooden rocking chair. His plaid shirt--unbuttoned at the neck, revealed a white tee shirt--his Wrangler jeans were thin at the knees. Ellie found it remarkable that his broad, calloused hands carved the intricate dogwood blossom and played the guitar with such ease. He accepted her without knowing her identity, leaving her to hope he wouldn't change his opinion of her--if he ever found out.

And then she began to write as if the pen in her hand could read her mind. It curved across the page forging words like *handsome* and *debonair*. Convinced she'd never show this to anyone, not even Dr. Shanks, she continued--mentioning her new love for God and adoration of Mohan. Then, she added a part about Jenna, and how she wished she could be more like her.

She closed her eyes, praying her father's inevitable wrath wouldn't outweigh the newfound joy of meeting Jesse and spending this time with him, even in the midst of the storm.

She began to write again. *Since no one will ever see this, I can let my imagination run wild. Maybe this is what it feels like to be a real princess, being in distress and danger. My castle in an enchanted forest is a cabin in a faraway place called Gabby Mountain. Confronted by a villain, my father, and rescued from the perils of the raging storm by a handsome cowboy prince... or in this case country boy. Do princesses always live happily ever?*

Suddenly the stillness of the night shattered with a piercing scream like a woman in dire pain.

"Jesse" Ellie leaped off the couch in frenzy, not noticing where the journal landed.

Mohan bounded to the door, barking and growling ferociously.

"Wahya. What happened?" Jesse sprung to his feet.

"There's a screaming woman outside."

"There can't be a woman outside. Not in this mess. You must have heard the wind." He grabbed Mohan by the collar.

Ellie raised her voice over Mohan's barking. "I *heard* her. Maybe it's Jenna. Go help her."

The trio bounded to the porch, peering into the darkness. Only the river in the distance could be heard above Mohan's continued low growl. Cupping his hands, Jesse whistled long and loud.

"Why are you whistling?"

"Listen." Jesse quieted her. "If Jenna's out there, she'll whistle back. I don't hear anything."

"Yell back at her. I heard her scream. Maybe she's too hurt to whistle back."

"Okay, Ellie. We'll make sure."

Again, Jesse cupped his hands and yelled, "*Heellloo.*" The only sound was his echo. "We'll stay out here as long as you want, but I think it was the wind."

"I know I heard a woman scream." Ellie brought her hand to her throat. "Mohan heard it, too. See the hair standing up on the back of his neck?"

"It could've been another animal, but the only animal that sounds like a woman screaming is a panther or a *painter* as the old folks used to say. Haven't heard of any panthers around here in years, but after a storm like this, you never know what might wander through these mountains."

"Maybe the animal Mohan chased out of the barn earlier tonight was a panther." Ellie backed toward the cabin door.

"I reckon it could've been. Dogs usually don't want *no* part of a panther. But Mohan *ain't* no ordinary dog. Being mostly wolf, he'd probably take one on. We better keep him inside the rest of the night."

Back inside the cabin, Ellie settled on the couch, and Jesse popped corn in the fireplace.

He dumped the savory heap in a metal bowl and filled two glasses with water. "It's too early in the morning to call this a midnight snack, but I like popcorn any time, don't you?"

Ellie simply nodded and reached for one kernel.

"What's on your mind, Miss Ellie?" Jesse spoke between

bites. "Don't care for popcorn?"

"Yes, but I'm thinking about panthers." Her voice dropped, "are they dangerous?"

Jesse took a long drink of water and wiped his mouth on the back of his hand. "Of course--they're wild animals."

"I mean, do they attack people?"

"As a general rule, I would say no, but they've been known to, especially people smaller than they are. Most wild animals don't like to be near humans, but a hungry animal of any kind is not one to be reckoned with."

Ellie chewed a few more kernels. She knew the animal that ran from the barn wasn't a bear. And the blood-curdling scream left a pit in her stomach. "Are there panthers around here?"

"I hear-tell there used to be. Franklin High School's mascot is the panther." Jesse raised his elbows above his head.

"But the last time one was seen here on Gabby Mountain, was right here *in this cabin*."

She stopped chewing as her stare penetrated the calmness in the room. The glow from the fire revealed a half-playful grin on his face. Time stood still, with only the ticking of the old mantle clock breaking the silence.

"Okay, Jesse. Are you teasing? I have to know if a wild panther was really in this cabin--where I'm sitting."

Plopping a few more kernels into his mouth, Jesse leaned toward her. "Well, Aunt Naomi mixed a bowl of biscuit dough. She put the biscuits in the oven to bake while she went to the springhouse--not more than fifty yards up the hill. She left a baby asleep right there in the chimney corner." He pointed.

"By *this* fireplace?"

"Yes, right here in this room. The baby was James, who was my great-great-grandfather. Anyway, Naomi wasn't gone very long, but when she walked back into the cabin, there was a panther reared up on the table, scratching the bread dough out of the wooden bowl. She got between the panther and the baby--afraid the baby would wake up and cry. Naomi stared that panther down and when it came toward her, she took after it with the broom and ran it out of here."

"You're teasing." Ellie closed her eyes and shook her head.

"I'm not teasing. That story's been passed down through my family for years. They kept the old wooden bowl with the scratches on it to prove it's true."

"What happened to the bowl?" Ellie's mouth formed a tight line.

"My grandmother has it packed away. You don't believe me, do you?"

"Wait. I do believe you. Naomi must have been an incredible woman. I'd like to hear more about her."

Jesse raked the dying embers in the fireplace. "If it hadn't been for Naomi, my family might not have been able to keep Gabby Mountain all these years. Her showing up changed the course of history for this family."

"Tell me."

"We'll have plenty of time for storytelling once we get packed up and on our way. It'll be daylight soon, and I want to get some gear together in case we have to walk off here."

When Jesse stepped into the back room, Ellie was grateful for a few minutes to sort her muddled thoughts. Her mind raced as she rehearsed how to explain all that had happened to her father. He wouldn't understand and no telling what his reprimand would be. The sickening feeling in her gut swelled, reaching into her throat. Only a few hours ago, she had risked her life trying to get off this mountain. Now, she was in no hurry to leave, and she felt as though she'd turned into someone else--someone free to relax in the comfort of a log cabin filled with enticing stories of long ago, patchwork quilts, hot bread with cinnamon apples, a warming fire, a wolf by her side, and a handsome cowboy prince who treated her like a princess. Did it all have to end now?

~~~~~

As daylight filtered through the windows, Jesse rummaged through the cabin, laying out things that might be useful for the expedition down the mountain. He didn't know what this day might hold. Even though he had walked off Gabby Mountain hundreds of times, this trek would be different.

As he slid a shiny, silver-handled revolver into a holster on his waist, he glanced toward the couch where Ellie brushed her hair.

"Not a gun," she gasped.

"Ellie, you don't have anything to worry about." He moved to the edge of the couch, next to her.

"Guns kill people." She held up her hairbrush as though it was a weapon.

"Look, I never come up this mountain without a gun." Jesse cleared his throat. "I'm not going to shoot another human being. A fellow never knows when he might have to fire a shot to
~~~~~

scare off a wild animal. I've seen a lot of wild hog sign this spring, and the rascals can be down-right ornery."

"I don't like guns." Her voice grew louder.

"I understand, but if I shoot this pistol, somebody may hear it. That way, they'll know where to come to meet us."

"Where did you get it?"

"Out of the drawer in the back room. Out here in the country, everybody has at least one gun, and they know how to shoot it. It's just part of how we live."

"Does Jenna shoot a gun?"

"Yes, she target practices with me sometimes, but I doubt she'd shoot an animal--even if it came toward her."

"Ellie, if this old pistol makes you uncomfortable, I'll leave it here. But I really want you to consider how it might come in handy. After all, you saw a wild animal at the old barn and heard something outside."

"I don't think we need a deadly weapon to get back to my car." She clung to her bag as if it was a shield.

"I'm sure we probably won't have to use it as a deadly weapon to get back, but there's always *just in case*." He tried to read her expression--half hidden by her hair.

"You ever been to New York City?"

"Yes. But what does that have to do with the situation we're in?"

With elbows on his knees, he leaned toward her. "Look at it like this, Ellie. If we were stranded—say, in New York City--I wouldn't know how to get to wherever we wanted to go. Not like you would. I wouldn't even know where the subway was or how to hail a cab." He attempted to laugh at his own remarks and Ellie tilted her head sideways, revealing a curious smile.

"Alright then, Gabby Mountain is my New York City. I may not be able to flag down a taxi or get on a subway, but I know this mountain and how to survive here. Bear with me--we'll get back safe and sound, in no time flat."

Ellie wrung her hands. "Okay."

Rising to his feet, Jesse patted her shoulder. "*Atta* girl, Ellie. Now let's get this show on the road."

"How long do you think it'll take us to walk back?"

"I don't know. It depends on what we find along the way. Shouldn't take more than a couple of hours, but we'll have to figure out the best route. We might make it by dinnertime. To be on the safe side, I'll pack something for us to eat."

"Dinner? That will be quite late, won't it?"

Jesse reached for a jar of peanut butter. "I keep forgetting.

I mean *lunchtime*. Up here on Gabby, we have dinner and supper. But, do you think you can walk well enough to start off the mountain?"

"We don't have any other options, do we?"

"We could stay here and wait until someone comes to rescue us, but it could take hours. I'm guessing there's a whole lot of timber down--the road will have to be cleared to get a vehicle up here."

"If I can't get my boot back on, how am I going to walk?" Ellie asked, leaving Jesse with the notion she trusted his judgment.

"Been thinking about that. Those are nice boots, they're pretty much ruined. I could rub them down with saddle soap, but they won't be pretty. I can make you a makeshift boot, but I'll have to cut this one." Holding up the boot, he added, "I'll buy you a new pair."

"No, that won't be necessary. I have other boots. Do what you have to."

He pulled a long hunting knife from his belt. He steadied the boot and knitted his brow as he sliced the front of the boot open, all the way to the toe.

"Can you get your foot in, now?" Jesse knelt and offered the boot to Ellie.

"Well, I got my foot in, but how will I keep it on?"

"That's where the duct tape comes in. I'll tape it to hold it on your foot."

Once the boot was secured on her foot, Ellie stood up. "Feels a little weird, but I suppose it'll do. What about these pants? They're too long."

"Ah, now. That's the good thing about overalls. You can adjust them. Here let me see these straps." Jesse fumbled with the buckles on her shoulders. "This took them up some, but they're still long on you."

Ellie took one of the straps off the Navè bag and twisted it through the belt loops circling her waist. "A makeshift belt to match my makeshift boot. I may not be a fashion icon, but this serves the purpose of a belt, don't you agree?"

Her beauty mesmerized him—and he wanted to tell her how pretty she looked, even in faded overalls with a tattered flannel shirt. But the belt she fashioned gave her the look of a character from the *Beverly Hillbillies*, and he couldn't resist the temptation to tease. "You look like Cousin Ellie Mae."

"Who's that?"

"You mean you don't know Cousin Ellie Mae from the

Beverly Hillbillies?"

"How should I know your cousin from Beverly Hills?"

The serious look on her face was too much for Jesse, and he chuckled. "You mean you went to Beverly Hills and didn't meet the Clampetts? Not even Jethro Bodine?" He guffawed, gasping for breath as she stared at him.

"I don't know what's so funny unless it's the way I'm dressed. Trust me. I'll be more than thrilled to change when I get back to my car. I must look like a scarecrow." She flailed her arms.

"Well until then, I can't resist calling you Cousin Ellie Mae." Jesse hooked his thumbs through the belt loops on his jeans.

"Fine with me. I doubt I'm your cousin, but if laughter helps us get off this mountain, so be it. Laugh all you want." She spun around, modeling her new get up. "Do I look hideous?"

Jesse's laughter subsided into a broad grin. "No Ma'am. You look fine. Exceptionally fine for where we're going, Cousin Ellie Mae." He added one last taunt.

"Please. Don't call me Ma'am. Cousin Ellie Mae will do. Actually, I like it." She said, as his eyes locked with hers.

He'd do anything in his power to please her, keep her safe, and get her back to the stable. He hoped this wouldn't be the last time they'd be together in the cabin.

꧁8꧂

Blue Skies

The climb to the top of the ridge left Ellie huffing for breath. The smell of wet dirt filled her head with a sense of earthy freshness as the cool, damp air chilled her lungs. They had no choice but to wade through knee-deep mud and storm debris to begin the journey off the mountain. Her feet were soaked, and the muddy legs of the overalls clung to her calves, leaving a cold, wet reminder as she trudged through the muck. Even with the makeshift boot, her ankle throbbed with each step.

But she was in awe of Jesse's continued kindness. He took her hand as they left the cabin--even offered to carry her, but she had insisted on walking. She felt protected by his firm grip as he guided her around rocks, through tree branches, and over slick leaves carpeting the rain-soaked dirt. She felt the part of a damsel in distress–Jesse her knight in shining armor. And she smiled to herself as he bent wet limbs and helped her over tree trunks--lifeless, scattered in all directions. Wet pine bows splattered cold drops onto her hair and face. Mud and pine rosin stuck each time she swept loose strands of hair out of her eyes.

Jesse had insisted she wear his old brown corduroy coat. And though it looked like nothing in her closet, she liked the warmth and comfort it afforded. The coat was like most everything else on Gabby Mountain--though worn, it served a basic purpose, and there was no need for a new one.

Mohan strode close by as they climbed the steep mountainside. Though coated in pasty, black mud, he rubbed up against Ellie when she propped against a huge rock. Stripping the mud-soaked gloves from her cold wet hands, she rubbed his head as her eyes surveyed the splendor before her. "I can see forever from up here. I've hiked to the top of a mountain," she exclaimed, still gasping for breath.

"That's right. You are now on top of Gabby Mountain." Jesse took binoculars out of his backpack.

"I see why you like to come up here so much." Ellie shielded her eyes from the brightness of the morning sun.

"Yeah, but I don't believe what I'm seeing." Jesse fumbled for his phone. "I've never seen anything like *this*. I'm going to take some pictures."

Offering the binoculars to her, Jesse pointed as he snapped pictures. "Look through here. The cabin and what's left of the log barn are the only things standing. Best I can tell, the mudslide ripped the whole side of the mountain--all the way to the river."

"This is horrible. It looks like a giant hand came through and cleared a path." Ellie handed the binoculars back to him.

"God gave us a miracle. The two big poplar trees fell and created a 'V' behind the cabin. Then, all the rocks, mud, and trees went down either side—leaving the cabin standing."

"You mean when the big rock hit the side of the cabin?"

"Exactly. We were spared, but my patch of young Christmas trees is gone. I guess that's the answer to that prayer. Looks like I'm getting out of the tree business." Ellie heard the down-heartedness in his voice.

"What do you mean? Aren't you upset your Christmas trees are gone?" Ellie strained to take in more of the scene.

Jesse propped on the rock beside her. "I've been asking God to give me direction in all the areas of my life. Looks like He's saying *no* to growing Christmas trees."

"Don't you like growing Christmas trees?"

"They're a lot of work, year-round. It can be a lucrative business, but a lot depends on the weather and how many beetles I have to spray for."

"You could always plant them back."

Jesse shook his head and went on, "It's not that easy. All the topsoil was washed away with the young trees. If Senator *Bottlestopper* Evan's legislation gets passed, I'll only be allowed to harvest half of my big trees. The other half of the patch will be controlled by government standards. He's probably never even got his exotic skinned slippers muddy. How does he know what a working man does?"

"But you'll still own-" Ellie cut her statement short, realizing she didn't want Jesse to know how familiar she was with the proposed legislation.

Jesse shot a doubtful glance at her. "What good will it do me to continue owning the property? I'll have to pay taxes on land

I can walk on but won't even be allowed to pick flowers on it, much less cut a tree."

Shocked by the loudness of Jesse's voice and the irritation she hadn't yet seen in him, Ellie sat speechless--her mind running rampant. Calling her father *Bottlestopper* was probably Jesse's way of swearing. But he was right, her father didn't get his slippers muddy. What would he say if he saw her now - drenched in mud?

She closed her eyes. In a few short hours, she'd have to explain all this to him. And she didn't want to face him alone. Her only hope was Dr. Shanks, and she prayed her father would listen to reason.

Jesse hadn't seemed to notice Ellie gave no response to his comments about her father. She sat quietly, rubbing Mohan's warm fur with her red, icy fingers while Jesse continued to scope out the terrain through the binoculars. But the longer she sat, the more her wet boots felt like blocks of ice. Each time the wind sliced through the trees, she felt even colder. Her head pounded, and her ankle throbbed. She wished she could take off the makeshift boot, but she willed herself not to complain and hugged the dog's head to her wind-chapped cheek, vowing not to tell Jesse how uncomfortable she was.

Turning his attention back to her, Jesse pointed again, this time in another direction. "Looking over this way is the Great Smoky Mountains National Park. The other side of that mountain range is Tennessee. From over here, you can see down into Georgia and even South Carolina."

"It's a breathtaking view. Layers and layers of mountains. With hues of blue and purple. I like taking in the whole panorama. No wonder you want to bring people up here to enjoy the mountain."

"Well, we've got a better view today than anyone has had in the last hundred years." Jesse pointed. "All this timber is destroyed. These hardwoods and pines will have to lay here and rot."

"What do you mean?"

"Everything you see, looking straight down the mountain this way, belongs to my family. All the way to the river. That's about two hundred acres. The land on the other side, going over the ridge there, belongs to the federal government. I can salvage some of the timber on my side, maybe get a few loads of logs for lumber, but the government won't let downed timber be removed on their side. No common sense about it."

He kicked his boots against the rock, and Ellie didn't know

if it was more out of frustration or an attempt to knock off the mud. But she kept quiet, choosing not to get into a discussion which might bring her father's name up again.

The silence was broken when Jesse whistled, long and loud. "I was hoping Tauga or Nanta might still be in earshot. Would be nice to get to ride off here."

"Do you think anyone's coming for us?"

"I don't see how they can. Looking through the binoculars, I can tell the old road's blocked with downed timber. It'll take days to cut it out enough to get a rig up here. I think the safest way for us to go is to follow the top of the ridgeline. We'll circle around under Buzzard Knob and down by Fish Hawk. Not as much damage that way."

Ellie stood, stepping closer to Jesse. "This is so weird. I mean, I was a nervous wreck last night, and it seemed like the storm was never going to let up. Just look at all this splendor today. The sun's shining--the sky's blue. Not a cloud in sight. It's as if nothing ever happened. I've never been in a place like this. I mean, we're so far away from civilization and we're all alone."

"Does this worry you?" Jesse's hand brushed her arm.

"Not really. I actually like being up here," she admitted, taking in the vast divide that separated his world from hers.

Gabby Mountain, even with its rugged terrain and mass destruction was a place that brought solitude and peace. Ellie knew her world was beyond the horizon. But being here was like looking at a picture of her life. On one side of the mountain, everything was destroyed beyond repair. Yet on the other side, the mountain looked as if no storm had ever hit.

"Here are the pictures I took." Jesse held the phone at an angle for Ellie to see.

"Did you take *my* picture?"

"Sure. Most people want a picture of themselves taken up here--with the view."

"You can't take a picture of me. Delete it now."

Jesse stared at her, and she knew he wanted an explanation.

She stepped back to gather her thoughts before speaking again. "Please. Don't take any pictures of me. I don't like to have my picture taken. Okay? Just don't."

"I'll delete it if you want me to. But take a good look at it first. This is really neat," he said. "The way the sun's shining, you and Mohan are silhouettes and the mountains are all that show."

The whole idea of Jesse having a picture of her made her uneasy. "That is an unusual picture. I do like it, but what will you do with it?"

"At least let me text it to your phone."

She knew he'd eventually find out who she was, but she didn't want him to find out now--not until they were off the mountain "All right here's my number. But you can't show the picture to anyone, and you can't give my number out. Promise?"

She watched as Jesse put her number in his phone and wondered if he'd ever try to contact her.

He looked at her. "First name, Ellie. Last name?"

"Why do you need my last name?" Her voice wavered.

"I don't have service up here, so I'll add you to my contacts list and send it later."

"Use my first name. You don't *have* to have my last name." She knew he wanted an answer and her heart raced, "Use Mae. I'm Cousin Ellie Mae, remember?" She looked away from him and focused on the treetops closest to the horizon.

She didn't like the look Jesse gave her. His stare was too long, and she hoped he wouldn't question her any further. Not right now, anyway.

"You don't want to tell me who you are. Are you in witness protection or something?"

Ellie looked away, knowing his deep brown eyes were fixed on her. Words didn't come, but Jesse waited for a response, with a sullen look on his face.

"Are you insinuating I'm in trouble with the law?" She timidly asked, trying to force a smile.

"I hope not, but don't you think you owe me an explanation for being so evasive about who you are?"

The seriousness in his voice jarred her. She looked down and wiped her hands on the front of her overalls, taking several seconds longer than needed. Finally, she stood and turned to face him.

"There's not much to tell. First and foremost, I'm not in trouble with the law." She stopped and realized she was taking too long to answer. "Like I've already told you--I was to meet my family, and some friends, to spend Easter weekend in a mountain home. I got here long before they did, so I decided to go for a horseback ride. You know the rest."

Jesse shifted his weight and clenched his jaw, and she knew he wasn't satisfied with the answer.

"Then at least tell me this much. Is there going to be some fellow waiting for me at the stable, wanting an explanation for why I've been on Gabby Mountain with his girlfriend?" He shoved his hands deep into his pockets.

"I don't have a boyfriend," she stated matter-of-factly, looking everywhere but into his face, hoping the conversation was over.

"I can't figure you out. Why all the secrets? Is there anything I haven't told you about me?"

Ellie forced a nervous giggle. "There's one thing I'd like to know."

"And what's that?" His mouth formed a straight line,

"Is there going to be some *girl* waiting for *me* back at the stable, wanting to know why *I've* been on Gabby Mountain with *her* boyfriend?" Ellie stammered.

Jesse's cheeks flushed. "I don't have a girlfriend."

"What about Cindi?" She pried.

"Cindi's like my sister." Jesse secured the straps on his backpack.

Ellie was surprised at her own relief in learning he didn't have a girlfriend. She slung her Navè over her shoulder and stood.

Jesse looked at her from the corner of his eye--then focused on her foot. "If you don't think you can walk, we'll stay. But there're lots of people worried about us. Are you up for it?"

"Let's go." She tried to sound strong.

As the two eased their way down the slippery slope in silence, she wondered what Jesse was thinking but vowed not to say a word. For now, she was hoping he wouldn't press for more answers.

After a few steps, Jesse reached for her hand again, still quiet. Her thoughts were consumed with the presence of the gentle man who escorted her down a path she'd never have chosen. Fate brought her here, and she felt content—the grandeur of the mountains, the warmth of the morning sun, even the frosty breeze that bit into her chapped face. The steady scuffs of their feet on the rocky path and the roaring of the river in the distance reminded her—father was nowhere to seen and he didn't even know where she was.

Ellie wondered if Jesse was praying and her thoughts turned to a prayer of her own. God, if this is what living for You is like, I'm glad I found You. I want You to always be in the midst of my life. I thank You I've come to know Jesus and Jesse. Amen.

~~~~~

On any given day, Jesse would've been pleased to take a quiet walk on Gabby Mountain, especially with a beautiful girl he
~~~~~

was becoming fond of. She was quiet, and he wanted to know what she was thinking. As he held her hand and guided her through the woods and along the trail, he wanted to feel the closeness of her touch. The way her small, soft hand clung to his told him she felt the same. She often smiled when he caught her gaze, and he enjoyed her company, even in these circumstances.

Neither spoke for several minutes. Thoughts of home lay heavy on Jesse's mind. He knew there was no end to his family's worries. They'd be searching for him, trying to figure out why he hadn't come home. Had Saja foaled?

He was growing concerned about Mohan's peculiar behavior--staying close to Ellie, as if trying to protect her, emitting low growls with the hair on his neck standing up. Suddenly, the dog barked and bolted into a clump of bushes.

Jesse whistled, but Mohan paid him no mind. He peered through the bushes to find fresh animal signs. This had been a big animal, but he knew it wasn't bear sign. More like that of a big cat. He grabbed Mohan's collar and pulled him back.

"What did Mohan find?"

"Not much. Some animal dug around a stump. Probably looking for grubs." He tried not to sound nervous. "I'm getting pretty hungry, myself. I've got some vittles in my backpack. Let's make it on over to the field where there's a spring."

"Sounds like a good plan." Ellie smiled up at him.

As they made their way out of the densely wooded thicket, Ellie took Jesse's hand. She hummed *In the Midst,* and Jesse sang along with her, laughing inside. Cold and wet. Tired and hungry—yet this girl made him feel like singing.

"I've got your song stuck in my head." Ellie tilted back her head.

"That's a good song to carry with you, Cousin Ellie."

"I like your music, but you're quite a good cook as well. I can't wait to see what we have for *dinner*."

"Sounds like you're figuring out how to talk on Gabby Mountain." Jesse gave her a good-natured pat on the shoulder.

"Sit here. It'll be a little drier, away from the spring." Jesse spread his coat on the ground for her, welcoming the warmth of the sun against the chill of the early spring air. "I'm going over to the spring to make sure Mohan drinks downstream and doesn't try to get in the water."

He knew Ellie was watching him, and he wondered what she was thinking. But when he came back he sat beside her--their arms touching as he sifted through his backpack.

"Here's the jar of pickles we opened last night, peanut

butter, and saltine crackers. Reckon this'll stick to our ribs." He'd scoured the cupboards for things that didn't have meat, especially deer meat, but stashed some deer jerky in his own coat pocket where she wouldn't see.

"I'm so hungry, almost anything will taste good." Her eyes twinkled.

"Let's say the blessing before we dig in." He bowed his head and removed his cap. "God bless this food we're about to eat. Simple as it is, we are thankful. And thank You for bringing us safe this far. Lord, we ask Your hand of mercy be on us. Bring comfort to those looking for us. Amen."

"I got fresh water in this canteen." He handed the water to her, then spread peanut butter on crackers.

"Thank you. It's been a long time since I've had peanut butter. I had forgotten how good it is." She popped half a cracker in her mouth.

"Eat all you can. I brought a jar of spiced apples for dessert. This will have to tide us over," he said between bites. After they finished the crackers and peanut butter, he pried the lid off the Mason jar of apples with his pocketknife.

Ellie spooned a scoop from the jar, then motioned to Jesse. "Aren't you going to have apples, too? It'd be a shame for me to eat all of them by myself. *Dig in*. Isn't that how we eat *dinner* on Gabby Mountain?" She giggled.

Though Jesse didn't mind sharing the jar of apples with Ellie, he hadn't expected her to be so lighthearted about them eating from the same jar.

Ellie tilted her head. "Come on, you better take a bigger bite than that. They're so good--I'll eat them all."

"This little dinner will have to tide us over until we get back to the stable. My family will be cooking for our Easter dinner, so we can eat plenty once we get back down the mountain."

She raised her chin and met his eyes. "I'd love to meet your family."

The look in her eyes caught him off guard. His heart raced, and the thoughts of introducing Ellie to his family seemed overpowering. He'd never brought a girl home to his family, but this time was different, in every way. Somehow, everything about Ellie mattered more than he ever imagined.

"Thanks for lunch, I mean dinner. Thank you for everything you've done for me."

"You don't have to thank me for anything." He cleared his throat uncomfortably, packing the remains of their picnic in his backpack.

She placed her hand on his arm. "No, really. I don't know how to say this to you, but I really like being on Gabby Mountain. It's so beautiful and tranquil. I want to drink it in. Like right now. It's so peaceful, and the warm sun feels good on my back. I can think and clear my head. This must be--what's the word? *Penial.*"

With his elbow on his knee, he leaned closer to her, hanging on her every word. "Glad you like it up here. Come back and it'll be a vacation."

"When I go on a vacation, there are always people around--agendas and schedules to keep. Sitting here in this secluded field and having a picnic is indescribable." She paused. "But there's something about me I think I should tell-" Her words were cut short by an overzealous Mohan who came bounding across the field, stopping short of knocking her over as he landed almost on top of her.

"Ahh. Mohan, stop." She laughed attempting to cover her face as the dog licked her.

Jesse grabbed Mohan's collar and pulled him off. "I'm sorry, Ellie. Mohan's in a playful mood. Now, you were saying-"

"It's nothing--telling you how beautiful Gabby Mountain is." She attempted to wipe her face on the sleeve of the old brown corduroy coat. "Awe, poor Mohan. He must be a hungry boy."

Jesse realized she wasn't going to pick back up where she'd left off, and he brought out a can of sardines for Mohan. "I'll feed him. His dinner won't smell too appetizing, I'm afraid."

Mohan sat at attention, with his eyes on the can, while Ellie rubbed his head. "I like you too, Mohan. *Please*, next time give me a warning. Don't come from nowhere and take me by surprise with so many kisses. Now, I *really* need my face washed." She giggled.

Jesse chuckled. "Yeah, sardines smell bad, but Mohan loves them. Rinse out this Mason jar in the spring and freshen up."

Jesse's eyes never left her as she walked to the spring. He noticed her auburn hair falling loosely around her face and over her shoulders. The saggy overalls dragging the ground, and the strap she had fashioned into a belt hardly held them around her waist. The flannel shirt under the corduroy coat hung over her hands as she walked. He thought a girl's look shouldn't matter, but he couldn't deny Ellie's attractiveness, the shine in her green eyes, and the song in her laughter. The way he felt when her eyes met his, or she reached for his hand.

The trio left the field and started up the ridge. "The storm probably didn't tear down as much timber on the other side of the ridge, so we'll start up here--cut through the old cemetery and go down the other side."

"I understand."

"Look." Jesse stopped, pointing toward the top of the tallest trees. "That's a red-tailed hawk. We don't see too many of them anymore."

"Oh, my. Can I see your binoculars?"

"Yeah, take a closer look. Would be a shame if they became extinct because somebody wanted to target practice."

"You believe in killing animals. Don't you?" Ellie scrunched her brow and handed the binoculars back to him.

Jesse stuffed them back into his backpack. "There's a difference. Killing an animal for food is one thing, but I don't believe in killing animals for sport. I don't need mounted deer heads to prove a bullet from my rifle is more powerful than the speed of a buck. And furthermore, I refuse to hunt doe. I can't kill a baby's mama."

"I don't like the idea of killing animals at all." Ellie shuffled her feet.

"I understand—but on a brighter note, look for pretty rocks. You know there are gems in these mountains, don't you?"

"Yes, but don't you have to go to the gem mines to find them?" Ellie stepped over a fallen log and reached for his arm.

"We've found lots of garnets in the creek. It's harder to find rubies or sapphires, but after a storm, like we had last night, there's no telling what we might run up on. Many years ago, my cousin went out to milk the cow one rainy night. He was holding up a lantern and saw something glisten in the mud in front of him. He found a pretty little rock and put it under his tongue, so he wouldn't lose it. Come to find out--it was a ruby. He sold it for enough to buy a new cow."

"I don't need a new cow." She giggled. "I'd like to find a North Carolina ruby. Is this why Franklin is called the Gem Capital of the World?"

"Sure is. If you see an interesting rock, pick it up."

"I doubt I'd recognize a valuable stone if I saw one. They all look the same to me." Ellie bent to pick up a rock. "What kind is this?"

Jesse took it from her hand. "I think I see red flecks. Might be a garnet or a ruby. Take it with you. You can have a gemologist look at it. It can be your souvenir from Gabby Mountain."

"Since there aren't any gift shops along the way, I suppose

I should gather some souvenirs." Ellie shrugged.

"Better start collecting now. Once we cross over on Uncle Sam, you won't be allowed to pick *anything* up. Senator Evan will have a hissy fit."

"Then I'll hide this little gemstone real deep in my bag where he won't find it." She announced with another giggle and took Jesse's hand as they continued up the ridge to the old cemetery.

"Let me carry your Navè. It's a hard climb from here, and it'll be easier if you don't have to carry anything."

"If you insist, Sir Jesse." She mimicked a bow and shifted the bag to his outstretched hand. "Last time I saw a guy carrying a Navè was in the movie *Black Knights Avenge.* Did you see that movie?"

"Sure did." Jesse slid the bag over his shoulder.

Ellie continued, "Remember the scene where Morgan Alexandria and Briley Scout jump out of the helicopter and land on the burning building? I don't know if you could tell just watching the movie, but they both had Navè bags, loaded with secret weapons. They tied their Navès together and hurled them to Breyer as he scaled the building to escape." She rattled on and on, a new light in her eyes. Jesse found her enthusiasm for the movie interesting as she gave in-depth details about the set, referring to the stars as if she knew them personally.

When Ellie paused to catch her breath and adjust her boot, Jesse commented, "Wow Ellie, I had no idea you were so into action films. Especially ones with guns and fighting."

Her enthusiasm mounted. "I would do it all again. This was the most amazing thing *ever*."

"What would you do all over again? Watch the movie?"

"No, be on the set and watch them shoot the movie!"

Jesse couldn't believe his ears. "Were you on the set of *Black Knights Avenge*?"

"Yes, and they ruined at least ten Navès trying to film one scene. I'm the one who showed the director how to rip the Navè cords and tie them together."

"Did you meet Breyer Montgomery?"

"Yes—along with Morgan and Briley."

"How did you manage to get to do that? Jenna'll be so jealous. She adores those three and has seen every movie Breyer ever starred in."

"My father's friends with the producer." She paused, leaving Jesse to wonder if there was more she wasn't telling.

"What about the guns and shooting?"

"Okay. I mean, it wasn't real, and besides, no one was going to get hurt. What about the gun you brought? Are you going to shoot it?"

"Now that we're at the old cemetery I think I should fire a shot if you're alright with it. I don't want to make you nervous, but this really is the only way we have to let anybody in earshot know we're okay." Jesse motioned to a mossy rock wall a few yards away. "Sit down on the rock wall and prop your foot."

"I still don't understand how this is going to help us get off Gabby Mountain any sooner."

"It's like this. I know my family's out looking for us. They may not know to come over this way since we've had to walk around the ridge instead of just down the mountain. From up here, somebody may hear the shots. I only have five bullets, and I'm going to shoot it four times." He pulled the revolver from its holster on his side.

"Why do you have to shoot it four times? Won't once be enough?"

"We have a code. If Dad hears this gun, he'll know I've been to the cabin, because this old Colt 45 always stays in the cabin. If I shoot two times, that means there's one person and I'm all right. If I shoot two more times, that means there's another person. He'll also be able to tell the shots came from the old cemetery If it works, then it works. If it doesn't, no harm done." He waited as she walked to the wall.

"Cover your ears," he called. Then drew the pistol and shot into the air four times.

She still had her hands over her ears, her face drawn tight when he came back to the wall--the pistol safely in its holster. He couldn't help but laugh. "That wasn't so bad, huh?"

"Glad it's over. Can we go now?" Jesse caught a hint of anxiety in her voice.

"We need to rest here for a little while and keep you off that leg." He sat beside her on the rock wall.

Ellie shrugged and ran both hands through her tangled locks. "I don't like being in a cemetery, and the thought of people being put in the ground."

"The people aren't here. They've gone on to heaven. Besides, there hasn't been a burial in this cemetery for well over seventy years. Most of these graves are people who lived up here. My family keeps the graves cleaned. It's our way of honoring their legacy. There's a story behind every soul represented here. Especially Aunt Naomi."

"Your fourth-generation grandmother, right?"

"That's right. My family might not even own Gabby Mountain today if it hadn't been for Naomi." Jesse pointed toward her grave. "When she died, she left a deerskin pouch filled with gold. It was worth enough money for Grandpa Jesse to buy out all the other landowners on Gabby, with plenty of money left over. He was known to be quite a wealthy man after that. That's how he sent Daisy Marie to college."

"Where did she get the gold?"

"That's part of the mystery. Nobody knows who she was, where she came from, or where she got the gold. She never told. And for many years, the family didn't tell anyone about the gold. They didn't want people coming in here demanding to dig for more."

"Is there more gold on this mountain?"

"Your guess is as good as mine. The Cherokee knew where gold was. Before they were run off their land, they hid it where no one would ever find it. They said if the white men ever figured out where it was, there would be more bloodshed."

"Where do you think they hid it? I may be standing on top of a gold mine." Ellie threw out her hands with a giggle.

Jesse didn't as much as offer a smile. This was no laughing matter to him. "Legend has it that it's buried in caves and rock cliffs, with laurel bushes and rocks over it where it'll never be found. They say the Little People guard the gold."

"Wait. Who did you say guards the gold? Little People? Who are they?" Ellie's mouth dropped in a puzzled look.

"Again, legend has it there are Little People living in the mountains. They look like the Cherokee, but they're only about knee high and have long dark hair. They like gold, so they guard it." Jesse simply stated the facts. "Next time you go through Atlanta, look at the gold dome on the capitol building. A lot of innocent blood was shed so that dome could be covered in gold from Cherokee land."

"Why didn't the white people take the gold and leave the Cherokee and the Little People alone?"

"The United States government got greedy and didn't give one iota how the Cherokee or the settlers who lived among them felt. Especially President Andrew Jackson. A lot of blood dripped from his corrupt hands. He could've stopped the Indian removal."

"*Andrew Jackson*." Ellie blurted. "He was known as the people's president."

"Oh Mohan, Cousin Ellie Mae needs to re-read her history book." Jesse lifted his hat and scratched his head. "I bet she thinks ole Jackson was some kind of hero. She doesn't know what a crook he was--does she, Wahya?"

Mohan let out his familiar *gr-howl* and stepped between Jesse and Ellie.

"I see I could never win this debate with you, especially when you've got Mohan on your side." Ellie playfully poked at him.

"Cousin Ellie Mae, we'll have a political debate another time. Don't get me started or we'll never get off Gabby Mountain. I guess that's why America is such a great country. We're all entitled to an opinion, whether it's right or wrong."

"Are you sure? I've never heard anyone say anything derogatory about President Jackson." Ellie shot a puzzling glance at Jesse. "Besides, what would you say if I told you President Jackson is one of my ancestors?"

"I'd say you're lucky you turned out as good as you are pretty. But I guess it explains why you have such a stubborn streak." Jesse laughed and extended his hand to her.

Taking his hand, she pulled herself up. "You're teasing me."

"Reckon I am." He slipped the backpack over his shoulder. "And I guess you're teasing me, too, aren't you, Cousin Ellie?"

"Maybe." She smiled, tilting her head to one side.

꧁9꧂

Escape

Ellie was glad when they left the cemetery. Being there flooded her mind with thoughts about her mother and one unanswered question--Where was her mother buried? Any time she questioned her father about the accident, he made excuses not to answer. Now, she was determined to find out more, visit her mother's grave and leave flowers. She needed complete closure from the empty longing in her heart.

Then, Mohan darted ahead, barking into a clump of bushes.

Ellie waited on the trail as Jesse ran ahead to see what Mohan had found. He motioned for Ellie to join him, and the trio peered into the underbrush to find a spotted fawn.

"How cute. I've never seen a baby deer in the wild. Where's its mama?"

"Not far away. Let's get Mohan out of here so she'll come back. I need to put a leash on him, but I don't think I brought one."

Mohan barked again and pulled out of Jesse's loose grip. "No use to call him back. Look who he's chasing."

"Is that the mama deer?"

Jesse nodded. "Mohan'll chase her until she outsmarts him. She'd rather have him chasing her than let him mess with her baby. Funny how mamas are like that. I know my mama's wondering where in the world I am. She's mighty protective. How about yours?"

Ellie stared at the ground. "I lost my mother when I was eight--a tragic car accident."

"Oh Ellie, I'm sorry."

"It's okay. I don't talk about it much. It happened a long time ago." Her voice trailed. "That's why I have a scar on my face.

I've had lots of surgeries, and I'm scheduled for another as soon as I turn twenty-one. I hate surgeries, doctors, and hospitals."

"I had no idea. I mean-" Jesse stammered.

"It's okay," she interrupted. "I know you saw the scar--thank you for not mentioning it. You told me you had cancer as a child. Are you cancer free?"

"Thank God, I am. I go for check-ups, but they always say I'm healthy as a horse." He stepped ahead, pulling a low-hanging limb out of her way.

"That should make your mama happy. About the cancer, I mean."

"It does, but what doesn't make her happy is the fact I don't want to go to college. Never have wanted to. College has been good for Jenna and Cindi, but I'm happy here with my horses."

"Must be nice to get to do what you want." Ellie brought her hand to her face.

"Has anybody ever tried to make you do something or be somebody you didn't want to be?"

"All the time," Ellie's voice rose. "This is how it is when you're raised by your father."

"Dads aren't so bad. It would've been hard, but my dad could've raised us."

"My father's different. He works all the time. I grew up with housekeepers, nannies, boarding schools."

"Personal question." Ellie swallowed hard, but Jesse went on. "Do you always call him *Father*? Do you ever use *Dad*?"

"After the accident, my brother and I were instructed to call him *Father*. We're reprimanded if we refer to him in any other way."

"What does your dad do?" Jesse reached for her hand.

"When I was younger, he was an attorney. Now he travels most of the time." Ellie cleared her throat. "Enough about me—what does your dad do?"

"Accounting. He stays busy during tax season. I'd hate for it to be like that all year."

"At least you've had one parent at home. What does your mom do?"

"Special education teacher. That's why she's so big on getting an education."

Wanting to keep the conversation away from her father, Ellie kept asking questions. "What about Jenna? Why does she want to become a doctor?"

"Since we were little, and I had cancer, Jenna has said she

wanted to be a doctor. To find a cure for cancer. And as determined as she is about everything, if there's a cure, she'll have her hand in it somewhere."

"Doesn't she realize there's more money in other areas of the medical field than research?"

"Money's not what drives this family. We've got God and each other. Way too many things to be thankful for than to worry about money." Jesse lowered his head under another low hanging branch before pulling it out of her way.

"And don't forget, you've got Gabby Mountain, the cabin, and the old barn."

"You're right. That old barn's been on this mountain for nearly two centuries. Nothing we can do about it now. All manmade things have to end, whether it's something big like a barn or little like a book."

"Sorry about *Althea Spineeta with Curls in Her Hair*. I didn't mean to throw it into the fire."

"I can't figure why a children's little book upset you so much."

"I had that book when I was a little girl, too. It brought back memories. Mama read it to me and after the accident, the book strangely disappeared. I hadn't seen it in years until--your copy."

"Ellie, I had no idea. If you want to talk about it, I'm a good listener."

"So why is that children's book important to you? You don't have curly, red hair, like me or Althea Spineeta." She reached for another rock from the mud.

"It was given to Jenna when I was bad off. I lost all my hair, it upset her more than anything else about me being sick."

Ellie touched his arm. "That would be hard."

"Dicie Kimsey Headrick, the lady who wrote the book, visited Jenna's preschool. Jenna cried so hard while Miss Dicie read the book, she stopped reading, prayed for me, and finished the story with Jenna and Cindi both on her lap."

"That's sweet," Ellie said and meant it. "I suppose Miss Dicie gave the book to Jenna."

"She did, and to this day, Jenna and Miss Dicie stay in contact. Miss Dicie brings her kids to ride horses and camp."

"Do you think you'll be bringing people up here again?" Ellie asked, stopping to adjust her makeshift boot.

"Sure--after a lot of cleanup. I'm going to have to reconsider my options after this storm. Looks like my Christmas tree crop is ruined, and who'd want to go to the cabin in all that mud? Besides, I'll have to do some repairs to the outside wall where the big rock grazed the corner."

"I'm sorry. I didn't realize how much work could be involved."

He stopped and turned toward her. "You'll come back up here with me, won't you? I mean, when I get the road cleared out. We can bring the four-wheel-drive truck or make Nanta finish the ride you were promised."

"I'd be honored to accompany you, hear more about the settlers on this mountain, and the Cherokee."

"You've got a deal. Want to shake on it?" She teased and grabbed his hand to mimic a handshake.

The walk on down the ridge put an extra strain on Ellie's ankle, but Jesse's hand kept her steady. They were quiet, but it was a comfortable quiet. Talking to him about losing her mother and giving him a few details about her father had come naturally. Years of talking to professionals hadn't brought such peace. Even Dr. Shanks referred to her life as a giant balloon filled with fears, hurts, and anxiety--a balloon Ellie needed to deflate. She told her talking to others and writing in her journal would prick pinholes in the balloon, and eventually, it would lose its power and fly away.

Ellie now understood what Dr. Shanks meant. She wouldn't tell Jesse about her balloon yet, but she knew when she did he'd understand. Now, if she could only figure out a way to reveal her last name to him.

Jesse stopped again. "Hear something? Sounds like a trapped animal."

Ellie stepped aside as he picked up a long stick, knocking the laurel bush limbs aside. "Good grief. That makes me mad. Don't worry little guy. I'll set you free." He pulled the laurel branches off a box trap to reveal a small red fox.

"Look at him. That helpless animal must be scared to death. You're not going to shoot it, are you?" Ellie cringed, backing away.

"No, I'm not going to hurt this little fellow, just set him free. I have an idea who set this trap, and I'm going to have a long talk with that fellow. We don't allow traps, and he had no right to cross over onto the Forest Service side, especially out of season."

Ellie held her breath as Jesse opened the trap door, and the fox ran for its life.

"Here's what I think of box traps." Jesse ripped the metal box from the ground and slung it into the laurel thicket.

"Why would anyone want to trap such a beautiful little

creature?"

"Hunters bring their hounds up here and turn the fox loose. It's their sport to watch the dogs chase it."

"That's cruel." Ellie's mouth flew open. "I'm glad you found it and set it free."

"I can't stand to see an animal mistreated." Jesse clenched his jaw. "Speaking of animals, I wish Mohan would get back here." He gave a resounding whistle, and in the distance, Mohan answered with a *gr-howl.*

"Let's head on down the mountain. Sounds like he's run on ahead of us. Maybe we'll meet him on his way back up." Without asking, Jesse slipped her Navè over his shoulder and reached for her hand.

Once again, Ellie marveled at his strength and courage. Maybe she was like the little red fox. Trapped. Hopelessly waiting for someone to set her free. Free from what? Free from whom? Free from her past hurts and fears? Free from the tears welled up inside, tears that had not been cried since she lost her mother.

The afternoon sun created shadows through the trees, promising to soon bring the budding foliage to life. The breeze lightened the air with its ever-present chill. Except for the wet earth, nothing on this side of the mountain seemed harmed by last night's storm. Flocks of birds flew from the branches overhead, with only the sounds of their wings fluttering.

Ellie could hear the roar of the river in the distance, and she knew they must be getting close to the place where it all had started. She couldn't help but wonder where she would be right now if things had gone as planned. *What if* the horseback ride with Nanta had been uneventful? *What if* she had simply enjoyed the natural beauty of the trail ride and made it back to the car without her father or Dr. Shanks ever knowing she'd taken off on this escapade? *What if* Jesse hadn't been at the stables when she returned Nanta after the ride? The whirlwind of *what-ifs* clouded her mind. That's not how the last twenty-four hours had played out, and she knew she'd have to find a chance to tell him—the dreadful Senator Evan was her father.

But the time hadn't been right yet. Plus, he hadn't asked any more questions since she told him about her mother, and she dreaded to bring it up herself. He seemed content to be holding her hand and guiding the way off Gabby Mountain. Or was *she* content to be holding *his* hand? Either way, he whistled and hummed tunes, having her guess the song, and told story after story about his ancestors and life on Gabby Mountain for the last century. He made her laugh more in one afternoon than she had laughed in the past ten years of her life, and she wanted to enjoy the time for as long as she could.

Jesse slid his backpack to the ground. "Sounds like a motorcycle coming up the mountain. You stay here by this big rock. I'll run to the top of the ridge and see if I can figure out what's going on. We may get rescued after all."

Ellie didn't take her eyes off Jesse as he sprinted through the trees. She didn't like being alone in the woods, even though he wasn't far away. He turned once and waved to her. She waved back, but what she really wanted to do was run after him. *He'll only be gone a minute. Relax, breathe.*

She propped against the boulder, stretching her aching foot in front of her, trying to relax. But something wasn't right. The silence was eerie, and she wanted to run and catch up with him. She drew in a deep breath, then blew it out. The air smelled of rank cat urine.

Her heart raced even harder when she heard a rustle in the brush, a few feet away, on the other side of the big rock. "Mohan. Come here, boy." She struggled to breathe under the heavy blanket of fear.

"Mohan. Wahya." She called louder. Fear rose in her throat as she stepped around the rock to see what was in the brush.

Her blood-curdling scream broke the silence in the exact same instant a black panther opened its mouth and growled, with one paw in the air, its glaring eyes fixed on her. In that same split second, Mohan leaped from out of nowhere and landed between Ellie and the panther as she struggled to climb atop the rock.

The panther gnashed its teeth, swatting toward Mohan, lowering itself to the ground preparing to attack. Mohan crouched even lower, dodging blows from the cat twice his size, darting backward--sideways, staying close to the base of the rock, between Ellie and the panther, the hair standing high on his back.

"Jesus," Ellie screamed, and then saw Jesse charging down the ridge. The panther lunged toward her as a shot thundered through the trees.

Jesse fired the Colt 45's single remaining bullet, hitting the panther in mid-leap, bringing death's claws inches from the intended target—Ellie. The panther fell to the ground, writhing and thrashing, blood gushing from the hole in its head. Mohan growled and snarled at the dying panther as his body went limp and he collapsed. The panther flailed one last time, ending up on its back.

Jesse reached for Ellie and held her close as she buried

her head in his chest. Her body shook as she gasped for breath. Her tears soaked his shirt, and her hands grasped his arms as if she would never let go.

As Jesse held her, he whispered in her ear over and over, “It’s all going to be all right. You’re safe now. I’m here with you. I won’t leave you again. I promise.”

After what seemed an eternity, Ellie let go of Jesse’s arms and her wails became sobs.

“What are you trying to say?” Jesse asked, without letting go of her.

“Jee-ss-ss, Jee-ss-ss.”

“Are you calling my name?”

“No,” she managed. “*Jesus*.”

“It’s all over now. You’re okay. I’m okay.”

“What about Mohan?” She loosened from his embrace and stepped back.

“Here, steady yourself by the rock, and I’ll go check on him.”

But Ellie hobbled behind Jesse and watched as he knelt beside Mohan, examining his wounds. The gashes looked deep, going almost to the bone, and blood-soaked his fur.

“I didn’t want you to come to this side of the rock. I mean, you don’t need to see Mohan or the panther.”

But she stood by his side, still trembling, as she looked at the bloody scene. The smells of cat, death, blood, mud—she pressed her hands into her stomach—afraid she’d throw up.

Then Jesse turned to her. “Do you have anything in your bag we can bandage Mohan with? Any kind of scarf or anything?”

She knelt and with shaking hands, went through her bag. “I don’t have anything,” she muttered, trying to keep the tears at bay, looking first at Mohan and then the panther.

“It’s okay. You’ve been through a horrible experience.”

“What if I never stop crying?” She wept. “What about Mohan? Is he going to die? It’s all my fault.”

“Nothing’s your fault. You can cry for as long as you want to, and I’ll hold you for as long as you want.” He moved closer to her.

“Take care of Mohan. Don’t let him die.” She cried harder. “He saved my life.”

Jesse wrapped her in his arms once more.

10

Teary

The last twenty minutes seemed like a lifetime passing in a flash. A dream. A nightmare. A news clip happening to somebody else. Jesse's mind reeled, and he wasn't sure he was thinking straight. He'd never been so scared--even more scared than when they were in the storm. There hadn't been time to think when he heard Ellie's screams, then the roaring and growling of the fight between Mohan and the panther. There had only been time for a split-second reaction. Pull the trigger- hit the panther- no second chances- only one bullet.

The storm must have steered the panther in this direction. There hadn't been panther sightings around here in years—now he knew why Mohan acted the way he did. No doubt the panther ran out of the old barn when Ellie let the horses out—and its scream was what she heard the night before. Now, it was all made sense.

Jesse wanted to hold Ellie longer, and he knew she wanted to be held. But he had to tend to Mohan, and she sat on the ground, hugging her knees to her chest--still sobbing. "As soon as Mohan's bleeding slows down, we'll head out for the old road. It's only about a hundred more yards. Whoever's on that motorcycle no doubt heard the shot. They'll come to meet us."

He stood, took off his coat and a long-sleeved shirt, pulled his white t-shirt over his head, and put the long-sleeved shirt back on. He knelt beside the wounded dog and started to unlace his boots.

"What are you doing?" Her voice shook with sobs.

"I'll tie my t-shirt around him--then wrap him in my coat. Maybe he'll let me carry him."

Ellie reached for her Navè. "No need to use a shoelace. I'll ravel cord off this bag."

"No, you've been through enough. I don't want you to ruin it." Jesse shot a glance in her direction.

Ellie moved beside him, hovering over Mohan. "Never mind the Navè. Mohan's more important." With trembling fingers, she unraveled the entwined cord along the edge of her Navè.

"I'll buy you a new one." Jesse took the cord with one hand while holding the t-shirt around Mohan with the other.

"No, it's not my only one." Ellie reached to help secure the t-shirt over Mohan's wound as Jesse wound the cord around the makeshift bandage. He could tell by the way she kept closing her eyes and clearing her throat--she was squeamish about blood.

"Hang on boy--hold still. We'll get you fixed up." Jesse tied the ends of the cord. "You were brave, taking care of Miss Ellie."

Ellie stood, her eyes widening as she glanced first at Mohan and then the dead panther.

"I know it's been a trying time for you, but we're nearly to the old road." Jesse placed a hand on her shoulder and looked into her tearstained face. "I hear the motorcycle again, but it sounds like it's still a way down the mountain. Let's head on out."

Mohan stood on wobbly legs, letting out a single sharp bark, followed by low growls. The hair on his neck rose--the growls came deeper and louder.

Jesse kept his eyes peeled for another panther. He was out of bullets, but the dog wasn't looking at the panther, but toward the back of the big rock. He staggered around the rock--Jesse and Ellie behind him. Jesse grabbed a long stick and listened.

"Ellie, hold Mohan's collar." Jesse knelt for a closer look under the rock.

"I hear a kitten. How could a kitten get way up here?" Ellie inched closer.

"It's a kitten all right. A panther kitten. It's not been born very long." Jesse stood, taking Mohan's collar.

Ellie brought her hands to her face. "You killed the baby's mama. You said you'd never kill a baby's mama. Now, look what you've done."

"But Ellie, you know yourself I had to shoot the panther. It would've killed *you.*" Jesse stared at her in disbelief.

She glared at him, tears streaming down her cheeks.

"I understand if you need to cry and if you feel sorry for the kitten. But we have to make it to the old road before the motorcycle gets up here." He draped his coat over Mohan's back.

"I'm not leaving the poor helpless baby here." Her voice

rose, and she stomped one foot.

"What else can we do? It's a wild animal." He lifted Mohan into his arms.

She put her hands on her hips--not budging. He hadn't seen her like this since the day before.

"What do you suggest?" Jesse tightened his jaw.

"I'm not leaving this mountain without taking the baby with me."

"What if it bites you or scratches you?"

"It's too little to bite me. I'll carry it in my Navè. See, I'll unfasten the liner and push it to the bottom of the bag to make a soft bed."

Jesse shook his head in both frustration and admiration as he watched her empty the fancy bag, stuffing the items into the pockets of his old brown coat. He placed Mohan on the ground. "All right then, hold Mohan's collar and try to keep him from getting up."

Ellie kneeled beside Mohan, and Jesse used a long stick to scoot the bundle of damp, matted leaves along with the kitten. When it was within arm's reach, he picked it up by the loose skin on the back of its neck, holding it up for her to see. Its eyes were closed and covered with faintly spotted, smoky gray fur.

"It doesn't weigh more than a pound, but are you sure you want it in your bag? What if it pees on you? Nothing smells worse than cat pee."

"Jesse, I don't care. I won't leave this poor motherless baby."

"What are you going to do with it?"

"I'll give it to a zoo where it'll be taken care of and safe from hunters." She stood, opening the Navè.

"Ellie, listen to me. It's against the law to catch wildlife on government land. If you take it, you'll be breaking federal law."

"I don't care about the federal law." Her lips formed a tight line.

"I still don't think this is wise." Jesse grimaced, slipping the kitten into her bag.

Ellie was quiet, and he wondered if she understood what the outcome might be.

With Mohan in Jesse's arms and the panther cub snug in Ellie's Navè, the troop made their way to the old road. Mohan seemed alert, but he'd lost a lot of blood, and the fact he was allowing Jesse to carry him attested to how weak he must be. The sixty pounds of dead weight tried Jesse's energy, but he was determined to keep going. He looked down at Ellie, and her eyes met his with silent tears streaming down her cheeks.

"It's not much further. Once we get on the old road, it's only about a quarter of a mile on down to where I left my old blue work truck. Do you think you can make it that far?"

"Yes. I'll make it."

"I bet you're as tired and hungry as I am." He slowed, shifting Mohan's weight.

"Granted, I'm tired, but I can't wait to tell Dr. Shanks I cried." She took a deep breath and kept talking, "I never cried when I lost Mama—and I haven't cried since. Until today. I was afraid to cry. I've seen all sorts of doctors and therapists. They all say I need to cry. Something as simple as *crying* is supposed to help get my life back on track."

"I'm sorry. I shouldn't have left you alone back there-- even to run up the ridge," he spoke with regret as they trudged on.

"I was so scared. Purely petrified. What was I to do? All I remember was screaming *Jesus*."

Jesse stopped and faced her. "Calling on the name of Jesus was the best thing you could've done. Hey, you handled it like a trooper. And you'll go down in the history of Gabby Mountain as being one of only two women to ever come upon a panther."

"Your grandmother Naomi and me, right? I can't believe all that's happened."

"You're a stronger woman than you give yourself credit for." He glanced over his shoulder at her. "You're tougher than a pine knot."

"Do you really mean that? No one has ever said those things about *me* before. People always treat me like a pitiful, sick little girl." Her voice broke.

"You're not a little girl. In fact, Cousin Ellie Mae, you're a beautiful woman—a real courageous one at that," he added, hesitating to catch her reaction. "Got mountain dirt on your boots, and now you're like all the other women from Gabby Mountain. You stand your own ground."

"Your words are very kind. I'll have to think on that. Right now, I'm too tired to put one foot in front of the other. So, how's Mohan?"

"Enjoying a free ride. He acts like he's asleep, but every time I jostle him, he kicks or opens his eyes. He'll make a quick recovery. Don't worry about a big boy like Mohan. How's that little kitten?"

"It's squirming but hasn't tried to climb out. It keeps

meowing, so I know it's fine."

"I would guess it's no more than a day old. If it was much bigger, you'd probably have quite a rascal on your hands." Jesse stopped, listening for the motorcycle again.

"I hear an ax. Whoever's on the motorcycle is stopping to chop limbs out of the road--then coming on a little further each time. I'm going to whistle and see if anybody answers." Jesse laid Mohan on the ground, then cupped his hands and blew a long, resounding whistling sound through his fists. From somewhere in the distance came an answer--the same whistling sound-- in three short blows.

Hearing the whistle, Mohan perked his ears. Jesse reached down and rubbed his head. "Wahya, I can tell by the way you're acting you know Jonathan's coming, don't you?"

"How does Mohan know who it is?"

"He's really Jonathan's dog, but he likes to be on Gabby and have the freedom to run free."

"Then I'm like Mohan. I want to be able to run free, too." Ellie pushed a strand of hair from her cheek.

Jesse took her hand. "You're welcome to come back to Gabby any time, and you can run as free as you want to. As long as you let Mohan and me run with you."

"I'll take you up on it. I'll even bring crackers and peanut butter. Maybe even a can or two of stinky fish for Mohan." She pursed her lips. "And you bring a jar of apples."

Mohan let out a *gr-howl* and feebly started walking. Jesse picked up his coat and took Ellie's hand. Everything would be over soon, but he'd become accustomed to the feeling that came over him each time he touched her.

~~~~~

Ellie had never been so happy to see a pickup truck--especially this old, blue one. It was the same truck she'd seen in front of the Navè boutique in Asheville. Now she felt guilty for finding the slightest bit of humor that day. As she watched Jesse lay the Navè with the panther kitten on the seat between them, she realized he was more fortunate than she'd ever been.

"Look what I found, Cousin Ellie." Jesse pulled a metal lunch box from behind the seat. "See if there's anything in this dinner bucket you'd like. Here's a Mountain Dew, a bag of chips, and a Butterfinger."

Jesse got in the truck and tried to start the engine, but it refused to crank. "I should've bought a new battery for this old rig
~~~~~

last week. Wouldn't you know it? When I really need it to start, it won't. Guess we'll sit here and rest until Jonathan gets here."

"Let's share this bag of chips." He ripped the top of the bag, stopping short of taking the first chip, removed his cap, and bowed his head. "Lord, thank you for protection and grace. Bless this food, Amen."

Ellie took the first chip from the bag. The salty goodness was satisfying, but her stomach was in knots, thinking about how to tell Jesse who her father was. Maybe she could begin by telling him about being the designer of Navè--not tell him about her father until later.

Jesse reached for the bottle of Mountain Dew and unscrewed the lid, releasing a hiss of carbonation. "Here you go. Have a swig." He offered the bottle to her.

Ellie took it from his hand and brought it up to her lips allowing the sweet, tingly drink to wet her throat. It had been so long since she had enjoyed a carbonated drink, she'd almost forgotten how it felt going down. And she didn't even care it wasn't cold.

She handed the bottle to Jesse. "You better have a swig, too."

He stopped chewing and looked at her out of the corner of his eye as he accepted the bottle and downed a long drink, before placing the bottle in the cup holder on the dash. She knew he did it on purpose, so she wouldn't be put on the spot if she chose not to drink after him. She never drank after anyone, but somehow it was different with Jesse.

Jesse rubbed his mouth on his sleeve before stepping outside the truck and giving another long, resounding whistle through his fists. This time, an answer came in the form of a yell. Jesse yelled back. "That's Jonathan and he's down about the switch back. He ought to be here in another ten minutes."

The thoughts of getting back to the stable and not being on Gabby with Jesse seemed surreal for Ellie. Tears ran down her cheeks, and she wiped them with the back of her hand.

Jesse reached across the seat and put his hand on her shoulder. "It's okay if you need to cry. Been a long day, and you've been through a whole lot. You'll be home soon, Cousin Ellie."

"It's not that. I need to tell you something I should've already told you." Ellie squirmed in the seat, turning to face him.

Jesse stopped chewing his half of the Butterfinger. She took a tiny sip of the Mountain Dew, looking straight at him as she screwed the cap back on. It was too late to back out--she had to tell him now.

"Jesse, the reason I know so much about the Navè bags, well, I'm the one who designed them." She stopped, looking deep into his eyes for a reaction.

"Hey, I think that's great. I mean, all the girls really like them, and yours sure has come in handy on this trip." She watched him--relieved he hadn't yet associated Navè with her father.

"Why did you keep it a secret from me? I've been on Gabby Mountain with a famous designer and didn't even know it." He chomped the remaining bite of the candy bar.

She let out the breath she'd been holding. "Most people don't know who I am. I designed the first one as a project in high school. My father thought I was too young to have the notoriety the bags might bring. I've never been allowed to associate myself with Navè, and I stay away from the media. It's awkward at times."

"Your secret's safe with me and Mohan. But I'm sure Jenna would like to know. She carries the one I bought for her all the time."

Mohan whined, and Jesse bounded to the bed of the truck. Ellie could hear him talking to the dog.

She was relieved he hadn't questioned her or even seemed surprised. Her heart raced as she tried to decide if this was the right time to tell him about her father. She watched in the side mirror as he stood by the truck bed looking at the wounded, exhausted Mohan. If she could've run away at that moment rather than face him with the rest of her story, she would have. He looked so innocent, yet rugged, and strong. Wisps of brown hair stuck out around the John Deere cap he'd worn all day. And she was convinced he was the most handsome guy she'd ever seen. It had been such a privilege to spend a day on the set of a movie, but that day didn't even compare to this one. Jesse was a different kind of hero. His bravery and strength had been real, not orchestrated by a director and displayed by a film crew. Jesse's attention had been on her, and her only.

Jesse let out a whoop, waving both arms as the motorcycle came to a stop in front of the truck. Ellie recognized Jenna as the passenger on the back, and she knew the dark-haired driver must be Jonathan.

Jenna wrapped her arms around Jesse. "Thank God. Jonathan and I knew we'd be the ones to find you two. Everybody and I mean *everybody,* is worried and out looking for both of you."

Then Jonathan nodded in Ellie's direction. "Jesse, aren't you going to introduce me to Miss Evan or do I have to introduce myself."

Jesse's face flushed beet red. "Jonathan, if this is some sort of joke, it's not funny."

"I'm not kidding, Jesse. This is Eloree, Senator Evan's daughter. He's been down at the barn since last night. The sheriff and rescue squad have been out looking for you two. He's even called in the National Guard."

Jesse squared his shoulders. "Jonathan, you better check on Mohan. He's hurt."

"What happened?" In one fluid motion, Jonathan leaped onto the back of the truck.

"Crazy panther nearly killed Mohan and would've got Ellie-- if I hadn't shot it."

"You killed a panther?" Jenna shrieked. "Where is it now?"

"Up yonder on the government side of the ridge. Guess I'm a poacher now." Ellie watched as Jesse turned and strode away.

Ellie felt as though a bucket of cold steel had been poured over her. Pulling her under with a smothering weight. She wanted to say something. Explain. Beg Jesse to understand.

"You must be exhausted. Come sit back down in the truck." Jenna put her arm around Ellie's shoulders. "Are you sure you're okay? I can't imagine the horror you've been through."

"Please. Tell Jesse I'm sorry. I wanted to tell him who I really was, but I know how much he dislikes my father. I didn't know how to tell him." Tears overtook her.

"He'll be okay. Give him a few minutes." Jenna reached into the glove compartment and pulled out a clean, white handkerchief. "By the way, do you want to be called *Eloree* or *Ellie*?"

"Ellie. Definitely, Ellie." She wiped her face with the handkerchief. "Jesse's been so nice to me, and we've had a great time—even though we were stranded in the cabin all night."

"Looks like Jonathan's going to talk to him." Jenna glanced over her shoulder. "They'll get the truck started, and this will all be over for you."

"I can't help what my father does. I'm always overshadowed by him. But while I was up here I escaped his rules." Ellie shrugged. "Will Jesse ever speak to me again?"

"Of course, he will." Jenna patted Ellie's hand.

"How did my father know where to look for me?" Ellie

muttered.

"Once the sheriff figured out who the Range Rover belonged to, he brought your dad and Dr. Shanks to the stables. The storm didn't let up enough for anyone to leave, so a bunch of us spent the entire night in Jesse's office at the stables."

"Is my father livid?" Ellie looked down.

"He's worried--like the rest of us, and he tried to do everything in his power to find you last night. Nobody knew for sure if Jesse and you were together or if you'd made it to the cabin."

"What did Dr. Shanks do?"

"Helped everybody stay calm and keep their wits. Such a nice lady." Jenna looked toward Jesse and Jonathan. "I'll go see what's keeping these two. Stay here."

Jenna stepped away and Ellie leaned against the dash and buried her head in her hands. She wished she was far away from Jesse. And most of all, she wished she didn't even know her father. Instead, she wished her brother, Terrance, was here. Even though he was ten years older than her, she longed to talk to him –have him as a friend--like Jesse and Jenna had each other.

She opened the glove compartment to look for another handkerchief, and a card fell onto her lap. She unfolded it and read--If you are weary and weak, God will give you strength and increase your power Isaiah 40:29. And Ellie needed strength and power.

Wiping her eyes, Ellie read the words again. She needed power and was reminded all she had to do was call on Jesus. She peered into the Navè. "I'm not like you, little kitten. I'm not going to be put away for the rest of my life like you'll be or snared in a trap like a red fox. I'm going to call on Jesus to help me find my way."

꧁11꧂

Yesterday's Gone

Jesse, you've got to understand where Ellie's coming from. She really likes you, and she's broken hearted to think you hate her."

"What she thinks won't matter. I shot an endangered animal, out of season, and on government land. Her daddy won't care why. I could go to jail for poaching, not to mention the ammunition he'll now have for taking mountain land." Jesse's eyes narrowed.

"Jesse, you've never been one to worry," Jonathan said. "Besides, the sheriff pretty much put the senator in his place."

"And, Dr. Shanks, the lady that's with him, steps in and keeps him out of a lot of trouble when he starts getting too pushy," Jenna added.

"What did the sheriff say?"

"The sheriff told him he better be glad his daughter was lost on Gabby Mountain with you because you at least knew how to take care of her." Jonathan grinned.

"And when he started getting haughty, prancing around saying I had set his daughter up to get kidnapped, I thought Daddy would throw him out in the storm." Jenna shrugged with a smirk.

Jesse almost laughed at the thoughts of such a scenario.

"That's not all. The house they were going to stay in, upon Buck Creek, got washed right off the mountain in the middle of the storm." Jenna's eyes grew wide.

"What's everybody saying about that?" Jesse asked.

"The senator kept strutting around saying *there has to be an explanation for this.*" Jonathan mimicked.

"Dr. Shanks cried and thanked God they were in the barn

instead of in the house. If they hadn't been with us and had been on Buck Creek as planned, it'd all be over." Jenna touched his arm.

As the three walked back up the old road, Jesse stared ahead. He saw Ellie in the truck with her head down, and he wondered if she was still crying. His mind was like two puzzles mixed together--one with pieces of his own mind and emotions--the other with his feelings for Ellie and her situation.

Jesse squinted into the late afternoon sun. "No telling what he'll try to do to me."

"Jesse, stop worrying. You're bigger than Senator Evan in every way, and his daughter's nothing like him. Ellie doesn't deserve to be punished because he's a jerk. Give her a chance." Jenna put her hand on his shoulder.

"How am I bigger than him? He has all the political guns in his corner."

"His bark is worse than his bite," Jonathan added. "He prances around like a peacock, but he's more like a little Banty rooster with his feathers ruffled up."

"It's okay. We're all tired. None of us have had any sleep. Let's get off Gabby. Too much drama for one day," Jenna concluded as they reached the truck.

"I think we can put Jenna behind the wheel and roll the truck off to get it started. What do you say?" Jonathan asked.

"Let's try it, but I want you to go on ahead and get the game warden. The sheriff needs to be there, just in case the senator decides to twist the situation to his benefit."

Jesse walked around to the passenger side of the truck where Ellie was. Her face and eyes were red and swollen from all the crying, but she managed a feeble smile as their eyes met.

"I'm sorry," she said. "I should have told you everything from the beginning."

Jesse took her in his arms. "You don't have to apologize."

"Do you forgive me?"

"Yes, Eloree Evan, I forgive you." Jesse pulled her closer.

"Please, don't call me anything but Ellie, or in your case, Cousin Ellie Mae. Eloree is weak and weary, but I'm Ellie and Ellie knows Isaiah 40:29." She held up the card. "I found this when I was looking for another handkerchief."

"See, I told you, you're an amazing woman. Let's get home now."

Once the truck started and Jesse got behind the wheel, Jenna hopped in on the passenger side with Ellie in the middle of the bench seat, close to Jesse. Mohan seemed to be comfortable, in the bed of the truck.

The ride down the mountain was bumpy as Jesse maneuvered the old blue truck around rocks and through the creek. The trek was slow and even though Jesse was anxious to get home, he wasn't looking forward to facing Ellie's father. He glanced at Ellie, but she was turned toward Jenna, engaged in lighthearted chitchat. He wished he could be alone with her - just long enough to say something, anything that would erase the last half hour. He put his hand over hers, grasping her fingers. She squeezed his hand and turned to smile at him.

He put both hands on the wheel as they started down a steep, muddy part of the road. "Hang on, girls. We may slide a little, but we're nearly home."

"I think there's something you two need to know." Jenna turned to check on Mohan. "The stable's crawling with television cameras and newspaper reporters. CNN pulled in as Jonathan and I left earlier this afternoon. The reporter was going to hike up to Bridal Veil Falls, looking for Ellie."

"Glad they won't find her over there." Jesse furrowed his brow.

"That's where the authorities got a ping on Ellie's cell phone." Jenna tilted her head, peering first at Jesse and then Ellie.

Ellie clutched her arms to her chest. "I'm sure my father thinks I fell over the falls."

"It's okay, Ellie. He'll be oh-so-happy to see you didn't." Jenna giggled.

"What made you and Jonathan take off to this side of the ridge?" Jesse asked.

"We were headed to the cabin, going up the other side, but the storm left too much damage. We couldn't even attempt to get through on foot. But you shot the old Colt 45 four times from the cemetery, didn't you?"

Jesse nodded.

"Dad told us he'd stay with the search party at the falls. But he figured if Jonathan and I headed up the old road, we'd probably meet you walking out. So that's pretty much what happened. We had to clear a lot of limbs out of the road, but you can tell the storm wasn't nearly as bad over here."

"What about on Buck Creek?" Ellie's eyes widened.

"There was quite a bit of damage on Buck Creek. Mostly trees down and some houses damaged, but nobody got hurt," Jenna answered.

Jesse was glad Jenna chose not to tell Ellie about the

house being destroyed.

"How's Dr. Shanks?" Ellie wanted to know.

"She weathered the storm out at the stables with the rest of us. We got caught out there and couldn't even get to Ma's house. Besides, Saja was about to foal and there was no way Daddy and I were going to leave her--storm or no storm."

"Did you try to call the vet?" Jesse asked.

"Yes, but we couldn't get through. Even the cell phones were out. All the power was off, but we got the generator started, so we at least had lights, and the sheriff's radio worked."

"I'm sure my father was quite upset with no phone service," Ellie almost whispered.

"He promised to see if he could get legislation passed so we can have more cell towers and get better service in the mountains." Jenna smiled. "Are you okay?"

"Yes, but I'm concerned about the media." Ellie closed her eyes. "I've spent my entire life hiding from them, and now look at me. My hair's a mess, and I don't have on any makeup."

"I've got a plan. We don't want them to see this bandage on your head. It makes you look like you're hurt worse than you probably are. Let's take Jesse's John Deere hat and pull it down over the bandage." Jenna swiped the hat from Jesse's head and placed it on Ellie's.

"Now, you really look like Cousin Ellie Mae from Beverly Hills." Jesse grinned.

"Seriously, how am I going to get away from them? I never talk to the media, and I don't like to be filmed."

When they got to the top of the hill, looking down on the stables, Jesse stopped the truck. "Looks like the carnival's come to Gabby Mountain." He whistled. "Let's do this. Jenna, you get in the back with Mohan. When we get to the gate on the backside of the barn, I'll slow down, then you jump off and open the gate. We'll cruise on into the backside of the entry. Ellie and I will jump out and duck into Saja's stall. If you want to talk to the media, you can. Don't tell them about the panther. That could stir up a lot of stink. We'll leave it to the game warden and the sheriff."

Jenna clambered into the bed of the truck with Mohan, and Ellie stayed put, sitting close to Jesse. As they neared the stable, the media frenzy came at them from behind. In the rearview mirror, Jesse saw Jenna with her arm around Mohan as he sat regally at attention. She waved with her palm cupped, swaying her wrist from side to side. "That silly girl's going to get us in a pickle. They think it's you back there with Mohan."

Jenna barely got the gate opened before the mob attacked

her, microphones in hand, cameras flashing. "You're on your own, little sister," Jesse said as he guided the truck into the entry. Once his feet hit the ground, he reached to help Ellie down. Her hands were on his shoulders and his hands grasped her tiny waist as he swung her out of the truck. They bounded into Saja's stall where the filly and foal were standing next to their mother.

"Look, Ellie. They're beauties." Jesse reached to stroke each one. "Saja, you did good. I'm sorry I wasn't here with you."

"The little filly is yours, right? Have you decided what to name her?" Ellie asked.

Jesse looked down at Ellie and back at the filly. "Well, she's so pretty. Let's name her Elise, after you and the song *Fur Elise*."

Ellie beamed. "Are you sure you want to name her after me?" She wrapped her arms around his neck. The stall door opened, and in stepped Senator Evan, followed a swarm of reporters with microphones and cameras.

"Eloree, there's an air ambulance waiting for you. Make your way over there *now*," her father ordered.

Jesse was shocked. Was that all he had to say to his daughter after all she'd been through?

The flashing cameras were blinding as Jesse grabbed Ellie's arm, and headed for the door, pushing through the mob.

Questions came from all angles, and there was no way to escape.

"Miss Evan, is it true you were thrown from a horse?"

"Miss Evan, how badly are you hurt?"

"Miss Evan, what was the worst part of this ordeal?"

Ellie pulled the old brown coat up over her head and hid underneath it the best she could, turning her back to the crowd. Jesse didn't know what to do. Still, he had to protect Ellie. His mom and grandmother were in the crowd, calling his name. Taking Ellie by the arm, he pushed through the sea of microphones without answering any questions or making any statements. The crowd was with them, filming every detail, as Jesse reached his dad, mom, grandmother, aunts, uncles, cousins, and well-wishers. His family cheered, hugged him, and hugged Ellie.

"Son, I love you. I don't know what I'd do if anything happened to you," his mom sobbed, taking his face in her hands, kissing his forehead. "We prayed so hard, and we knew God would bring you and Eloree back."

The attention was all from Jesse's family until finally, a woman made her way through the crowd, reaching for Ellie.

"Dr. Shanks." Ellie threw out her arms.

"Eloree. You're safe," the woman cried, embracing Ellie.

Much to Jesse's relief, he spotted Jonathan talking to the sheriff and the game warden. He wanted to talk to them, but he didn't want the throng of reporters to follow him or hear any mention of the panther.

Jesse scanned the crowd for Ellie's father and was stunned to see him giving an interview to a group of reporters. He hadn't so much as offered his daughter a hug or told her it was good to see her alive. Then, a tall bald-headed man in a dark suit approached them, looking straight at Jesse. "Eloree, your father wants to speak with you," the man said with a heavy French accent.

"Gustave, this is my friend Jesse," Ellie stammered. "He rescued me from the storm. Jesse, this is my father's assistant, Gustave."

Jesse didn't like the nervousness in her voice. "Nice to meet you, Sir." He swallowed hard, offering a handshake. Was he going to be arrested?

Gustave didn't acknowledge Jesse's hand or take his eyes off him. "Senator Evan will compensate you well."

Turning to Ellie, he scowled. "Come on. *Vous devez exécuter à votre père maintenant.*"

Jesse knew exactly what Gastave had spoken in French. "You must run to your father now," he repeated to himself, wondering if he'd heard it right.

Jesse saw tears well up in Ellie's eyes as she turned to go. She didn't say a word or even offer a smile. All expression left her face, even though she had been laughing and smiling only minutes ago. Anger rose up in him. He wanted to run after her and get her out of Gustave's clutches. But she was trapped, and there was nothing he could do.

Jenna came over and hooked her arm through Jesse's. "What's going on over here?"

"*Vous devez exécuter à votre père maintenant*," Jesse answered.

"What? *You must run to your father now*. That makes no sense. What are you talking about?"

Jesse and Jenna were speechless as they watched Gustave escort Ellie toward her father. With the reporters' microphones and cameras in place, Ellie threw up her arms and ran toward her father, as he opened his arms to embrace her for the entire world to see.

"Are you telling me that was staged?" Jenna frowned.

"Afraid so. Her father hasn't spoken a kind word to her since we got back. He opened Saja's stall door, told Ellie to get to the air ambulance, and disappeared with all those reporters. I can't believe he treated Ellie like a stranger."

"You mean to tell me Senator Evan didn't even say *hello* to her?"

"That's right. Maybe he was ticked off because she had her arms wrapped around my neck when he opened the door." Jesse's jaw tightened.

"Ahhh, Jesse. What was that all about?" Jenna pinched his arm.

Jesse pulled away from her. "Don't aggravate me right now, Jenna. Ellie was really excited I named the little filly Elise. That's Ellie's middle name."

Looking around, Jesse realized a small group of his family and friends had gathered near the air ambulance. Dr. Shanks was giving a *thank you* speech to everyone who'd been instrumental in Ellie's rescue. Jesse figured she'd rehearsed her lines since she was thanking all the different local and government agencies. Spotting Jesse and Jenna, she motioned for the cameras to cut and darted to them. First, she hugged Jenna and then Jesse, telling them how much she and Senator Evan appreciated everything they'd done for Eloree. "Jenna, I know you've already addressed the media. Is there anything you'd like to say, Jesse?"

"No, Ma'am. Not much left to tell." Jesse's eyes were fixed on Ellie.

Dr. Shanks placed her hand on his shoulder. "You're being modest, but without you, Eloree wouldn't be alive. We all have you to thank."

"All thanks goes to God," Jesse said and turned.

Jonathan made his way through the crowd. "Jesse," he whispered, "The sheriff says it'd be a good idea for you to give a brief statement to the media"

Jesse took in a deep breath. Talking to the media was one thing he wasn't looking forward to. If it had to be done, he'd do it. But, only after Ellie had gone.

Like a bad dream, Jesse watched Ellie approach the helicopter with Gustave on one side and her father on the other. The cameras and reporters rolled in full swing, once again. Jesse and Jenna looked at each other and pushed through the reporters for one last glimpse of Ellie.

She was already seated in the helicopter, and the medics hovered over her. The old, brown corduroy coat lay across her lap. Her head was down and the strands of auburn hair that fell across her face made her resemble the little red fox he had set free from the box trap. More than anything, Jesse wanted to set Ellie free.

"Ellie," Jesse shouted over the sound of the helicopter.

Ellie looked up and timidly waved. "Bye..." Her voice trailed as the door shut.

As the helicopter flew out of sight, Jesse felt a familiar hand on his shoulder. "I love you, Son. I'm proud of you. This world would be a better place if every daddy had a son like you."

"And this world would be a better place if every child had a daddy like you."

꧁12꧂

Simple Notions

Ellie awoke the next day in a hospital room. Dr. Shanks napped in a recliner beside her bed, an open book in her lap.

There had been too many hospitals and doctors. The nightmare never ended. But as always, her father saw she was taken to highly respected facilities. The Branches was no exception—with its suites decorated by oil paintings and mahogany furnishings, and the smell of antiseptics masked with fresh flowers.

Ellie propped on one elbow and watched Dr. Shanks sleep. She'd been her therapist for only a few weeks, but Ellie was beginning to relate to her. Most therapists didn't last more than a few days. Either she was accused of not cooperating, or her father dismissed them for telling him he was part of Ellie's problem.

Dr. Shanks was different. She even looked different than other therapists--dressing in blue jeans with trendy blouses and clunky jewelry--her shoulder-length, blond hair pulled into a ponytail at the nape of her neck. Ellie knew she was forty, though she looked younger. So far, she hadn't hesitated to let Ellie try new things and act more like a young woman rather than a sickly child.

"Eloree, you're awake." Dr. Shanks stretched.

"It's fine if you call me Ellie. I like it better than Eloree."

Dr. Shanks raised an eyebrow. "Then Ellie you shall be."

"Where's Father?"

"He was called away and won't be back for several days. I'm to stay with you, and Gustave is right outside if we need anything."

Ellie closed her eyes and shook her head, wishing her father was here. Not because he'd dote over her, but to get the dreaded reprimand over.

The door opened, and a middle-aged doctor with long, blond hair entered the room, accompanied by a nurse pushing a cart filled with medical equipment. "Good morning, Eloree. Let's get your vitals and check you out. How do you feel?"

"Good morning, Dr. Link. I'm a little groggy. How long have I been asleep?" Ellie grimaced, as the blood pressure cuff tightened on her arm.

"About twelve hours—you must have been tired. The CAT scan showed a mild concussion. With a day or two of rest, you'll be your old self again."

"Will I have another scar?"

"Not much of one."

"What about her ankle?" Dr. Shanks asked.

"Nothing a few days rest and an ice pack won't cure." Dr. Link peered over the rim of her glasses. "However, Senator Evan insists she stay here until he comes back next week."

"Not stuck here again." Ellie fell back on the pillow.

"Since you're not physically sick this time—pretend you're on vacation." Dr. Shanks smiled.

Ellie crossed her arms. "I was having a vacation until—"

"You wound up back at The Branches," Dr. Link laughed and patted her arm. "How about something to eat? Dr. Shanks has our vegan gluten-free list."

"I used to eat only vegan, gluten-free, but not anymore." She wrinkled her nose. "I'm starved, and I want real food."

"Take the vegan, gluten-free subject up with your father." Dr. Link said as she headed toward the door. "Have whatever you want."

Dr. Shanks picked up a notepad and pen. "What'll it be?"

Ellie rattled off her recent delicacies--fried potatoes, green beans, cornbread, cinnamon spiced apples, ham, and turkey.

Dr. Shanks lowered her head, peering over the rim of her reading glasses. "Ham and turkey?"

"Sure, today's Easter, and that's what Jesse and Jenna are having. With all the trimmings. I want it, too."

Dr. Shanks tucked the pen behind her ear. "So how did we get from vegan and gluten-free to ham and turkey?"

"The last therapist suggested an all-natural diet. I never thought eating nuts and drinking disgusting herbal teas would solve anything. Father agreed to it."

"Okay, let's see what happens when you eat differently." Dr. Shanks picked up the phone to order the meal.

Ellie showered and dressed in her own clothes, tossing the hospital gown into a hamper. And when the food came, she and

Dr. Shanks sat in the suite's main room at a large wooden table covered in a linen tablecloth, with a vase of fresh flowers in the corner. Before either of them lifted the silver covers from the dinner plates, Ellie bowed her head to pray, "Lord, we thank You for this food--I ask You to bless it. Bless Jesse and all his family on Gabby Mountain. Amen."

"You're saying grace now." Dr. Shanks placed her napkin in her lap, then lifted the silver dome from her plate.

Ellie smiled. "You're having the same thing I am."

"Of course." Dr. Shanks winked. "Why eat nuts and berries when there's a feast?"

"I hope they fixed plenty--I may have seconds." Ellie giggled.

As they neared the end of the meal, the TV in the corner caught Ellie's attention. "I hope I'm not on the news." She picked up the remote and searched for a news channel.

She sunk onto the couch and sat motionless as she watched herself run along the fence to her father's open arms. Tears welled in her eyes, as she only wished her initial greeting with her father had been warm and inviting. Jesse's family had been real, genuine in their reactions. Warm tears slid down her cheeks, but the sound of Jesse's voice brought her attention back to the screen.

The reporter held the microphone in front of Jesse. "Miss Evan is quite an amazing young woman. Throughout the whole ordeal, she showed immense courage and strength, never giving up."

The reporter asked, "Is it true Miss Evan had contact with a wild animal?"

"My dog, Mohan actually located Miss Evan. Some people believe he's part wolf. He and Miss Evan have a friendly bond."

"Is it true the animal was injured during Miss Evan's rescue?"

Ellie loved the way Jesse sidestepped the question. "Mohan's an adventurous animal. I have no further comments," he said, tilting his head with a nod.

Dr. Shanks didn't say anything but listened as Ellie rambled, recounting details of what Jesse said and did, describing how he looked, the way he spoke French and knew about high tea.

"Today's his birthday, and I want to talk to him. I'll grab my phone." Ellie dug through her suitcase.

"I thought your phone went over the falls."

"*That* phone did go over the falls, but *this* phone was in my suitcase the whole time. This is the number I gave Jesse. He was going to text a picture to this phone. Let's see if he did." She scrolled through the messages.

"He texted it to me last night. The message says, *Cousin Ellie Mae - hope you like the picture. Had a great time with you on Gabby. Save my number. Call to check on Elise. Jesse."*

Ellie held up the phone for Dr. Shanks to see the image. "Here I'm sitting on a big rock with Mohan beside me. The way the sun's coming in, Mohan and I are silhouettes. You can see the mountains and pockets of fog down in the valleys. May I call him?"

"You're a grown woman. Only you can make the decision to call a handsome young man." Dr. Shanks folded her arms. "Especially one who calls you *cousin*."

For well over an hour, Ellie's sprawled on the recliner, legs dangled over the arm—phone cradled to her ear—as she and Jesse conversed like the old friends they'd become. And she ignored the fact Dr. Shanks was in the adjoining room, gleaning a wealth of information by what she was overhearing.

"Dr. Shanks," Ellie held the phone down.

"Yes?"

"Am I allowed to have company at The Branches?"

"Who?"

"Jenna and her friend Cindi are leaving Franklin early tomorrow morning. They can stop on their way to Chapel Hill. And if you approve, Jesse can drop by Tuesday."

"Company is a fine idea." Dr. Shanks agreed.

~~~~~

During the night, Dr. Shanks was awakened more than once by Ellie crying out. Each time she rushed to Ellie's side, she could barely make out the words *...panther...kill...Mama...gun.* Finally, she shook Ellie. "Honey, wake up. Are you having a bad dream?"

Ellie sat up, as tears streamed down her face. "It was a scary dream."

"You've been through a horrible ordeal, so having a bad dream is to be expected."

Reaching for a tissue, Ellie began, "It was so real--like living through it all over again."

"It'll help you to talk about it. Tell me everything."

"Dr. Shanks, I can't tell you everything."

"Why?"

"I promised Jesse I wouldn't," Ellis's voice quivered.
~~~~~

“Is someone in trouble?”

“I don’t see how it could get Jesse or me in trouble, but he’s worried about it and asked me not to tell.” Ellie hugged a pillow to her chest.

“Tell me about the dream and what happened.”

“It wasn’t only me in the dream. It was Mama, too. A panther was chasing her. She was falling, and the panther got closer. I had a gun--I had to shoot it--to keep it from getting Mama. After I shot at the panther--Jesse ran out and fought with it,” Ellie blurted between sobs.

Dr. Shanks put her arms around Ellie. After several minutes, she whispered, “It was only a dream. Dreams can help us heal. It wasn’t real.”

Ellie cried harder and clung tighter to Dr. Shanks. “It was real. There really was a panther.”

Catching her breath, Ellie finished, telling Dr. Shanks everything.

“That was heroic of Jesse. Why did he think *anyone* would get in trouble? Maybe Jesse meant he didn’t want you to tell the media. It’s fine for you to tell me. After all, this is a terrible thing to keep to yourself.”

“It’s all because of Father. Jesse doesn’t trust him and thought charges would be pressed for shooting the panther on government property.”

“Your father wouldn’t press charges against someone for protecting you.”

“Then why doesn’t he act like a real *daddy*? Jesse’s dad spends time with Jenna and him. Even takes care of Cindi, and she’s not even his daughter. I wish I had a normal dad,” Ellie ranted, burying her head on Dr. Shanks’s shoulder.

“I understand. You’re frustrated--we’ll address this with your father when you’re ready.”

“He’s never here. Why’s he always gone away on business? I never know where he is or why he’s gone. I don’t even care anymore.” Ellie closed her eyes. “I want to go away like Terrance. Do what I want to, and never come back.”

“I’m hearing you say you’d like to do more things on your own. Right?” Dr. Shanks handed Ellie a tissue.

“Yes, I want to be a normal girl who does normal things. I need to talk to Terrance more often. I want to have a relationship with him like Jenna has with Jesse. After all, he is my brother.”

‘You’ve brought up issues we need to work through.”

Ellie’s sobs had quieted to tears trickling down her cheeks.

“Go back and tell me about your original fall--when your

phone went over the falls."

Drawing in a deep breath, Ellie began again, "Jenna told me to stay on the Fish Hawk Trail and I'd be okay. As you know, I didn't heed her advice. I got off Nanta and tried to climb down to take a picture. That's when I fell."

Dr. Shanks nodded.

"I don't remember much about being rescued by Jesse. But I do remember Mohan standing over me, barking. I had no idea what was going on or that Jesse was nearby. All I saw was this wild animal I thought was about to attack me."

"What did Jesse do?"

Ellie rambled on about Jesse getting her into the cabin and how she had darted out into the storm.

"Why did you do such a dangerous thing?"

Ellie sat straighter. "Don't you understand? I *had* to get back to the car, no matter what. Father would be furious with me for being late. The whole time I was on Gabby Mountain, I worried about having to face Father and his punishment."

"What made you think you could ride a horse off the mountain during such a storm?"

"Before my ride, Jenna told me Nanta could find her way back from anywhere on Gabby Mountain. This was my only option."

"What are your overall feelings about Jesse?"

Ellie rubbed her face with her hands, allowing her fingers to stroke the mark on the side of her cheek. After a moment, she turned to Dr. Shanks. "Promise you won't tell Father?"

"You can tell me anything. I'm here for you."

"He asked if I had a boyfriend." She giggled and brought her hand to her mouth. "Then he told me he doesn't have a girlfriend."

"Tell me more about the brunt of the storm, when you were in the cabin with him."

Ellie hesitated. "Dr. Shanks, do you know about God? Do you know Him as your personal Savior?"

"I've known God since I was just a child."

"That's not what I mean. If you died right now, would you go to heaven or hell?"

"Heaven." Dr. Shanks brought her fingertips together.

"That's the only right answer. I didn't know about God and heaven in that context until Jesse shared it with me. During the storm, we were under the bed with Mohan, of course. It was so scary, but Jesse prayed and called out *Jesus, Jesus*. Right there under the bed--I called on Jesus and gave my heart to Him. I know it's only because we called on Jesus that we were spared."

"You've been through some trying situations and I agree with Jesse. You are strong and courageous. But you have visitors coming in a few hours. Do you need to rest?"

"Maybe if I read, I can go to sleep. Do you have a Bible? Jesse says to read Psalms for comfort and Proverbs for wisdom. I need both."

Turning to go, Dr. Shanks handed her personal Bible to Ellie and gave her one last hug. "Call me if you need anything."

~~~~~

At 10:00 a.m. the next morning, Gustave escorted Jenna and Cindi to Ellie's suite.

Ellie took a seat across from Jenna. She noticed Cindi and Jenna both wore tight fitting jeans tucked into boots, and sweaters accessorized with colorful scarves. Jenna's hair was bobbed neatly at her shoulders. And Cindi's was shorter--styled with an asymmetrical cut laying neatly against her cheek.

"Jenna, I like your new hairstyle," Ellie commented.

"Thanks. Cindi and I both had our hair cut to donate to Locks of Love."

"Cindi, how long was your hair?" Dr. Shanks asked.

"Nearly to my waist. Ellie, have you ever thought about donating to Locks of Love?"

"No, but I'd consider it." Ellie ran her hand over her hair.

Jenna's phone rang. "Excuse me, but I need to grab this." She raised the phone to her ear. "Hi, Daddy...Yes, Cindi and I found the place just fine..." She paused, smiling as she listened. "Bye Dad. I love you, Dad."

"Is everything okay?" Cindi asked.

"Daddy was checking on us." Jenna shoved the phone back in her pocket.

Jenna's words rang in Ellie's head. She would give anything to have a phone conversation like that with her father. *I love you, Dad...*

Then a knock at the door brought Dr. Shanks to her feet. "Come on in," she called, as an attendant stepped into the room.

Dr. Shanks insisted Jenna and Cindi serve themselves first. And Ellie watched as they filled china plates with meat, cheese on crackers, fruit, and vegetables cut in floral shapes.

Once they were seated, Dr. Shanks directed the conversation back to Jenna and Cindi. "I understand you girls are getting ready to graduate. How did you decide which college to
~~~~~

attend?" Dr. Shanks asked.

Jenna pushed back a strand of hair. "First, we decided we weren't going to play Division I basketball. As heart-wrenching as that decision was, we agreed basketball would consume so much of our time we wouldn't get to go home often enough. For years, I couldn't wait to get away from Gabby Mountain. I wanted to live where all the roads are paved, and there's no stench from a barn. But, when it came right down to it, I realized nothing--absolutely nothing--will ever be more important to me than my family."

"We chose UNC because they offered the best academic scholarships. I had no way to pay for college. I'll always be grateful to Jenna's family for taking me in the way they did. When I was still in high school, her parents saw I had the same things Jenna did. They bought this outfit for me because Jesse and Jenna got new things for their birthday, and they wanted me to have something new, as well. There's no way I can ever repay them," Cindi's voice quivered.

Jenna patted her arm. "Ah, come on, sister. You got as much scholarship money as I did. As determined as you are, you'd have made it happen."

"It's not about money. It's about love and encouragement. Your parents make me a part of their family. You can't put a dollar amount on love." Cindi dabbed at the tears welling up in her eyes.

"What are your plans after graduation?" Dr. Shanks filled her glass with more Coke.

"We're moving into our own apartment in Knoxville. I got into medical school—Cindi got into vet school at the University of Tennessee." Jenna turned, to playfully give Cindi a high five.

"Congratulations to both of you. UT is a great choice. I'll be going there in a few weeks for a symposium," Dr. Shanks said.

"Awesome," Jenna exclaimed. "Maybe Ellie could come with you and hang out with us."

"Yeah, Ellie. We could have a wonderful time. Shopping. Movies. Will you be finished with school by then?" Cindi turned to her.

"I'm not enrolled in a college." Ellie sat straighter. " But I've studied at Highland Piano with Patrick Lee Hebert."

"I'm sure the Navè bags keep you busy," Jenna commented.

Ellie's mouth formed a line, hardly showing her teeth. "I'm ready for some new adventures."

The conversation became awkwardly quiet and Jenna and Cindi looked at each other.

Jenna broke the silence. "Speaking of adventures, we need to go. It's another three hours to campus."

What started out to be a formality of thank you and goodbye, turned into a round of hugs and giggles, with promises to stay in touch. When Gustave came to escort Jenna and Cindi out, Ellie insisted she and Dr. Shanks go along. As they arrived at the last set of glass doors, Gustave wouldn't allow Ellie to leave the building or walk into the parking lot.

Ellie and Dr. Shanks stood behind the glass wall separating them from the world of Jenna and Cindi. As they watched the Ford pickup truck maneuver out of sight, tears trickled down Ellie's cheeks.

"Is there anything you want to talk about?" Dr. Shanks asked.

Ellie choked back sobs as they made their way back to her small world. A *world* that offered no freedom. A *world* surrounded by attendants, doctors, confinement, and regulations. A *world* Ellie had come to despise more with each stay. A *world* ordered by her father.

13

Restless Days

Gustave followed Dr. Shanks and Ellie back to the suite, keeping ample distance behind them as if a perpetrator lurked in the hallways. Ellie bolted into her room and slammed the door—wanting to be alone. But she heard Dr. Shanks and Gustave talking in the adjoining room. She couldn't make out all they said, but as Gustave raised his voice, Dr. Shanks responded in her usual quiet tone.

Ellie always felt threatened by Gustave's stern look--well over six feet tall with broad hands hanging from his coat sleeves like a human robot--eyes forming rectangular lines under heavy, dark brows, and high cheekbones. And she knew he resented being assigned to her care, instead of traveling with her father's entourage.

Ellie also knew he had a teenage daughter in France. And as domineering as her own father was, she couldn't imagine having Gustave as a father. Or—on the other hand--parents like Jesse and Jenna's—with all they've done for Cindi.

"I'd like to sit out on the patio and have some alone time," she said when Dr. Shanks stepped into the suite. "I've been cooped up for two days."

"I couldn't agree more. Alone time is part of the plan for you. I'm glad to see you taking advantage of the opportunity."

Ellie squinted as her eyes adjusted to the blinding sun. The gentle breeze reminded her of being on Gabby Mountain. As she stared out over the neatly manicured gardens, her mind raced to encompass the events of the last few days. This place was nothing compared to where she'd been. Even with the destruction of the storm, Gabby Mountain's beauty was natural, not ordered by a groundskeeper. She felt free when she was there-- no one had pruned her or made her fit into a mold. She laughed to herself.

In one way, she felt like the little red fox Jesse set free from the hunter's trap. In another, she felt like she was still trapped, waiting for someone to set her free, yet in fear the hunter would come first. Maybe she was like the baby panther, having its mother taken away. Now it would grow up, cared for by zookeepers and would never know its mother--just as she no longer knew her mother.

Thoughts of her mother brought quiet sobs. Crying was a relief, and she watched tears splash onto the patio floor. She gazed upward, not seeing the blueness of the cloudless sky. "Oh Jesus, I miss Mama," she began. "I know she must be in heaven with You. Did You tell her You kept me safe from the panther? Tell her I finally got to read *Althea Spineeta with Curls in Her Hair*, all by myself. She always said I'd be able to read it someday, and she'd be so proud of me. Tell her I like the scar on my face. It reminds me of her, and I'm going to keep it. Tell her I'm going to bring lots of flowers to her grave. And tell her I will play *Fur Elise* more beautifully than ever, just for her, the way Jesse plays it for his mother."

She sat on an ornate wooden bench and hugged her knees to her chest. Jesse said the Bible speaks of peace that passes all understanding--in her heart, she felt an unusual peace. The gentle breeze whipped her hair across her face, catching strands in the wet tears. Now she knew why crying was good therapy. She could breathe easier, and her heart beat stronger.

A cardinal lit on a low hanging branch and chirped. She listened to its song. "Ahh, little cardinal. Your song is so pretty. You can go wherever you want and sing. Little bird, fly to Gabby Mountain and sing a pretty song to Jesse, Mohan, Saja, and the babies."

The suite door opened, and Dr. Shanks stepped onto the patio. "Are you getting chilly out here? I brought your jacket."

Shoving her arms into the jacket, Ellie stammered, "I miss Mama. Father doesn't want me to talk about her, but I need to."

"You can talk about anything you want to. These are natural feelings." Dr. Shanks sat on the bench, wrapping her arms around Ellie. "I'm here for you. Let your feelings out," she whispered as Ellie clung to her, her body quaking with each sob.

Ellie released herself from the embrace. "I'm sorry for crying and acting childish."

"Crying is good. How long has it been since anyone hugged you?"

"After Jesse shot the panther, I cried for the first time

since Mama's accident. Jesse held me for a long time and kept telling me everything would be all right."

"Before that, how long had it been since anyone showed affection toward you?"

"I don't remember. A few housekeepers and nannies hugged me. But Father frowned on it. He thought physical affection was inappropriate, and crying was forbidden." Ellie drew her knees to her chest.

"How does your father show affection?"

Ellie laid her head on her knees, rocking back and forth. "Frankly, he doesn't show physical affection. His answer to any situation is money. He always uses money as a form of mind control. Jesse told me that the love of money is the root of evil. He says that's in the Bible."

Dr. Shanks nodded, and Ellie continued telling how her father would hold her hand when they were in front of a crowd or put his arm around her for pictures. Other times, he was too busy for childish antics, as he called it.

"How does all this make you feel?" Dr. Shanks asked.

"Confused. Disappointed. Angry, perhaps. I'm not sure how to explain it. This is how my life has always been. Until I met Jesse, I didn't realize how much different life should be. His life is nothing like mine," Ellie confessed.

"Let's go inside. We'll make a list of questions you need answers to and write down things that are important to you." Dr. Shanks stated, leading the way back into the suite.

Seated at the wooden table, Ellie scrawled ideas onto a legal pad. The first item--ask her father about her mother's burial place. She paused to explain how she'd never asked to visit the site because her father refused to talk about her mother or the accident.

The next item involved a discussion with her father about her brother, Terrance. She rambled on about how she wished she had a brother like Jesse. Even though Terrence was ten years older, she needed more contact with him. Terrence had gone away to college shortly after the accident. Ellie was unsure of the reasoning behind her father's decision to practically alienate his only son. When she asked her father about it, he had simply replied that if she disobeyed, he would treat her the same way he had Terrance. Ellie thought the conflict could have stemmed from the fact Terrance became an archeologist instead of following their father into politics.

Dr. Shanks listened, asking a few questions as Ellie paused to elaborate. "Yes, I want to know about Mama and

Terrance. But I can't stop thinking about Jesse and I'm glad he's coming to visit tomorrow. You're not going to let Gustave stop him, are you?"

"No." Dr. Shanks shook her head. "Jesse's visit is much too important. I'm sure he's a fine young man, or you wouldn't be so impressed with him."

"Thanks again for allowing Jenna and Cindi to visit. I'm going to strive to be more like them. When they were here, I yearned to leave with them. Even without lots of money, they have the freedom to go places and enjoy a normal life. No one's watching their every move. They are best friends--like sisters. I can only dream of such a life. I'm envious of them."

"What do you think you should do?" Dr. Shanks asked.

"What are my options? I don't want to be like a trapped animal. I'd give all the money I have to simply be set free."

"This is why I'm here, and I couldn't agree with you more. You have a special visitor coming tomorrow, young lady. Have you decided what you're going to wear and how you'll fix your hair?"

Ellie pursed her lips. "Jesse has seen me at my absolute worst. In fact, he's never seen me when I wasn't at my worst."

"He must be a remarkable guy. So how did you get the nickname *Cousin Ellie Mae*?"

"When he tried to tell me, he was laughing so hard I couldn't figure out what he meant. He referred to his cousins from Beverly Hills, saying I looked like Cousin Ellie Mae because I used a strap off the Navè to tie around the waist of the overalls." Ellie twirled the pen with her thumb and forefinger.

"He meant you looked like Ellie Mae Clampett on the Beverly Hillbillies. That old TV sitcom came on back in the 60's. Maybe we can find it on TV."

"I'm flattered Jesse considers me a movie star," Ellie giggled. "I know one thing, I'm not going to use concealer or makeup on my face when he comes. He never said anything about my face or stared at me when all the makeup wore off. I know he won't tomorrow either."

Before Dr. Shanks could respond, Ellie's phone rang. "It's Jesse." she gasped.

Dr. Shanks winked at her and excused herself from the room, and for over an hour, Ellie lounged in the chair beside the bed with the phone pressed to her ear. There were moments of silence, followed by a giggle, and then Ellie's voice could be heard in response. Each time Dr. Shanks peered in, Ellie was smiling completely immersed in the conversation.

After she hung up, Ellie darted to the door of Dr. Shanks's room. "He had to go. It's time to feed the horses, but he's going to text more pictures of Tanasi and Elise. He'll be here at two o'clock tomorrow."

"That must've been an exciting conversation. I don't think I've never seen you so enthused." Dr. Shanks grinned, raising her brow.

"Go ahead. Tease me. I don't care. I'm so excited to see him." Ellie turned with a light, bouncy step. "He's a great guy—he helps me see how to choose joy even when things aren't going my way. He points me toward God and His will for my life."

~~~~~

"I hope you set *The Beverly Hillbillies* to record again. That was the funniest show," Ellie commented over breakfast. "I'm flattered Jesse thinks I look like Ellie Mae. She's very attractive but she sure isn't as thin as stars today. By the way, may I have seconds on bacon and eggs?"

"Do you feel any differently since you're no longer sticking to your old diet?"

"I feel fine and I want to eat this way. You'll be my ally when Father finds out, won't you?" Ellie spooned another helping of eggs onto her plate.

"Of course." Dr. Shanks tapped her fingers on the table. "But I want to speak with your father, alone before you talk with him about these issues."

"Fine with me--I want to get the punishment over." Ellie hesitated. "What do you think Father will do to me?"

"We discussed it the night of the storm. He blames me, not you. He says he should never have let me talk him into allowing you to drive in the mountains alone. Be patient, even if he wants Gustave by your side at all times for a while."

Ellie closed her eyes, crumpling a napkin in her hand. "He shouldn't blame you. It's my fault. I did go to the mountain home. But, when I got there the gate was locked. I decided to drive around until I saw the sign for horseback rides."

Dr. Shanks placed her coffee cup on the table. "Do you know what happened to the mountain home?"

"No, what?"

"The house slid off the side of the mountain in the storm. There's nothing left of it."

Ellie's eyes grew wide. "Are you saying if you hadn't been at the stables, looking for me, you would've been *killed*?"
~~~~~

"Exactly. I firmly believe God protects us, though sometimes in unusual ways. He used you and the circumstances you were in to make sure no one was in that house." Dr. Shanks wiped a tear from the corner of her eye.

"What did Father say about all that?" Ellie swallowed hard.

"Once we knew for sure you were somewhere on Gabby Mountain, presumably by the falls, we weren't leaving." Dr. Shanks leaned closer. "And to your father's credit, I've never seen a parent more concerned. He paced the floor, unable to do anything, but worry."

"What did Jesse's family do?" Ellie drew in her bottom lip.

Dr. Shanks poured another cup of coffee. "Prayed without ceasing, as the Bible says."

"I can't imagine Father in that situation. Was he rude?"

"Let's say he was especially nervous. The sheriff told him over and over that Jesse was out in the storm, too, and his family was just as concerned about their son."

"I caused quite a commotion, didn't I?" Ellie crossed her arms.

"Things work out for the best."

"Why did Father leave?" Ellie scowled, staring at the half-eaten food on her plate.

"Your father has responsibilities and obligations." Dr. Shanks took a slow sip of coffee. "But you'll be having a guest in a few hours. Let's get ready."

Ellie closed her eyes and drew in a deep breath. She knew Dr. Shanks wasn't telling her everything, but this wasn't the time to push the issue.

"Go take a shower." Dr. Shanks patted her shoulder. "I'll have Dr. Link's assistant come in to change the bandage on your forehead and shampoo your hair."

After Ellie showered and her hair had been shampooed, she searched through her suitcase, but nothing came close to what Jenna or Cindi wore the day before. No matter what she chose, she'd be overdressed, so she settled for black linen slacks with a royal blue silk sweater and black flats. Instead of matching earrings, she decided on oval silver hoops.

Then she stared in the mirror. The scar shone as vibrant as ever--on any other day, she'd cover it with concealer and makeup, but it was different with Jesse. She knew he wouldn't mention it. Settling for only mascara and lip-gloss, she put the makeup bag away.

Dr. Link stepped into the room. "My, you look spiffy.

Something special happening today?"

"Thanks, I'm expecting a visitor."

"Then you've something to look forward to. Let me get a closer look at your scar." She held a magnifying instrument above Ellie's face.

"I've decided against another surgery." Ellie turned away.

"Why's that?" Dr. Link stepped back. "You're almost twenty-one--time for final reconstruction."

"I can live with the scar." Ellie pressed her lips together.

"Senator Evan has requested a prestigious team of cranial surgeons who only take high profile patients. Does he know about your decision?" Dr. Link looked concerned.

"No." Ellie cut her eyes toward Dr. Shanks.

"I suggest we listen to Ellie." Dr. Shanks stepped closer.

"You may want to discuss this further before Senator Evan returns." Turning to Dr. Shanks, she added, "I understand you've seen a partial set of Eloree's medical records. Here's her medical portfolio." She handed Dr. Shanks a thick leather binder.

"I'll review this, but do you see any reason Ellie can't leave the facility for a few hours? Maybe go shopping."

"If she feels up to it, I have no problem with the two of you going out for the day." Dr. Link waved, as she left the room.

"Shopping? Are you serious?" Ellie bounced on the balls of her feet.

"Tomorrow, we'll drive into Asheville--check out the boutiques and shops. And have lunch, if you're up to it."

"What about Gustave?"

"He'll go with us but trust me on this one." Dr. Shanks winked. "Is there anything you'd like to chat about before Jesse comes, or would you like to have alone time?"

"Alone time. Do you mind if I borrow your Bible again?"

"Of course, but I'm curious, do you have a Bible at home?" Dr. Shanks pressed her thumb to her cheek.

"I think there's one in Father's study. Mama had several--I haven't seen those in years."

Nestled in an overstuffed chair, Ellie opened the Bible. Her eyes fell on a handwritten page that read:

> *Presented to: Our daughter, Susan. Congratulations on your Doctorate. We've always been proud of you, but today we're especially blessed as you prepare to speak into the lives of others. God will bring His hurting children to you for comfort and refuge. Psalm 91:1*
> *By: Dad and Mom Date: April 3, 1999.*

Ellie stared at the page until tears blurred her vision and rolled down her cheeks. *April 3, 1999, was the day of the accident.* The day her whole life fell apart. How could this be? How could life be so unfair? What had she done to cause her life to crumble the way it had?

Dr. Shanks stepped into the doorway. "Ellie, are you okay?"

"No." Ellie bit her lip.

Dr. Shanks sat on the arm of the chair. "Want to share?"

"No." Ellie handed the Bible back to her. "I need to talk to Jesse."

"I understand, but..." Dr. Shanks hesitated.

Ellie broke in, "Will you allow Jesse and me to walk down to the fountain?"

"Of course."

"Then ask the staff to pack a picnic. Jesse and I like Mountain Dew, ham and cheese sandwiches, along with potato chips and pickles. Ask if they have Butterfingers."

"First, you're eating meat and now junk food." Dr. Shanks smirked, with a playful gesture.

"It's the new me—Ellie. Not Eloree."

"Sounds like a great plan. I'll check with the staff. Decide how you're going to fix your hair while I'm gone," Dr. Shanks called as she left the room.

Alone in front of the mirror, Ellie stared at her image. "Maybe life's been unfair, but I know what I want. I'm going to be an ordinary girl, living an ordinary life with a scar to remind me of Mama. Little cut on my forehead, you're a reminder of the time I spent with Jesse. Frizzy hair, how about a side ponytail? You won't be hiding my face anymore. And I might share you with Locks of Love. Someone with no hair would be delighted to have you," Ellie whispered aloud.

Her phone rang--Jesse's name flashed on the screen.

"Jesse. How far away are you?"

"I'm here. The Branches isn't far from Mohan's vet, and we got finished with his appointment sooner than I expected. I don't mind to wait--since I'm early."

"No reason to wait. I'll have Gustave escort you in. See you in a bit." Tossing the phone aside, she brushed the strands of curls sweeping across her shoulder, one last time.

"Gustave," she called around the corner. "Jesse is here. Will you see him in, please?"

"He's not expected for another thirty minutes," Gustave

stepped into the doorway, a staunch look on his face.

"I'm ready for his visit." Ellie's heart sunk with the idea Gustave might keep Jesse waiting, or even worse forbid him to come in.

Dr. Shanks came down the hallway. "What's going on?" Her gaze shifted from Ellie to Gustave.

"Jesse is here. I asked Gustave to see him in." Ellie tried to mask her frustration.

"Gustave, is there some reason Jesse shouldn't be escorted in *now*?"

"Not time for his appointment," Gustave countered.

"I'll escort him myself. Come on Ellie, you may go with me." Dr. Shanks stepped around Gustave.

Gustave put his hand out. "No. Miss Evan's father is not pleased with this visit."

"Then Miss Evan's father needs to speak with *me* if he has concerns regarding *my* treatment plan for *his* daughter," Dr. Shanks's voice came across smooth and steady.

"That farm boy has no right to come here." Gustave's jaw twitched.

"That's for Ellie to decide. She spent twenty-four hours alone with this young man--on top a deserted mountain. Not to mention, he saved her life more than once," Dr. Shanks spoke, with authority."

"I won't jeopardize security."

"This place is filled with security cameras. How could Ellie's safety possibly be an issue? Besides, neither she nor I have heard from the Senator since he left."

"Rest assured, Senator Evan will be in touch," Gustave scoffed, then turned and strode down the hallway, as if on a mission.

Ellie squeezed her temples. "Oh no. He'll send Jesse away."

Dr. Shanks put her arm around Ellie's shoulders and led her back into the room. "Listen to me, Ellie. Gustave won't send Jesse away. He's only trying to do his job. I spoke with your father at length before he left for this trip. All you need to do is enjoy this visit with Jesse."

Ellie stared at her in disbelief. No one ever stood up to Gustave or her father the way Dr. Shanks did. Would Dr. Shanks help to turn her life around?

ᘛ14ᘚ

Blue Skies

Hello Ellie. Dr. Shanks." Jesse nodded as if tipping an invisible hat to distinguished ladies.

"Hi, Jesse." Ellie clasped her hands behind her back, shifting from heel to toe. She stared at him like she was meeting him for the first time.

"Glad to see you're feeling better."

Dr. Shanks stepped forward, extending a handshake. "I'm pleased to officially meet you, Jesse. Please, have a seat."

Jesse took a seat on a leather side chair. And Ellie perched on the sofa where she saw Gustave outside the door, leaned against the wall--his arms crossed like a locked iron gate.

"You're quite a hero," Dr. Shanks said, closing the door where Gustave stood.

"No, Ma'am. I'm no hero." Jesse blushed. "Mohan's the hero--he sure took a liking to Miss Ellie."

Ellie piped in, "I love Mohan. How is he? What did the vet say?"

"Got several stitches, but he'll make a full recovery and be chasing rabbits again in a few days."

"Tell Mohan I want to give him a big, juicy bone." Ellie smoothed her side ponytail.

"You can tell him. He's waiting in the truck."

"I want to see him. You too, Dr. Shanks. You have to meet this dog."

Before the conversation went any further, an attendant delivered a picnic basket. "I'm sorry, Miss Evan. We were able to pack everything you requested except the Butterfinger candy bars. But we included several other candies."

"Thank you." Ellie stood and reached for the basket.

Jesse took the basket and held the door for Ellie as they stepped through the door leading outside to the gardens.

Ellie turned to see Gustave step into the room and attempt

to follow them, but Dr. Shanks stepped in front of him.

"You two enjoy fresh air and sunshine," she called. "Gustave and I'll wait here for you."

Once they reached the walkway leading to the garden path, Jesse turned to Ellie. "Is there something going on I should know about?"

"What do you mean?" Ellie stammered.

"Gustave doesn't want me here and neither does your father."

"Did Gustave say that?" Ellie looked back over her shoulder.

"Look, don't tell Gustave I understand everything he says. He mumbled in French as we were walking down the hallway, and I didn't let on I knew what he said."

"I don't want this to be uncomfortable, but please stay. I need to talk to you."

"Well, I'm here as long as he doesn't run me off."

"This is my life--someone always watching me or telling me what I can and can't do. Do you realize the twenty-four hours I had with Mohan and you was the most freedom I've had in my entire life?"

"What are you going to do?" Jesse took her hand as they continued along the path.

"Can you hide me on Gabby Mountain where Gustave and Father won't find me?" Ellie wrinkled her nose.

"I don't think Gabby Mountain's big enough to hide you from Gustave. He seems downright determined to keep an eye on you. How about Dr. Shanks?"

"Dr. Shanks is wonderful. No other therapist has ever worked with me like she does.

"My family thinks highly of her. They all call her Susan. From what I hear, she kept everybody settled down during the storm and even helped deliver Saja's babies."

"She understands how I feel--even holds me when I cry." Ellie stared straight ahead. "Every therapist tried to help me learn to laugh and cry. Now I laugh and cry—mostly cry."

"Crying's good for you, I guess." Jesse placed the picnic basket on a bench near the fountain.

"I hope to soon stop crying over *everything*. Like this morning, Dr. Shanks let me borrow her Bible--when I opened it up to the front, I almost cried reading the dedication page," Ellie confessed as they sat on the bench.

"The *dedication* page?" Jesse took both her hands.

"Dr. Shanks's parents gave her the Bible as a gift on the

date of *my* accident, April 3, 1999. They wrote how proud they were of her. She grew up with two parents. I miss Mama," Ellie's voice cracked, and she rested her head on Jesse's shoulder.

"Ellie, I wish I had all the answers for you." Jesse put his arm around her. "But I don't. We have to look to God when storms come our way."

"Why do bad things happen to good people? Why did Mama have to leave me?"

"That's a tough question. But while we're here on earth, we're in a spiritual war. Good against evil. God is good, Satan's evil. The Bible tells us God will win the war, but while we're in the battle, there'll be casualties. We don't understand why, but we have to trust in God," Jesse paused. "Like when I shot the panther. I only had *one* bullet. It was my intention to run to the top of the ridge and shoot the last bullet to signal whoever was on the motorcycle. I heard you scream, a split second before I pulled the trigger. That was God looking out for us. He knew I had to have the bullet. We have to trust Him and His word to give us strength to fight our battles."

"I'm sure you're right. I remember what you said about reading the Bible, and I borrow Dr. Shanks's Bible every day."

"Don't you have a Bible of your own?"

"No, but I intend to ask Father where Mama's Bibles are."

"I have one in the truck I'd like to give you. That way, you'll have a Bible of your very own."

"Thank you." Ellie opened the picnic basket. "I'm sorry to be asking so many questions. We're supposed to be having a picnic and having fun. Guess what's in this basket?"

"I've already had lunch but surprise me." Jesse crossed his arms.

"Mountain Dews, ham sandwiches, chips, and plenty of candy." Ellie closed her eyes and took Jesse's hand. "You ask the blessing."

Jesse bowed his head, thanking God for the food, ending the prayer by asking God to renew Ellie's life with His peace.

As they munched on the picnic goodies, Ellie said, "I've never had anyone say a prayer with my name in it before. Thank you."

"Does your father not pray for you?"

"I don't think so, but I'll put that on the list of things to ask him. I'd like to know what he thinks about God and the Bible." Ellie reached for another chip.

They laughed and talked, but Ellie hardly ate, instead taking every opportunity to look deep into his warm brown eyes, believing he enjoyed being near her as much as she enjoyed being beside him.

"Let's throw coins in the fountain and make a wish," he said, finishing off the last of his Mountain Dew.

"Sounds fun to me."

Jesse shoved his hands in his pockets as they neared the gurgling water. "I don't have a penny. Take this nickel. Maybe you'll get five wishes, or one wish will come true five times faster."

"I'll take the nickel and make it five times faster." Ellie tossed the coin into the spray.

"Watch this, Cousin Ellie Mae." Jesse flipped a quarter high into the air and watched it splash in the ripples.

"Does this mean you want twenty-five wishes?" She beamed up at him.

"Nope, I'll make one great big wish."

"Tell me what it is," Ellie begged, putting her hands behind her back and swayed from side to side.

"All right." Jesse pointed. "See the top of the big building over there. That's the Biltmore House. I wish we could spend a day there."

"I'd like that, too. I'll ask Dr. Shanks if she can arrange it." Ellie grabbed his arm.

"Should I mention it to her when we get back?" Jesse wrapped his fingers around hers.

"No," she hesitated. "Let me ask her when Gustave isn't listening. He tells my father everything."

"I'd want your father's approval, but don't tell me I have to get Gustave's permission first," Jesse half-joked.

Ellie tightened her lips, furrowed her brow, and mumbled in French.

"You don't do a very good job of looking like Gustave. You're way too pretty." Jesse laughed, reaching for the picnic basket.

"Thank you." She tucked her hand into the bend of his elbow as they started back up the path.

"By the way, Miss Ellie. What was your wish?"

"If you honestly want to know, I'll tell you. But you have to promise not to laugh."

Jesse shrugged. "I promise unless it's so funny I can't help it. I've seen your playful side today."

"I wish I could be an ordinary girl, like Jenna and Cindi. Go shopping." She stopped. "Have my own car. Go to movies and hang out with friends."

Jesse saw the seriousness on her face. "Go on, what else

do you want?"

"I'm not happy always being cooped up and having people making a big deal over me, because I'm Eloree, Senator Walton Evan's daughter. I left Eloree on Gabby Mountain, and I walked off as Ellie."

"You content to be Ellie?"

"Yes, Dr. Shanks and I watched the *Beverly Hillbillies* and we laughed like kids."

"What did you think about Ellie Mae?" Jesse slowed the pace.

"I think she's funny and beautiful. I'm going to gain weight and look more like her. Maybe even cut my hair a bit or dye it blond." She tilted her chin at him.

"You mean you'd cut your hair or dye it to try to look like an old-fashioned movie star?"

"Hmm, I'm thinking about getting it cut for Locks of Love, like Jenna and Cindi." Ellie ran her fingers through the side ponytail. "I liked the highlights in Cindi's hair. I've never had highlights. Most girls, my age, do different things to their hair all the time. I want to try it, too."

"You sound serious." Jesse opened the door for her.

"I am," she whispered, stepping ahead of him.

Dr. Shanks came into the room. "Hi, you two. Jesse put the basket on the table. Would you like to sit down and visit here for a while?"

"Thank you, Ma'am. I better go. Don't want to leave Mohan in the truck too long."

"We're going out to see Mohan, right? Both of us?" Ellie's eyes lit up.

"Absolutely." Dr. Shanks pulled on a sweater. "I want to meet this heroic wolfdog, you call *Wahya*."

Gustave scowled as he led the way through the series of locked doors with keypads. Ellie kept quiet while Dr. Shanks made small talk with Jesse. When the party reached the last set of doors to the parking lot, Gustave stopped and opened the door. Jesse stepped aside for Dr. Shanks and Ellie to walk through first, but Gustave motioned for him to go on out.

Dr. Shanks stepped between Jesse and Gustave. "Excuse me, Gustave. Ellie and I are going to Jesse's truck. Do you want to come with us?"

"*Non, il apportera le camion ici*," Gustave demanded in French.

Turning to Jesse, Dr. Shanks interpreted, "Jesse, Gustave would like you to bring the truck over here."

As Jesse drove the truck across the parking lot, Ellie saw Mohan's head out the window. As the truck came to a stop in front of the side entrance, Mohan gave his usual *gr-howl.* When Ellie stepped into view, he threw his head back and howled. She darted around Gustave and flung the truck door open.

Before Jesse could make his way around the front of the truck to the passenger's side, Ellie was on the ground--Mohan on top of her, plastering her face with kisses. Ellie laughed and tried to sit up.

Then Gustave yelled obscenities in French--Jesse lurched between Mohan and Gustave. "No. Don't you kick my dog." Jesse roared, his face no more than a few inches from Gustave's.

Jesse grabbed Mohan by the collar and stood face to face with Gustave. Dr. Shanks darted between them. "Gentlemen. Gentlemen. There's been a misunderstanding."

Gustave continued to swear in French.

"Gustave, that's enough. I've got control of this situation," Dr. Shanks demanded. "The dog wasn't hurting Ellie. He was only—" but her words were lost as Gustave maintained his stony stance.

Jesse held Mohan's collar with one hand, his other arm around Ellie's shoulders. "Mohan didn't hurt you, did he?"

"I'm fine. He caught me by surprise when he jumped out of the truck, and I fell," she whispered.

Gustave's defiant stare compounded with more French swears--his glowering eyes darted between Dr. Shanks, Ellie, and Jesse.

"If he doesn't hush, I'm going to say plenty," Jesse stated. "I will not stand by and see a woman disrespected."

"No, Jesse, no." Ellie tugged his arm. "No one ever talks back to Gustave."

Jesse put Mohan back in the truck and stepped in the direction of Dr. Shanks and Gustave. She motioned for Jesse to stop. "Gustave, you're dismissed for the day. You may not speak to me in such a manner in front of Ellie and her friend."

"I'll speak to the senator about this matter." He turned on his heel and stepped aside, cell phone in hand.

"I'm sorry Dr. Shanks, Ellie. I had no idea Mohan would cause such a ruckus," Jesse apologized. "If Gustave had kicked him, it would've ripped the stitches on his side."

"I apologize to the both of you. Gustave's actions were uncalled for. Now, where were we? I want to pet this fellow." Dr. Shanks reached in the window and rubbed Mohan's head.

"See how soft his ears are." Ellie climbed on the running

board.

Jesse asked, “How much longer will you be staying here?”

Ellie stepped off the running board. “Father returns on Monday--I’m leaving then.”

“I was wondering if you’d like to come to the stables to see Saja and the babies.” Jesse pushed his hands into his jeans pockets.

Ellie gasped, “Oh Dr. Shanks, may we? I’d love to go see the babies.”

“You have a consultation with Dr. Link tomorrow.”

“Maybe we can go the next day.” Ellie bounced from foot to foot.

“How about the day after tomorrow?” Jesse went on. “Mama’s on break this week--she’d like to see you. And Miss Dicie is bringing her kids to see the babies.”

“Please, Dr. Shanks.” Ellie wanted to get on her knees and beg. “I want to meet Miss Dicie.”

“I hope we can.” Dr. Shanks cut her eyes toward Gustave. “We’ll see how things work out.”

“Call and let me know.” Jesse opened the glove box and pulled out a small leather Bible.

“This is for you, Ellie.”

“I can’t take your Bible.” She brought her hand to her mouth.

“I’m giving it to you--got plenty of other Bibles.” He grabbed a pen and wrote on the inside cover.

To: Ellie   From: Jesse
You can do all things through Christ who gives you strength.
Philippians 4:13

“Thank you. This is special.” Ellie hugged the gift to her chest.

“Well, ladies. I’ve got horses to feed. Hope to see you later this week.” Jesse grinned.

Ellie didn’t take her eyes off him until the truck went out of sight.

~~~~~

Ellie sunk into the chair beside the bed, still hugging the Bible to her chest. For well over an hour, she thumbed through the Bible—reading passages and notes Jesse had written. If having a Bible was supposed to give her strength, she wished for
~~~~~

the tenacity to stick up for herself the way Dr. Shanks did with Gustave. If only she had the nerve to tell her father how she felt, but the day would come, and Dr. Shanks would be on her side.

Dr. Shanks stepped into her room wearing gray sweatpants and a pink t-shirt, her hair loose around her face, no jewelry or make-up. "Hey, Ellie. What do you say we get comfortable--have dinner in front of the TV, again?"

"You mean you don't dress for dinner every evening?"

"Heavens, no. When I'm home, this is how I dress. I'm an *ordinary* person, doing what *ordinary* people do. Have I heard the word *ordinary* from someone else lately?"

"I thought we were supposed to have a therapy session after Jesse's visit."

"Let's have a pajama party. I'll set *The Beverly Hillbillies* to record." Dr. Shanks picked up the TV remote.

Ellie grinned. "Should I wear, pajamas? I don't own any comfortable clothes like you have on."

Dr. Shanks threw out her hands. "Pajamas sound great."

"I've never been to a real pajama party."

"Then you're about to have an *extraordinary* time being *ordinary*. This will be fun therapy. Get changed and I'll tell the dining room staff we won't need their services." Dr. Shanks stepped to the door. "Oh, by the way, I hope you don't mind we're having pizza delivery for dinner."

"Sounds delicious. Is it okay if I call Jesse?" Ellie called after her.

"What are you asking *me* for? He's *your* boyfriend." Dr. Shanks stuck her head back around the door and laughed.

My boyfriend. The words rang in her head, and blood rushed to her cheeks. Her fingers trembled as she dialed Jesse's number. The phone rang. He didn't answer. Four more rings--still no answer. Ellie's heart sank. What if he never wanted to talk to her again? What if he thought she had too many issues?

Dr. Shanks was humming a tune, as she strolled back into Ellie's room. "What's wrong? You look like you just lost your best friend."

"It's Jesse." Ellie looked down at her phone. "I tried to call him--he didn't answer. Maybe he doesn't want to talk to me again."

"Let's think about the situation before you jump to conclusions." Dr. Shanks propped in the doorway. "Did Jesse say anything leading you to believe he doesn't want to talk to you?"

Ellie shook her head. "No, but Gustave tried to kick Mohan. That made Jesse angry, and he wanted to stop Gustave from cursing at you."

"Those things happened, but Jesse seemed fine as he left. After all, he invited us to come see Saja and the babies."

"Why won't he answer?" Ellie tossed the phone onto the bed.

"We'll work on this--you should wait before getting worked up over any situation. This is a life skill everyone should practice."

Ellie wrung her hands. "I don't understand what you mean."

"Here's an example. Remember how Gustave reacted this afternoon. That whole situation upset you, Jesse, and me. I'm choosing to walk away from it for the rest of the day and have some peaceful harmony in my life." Dr. Shanks's mouth curved into a precarious smile.

"How can you simply forget about what happened? Even Father would be displeased with Gustave's swearing."

"I'm choosing to unwind and deal with it tomorrow. Both Gustave and I will have a chance to settle down and clear our heads. Tomorrow, we'll come to terms."

"Are you always this calm? I feel like ranting when things don't go my way." Ellie smoothed a strand of hair from her face.

"Most people feel like ranting. It's not human nature to be calm when we're facing tough situations. It takes practice and self-control. Once you learn to cope with yourself and maintain self-control, you'll gain control over tricky situations instead of losing control."

Ellie crossed her arms. "Do you think I'll master that?"

"Ever heard the old cliché *practice makes perfect*? Life's always going to give you lots of practice in this arena. The better you become at remaining calm, the happier you'll be. Trust me."

"I wish I'd known this before I went to Gabby Mountain. I didn't use self-control, but Jesse was nice to me--even after I was rude to him."

"Why do you think he was nice to you?"

"Well ..." Ellie paused. "At first, he said he was treating me the way he would want my brother to treat Jenna if they were in the same situation."

"Jesse treats others the way he wants to be treated."

"That's right. He's an all-around happy person."

"Why do you think he's so happy?"

Ellie looked at the ceiling. "He has everything he wants. It's all there on Gabby Mountain."

"Jesse was born into a family with that particular lifestyle.

None of us control the family or the lifestyle we're born into." Dr. Shanks leaned closer to Ellie. "How do you feel about your family?"

Ellie stepped over to the dresser, staring at herself in the mirror before picking up a hairbrush. She aimlessly tugged at the strands of hair falling around her shoulders. "I don't feel like I have a family," her voice elevated.

"Why?"

Ellie took in a deep breath and held it as she stared at Dr. Shanks. "You already know everything there is to know about my family. Father is paying you to fix everything--It's *his* problem, not *mine*."

"Let's assume I'm your fairy godmother, and I have a magic wand to fix your family. Where do want me to start? With whom?"

"Ugh..." Ellie groaned. "Okay. Start with me. Father wants me to be a puppet on a string with a painted-on smile. But to stay out of sight until he takes me off the shelf. Then, I'm only supposed to do what he tells me to, or whatever it may be that furthers his political agenda."

Ellie yanked the hairbrush, pulling at the tangles, carelessly breaking strands. Her face turned red--her sighs became heaves. "Why are you looking at me like that?" Ellie flung the hairbrush onto the floor.

Ellie held her breath as Dr. Shanks waited. "I was wondering what you were thinking that caused you to overreact."

"Does it matter? Father will be back in a few days--my *nice* little stay in this *beautiful* facility will be over until father finds another facility to get me out of his way," Ellie sneered, placing her hands on her hips.

"Do you want to stay here?" Dr. Shanks lowered her voice.

"It's better than going to my so-called home. Evan Manor is nothing but a dungeon that needs a moat. Gustave and the rest of the staff are dragons watching my every move, and Father's worse than a wicked stepmother. He's already dispensed of Terrance."

"How do you feel about that?"

"If I don't do what Father says, I'm next. Give me the poison apple. Take me into the woods and leave me. Maybe I shouldn't care. Fix that Dr. Shanks, *my fairy godmother*." Ellie roared, throwing herself across the bed in a fit of tears.

Once the crying subsided to faint sobs, Dr. Shanks touched Ellie's shoulder. "You've brought up some interesting points. I have a plan for when your father returns."

"No plan will work with him. He's hopeless." Ellie turned to face Dr. Shanks.

"Lots of things have changed since the first day I met you. If you'll make one promise to me, together we can make some things in your life change. Are you willing?"

Ellie raised up on her elbows. "I guess."

"The one thing you must do is remain calm. No matter what your father says or does--you need to remain composed. If you feel like shouting at him, simply force yourself to speak a bit softer. When you whisper, others must listen intently to hear you. That's a powerful weapon," Dr. Shanks whispered.

"I'm sorry I yelled at you. I shouldn't have."

Dr. Shanks smiled at her. "Next lesson--always have a friend you can vent to. Someone who'll listen, whether you're glad or whether you're mad. Helps settle the dust. You've got my number, so even if I'm not around, call me."

Ellie craned her head. "You're not leaving, are you?"

"Not until we get these issues resolved with your father."

"What's your plan? Will you ask him to buy me an enchanted mountain and a wolf-dog?" Ellie wiped her face.

"Oh-fairy tale princess, you've left characters out of your story. Not to mention a tall, brown-eyed knight in shining armor wearing Justin boots, Wrangler jeans, and driving a white Ford pickup truck that still smells new," Dr. Shanks teased.

Ellie closed her eyes and shook her head. "Stop teasing me, Dr. Shanks."

"You're trying hard not to smile. You know you love being teased about a certain young man, especially one that's calling you right now. I hear your phone in the bathroom." Dr. Shanks pointed and headed for her own room.

Ellie dashed for the phone. "Hello, Jesse."

"Hey, Ellie. Saw I had a missed call from you. Everything okay?"

"Yes, I wanted to thank you for coming by today and bringing Mohan. How are Saja and the babies?"

"I'm not home yet. Had to make a stop in town on my way back through. Picked up a little surprise for you."

"For me? Tell me what it is!"

"If I tell you, it won't be a surprise. You'll have to come to Gabby to get it. Let me know as soon as you find out if you're going to get to come."

"I will. We should find out for sure in the morning when Dr. Link comes back in. I already have approval to go to Asheville tomorrow."

"There's a lot to see and do around Asheville. I only go when I have business, but Jenna and Cindi go every time they can come up with an excuse. They even drive all the way over there to get their hair cut sometimes."

"Don't they have a hairdresser in Franklin?"

"Sure, but they like to go to a girl named Shelby. Actually, her shop's not far from where you're staying."

"What's the name of the shop?"

"Happy Hair Fashions. But you're not thinking of doing anything to your pretty hair, are you?"

"Actually, I'm considering having it cut for Locks of Love."

"Have you ever had short hair?"

"No, but my hair's thick and grows fast. I'm ready for a change."

"No matter what you do with your hair, you'll still be a pretty girl, and Mohan will be more than happy to see you." Jesse laughed. "I'm going to lose you any second now. I won't have service again until I get to the barn..." Static came on the line and the call was dropped.

Ellie closed her eyes and let the conversation soak in. Jesse said she was *pretty*. Her stomach fluttered.

Dr. Shanks stepped into the doorway. "Pizza's here, and I've got the TV ready for *The Beverly Hillbillies*."

"Where are we sitting?" Ellie asked, seeing the table had been pushed aside.

"I thought you'd like to eat on the couch and watch TV."

"I don't recall ever having dinner away from a table."

"Eating on the couch is taking you out of your comfort zone, isn't it?"

Ellie nodded, "But this is fine. I want to do what ordinary people do. I'm not dressed for dinner. Why should I sit at the dinner table to eat from a cardboard box with my fingers?"

Dr. Shanks laughed. "We're drinking out of bottles. Coke goes great with pizza. We can ask for glasses if you'd like."

"No, I want it this way." Ellie settled on the couch with the pizza box on the coffee table between them.

"Jesse always says a blessing. Even today, when we had the picnic by the fountain. May we ask a blessing now?"

They closed their eyes and bowed their heads as Ellie asked God to bless the food--continuing with the mention of Jesse and how she was thankful he'd come to visit.

When the prayer was finished, Dr. Shanks smiled at her. "Was he mad at you?"

"No," Ellie swallowed a bite of pizza. "He said he picked

up a surprise for me on his way back home. He wants us to visit."

"We'll work on it tomorrow. For tonight, let's finish our party."

"What will we do after this?" Ellie wanted to know.

"I found some games in the credenza. Maybe we could play checkers. It's my goal to teach you simple pleasures in life. People relate to each other and carry on conversations while playing games. Watching TV is fun, but it doesn't allow you to relax and still interact."

"I don't watch much TV. I like *The Beverly Hillbillies*, but it seems ironic they went from being poor to filthy rich, yet they're still made fun of. All these people befriend them because of their wealth. I realize it's a comedy, but the reality is people treat me differently because of Father and his wealth."

"What would you like to do?" Dr. Shanks dabbed the corners of her mouth with a paper napkin.

"Go through life without people knowing who I am or that Father is so wealthy."

"But you are Eloree Elise Evan--daughter of Senator Walton Evan. How do you think you can combat that?"

"Maybe like Terrance--he moved to Europe, where few people had even heard of Father. He travels all over the world and lives his own life." Ellie reached for another slice of pizza.

"What do you propose for yourself?"

"For starters, someone should come up with a TV show depicting the flip side of being rich and well known. The characters should be rich and discontent. Then, they could become like ordinary people, with little or no money. At least have happiness that doesn't hinge on money."

Dr. Shanks placed a half-empty soda bottle on the floor. "Maybe a career in the entertainment industry would be exciting, but what can you do today to change things?"

"I've thought it through--I know what I want to do."

"I'm listening."

"I'd like to change my appearance. Jesse told me about a salon called Happy Hair Fashions, not far from here. He says there's a stylist there named Shelby who does Jenna's and Cindi's hair. I want to cut mine for Locks of Love and get a new style."

"Commendable, but a bit drastic. Have you ever had short hair?"

"No, and I'm sure Father wouldn't approve. I used to beg him to let me get it cut and styled. He said I could when I'm grown up--but not as long as I'm his little girl. I'm almost twenty-one. Don't you think I'm old enough to decide how I want to wear my hair?"

"Better think this one through. What else do you plan?"

"Go shopping for jeans and sweaters--not designer originals or imported of exotic fabric. I want to walk through a store myself and look for things. I'm tired of having clothing delivered for my approval or being tailor-made. Is that asking too much?" Ellie held her breath, seeking approval.

"Let's see what tomorrow holds." Dr. Shanks smiled at her with a reassuring look.

꧁15꧂

Changes

Ellie squinted as the blinding sun glared through the windshield of Dr. Shanks's car. Dr. Shanks seemed like her usual cheerful self, so Ellie assumed the discussion with Gustave must have gone well. She was glad Gustave had chosen to drive alone. She laughed under her breath--thinking it funny no one realized Jesse was fluent in French.

"What's so funny?" Dr. Shanks turned the volume down on the radio. "We're not even to Happy Hair Fashions, and you're already acting happy."

"You're right. I'm happy because today is the first day of the rest of my life. Now I know what that expression means. Today is the first day of my *ordinary* life. Do you think anyone will recognize us?'

"I doubt it. Most people notice your father rather than you. I still haven't figured out why he wants to keep you under surveillance the way he does."

"He says he's afraid someone will kidnap me and hold me for ransom."

"Are you concerned?"

"No, it drives me bonkers."

"What will you do if someone does recognize you?" Dr. Shanks lifted her eyebrows.

"Maybe I'll talk to them. I don't think anyone will try to harm me simply because they recognize who I am. Besides, Gustave will be nearby, whether I want him there or not." Ellie pursed her lips.

"Here's to your *ordinary* day." Dr. Shanks maneuvered into a parking space near Happy Hair Fashions.

Ellie's heart pounded as they walked across the parking

lot. "This is the next step. I've already changed my name from Eloree to Ellie, and now I'm changing my appearance," she said aloud.

"You're making this decision on your own. It's your hair." Dr. Shanks shrugged—with a knowing look.

When they opened the door to the shop, Ellie stopped, taking a deep breath as she rubbed her sweaty palms against her pant legs. At last, she could choose what she wanted, but the tingling in her chest and her clenching stomach made her feel lightheaded.

"Good morning. Welcome to Happy Hair Fashions," the girl behind the counter piped, tilting her head as she smiled. "Who are you here to see?"

Ellie took note of her short, stylish blond hair, dangly earrings, and bright lip-gloss. Her name tag said, *Adrianna.*

Dr. Shanks placed her hand on Ellie's shoulder. "Hi," Ellie stammered. "I'd like Shelby to cut my hair today."

"Shelby's booked up." Adrianna tossed her head, swinging her earrings, as she peered at the computer screen. "But it looks like this is your lucky day. Come back in an hour. Shelby's had a cancellation and can work you in."

Ellie turned to Dr. Shanks for a nod of approval.

Dr. Shanks stepped forward. "Do you have an opening for a manicure and pedicure?"

"I'll put you down with Sheila. Your names?

Ellie froze, not knowing what to say.

"I'm Susan--this is Ellie."

"Last name?"

"Shanks."

"Okay, Susan and Ellie. We'll see you in two hours." Adrianna still smiled. "By the way, who can Shelby thank for the recommendation?"

"Jenna Woods," Ellie said.

"I know Jenna." Adrianna flashed a wider smile. "Tell her I said *hi*."

Closing the door behind them, Dr. Shanks laughed. "I doubt Adrianna ever takes her smile off. Working in Happy Hair Fashions obviously makes her happy."

"Thanks, Dr. Shanks. I didn't want to give Adrianna my name," Ellie commented as they strode along the storefronts.

"Be yourself. You may be recognized sometimes, but you don't have to treat others differently because of who you are."

"I'd never want to do that." Ellie paused in front of a shop. "Look at the brown coat in the window. It looks like Jesse's coat I wore."

"Let's go inside. I'll make sure Gustave knows which store we're in." Dr. Shanks reached under her jacket for the mic. "We're going into a store called Judy Ann's"

"Do you mean to tell me you're *wired*?" Ellie stepped back and threw out her hands.

"It's all right. You have to give and take in most situations," Dr. Shanks added with a smug smile. "This little wire appeases Gustave. He can't hear what I say unless I switch on the mic."

"If you're wearing the mic to keep Gustave happy, what does he have to do for you?"

"He's going along with our plans to visit Jesse tomorrow."

"You're a wonderful fairy godmother." Ellie held her arms out wide as if to hug the world.

"I like to think so." Dr. Shanks held the door.

"Hello, ladies," a woman called, from behind the counter. "I'm Judy Ann. Got more of my new spring line. Let me know if I can help you."

"Go ahead," Dr. Shanks prodded in a whisper. "Tell her what you want to see."

"Yes, Ma'am. I'd like to see the brown jacket in the window."

Judy Ann made her way to the display in the window. "That's the last one of these jackets. I couldn't keep them this season."

Judy Ann held the jacket as Ellie slipped her arms into the sleeves. "There's a mirror by the dressing room." Judy Ann gestured to the other side of the shop.

When Judy Ann stepped away, Dr. Shanks whispered, "Let's practice making small talk. She seems friendly. Ask questions about the jacket and let her show you around the shop."

Ellie nodded. "I love this jacket, but the sleeves are a bit too long."

"Let's ask Judy Ann's opinion. Remember, she doesn't know who you are, and probably wouldn't treat you any differently if she did know."

"Do you suppose the jacket can be altered?" Ellie asked when Judy Ann came by carrying several sweaters.

Judy Ann stacked the sweaters on a nearby table. "Most of the college girls bought these a little big and rolled the cuffs up so the sleeves of their sweaters showed."

Ellie was on her own. Soon, she and Judy Ann had their arms loaded with the latest styles of spring tops, jeans, and accessories. Judy Ann's attention reminded Ellie of shopping with her mother. Memories-oh sweet memories.

"Do you want to get your mother's opinion?" Judy Anne looked out over the rim of her wire-rimmed glasses.

"She's not my *mother*. Just a friend." Ellie tightened her lips.

Judy Ann smiled as if no further explanation was needed and held the blue floral print curtain separating the dressing rooms. It reminded Ellie of the curtain over the doorway to the backroom of the cabin. She closed her eyes and remembered the cabin...the fire...Jesse.

"Is everything okay?" Judy Ann called out, after several minutes.

"Yes, I'm fine. I'll be out in a minute."

"Maybe you should try on the coral, striped short-sleeved top with straight legged jeans. I've got a pair of boots you might want to try with it. That way you'll have a better idea of how it all goes together."

Ellie called back. "Boots would be great. Size 5."

Dr. Shanks was waiting by the three-way mirror when Ellie stepped out of the dressing room. "Look, Dr. Shanks. Everything is my size. No need for tailoring."

"You look nice."

"Everything fits. Jeans. Boots. Jacket. Tops. Even the accessories. I'll take it all." Ellie pulled off the jacket and draped it on her arm.

Looking first at Dr. Shanks and then Judy Ann, Ellie went on, "Do I have to change? I'd like to wear this the rest of the day.

"Okay by me." Judy Ann picked up a pair of silver-handled scissors and began snipping the tags. "You must be on spring break. Where do you go to school?"

Ellie swallowed hard. "I'm not in school right now. I've studied at Highland Piano."

"Oh my, Patrick Lee Hebert. Did you study piano or guitar?" Judy Ann's face lit up.

Ellie hugged the jacket to her chest. "Piano and voice, but I love guitar. Do you play?"

"Guitar." Judy Ann motioned in the direction of a beautiful two-toned guitar with an antique, hand-tooled leather strap, on a shelf behind the counter.

"That's a striking guitar. I see it's for sale." Ellie awed.

"Yes, I bought a new one and decided to sell this one."

"May I see it?"

Judy Ann placed the guitar in Ellie's hands. She felt like

dancing—bubbly and light. She'd learn to play and surprise Jesse. But what would her father say? He'd forbid her to take up the violin. Would guitar be any different?

"Go ahead, strum it," Judy Ann invited.

"I can't play, would you?" Ellie handed the guitar back to her.

"This is *Wildwood Flower*." Judy Ann looked down at her hands, the way Jesse did—and the folk tune took her back to the stormy night in the cabin.

"You play well. Do you give lessons?"

Judy Ann furrowed her brow. "I couldn't teach anybody. I play by ear."

"Ellie has a musical ear." Dr. Shanks interjected. "Bet she'd pick it up in no time."

Ellie blushed, but inside she relished the attention and reached to squeeze Dr. Shanks's hand.

"You have to hear the music--feel it in your soul, then start strumming and use your fingers on different strings until you learn how they sound in different combinations. It just happens."

"I could listen to you play all day long." Ellie ran her hand along the neck of the guitar.

"You're kind. Everybody can't play by ear, though. It's a God-given gift." Judy Ann winked at Ellie. "Tell you what. You come to work for me and run the shop. I'll sit and play all day."

Ellie liked Judy Ann's light-hearted humor and pleasant smile. Is this what it would be like to have an aunt or grandmother?

"Better watch out. She'll take you up on it." Dr. Shanks stepped closer.

"I want the guitar." Ellie stared at the instrument, then at Dr. Shanks.

"Honey, this guitar's a Martin. You don't want to pay this much for one to learn on."

"But it sounds fantastic and it has a *really* unique strap. Tell me your price."

Ellie blew out a sigh. "Dr. Shanks?"

"This is between you two. I know nothing about guitars." Dr. Shanks stepped aside--turning to a display of earrings.

"I'll pay whatever you're asking. If I decide against learning to play, I have a friend who'll like it."

"Maybe you should get prices at one of the guitar shops before you decide. I don't want you to get home and regret buying the first one you looked at. This one isn't new--you might rather have a new one, not one made in '99."

"1999 was a significant year for me. I'll take it." Ellie's voice trailed, as she rubbed her fingers along the strings.

Judy Ann stood behind the mound of clothes, staring at Ellie. "I'm asking $900 for it. I can't take less than $850 with the case. You probably don't want the strap. It's for a much larger person."

"$900 is fine--I'll give the strap to a friend."

"Well, only if you're sure." Judy Ann began to fold the mound of clothes.

"Oh, my. We've lost track of time. Ellie, it's almost time for our appointment at Happy Hair Fashions," Dr. Shanks chimed in. "I'll help fold all these clothes and we'll scoot on out of here."

"I hate to charge a young person that much for anything," Judy Ann declared, adding up the last of Ellie's purchase. "Honey, that'll be $1287.65 for everything, if you're sure you want the guitar."

"I'm totally sure." Ellie handed a debit card to Judy Ann.

Judy Ann looked at the card, then back at Ellie. "Eloree Evan." She paused. "That's a pretty name. Are you any relation to Senator Evan?"

Ellie's heart fluttered. She looked at Dr. Shanks but only got a smile and nod for an answer. "He's my father."

"Well, I'm sure he'll be pleased you're going to learn to play the guitar." Judy Ann handed the guitar case to Ellie. "Now you be sure and come back in and let me hear how you're coming along with your playing. It takes lots of practice to make perfect"

Ellie shrugged, with a short laugh. "There are lots of things I have to practice to become more perfect. Thank you, Judy Ann. I'll come back to see you."

Once they were on the sidewalk, Ellie asked, "How did I do?"

"You did great. Judy Ann came right out and asked if you were related to Senator Evan. You simply answered the question and the conversation went back to being about *you,* not your father." Dr. Shanks shifted the weight of the bags. "There's Gustave. Do you want him to carry the bags to the car?"

"Let's carry them ourselves, like ordinary people." Ellie edged her way along the sidewalk.

As they made their way in front of a dog grooming shop, an older, gray-haired woman approached, cradling a white poodle with bows in its hair. She didn't step aside but looked at Ellie and Dr. Shanks, with a scowl. They stepped aside and let her pass. After the lady had gone, Ellie giggled, "That woman was so funny. She's a Mrs. Drysdale, from *Beverly Hillbillies* look alike *and* act alike. Not me. I'm going to look like Ellie Mae and be funny and happy."

~~~~~

"Hi ladies." Adrianna beamed, the dangly earrings accenting her dramatic smile. "Here comes Shelby."

As Shelby came around the counter, Ellie noticed they were wearing practically the same outfits, right down to the jeans tucked into boots. Her long brown hair was pulled into a precarious ponytail, and the corners of her eyes widened as she smiled. "I'm Shelby," she held out her hand.

Ellie shook Shelby's hand with what she hoped was confidence. "I'm Ellie and this is Dr.--" she caught herself, "Susan."

"Hello Shelby," Dr. Shanks began. "Do you mind if I come along for Ellie's haircut?"

"Sure. Come on back." Shelby led the way to her station near a sitting area with couches, overstuffed chairs, and small tables with neatly stacked books and magazines. "Adrianna will let Sheila know you're here."

Dr. Shanks settled into one of the chairs and picked up a magazine, while Ellie took her seat at Shelby's station.

"How would you like your haircut?" Shelby spread a drape over Ellie's shoulders and fastened it at the neck. It wasn't too tight, but she struggled to catch the next breath—her insides quivering.

"You have healthy hair and lots of it. Pretty color, too. Natural curl." Shelby raised the chair higher, and Ellie felt as though she was dangling from the top of Sears Tower with no lifeline.

Ellie's stomach played tag with her heart, and she looked to Dr. Shanks. She needed to pinch herself to see if this was happening to her or someone else.

Dr. Shanks met her gaze with a tight smile. "This is completely your decision. Are you sure?"

"I'm sure." Ellie took a deep breath. "I want to have my hair cut for Locks of Love."

"Locks of Love requires at least ten inches. If you cut that much, it'll be right at the top of your shoulders."

"I see," She cleared her throat during the fleeting moment of indecision.

"With your features, almost any style will be flattering."
~~~~~

Shelby flipped through a styling book. “A layered cut like this one would do well with your curl, and you can still pull it up.” She swooped Ellie’s hair off her face.

Ellie’s heart did double-time—*the scar*. She forgot to reapply concealer and makeup after trying on clothes.

“Give me a minute.” Ellie grabbed her Navè and dug for concealer but came up empty-handed.

Shelby turned away and rearranged the magazines in the waiting area, and Dr. Shanks stepped to Ellie’s side. “Okay, Ellie this is decision time. You don’t have to get your haircut. We can leave, no harm done.”

“It’s not that,” Ellie whispered, lowering her chin. “Shelby saw my face. Judy Ann probably saw it, too. I don’t have any concealer. Everyone’s going to see my scar if I stay.”

Dr. Shanks spoke in a low tone. “It’s *ordinary person* decision time. Your choices are leave and never come back. Leave and come back later. Stay here and face life, head-on.”

Ellie clenched her jaw. “Shelby didn’t act like she even noticed. I’m staying.”

Dr. Shanks patted Ellie’s shoulder. “You’re a brave girl. *Queen of Ordinary*.”

Dr. Shanks gave Ellie a thumb’s up and stepped away with Sheila. But Ellie could see her from the sink where Shelby washed her hair. Reclining back in the chair, Ellie stared at the ornate black lettering on the wall in front of her.

Ecclesiastes 3 ~

A Time for Everything
There is a time for everything,
and a season for every activity
under heaven,
a time to be born and a time to die,
a time to plant and a time to uproot,
a time to kill and a time to heal,
a time to tear down and a time to build,
a time to weep and a time to laugh,
a time to mourn and a time to dance,
a time to scatter stones and a time to gather them,
a time to embrace and a time to refrain,
a time to search and a time to give up,
a time to keep and a time to throw away,
a time to tear and a time to mend,
a time to be silent and a time to speak,

a time to love and a time to hate,
a time for war and a time for peace. (NIV)

"I like the poem." Ellie motioned, as Shelby draped a towel over her shoulders.

"Ecclesiastes is one of my favorite books of the Bible." Shelby led the way back to her station.

Ellie opened her mouth, but nothing came out. At that moment, those words gave her the same peace she felt the night of the storm, huddled under the bed. This was *her* season, *her* time to heal, laugh, dance, embrace, love. A time to gather stones. She closed her eyes--content with this decision.

"Are you in college with Jenna and Cindi?"

"No, I don't go to UNC. Did you play basketball with them?"

"I was a cheerleader, so we hung out a lot. I still can't believe they passed up the chance to play basketball for the Lady Vols, but life's full of decisions." Shelby wrapped a ponytail holder around Ellie's hair and snipped it off, then dropped the locks into a plastic bag.

Ellie brought her hands to her throat and squeezed her eyes shut to ward off tears. What had she done? Betrayed her father? Or made a decision on her own--one she couldn't reverse.

Ellie closed her eyes as Shelby continued the transformation. With each snip, thoughts bombarded her mind. What would her father say?

After minutes, which seemed like hours, Ellie opened her eyes and was met with the flowery smell of gel, as Shelby worked it through her hair. Then Ellie watched as she used a blow dryer and round brush to create side-swept bangs feathered along her forehead and soft curls along her face.

"What do you think?" Shelby handed Ellie a mirror.

Ellie tilted her head and held the mirror at an angle.

"I love it. If I'd known my hair would do this, I would've cut it years ago."

"*My dearie stars.* Nanna. Aunt Sheila. Come look at this." Adrianna stopped with an armload of towels. "Ellie, you're so cute. Aliyah, come see Ellie's new-do."

Within seconds of Adrianna's bold announcement, a host of onlookers surrounded Ellie.

"This cut's so flattering."

"Wish my hair was that color."

"You're so beautiful."

Ellie sat spellbound, not knowing what to say. "Thank

you," she finally muttered.

"Here comes Sarah, the shop owner. Let's see what she thinks." Shelby turned the chair, facing Ellie away from the mirror.

"It warms my heart you're willing to share your pretty hair with some child," Sarah said. "In fact, I want to buy your lunch." Sarah continued before Ellie had a chance to respond. "Adrianna. Get money out of my purse and take Ellie to Wendy's"

"Thanks, Nanna," Adrianna beamed. "Can Aliyah come too?"

"Sure. Take your sister with you."

"Thank you," Ellie managed, not sure how to accept or decline the offer.

When Adrianna stepped away to get the money, Ellie darted across the shop to Dr. Shanks. "Like my hair?"

"I do, but are you satisfied with it?"

"Yes, but I've been invited to go to Wendy's with Adrianna and her sister."

"Would you like to go?" Dr. Shanks shifted in her seat.

"Sure, but what about Gustave?" Ellie's voice trailed.

Dr. Shanks winked. "Use my phone and send him a text so he'll know we won't be meeting him for lunch."

Ellie's fingers felt numb as she fumbled to text the message, trying to thwart butterflies in her stomach—knowing Gustave would be furious.

Ellie met the two girls at the front of the shop.

"Ellie, my sister, Aliyah," Adrianna introduced with a flourish. "Aliyah, Ellie. She's a friend of Jenna Woods."

"Nice to meet you." Aliyah held the door. "I haven't seen Jenna or Cindi in a while."

"I heard Nanna saying the storm that hit over the weekend was really bad in Franklin. Maybe that's why Jenna and Cindi didn't come by. What if they got carried away in the storm." Adrianna piped.

Ellie didn't want to think about the storm or even comment on it. She changed the subject. Aliyah, what do you do at the shop?"

"Adrianna and I share front desk duties, greeting people, and taking appointments. She likes the job better than me. I prefer washing brushes, sweeping, whatever needs to be done out on the floor."

"Aliyah thinks she's the maid or Cinderella." Adrianna quipped.

"Go powder your nose, Adrianna." Aliyah teased. "What

do you do, Ellie?"

Never knowing how to honestly answer the question, Ellie took a deep breath. "I study piano and voice."

"Oh, I'd love to play the piano and sing. Will you teach me?" Adrianna tilted her head toward Ellie, swiping a strand of hair off her face. "Seriously, you could teach Aliyah how to play the piano and me how to sing. We could be famous like Morgan and Briley."

Aliyah wrinkled her nose and poked at Adrianna. "See what I have to put with, Ellie. Little sister, always trying to get me into something. Stop daydreaming, Adrianna. Go become a rocket scientist or farmer. Make yourself useful instead of cute."

Ellie wondered how life would be if she had a sister like one of these girls or even a best friend like Jenna and Cindi.

Standing in line, Adrianna shifted her shoulders, causing the dangly earrings to dance with her chin. "Look what Nanna gave me. Two twenties. We can have *anything* we want," she announced, twirling the bills with her finger and thumb. "What would you like, Ellie? Thanks to you, this is Nanna's treat."

"I'll have what you're having." Ellie bit her bottom lip.

"I get a number three with Coke. How about you, Aliyah?"

"Since you're paying, I'll have a number four, with water." Aliyah stepped aside. "Come on Ellie. Let's get a booth by the window. I like to watch the cars come through the drive-through."

"Why do you watch cars?" Ellie remembered what Dr. Shanks had told her about keeping conversations alive by asking questions.

Aliyah gathered a collection of straws and napkins. "I'm getting another car soon. Big difference between what I can afford and what I'd like to own. I'll be happy with most any car, but it's nice to window shop. Maybe someday, money won't be an issue."

"What kind do you want?" Ellie slid across the seat, trying to comprehend how it would feel to not have enough money to buy whatever you wanted.

"I really want a used VW Beetle convertible. You know, like the one in *Black Knights Avenge*. Did you see that movie?"

Ellie nodded, choosing not to tell Aliyah about being on the set when the movie was filmed.

"Well, I'm simply mad about that cute little car."

Adrianna arrived with a tray piled with steaming hamburgers and fries falling out of their containers. Ellie barely closed her eyes when Aliyah asked the blessing, for she saw Gustave outside talking on his cell phone--no doubt reporting her whereabouts to her father.

"Is everything okay, Ellie? I've got plenty of money. I can get you something else." Adrianna plopped a fry in her mouth.

"No, everything's fine." Ellie took a sip of Coke. "I was thinking ... about Aliyah's car."

"I wish she'd go ahead and get a VW Beetle. I'd look like Briley Scout riding around with the top down."

"This little sister thinks she's a Briley Scout look-alike. Honest opinion, Ellie, what do you think?" Aliyah made a face at Adrianna.

Adrianna sat straighter and tilted her head to one side as if striking a stunning pose for the camera. "Ellie, do I get your vote in a Briley Scout look-alike con-" She paused. "Don't look now, but there's a man at the corner table staring at us. He's not even eating, just staring at us." Adrianna declared in a whisper, rolling her eyes.

Aliyah turned around to get a look for herself. "Don't be ridiculous. He's probably waiting on somebody. Don't stare back."

Ellie took a bite of the hamburger and stared at the table in front of her to avoid eye contact with Gustave. Why couldn't he let her enjoy this lunch and be an ordinary girl for one day?

"Well, what do you think, Ellie? Would I get your vote?" Adrianna chattered, taking a long sip of Coke. "Maybe I should go ask the guy in the corner if he's the paparazzi."

"You'd get my vote." Ellie forced a smile and decided to change the subject. "How do you two know Jenna?"

"We lived in Franklin until our brother, Aiden, was in middle school. Her brother, Jesse, was Aiden's best friend." Aliyah answered.

"I see." Ellie took another bite of hamburger. She wanted to hear about Jesse.

"Aiden started racing motocross, and we moved over here for him to be closer to his sponsors," Adrianna added.

"I thought that kind of racing is dangerous," Ellie commented.

"You can't be afraid of what you love. And Aiden loves racing. You have to go on faith. If someone told Aiden he couldn't race, it'd be like putting him in a cage and throwing away the key," Aliyah said. "Same way with me."

Ellie cleared her throat. "Do you do something dangerous?"

"I'm getting ready to. I'll finish cosmetology school soon, and I'm taking part of the cash I've saved up to go on a mission trip to Nigeria."

"*Some* people in our family don't want her to go,"

Adrianna snapped with no trace of a tease or giggle.

"Will you go if your family doesn't want you to?" Ellie cut her eyes at Aliyah.

"Yes, it's what I want to do. I know God's calling me there. Only I can decide which is bigger--my faith or my fear. I'd rather have my faith control me than my fears or my family's fears. I'm twenty and making this decision on my own. Aiden makes his own decisions," Aliyah concluded. "Even my *baby* sister gets to make decisions on her own, don't you?"

"You better be nice to me, Aliyah. I've got the money to get our Frosties." Adrianna put her hands on her hips as she stood and started toward the counter.

"Here's my secret." Aliyah leaned across the table. "Adrianna's sixteenth birthday is next Saturday. If I have another car by then, I'm giving her my old one. She doesn't know it, but we're having a party for her at the shop next Friday night at eight. I'd like you to come. Think you can make it?"

"I'd love to." Ellie forced a weak smile. "I'll have to check ..." She paused, wishing she could say she'd be there.

"Let's take our Frosties to go," Adrianna said. "I'm afraid the weird guy's going to come over here and ask for my autograph."

They laughed, but Ellie cringed. Oh, to be carefree like Adrianna or free to make decisions like Aliyah and their brother.

ꙮ16ꙮ

Simple Notions

*E*llie glanced over her shoulder as the trio made their way back to Happy Hair Fashions. Gustave followed far enough not to be noticeable. When they stepped into the shop, Sarah and Sheila were seated near the door, crying.

"What's wrong, Nanna? Aunt Sheila?" Aliyah bolted to their side.

"It came," Sheila sobbed, handing Aliyah a large brown envelope.

Aliyah cradled the envelope in one arm. Sheila and Sarah wrapped their arms around her. Tears trickled down Adrianna's face, and she crooked her arm through Ellie's. The two stared at the emotional commotion. "Come here, Baby," Sheila sniffed, freeing one arm to reach for Adrianna. "We never want to leave you out."

Adrianna sprung into the group hug, dragging Ellie along with her. The next thing Ellie knew, she was caught up in a flurry of hugs, crying, and forced laughter. "I'm sorry, Ellie. You must think we're nuts." Sheila forced a weak laugh through tears as the party split up. "I'm having a hard time thinking about Aliyah going to the other side of the world without me."

Aliyah ripped the envelope open. "My passport. Looks like I'm legal and official now." She turned to Sarah and Sheila. "I'll be fine. Besides, I'll only be gone ten days. Those children at the orphanage need me, and I need them. Remember, this was my decision."

Sarah reached for a clean tissue. "I know you'll be fine, but I hate to see you go to such a dangerous place. Can't you go on a mission trip to a safer place, like Myrtle Beach?"

With that comment, the cries broke into laughter. "Okay, this is what I'm going to do. Adrianna, keep the appointment book clear for the week after Aliyah gets back. We're all taking the week off," Sarah declared, taking control of the situation. "Sheila, book a beach house for us. I don't care how much it costs. I'll come up with the money, even if I have to stay in this shop until midnight every night. I'll be awake praying for Aliyah, may as well be at work."

Ellie wanted to say her father owned resorts in Myrtle Beach, and they could go there for free. But she reminded herself--the resort belonged to her *father*, not *her*, and he would never approve of her making a decision

"Where's Dr.—I mean Susan?" Ellie craned her head.

"She decided to get a massage and will be finished in about fifteen minutes." Sheila pointed toward a door marked *Private*.

"Come over here with me while you wait," Aliyah invited. "Got somebody I want you to meet."

Ellie followed Aliyah to another area of the shop. "Ellie, meet my brother, Aiden."

Aiden grinned, cutting his eyes in Ellie's direction. "Nanna, how do you get the *pretty* girls to come to your shop?"

Sarah laughed and readjusted the towel around his neck. "Hundreds of girls come in here wanting their hair the color of yours, Ellie. Don't let anybody talk you into coloring it."

"I like the new style. Thank you for lunch, as well." Ellie smiled up at her.

"My treat. If you can keep Adrianna and Aliyah in line, I'll buy your lunch any time," Sarah teased. "By the way, I give free product to patrons who donate their hair."

"Thank you." Ellie took a seat in the sitting area and thumbed through a magazine.

Adrianna escorted two girls to the waiting area. "Look who's here, Nanna. Taylynn and Amber." Adrianna tossed a newspaper onto the table.

"Got to get our manis and pedis before we head back to school," the tall girl with dark hair said. "Would've come sooner, but the monster storm tore up jack between here and Franklin."

Monster storm. Franklin. Ellie brought the magazine closer to her face and leaned away from the others.

"Hey Sarah, have you seen the insert in today's paper about the storm?" Taylynn held up the newspaper.

"No, what does it say?" Sarah called.

Taylynn read parts of the article, pausing to read the captions under the pictures. Ellie wanted to run away. Surely her name wasn't mentioned, or her picture published.

"Remember the girl who was lost out in the storm? Well, here's a picture of her with Jesse Woods." Taylynn waved the paper.

Ellie's heart sank like a lead ball, and blood rushed to her temples. The closeup colored picture revealed the scar.

"Jesse Woods," Aiden blurted. "Let's see that."

Taylynn thrust the article to him. "Tells right here, he found the girl out in the storm and rescued her. Look at the caption. They're calling him a hero."

Aiden studied the picture, then cut his eyes at Ellie. She lowered her gaze and looked toward the door. There was no sign of Dr. Shanks and tears stung the corners of her eyes.

Amber leaned in and whispered, "Let's get some water."

Ellie followed Amber to a water cooler, grateful for the escape. But she could hear Aiden's remarks, "If I was lost on Gabby Mountain, in a storm, I'd want Jesse Woods there. He knows that mountain like I know a race track."

Ellie's legs felt like rubber bands, and the cup of water in her hand never made its way to her lips. She leaned against the wall as tears flowed.

Amber put her hand on Ellie's arm. "You must've been scared. I can't imagine being in such a predicament, but you're okay, aren't you?"

"Yes, but I don't know what to say to them." She willed to corral her emotions.

"Come on. I'll go with you. If they ask anything you don't want to answer, just shrug your shoulders. Works like a charm," Amber consoled.

As they approached the group, Adrianna wheeled to Ellie. "My dearie stars. You didn't tell us you were lost with a cute guy. Aren't you glad an ugly guy didn't try to rescue you? Like the paparazzi dude, we saw at Wendy's." Adrianna made a face.

"You're a mess, little sister." Aiden put his arm across Adrianna's shoulders. "Ellie, does Jesse still have horses?"

"Yes, one of the mares gave birth to twins while we were on the mountain." Ellie couldn't believe it was her own voice giving information about Jesse.

"Tell him to call me. I'd like to go camping on Gabby." Aiden reached for his motorcycle helmet.

"Well, look at you." Ellie turned when she heard the familiar voice.

"Dr. Shanks." Ellie's voice rose.

"A long over-due massage." Dr. Shanks sighed. "Ready to pay out and go on to the next adventure?"

"Actually, everything for Ellie's on the house. We can't do enough for our Locks of Love girls," Sarah said.

"But I—" Ellie started.

"Don't try to pay," Sarah cut in. "Come back and see us. Don't wait until time for another haircut."

"Thank you," Ellie said and followed Dr. Shanks.

Adrianna and Aliyah stood in the door as Ellie and Dr. Shanks made their way out. "See you soon. You know what I'm talking about." Aliyah winked, pointing to Adrianna.

~~~~~

On the way back to The Branches, Ellie rambled about the events of the day--leaving out few details of everything Adrianna and Aliyah said or did. She elaborated on how they love to tease each other. "I'm amazed," she said. "I thought Jesse and Jenna must be part of the happiest family ever. But look at these people. They're just as happy. Although Sarah and Aunt Sheila don't want Aliyah and Aiden to do dangerous things, they don't try to stop them. Even Adrianna gets to make decisions on her own, and she's just turning sixteen. By the way, Aliyah invited me to Adrianna's surprise sixteenth birthday party. I really want to go."

"Did you accept the invitation?" Dr. Shanks pushed her sunglasses up.

"I didn't know if I'd be allowed. I mean, Father will be back by then."

"I'm giving you a homework assignment," Dr. Shanks instructed. "Decide the number one thing you'd like to be allowed to do on your own."

"New things have come up. I want a car of my own, not one of Father's, but an ordinary car. Did you know Aliyah's getting another car and giving Adrianna her old one? Isn't that sweet of sisters?"

"Remember, you can't always replicate what others do. You're who you are, and you should make decisions accordingly."

Dr. Shanks adjusted the sun visor against the afternoon sun glaring through the windshield.

"Life's so confusing. Think about Aliyah. She's spending part of the money she's saved for a car, to pay her own way to Nigeria to help orphans. She's giving Adrianna her old car instead of applying it to the down payment on the newer one. Their nanna will work overtime to rent a beach house in Myrtle Beach when Aliyah returns. Why can't I give her the money she needs or have them stay at Father's resort for free?"
~~~~~

"I see where you're coming from but listen carefully. Some people don't keep score with money. Others do. If you have money and you offer to give it to others, it changes the relationship. Right now, your friends see you as one of them. Sarah bought your lunch and wouldn't charge you. If you start throwing your money into the mix, you'll no longer be their equal. Does that make sense?"

"Are you saying they like me for who I am, not for what I have? No one mentioned Father even after they found out who I am. All they talked about was Jesse."

"Bingo. Isn't that the way you want it? Jesse is the one who deserves attention. He rescued the damsel in distress. It doesn't matter she's the daughter of a senator. Have you met anyone today who cared who your father is?"

"No, no one. Not even Judy Ann," Ellie chuckled. "What do you think he'll say about me buying the guitar?"

"I don't know what he'll say, but I *Googled* it on my phone--even at $900, you got a bargain."

"Oh no," Ellie pondered. "Do you think I should go back and give Judy Ann more money?"

Dr. Shanks laughed. "Again, don't put money between you and the other person. Go back and visit Judy Ann—but don't mention money."

"I will. If she helps me get started, I know I can learn to play. How much do you think I should offer to pay her for lessons?"

"Stop and think, Ellie. We want people to like *you,* not how much money you have. Didn't Judy Ann say you could run the shop, and she would sit around and play the guitar? Take her up on it. Offer to help her out when you visit."

"This has been a wonderful day," Ellie concluded as they neared The Branches. "What about tomorrow? Are we going to see Jesse?"

"That's the plan as far as I'm concerned." Dr. Shanks pulled into a reserved parking space. "Let me guess. That's still what you want."

"Absolutely." Ellie grabbed the guitar case in one hand and a bulky Judy Ann's bag in the other. She couldn't wipe the grin off her face. This had been a day she would never forget. A day when she'd made decisions on her own and made new friends. Friends who knew who she was and hadn't asked about the scar. Friends who liked the fact she knew Jesse. And friends who didn't even care she was the daughter of Senator Evan.

♐17♑

Then

The trip from The Branches to Franklin took longer than Ellie imagined. Gustave insisted he drive the Range Rover with darkened bullet-proof windows. Ellie would rather have taken Dr. Shanks's BMW convertible, and Gustave follow like the day before. But she could tell he wasn't pleased about this outing. And since Dr. Shanks confronted him when Jesse visited, he'd been overly reserved.

Dr. Shanks sat in the front with Gustave and tried to make conversation with him. Ellie listened as he spoke about his daughter. Apparently, she was in some sort of trouble, and Gustave was planning to take a furlough to go see her. Dr. Shanks chatted about her own daughters but soon gave up as the conversation became one-sided.

Ellie suggested they listen to a CD of Patrick Lee Hebert, and the lively tunes drowned out the deafening silence. Since she couldn't see through the darkened window very well, she closed her eyes and let the music enthrall her.

"You've been rather quiet, Ellie." Dr. Shanks turned the music off.

"I hope this is the last mountain we have to cross," Ellie said. "How much further is Gabby?"

Dr. Shanks held up a map. "Once we pass through Franklin, it shouldn't take more than fifteen or twenty minutes. Do you want to see the map?"

Ellie took the map and studied the region Dr. Shanks had circled with a highlighter. "Look, Dr. Shanks. All these places have Cherokee names. Jesse is passionate about his Cherokee ancestry. He gets angry talking about the removal. He looks at these wondrous mountains and says he can't imagine how the Cherokee must have felt to be run off their own land by the

Federal Government, at the hands of President Andrew Jackson. Jesse says the government shouldn't try to take so much control of people's lives or their private land, the way they did with the Cherokee. What do you think about that, Dr. Shanks?"

Gustave shot a menacing glare over his shoulder in Ellie's direction.

"That's a heavy subject. I'm not much for debating politics. I like to think our U.S. government is working in our best interest, but I do have deep-seated feelings about the Cherokee. My great-grandmother was half Cherokee."

"Oh look, there's the sign for *Franklin High School - where the Panthers excel.* The panther may be their mascot, but I bet none of those high school girls ever warded off a wild panther the way I did. Simply terrifying. Jesse killed—"

Ellie stopped mid-sentence. Gustave glared stone cold at her in the rear-view mirror, and Dr. Shanks turned with a piercing stare.

Dr. Shanks tried to change the subject by luring Gustave into a conversation about his heritage. He mumbled something in French, and Dr. Shanks turned the music back on.

Ellie felt a searing sword in her heart. She couldn't take the words back. She hadn't talked about the panther much, even to Dr. Shanks, and she surprised herself talking about it the way she had. The whole ordeal with the panther seemed surreal. For the most part, she felt numb, like the panther tried to attack somebody else, someplace else. When she closed her eyes, she could see Mohan crouching and lurching between her and the black monster, bleeding and writhing on the ground. She still heard its growl and the shot from Jesse's pistol. Then, there was the panther baby she'd rescued in her Navè. Her tears weren't only for herself but for the baby panther that would never know its mother. She remembered Jesse telling her how strong and courageous she was. In the midst of all the feelings of fear and remorse, Ellie felt a sense of triumph--not because the panther was killed, but she'd overcome an inward battle, a thirteen-year battle.

Ellie folded the map on top of the guitar case on the seat beside her and pulled her Navè onto her lap. She pulled out her makeup bag and mirror, reapplied concealer, blush, and lip gloss, then ran her fingers through her hair. She loved the way it fell into place with waves--not frizzy, uncontrollable curls. In her mind, everything would be all right. Dr. Shanks would handle Gustave, and in a matter of minutes, she'd see Jesse.

Gustave turned onto the one lane road that wound toward

the stables, where Jesse waited in the entry of the stables, Mohan close by his side. He made his way to open the car doors for Ellie and Dr. Shanks. "Hey, Ellie. Dr. Shanks. Gustave."

Dr. Shanks stepped out. "Hello Jesse, good to see you."

Ellie bounded to the ground. "Hi," she tried to control her delight as she knelt and hugged Mohan--her head on top of his.

"I've never wanted to kiss a dog before, Mohan, but if I did, it'd be you. Do you know I love you, big boy?" Ellie laughed as Mohan tried to lick her face.

"Ma and Mama are in the house. Would you like to come on in?" Jesse asked.

"Let's see the horses first. I especially want to see Elise." Ellie let go of the grin she couldn't contain any longer.

Jesse grabbed Mohan's collar and headed for Saja's stall, Dr. Shanks and Ellie by his side. Gustave tried to make a call from his cell phone. "Hey, Gustave," Jesse called over his shoulder. "You can't get cell service except in the barn loft. You're welcome to go up there if you need to make a call. It's right up those steps. Watch your head. Got some low-hanging rafters."

"Do you mind if I use your restroom?" Dr. Shanks asked as they passed by the door to Jesse's office.

"Make yourself at home." Jesse opened the door for her.

"You two go on. I'll be there in a few minutes."

Turning the corner, Jesse took Ellie's hand. "Ye' look *real purty* today, *Cousin Ellie Mae*. 'At new hairdo suits ye', and ye've got some mighty fine-lookin' boots," Jesse jaunted with a heavy country drawl.

Ellie blushed. "Thank ye', *Cousin Jethro Bodine*. You won't be getting that one over on me, anymore. Dr. Shanks and I have been watching the Beverly Hillbillies." She laughed.

They stepped into Saja's stall, and Ellie blinked hard as her eyes adjusted to the dim light. "They're both so cute." She ran her hands over the coats of the filly and colt at the same time.

"Saja must be one proud mama, but I can't tell which one is Elise."

"She's the one that's giving you this." Jesse pulled a smooth stone out of his pocket and placed it in Ellie's hand.

"What's this?"

"The rock you found on Gabby Mountain. Jonathan got it out of your old Navè when the game warden took the panther kitten. I took it to a gem shop in town. They turned, cut, and polished it. Turns out, it's a quality ruby."

"Do you mean it's valuable?"

"Don't worry about how much it's worth. It's your gift

from Elise for letting her use your name." Jesse beamed.

"Thank you. I see there's a bracket, so it can be worn as a necklace." Ellie rubbed the dark red stone with her fingertip.

"The guy at the gem shop said it was too big to make into a ring. I thought you'd like to wear it for a necklace." Jesse reached for a long, thin leather cord hanging by the door. His fingers brushed Ellie's hand as he took the ruby from her. "This came off one of Saja's saddles. She won't need it for a while. It'll make a fine necklace until we can do better." He tied the cord through the bracket.

Ellie looked up at Jesse as he slipped the leather cord over her head. "Thank you." She leaned in, and he wrapped his arms around her.

The stillness of the moment was shattered by the sound of someone or something landing hard, followed by a series of French slurs and profanity. Jesse and Ellie bolted toward the steps leading to the barn loft, Mohan at their heels, barking with all his might.

"What's going on?" Dr. Shanks scrambled out of Jesse's office.

Jesse sprinted ahead of Dr. Shanks and Ellie, leaping up the stairs to the barn loft. "Gustave, you okay?"

Gustave's loud voice boomed in French, followed by Jesse's reply in English. "You can cuss at me all you want to, but you can't take the Lord's name in vain. That kind of language is not allowed around here."

Jesse shook his head as he came back down the steps. "I tried to warn him about the low hanging rafters."

"Is he okay?" Dr. Shanks wrung her hands.

"I think so. He wouldn't let me see, but the best I could tell he whacked the top of his head. Most fellows only hit their head on that rafter one time. They know to look out for it the next time."

Dr. Shanks stepped around Jesse. "I'll go up and check on him."

Jesse took Ellie's hand and started out of the barn. "Guess Gustave's still ticked at me for getting in his face the other day, huh?"

"Dr. Shanks can handle him. Besides, he's getting ready to leave soon to visit his family."

"Will you be on your own then? I mean, do you think we'll still get to meet at the Biltmore House on Saturday?"

"Yes, Dr. Shanks thinks it's a great idea, and Father's not scheduled to be back by then, so she's in charge."

"He must've had someplace important to go, with you being in that fancy hospital and all." Jesse kicked at a clump of fresh sawdust carpeting the dirt floor of the entry. "When's he coming back?"

"Monday." Ellie made a face. "Gustave constantly speaks with him on the phone, but Father hasn't called Dr. Shanks or me. So, we've had a wonderful time this week."

"Dr. Shanks is nice. Mama and Ma say she's like family."

"Bet *you* can't guess who treats *me* like family." Ellie teased. "All the folks at Happy Hair Fashions. I got to have lunch with Aliyah and Adrianna and Aiden. He said for you to call him--he'd like to see you again."

"I haven't seen him in years. Figured he was too busy becoming a famous motocross racer. Hey, if he wants to bring his little sisters, we'll all go up the mountain and have a cookout. Sound like something you'd like to do?"

"Yes, but, right now, I have something special I can't wait to show you. Come on, we'll get it out of the car."

Jesse opened the rear door of the Range Rover, and Ellie reached across the seat for the handle on the guitar case. "Here, let me get that for you." Jesse took the case. "Is this a guitar?"

"Wait until you see. It's a *Martin*." Ellie beamed as they made their way toward Jesse's grandmother's house.

"I didn't know you play the guitar." Jesse kicking his boots on the stone walkway as they made their way to the door.

"I don't, but you could show me the chords."

"I'll be glad to, but let's get on in here and say *howdy* to Ma and Mama. They're getting dinner ready." Jesse held the kitchen door for Ellie.

Ellie was greeted by smells of apples stewing and bread baking. Steam escaped pots on every eye of the stove. She'd never been in a kitchen like this and needed a moment to take it all in. A white, lacy tablecloth and vinyl placemats with red birds adorned the table.

"Ellie, do you remember, Ma my grandmother, and my mom Darlene?"

"Hi." Ellie smiled, acknowledging the older gray-haired woman. Silver hair formed waves and flanked her deep blue eyes. Her floral print of her dress resembled the curtain in the cabin.

"Come on in. Make yourself at home. We've nearly got dinner ready, and Dicie and her children will be here pretty soon." Ma set a stack of china plates on the table.

Jesse's mom dried her hands on a towel and made her way toward Ellie. Silver hooped earrings glistened under her short blond hair. She resembled a female version of Jesse, wearing slender-fitting jeans and a knit top, almost like the one Dr. Shanks wore. "Hello, Ellie. We hardly had a chance to meet the other day with all the commotion going on. I've heard so much about you from Jesse, as well as Jenna and Cindi. Are you doing well?"

"Yes, Ma'am. And you?" Ellie felt blood rushing to her cheeks.

"Happy to be out of school this week for spring break." Her smile stretched across her face causing her blue eyes to crinkle at the corners. "You two go on in the living room. I'll help Ma finish up. Can I get you something to drink, Ellie? Maybe some sweet tea?"

"No, thank you." Ellie swallowed, almost speechless in front of Jesse's mom.

Jesse and Ellie sat on the pink and green floral couch with the guitar case between them. "Go ahead. Open the case," Ellie invited. "This strap came on it, but I want you to have it."

"Now, this is the neatest guitar strap I've ever seen, and I've seen lots of them. Is it handmade?"

"Yes." She smiled, placing her hand on the ruby adorning her chest.

"All I can say is *thank you.*" He squeezed her hand. "Let's get a good look at this guitar."

"What do you think?" Ellie moved closer.

"If you got this guitar for less than twelve hundred dollars, you stole it." Jesse plucked the strings. "Martin is a pricey guitar."

Jesse's mom stepped into the living room and took a seat in a rocking chair by the window. "Susan's helping Ma finish up in the kitchen. Do you play the guitar?"

"No, Mrs. Woods. I play the piano."

"Please, call me Darlene. *Mrs. Woods* is my school name."

"What should I play?" Jesse flashed a grin, first at Ellie and then his mom.

"Jesse goes to Children's Hospital to pick and sing to the kids and their parents. Son, play one of those medleys for Ellie."

"All right, here we go. These songs will make you happy." Jesse winked at Ellie, as he began to pick the tunes of *Froggie Went A-Courtin', She'll Be Comin' Round the Mountain,* and *Turkey in the Straw*. He nodded and tapped his foot as his mom sang along, clapping to the beat.

Ellie didn't remember ever hearing these tunes before, but she liked them. "I'm sure the children like those lively tunes."

"They do, but now it's time to hear you play, *Cousin Ellie*

Mae. Sashay over to the piano and show Mama what you can do." Jesse winked.

"Don't be aggravating her, Jesse," his mom scolded as if she was going to swat him.

"It's okay, Darlene. He calls me that all the time."

"Jesse always has been one to tease. On a serious note, he tells me you studied at Highland Piano with Patrick Lee Hebert. Can you play *Fur Elise* the way he does? I've got a music book with Beethoven's masterpieces."

Jesse put his arm around his mom's shoulders. "You'll love the way Ellie plays *Fur Elise*, and she doesn't even need a book."

Ellie lost herself in the moment as her hands glided across the ivory keys. She swayed as her hands reached, striking every key, capturing the beauty and essence of the piece. When she was finished, she found not only Jesse and his mom standing beside her but Dr. Shanks and Ma, as well. She blushed as they clapped.

"What did I tell you?" Jesse boasted. "Ellie's awesome."

"You're really talented, Honey." Darlene smiled. "Quite a virtuoso."

"That was a stellar performance." Dr. Shanks gave Ellie thumbs up.

"Thank you." Ellie tried to hold back the rush of elation for the way Jesse praised her performance.

"Ellie, you can play the piano better than anybody I've heard in a long time." Ma turned to go back in the kitchen. "Come on in here. I've got something Jesse wants to show you."

They followed Ma into the kitchen. "This old wooden bread bowl belonged to Jesse's great-great-great-grandmother. She found a panther in the kitchen scratching bread dough out of this very bowl. She was a mighty brave woman to run that varmint out the door with a broom."

Ellie started to speak but stopped short when a booming knock shook the front door. Shivers ran up her spine when she saw the troubled look on Dr. Shanks's face.

Jesse scrambled to answer the door, with Dr. Shanks close behind him. It was Gustave. He didn't say a word to Jesse but motioned for Dr. Shanks to come outside. She stepped around Jesse and closed the door behind her.

Ellie darted into the living room. She couldn't control the tears escaping down her cheeks as she heard Dr. Shanks and Gustave on the front porch. She couldn't make out what they were saying, but she could tell from the tone, Gustave was upset.

Jesse took her hand and led her to the couch. He put the

guitar back in its case. "I don't know what's going on but hopefully, it doesn't have anything to do with you."

"Rest assured. Whatever is going on, has *something* to do with me. It *always* does."

"If there's anything I can do--" Jesse started, but Dr. Shanks stepped back inside.

"Ellie, I'm sorry but we have to go now," she spoke in an overly composed tone as if she was forcing calmness on herself.

Ellie couldn't gain composure and buried her head in her hands and wept. "I don't understand. Can't we at least stay until after lunch? I've hardly had any time with the horses--I haven't even met Miss Dicie."

"Dr. Shanks, if Gustave needs to go in such a hurry, I'll be glad to drive Ellie and you back to Asheville."

"Thank you, Jesse. I'd love to take you up on it, but Gustave insists there's an emergency requiring Ellie and me to get back to Asheville as soon as possible."

Dr. Shanks knelt on the floor beside Ellie. "We'll plan another time to come back, but we have to leave *now*."

"What could be so important? We just got here and I'm not in any kind of danger."

"This was not my idea. I tried to convince Gustave otherwise, but he insists we leave. Take a moment to tell Jesse good-bye, and I'll explain to Ma and Darlene."

"Go ahead and do what they say, Ellie. It's only two more days until we go to the Biltmore House. Then, we'll be together all day."

Jesse pulled a white handkerchief from his pocket. Ellie attempted to dry her face, as they started toward the kitchen door. Jesse's mom stood by the door and wrapped her arms around Ellie. "You're welcome to come back *anytime*. You're very special to Jesse--that makes you special to me."

All Ellie could do was nod as Ma stepped up. "I hate you have to go, Ellie. I wish you could stay for dinner. I've got some homemade jelly I want to send with you. Here's a jar for you and a jar for Susan. Do you reckon that *Goost-aig* fellow would like a jar?"

"No." Ellie gritted her teeth.

"Well, then, here are two jars for you. Be careful and come back as soon as you can." Ma hugged Ellie and placed the jars in her hand.

Gustave pulled the Range Rover closer to the kitchen door and honked the horn.

Jesse carried the guitar and walked out with Ellie. He

opened the door and slid the guitar case across the seat. She choked back sobs. “Bye, Jesse,” she whispered, offering the handkerchief back to him.

“Bye, Ellie. Keep the handkerchief.”

ꙮ18ꙮ

For Susan

Huddled in the back seat, Ellie gripped Jesse's handkerchief with one hand, and the ruby in her other. As tears trickled down her cheeks, she willed herself not to sob. Her mind was a blur of everything that had happened. She would never forget the way Jesse looked at her when he gave her the ruby and how he boasted about the way she played *Fur Elise*. She tried to relive the elation of giving him the guitar strap, the way his mom hugged her, and the words--you're special to Jesse.

After several miles, Dr. Shanks asked Gustave about the nature of the emergency. The only explanation he gave was Ellie's father would arrive within the hour.

Ellie wished she was someone else, not the girl trapped in a life she had no control of. She stared out the window as farmhouses with weathered barns came and went from view. She'd give everything her father's wealth ever afforded to be free to live in one those houses. Drive a pickup truck. Wear jeans every day.

The daydream was over by the time they arrived back at The Branches. And Ellie knew by the way Gustave bounded toward the door, her father was here.

Dr. Shanks motioned for Ellie to linger behind. "Remember, you have to remain calm--no matter what happens, Ellie."

"I understand, but I'm going to convince Father to drop the legislation. It's the least I can do for Jesse and his family."

"Listen to me and listen closely. You're not to mention anything even remotely defending Jesse or condemning the legislation. We win wars by fighting one battle at a time, and today our mission is to get more freedom for you. Let's strive to get a car and personal privileges. Let me do as much of the talking as possible, even if it requires both of us listening to things we don't want to hear. Control your anger and frustration. The more out of control you become, the more control the other person has over you."

"What about Gustave? He messes things up by reporting everything to Father."

"He's upset with his own daughter and some bad choices she's made. He's anxious to leave. Besides, you have to learn to forgive, even though others may have been wrong."

"How am I supposed to forgive Gustave?"

"Every time you think about him, ask God to bless him. That helps take the resentment away from you—so God can work in Gustave's life."

"Now that Father's back, will I still be allowed to meet Jesse at the Biltmore House on Saturday?"

"Let's not get ahead of ourselves. Remember, one battle at a time. I still think it's a splendid idea, but in light of whatever Gustave's told your father, we'll have to wait and see."

Dr. Shanks quickly closed the door to Ellie's suite behind them. "Get changed into your other clothes before you meet with your father."

"Why? I like these clothes, and everyone says I look nice."

"Remember, one battle at a time. Your father's going to need time to get used to your new hairstyle. Even though it's flattering, he didn't approve having it cut. We'll introduce your new wardrobe later."

"Where's Father?"

"I'm sure he's meeting with Gustave. We'll all be happier once Gustave is on his way. I'm going on out, so I can meet with your father next. I want to speak with him before he meets with you. Everything will be just fine, and you'll present yourself well." She flashed the thumbs up and darted out the door.

Ellie wanted to whine—grumble—pout, but it would do no good, so she changed into tailored linen slacks and a pink silk sweater with an open neck. When she bent over to adjust the straps on her shoes, the ruby dangled in front of her. She couldn't bring herself to pull it off. Instead, she tucked it under her sweater, unaware the leather cord showed around her neck.

At first, Ellie paced back and forth trying to tame the nervous monster lurking in her stomach. Her heart beat double time. She wanted to call Jesse and pour her heart out to him—find comfort in his voice, but she feared what her father might do if he found out. Instead, she opened the Bible to Ecclesiastes 3 - a time for everything, and read it over and over hoping to smother the anxiousness. After twenty minutes, she picked up the piece of paper with her notes and paced.

"Jesus, Jesus, Jesus." She whispered aloud, marking a trail from the window to the door. "I have to trust in You, God. This is the time for a change in my life."

Voices echoed from the next room, and Ellie knew Dr. Shanks and her father were having a discussion. *A discussion about her.* Her stomach and heart were on a rollercoaster spiraling out of control. She couldn't help but hear what they were saying. Her father's loudness boomed over Dr. Shanks's calm tones.

"Are you implying my daughter's problems have all gone away because she was nearly killed on a mountain, with some ruffian? Do you think she found what's missing in her life by nearly being killed?"

Dr. Shanks's calm, professional voice was barely audible, but she heard her remind her father how they'd been treated by Jesse's family. With each statement, her father interrupted, scorning Dr. Shanks for allowing such a horrible turn of events.

At last, Dr. Shanks raised her voice, the same way she had with Gustave. "If I may speak *uninterrupted*, I'll discuss the results of my findings and reports with you. May I remind you, we *are not* in a court of law, and you *are not* presenting a case before a judge or jury involving the betterment of your daughter. She's a precious young lady who's been through years of trauma that, quite frankly, could've been avoided had you, *Sir*, chosen to be honest with yourself and her. Don't you think it's time you stop this charade and tell her the truth about her mother? She deserves to have closure."

Honest? Charade? Closure? What did Dr. Shanks mean?

Once again, her father interrupted, but Dr. Shanks didn't stop. "You have a choice. Discuss my findings and report now or read it after I'm gone. Either way, my findings are in the best interest of your daughter. She must be allowed to have the same rights and privileges as other girls her age. You can't keep her in seclusion from society. She deserves friends of her own--not just those you choose for her."

"This is *my* daughter. I love *my* daughter. No one will come in here and tell me what I can and cannot do with her."

"You're right, Sir. She is your daughter. Not your possession. You are her father, not her warden. She needs to hear you say you love her. If you don't, you *will* lose her the same way you lost your son. You hired me to bring your family back together. That's what I'm trying to do, with a little help from you."

"Don't you see both sides of the issue? I'm concerned something will happen to her. She's all I've got left. Besides, since the accident with her mother, Eloree's been a frail child requiring constant medical attention."

"Do you realize she hasn't had her medications since the incident on the mountain?"

"Who made that decision? She's always depended on medications to control her angry rages and be able to sleep."

"Dr. Link and I discussed the fact Ellie didn't have her medications while on the mountain, and she came through just fine. Dr. Link reviewed Eloree's situation with a panel of colleagues, and the consensus to take the medications away on a trial basis was unanimous."

"Ludicrous. I'll speak with Dr. Link. Eloree hasn't been off these medications in years." Her father snapped.

"I understand your concern, but without the medications, Ellie has eaten heartily, slept well, and been emotionally stable."

"What about her outbursts of rage and uncontrollable temper? According to Gustave, she's been out of control on several occasions, and you simply give in to her." Ellie could feel the agitation in her father's tone.

"I choose to differ," Dr. Shanks went on. "Gustave provoked her on more than one occasion, and she conducted herself well. My theory on the tantrums is fully addressed in my reports. Eloree's under a great deal of emotional anguish. When the issues in her life aren't dealt with, she exhibits anger in unacceptable ways."

"How will I know how to deal with these issues once you're gone? I'll double your salary if you'll stay," he offered.

"Money. He thinks he can control others with money." Ellie whispered as she folded the paper in her hand.

"I'm committed to a series of lectures and symposiums in Europe which I can't cancel. I'll be happy to take Ellie with me, but my job here is finished. I've recognized the problems and given you a clear path for the solutions. Your daughter needs *you* and *you* must work some quality time for her into your schedule."

"Quality time? All my time is quality time. I help run this great country of ours. Eloree seems to have little interest in political affairs or my personal business dealings. What can I possibly do for her that I haven't already done? I give her everything money can buy."

"For starters, listen to her. I'm encouraging her to write down her thoughts and feelings. She's compiled a list of ideas and things she'd like to discuss with you."

For what seemed an eternity, her father's voice went away as if he wasn't even in the room. All Ellie could make out was the softness of Dr. Shank's voice and a few half-hearted laughs. Either Dr. Shanks had convinced him, or he was up to something. Ellie knew her father only too well. If he became excessively quiet and sullen, he was not defeated. The worst would come.

When the door opened, Ellie jumped and squeezed the piece of paper in her hand. Was she beginning a new journey or hurling herself into the midst of a new storm?

"Your father's ready to see you now," Dr. Shanks said.

When Ellie entered the room, her father put down his cell phone. She felt self-conscious as his gaze scrutinized her from head to toe. "Hello, Eloree. Have a seat." He pointed to the leather sofa facing him. Ellie crossed her ankles and folded her hands in her lap to cover the folded paper.

"So *this* is my new daughter." His nostrils flared and the muscles of his lower jaw twitched. "You certainly do look better than you did the last time I saw you."

Ellie sat motionless, knowing this was a sign of his irritation. "Thank you, Father. I trust your trip was productive," she spoke through the tightness in her throat.

"I understand you've been making decisions of your own?" Her father jeered with a grim twist of his mouth. "Eloree, I suppose *you* made the decision to drop your given name since Dr. Shanks keeps referring to you as *Ellie*."

"I apologize if you're offended. *Ellie* is simply short for *Eloree*. I've heard others refer to you as *Walt* instead of *Walton*. Dr. Shanks tells me she's often called *Sue* instead of *Susan*." Ellie's cheeks burned.

"You are to be called *Eloree* when in my presence. Furthermore, I see you took it upon yourself to have your hair cut. I thought you understood how I feel about your hair and my wishes for it to never be cut."

"I'm sorry if I've disappointed you by having my hair cut without your permission, Father. I hoped you'd like it. I kept as much length as possible. Are you aware I donated to *Locks of Love*?"

"Yes, I'm aware of your charitable contribution. Perhaps we could have discussed a new hairstyle *after* your facial surgery. Now, I understand *you've* made a decision against the surgery without consulting me."

An unnatural stillness gripped every morsel of Ellie's courage. "Yes, that's correct, Sir."

"Perhaps you don't understand the significance of this

surgery. Dr. Link has arranged the most prestigious team of surgeons in the world. The surgery could not be performed prior to your twenty-first birthday, and I've waited all these years to have that scar removed from your face," he glowered.

"Ellie, explain your feelings to your father," Dr. Shanks's voice rose.

"Father, please understand. I know how invasive the procedures will be, and I'm not willing to go through the surgeries and recovery periods. The scar doesn't bother me as much it does you. Besides, it reminds me of Mother, and I never want to forget--" Ellie stopped.

He gripped the back of the chair, scowling first at Ellie, then Dr. Shanks. The seconds before he spoke felt like daggers surging into Ellie's heart. "Eloree, you do realize there are certain ambiguities in our family we have no resolutions for, and by no means ever will."

Ellie cringed as his tone became overly composed as if she was his opponent in a political debate. "I'm almost twenty-one, and I hoped you'd share more family details with me."

"Eloree, what happened to your mother is a very painful, private affair. I established long ago it's best to leave the issue alone. Discussion won't change the matter." His eyes narrowed. "What's that *thing* around your neck?"

Ellie brushed her hand over the leather cord. "A necklace," she gulped, fearful he might demand she take it off, or even worse, take it from her.

"Dr. Shanks, do you know about this so-called necklace and where it came from?"

"Yes, it's a native North Carolina ruby that Ellie found on Gabby Mountain."

"Don't let me *ever* see you wear some piece of cheap rubbish. You own plenty of exquisite jewelry," he scoffed with a condescending tone.

"Regardless of where the gem came from, Ellie has every right to wear it if she so desires," Dr. Shanks retaliated.

"No doubt that backwoods boy had something to do with it." He shot a downward gaze at Ellie. "What's this I hear about an endangered wild animal being killed on government property and removing its young? Can you confirm that this either *did* or *did not* happen?" His stare shifted from Ellie to Dr. Shanks.

"Sir, you must remember Ellie has been through quite an ordeal. Please speak to her calmly, and she'll gladly give you any details you request. Won't you, Ellie?" Dr. Shanks crossed her arms.

Ellie forced herself not to look away. "Yes, Father. You're correct. Jesse did kill a wild animal. He only had one bullet in his gun and if he hadn't shot the panther, it would have attacked me."

"What was his purpose for carrying a loaded weapon on government lands?" He stepped closer to Ellie.

"Since there's no cell phone service on the mountain, Jesse fired the gun to signal others as to our whereabouts, making it possible for us to get help sooner. Before we left the cabin, he assured me he had no intentions of harming anyone or any animal."

"What about the animal's young? Does this young man know it's a federal offense to harm the young of a dead animal?"

Dr. Shanks started to speak, but Ellie held up her hand to stop her. "Father, I'm the one who insisted on carrying the baby panther off Gabby Mountain. I know how it feels to lose a mother. If you choose to charge someone with a federal offense, charge me." Ellie started to cry.

She felt lightheaded, and her heart pounded in her temples. "Jesse tried to talk me into leaving the kitten, and he told me the same thing you did--*it is a federal offense*. He had his cousin arrange for the game warden to take the baby. It would've died if I hadn't made the decision to rescue it."

"I hope this whole ordeal has been a valuable lesson to you. Perhaps you'll take heed to stay away from this kind of people in the future. They're nothing but trouble."

Hot tears streamed down Ellie's face onto the leather cord holding the ruby, and Dr. Shanks slipped her arm around her shoulders. "Eloree cries easily now, and that's good for her. It's an integral part of her therapy."

He glanced at his watch. "I see no need for this childish behavior. Crying doesn't solve anything. I suppose Eloree will probably never be the same again."

Dr. Shanks looked up at him. "That's one thing you're definitely right about. *Ellie will probably never be the same again*. She's become a self-assured, young woman who makes decisions on her own. She laughs and cries just like others her age. And, she has some great ideas, which I'm sure the father of any young woman would find fascinating."

Dr. Shanks patted her arm. "Perhaps you'd like to share some of your ideas with your father. I'm sure he'd be interested in knowing about your proposed business venture."

"Business venture? Now what?" He hissed, crossing his arms.

Ellie unfolded the paper in her hand. "I've been thinking

about having my own music studio. I could teach voice and piano. Other instructors, perhaps from Highland Piano, could teach guitar and violin."

"So, you're getting a business head about you." He raised his eyebrows. "I'm sure I can arrange for you to tour a music facility as early as tomorrow."

He stepped closer, taking the paper from Ellie's hand.

"Oh, Father. I really don't think you want that paper. It's just notes I've written." How would she get it back? Too much was written—about him, Terrance, Mother, and Jesse.

"Don't fret, now. I always want to know what's on my daughter's mind." He stuffed the paper in his jacket pocket.

Dr. Shanks put out her hand. "Sir, I suggest you give the paper back to Ellie. I've taught her to write private thoughts. Things she may be ready to discuss in due time, but not now."

He ignored her, addressing Ellie, "I'm also aware Dr. Shanks and you have made some other decisions while I was away. I understand you'd like a car of your own."

"With your permission, Sir." Ellie's voice trembled.

"I've made the decision to allow you to have your own car. I'll have one brought to the estate for you, and I'll assign a personal assistant to accompany you. I can't have you going out alone."

Dr. Shanks cut her eyes at Ellie. "Tell your father what you *really* want."

"I want to pick out my own car. I prefer one that's not black with tinted windows. I want an ordinary car, like other people my age." Ellie gathered unbelievable courage to oppose him on the two topics at once. "Also, I prefer to go places on my own, without an assistant."

With his chin tucked on his shoulder, he cut his eyes toward Ellie and formed a hard, straight line with his mouth, like a biting smile. She had seen that look too many times--it meant that he did not agree.

He opened his briefcase and placed the file with Dr. Shanks's report inside. "Okay, you've won me over. Dr. Shanks, you may take Eloree car shopping before you leave. Purchase whatever vehicle she wants. Good night, ladies." He grabbed his briefcase as he turned to go.

"Will you be having dinner with Dr. Shanks and me?" Ellie followed him.

"Not tonight," he called over his shoulder. "By the way, have a good time at Biltmore House. Tell your friend his reward for *my* daughter's safe return is on the way."

Ellie stared as the door swung behind him. She felt a hot brick land in the pit of her stomach. Would he come back and change his mind? He never admitted to being won over.

Dr. Shanks placed her arm around Ellie's shoulders. "What's wrong? You should be happy. You're getting a car tomorrow and going to the Biltmore House on Saturday with Jesse."

Ellie's legs felt too heavy to move. "I'm too scared to get excited about anything right now. I've seen Father change his mind before. He didn't say I could drive alone or the conditions for me to go to the Biltmore House. I don't want to provoke him, but he has my personal notes. I don't want him to see what I wrote."

Dr. Shanks put both hands on Ellie's shoulders. "I understand where you're coming from, but let's think on the positive side of things. After all, your notes were only things you wanted to mention to him at some point, right?"

Ellie made her way to the glass doors overlooking the garden before answering. "No, Dr. Shanks. I poured my heart out and listed too many issues. I never intended to hand it over to him."

"Ever heard the old expression, *let the chips fall where they may*? Well, that's how it is this time. Your father will bring up the subjects he chooses to address with you."

"I want to believe time will heal everything, but Father loves power and influence." Ellie stared into the distance. "Besides, do you know what the issues are about Mother that Father won't discuss?"

Dr. Shanks lowered her head. "Ellie, I wish I could discuss it you, but I've sworn to your father I won't. I have to keep my word."

"This is not fair. I know these issues involve me, but I don't even know what they are." Ellie felt emotionally drained.

"Come on, I'm sure dinner is ready. I had the staff set it up in a private dining room across the hall."

"I hope Father hasn't requested I have some despicable diet."

Dr. Shanks's mouth curved into a slow smile. "I took it upon myself to order the same dishes Ma and Darlene were preparing for lunch. I know you must be starved since we skipped lunch today."

The smells of cornbread and cinnamon spiced apples greeted Ellie as they stepped into the dining room. Ellie took a seat at the table. "I'm not sure if I can eat."

"I understand. You've been through quite an ordeal today, but you held your own with your father."

Ellie took a long sip of iced tea. "How did you convince Father to let me meet Jesse at Biltmore House?"

Dr. Shanks unfolded her napkin. "It wasn't as difficult to persuade him as I thought it'd be. I stressed how vital it is for you to maintain a connection with Jesse since you shared a traumatic experience with him. He seemed to understand how Gustave had interrupted the flow of my therapy by demanding we leave before our session at Gabby was finished."

"Father actually bought that line?" Ellie's jaw dropped.

"Ellie, that's not a line. You should be the first to agree that a connection with Jesse and Jenna has been therapeutic for you. You made my job easy when you asked to invite them here, and Jesse invited you to visit Gabby."

Ellie plopped a bite of mashed potatoes in her mouth. "I really wanted to meet Miss Dicie. *Althea Spineeta* brought back memories of Mama."

"My therapy is non-conventional. I like to take patients where they need to be. If I had my way about it, we'd even go back to the cabin on Gabby Mountain."

"*Really*?" Ellie almost choked. "Jesse would take us up there. Can you *please* stay so we can go?"

"I wish I could, but my obligations can't be changed. I've written all my recommendations and going back to the cabin is on the list. I even suggested visits with Mohan, considering you love him so much, and he did save your life more than once," Dr. Shanks said with a wink.

"You're the best doctor ever. I wish you weren't going, but I understand."

"I told your father you're welcome to come with me. He didn't *buy that line*, as you say. But you'll be fine. Remember everything we've gone over, especially to give and take. Also, don't forget to forgive others. Forgiveness gives God the opportunity to fine tune the person who hurt you. It gives you a chance to heal."

"Do you think Father will send someone with me to the Biltmore House or make me go wired with a radio?"

"If he does, simply go along with it. Fewer restrictions will follow. There's a time for everything, just like you found in Ecclesiastes." Dr. Shanks dabbed the corners of her mouth with the napkin.

After dinner, Ellie went for a long walk in the garden until Jesse called. They were on the phone well over an hour, reminiscing about the events of the day. Ellie went on to tell him she'd be car shopping, and how her father would make arrangements for her to visit a music studio. As the call ended, they agreed to meet at the ticket counter of the Biltmore House at ten o'clock on Saturday morning.

~~~~~

After breakfast, the next morning, Ellie and Dr. Shanks packed their bags and headed out to buy Ellie's car. As they cruised through the lots of the dealerships, Ellie felt overwhelmed until she spotted just the right vehicle. "This one," she squealed, pointing to a blue Ford pickup truck. "It'll be perfect for me."

"Are you pointing at the pickup truck that looks like an SUV?"

"Yes, the blue one. Jenna drives a red one like it."

"It's a used--your father probably wants you to choose a new one."

"I don't care if it's new or not. This truck will be perfect, and when I get a wolf-dog like Mohan, he can ride in the back seat."

"I can see the look on your father's face when he finds out *his* daughter went shopping for a pickup truck instead of a Mercedes or Lexus."

"I don't want a flashy car. I want a snazzy truck, like this one. It even has a sign on the front that says *Country Girl*. That proves it. It's a girl's truck." Ellie giggled.

Dr. Shanks tried reaching Ellie's father, but his secretary kept saying he was in a meeting and instructed Dr. Shanks to close the deal. By lunchtime, Ellie was the happy owner of a blue Ford pickup truck.

"Are you sure you don't want me to go with you to your father's office to show him your truck?" Dr. Shanks asked as Ellie piled her bags in the back seat of the truck.

"No, I'll be fine." Ellie placed the guitar case on the front seat. "Father said I could have whatever I wanted, and this is what I want. He hasn't tried to intervene all day, so you were right. He's had a change of heart and is giving me *freedom*."

Dr. Shanks placed her hand on Ellie's shoulders. "Ellie, it's been my privilege to get to know you. I hope I've helped you."

"And it's been my pleasure to have you here. You've helped me in every way imaginable." Ellie rubbed her hand along the side of the truck. "Right now, I'm happier than I've ever been, and it's all because of you. Thank you for making Father
~~~~~

understand, and now I can be an ordinary girl."

"My email and phone numbers are in your phone. Let me know how things go." Dr. Shanks and Ellie hugged as they said their final goodbyes.

Ellie watched Dr. Shanks drive away.

Then, with trembling fingers, she started the truck. Nervous excitement raced through her entire body. The salesman had shown her all the operating features of the radio, air conditioning, and made sure the owner's manual was in the glove box. Now it was her baby, and she was on her own.

She grabbed her phone and attempted to get a call through to Jesse. It went straight to voicemail. "Hey, Jesse. Wanted you to be the first to know. I just bought a Ford Explorer Sport Trac. It's only two years old, and it's blue, just like your other truck. It's a 4 by 4. Can't wait for you to see it tomorrow. Call me when you get this message. Bye."

The warm spring sun came through the open window as Ellie pulled onto the street. She'd never been more elated in her entire life. Where would she go, and what would she do first?

Realizing she hadn't had lunch, she turned into a Wendy's and guided the truck into the drive-through lane. Her sweaty palms clung to the wheel as the voice came over the speaker, asking for her order. She repeated what Adrianna had said when she ordered. *A number 3 with Coke.* She searched through her wallet, finding only ten dollars in cash. To her relief, that was enough to pay for the meal. She dropped the loose coins and bills in her Navè. She maneuvered into a parking space, enjoying the privilege of having lunch in her very own vehicle. No one knew who she was or even cared. Just an ordinary girl, in an ordinary truck, having an ordinary lunch.

꧁19꧂

Teary

Senator Evan, your daughter's here." the receptionist spoke into the phone. Then, like a robot in a black business suit, she escorted Ellie to a black leather sofa. "Senator Evan will be with you monetarily."

Ellie wanted to scream. Mrs. Ranora had been her father's secretary at least ten years. And like all the other staff, she treated Ellie like an outsider—never referring to their boss as *your father*. Their black suits, white shirts, and black ties were her father's way of bringing conformity to the workplace. But Ellie figured this was another control tactic, the same way he controlled what she wore. But today, she'd find out what he thought of the ordinary clothes she had chosen.

The office looked like an Andrew Jackson museum. Her father took considerable pride in the fact President Jackson was his ancestor. Paintings hung alongside display cases with artifacts depicting historical events of the president's life. Having little interest in history, Ellie never paid much attention to the paintings, but now one painting caught her eye. The artist captured the look on Andrew Jackson's face as he fought Indians, no doubt Cherokee. Her heart sank, remembering how Jesse felt about Andrew Jackson. *He could have stopped the Indian removal if he hadn't been so greedy.*

Ellie jumped when her name was called, and her father stepped alongside her. "Eloree, I understand Dr. Shanks and you purchased a vehicle. Is that what you want to show me?"

"Yes, Father. It's parked right outside." Ellie stood on her tiptoes, giving him the usual slight peck on the cheek.

"Where did you get those clothes?" he asked as they stepped onto the elevator.

"Dr. Shanks and I went shopping."

"You should be dressed in the nice clothes you already have," he said, as his phone rang.

He continued to talk on the phone as they walked across the parking lot. He finished the conversation and slid the phone onto a clip on his belt. "Where's your new car?" He frowned.

"Here, Father." Ellie stopped by the truck. "Will you go for a drive with me?"

"I don't have time for a drive. But I see this contraption, whatever it is, makes you happy." Ellie flinched at his tone.

"Dr. Shanks tried to call you numerous times, but your receptionist gave her the message to go ahead and purchase whatever I wanted. You did say I could have any car I wanted, didn't you?"

"A car, not a rattletrap. Dressed the way you are and driving this *thing*, makes you look like someone who *works* at the country club, not someone who *owns* the country club."

His berating comments seared her heart like a dagger, but she vowed not to cry.

"When you decide this contraption no longer makes you happy, I'll get you a *real* car."

His tone sent chills up Ellie's spine, but she mustered the courage to answer, "I'm sorry to disappoint you, Sir."

He rubbed his brow as if to ward off a headache. "I've arranged for you to go to a music studio this afternoon. Pierre's taken over Gustave's duties, and he'll drive you."

"If it's all the same, I'd like to drive myself. Perhaps Pierre could show me the way." Ellie bit her lip and tugged at the cuff of her sleeve.

"Very well, then. You may follow Pierre's car."

Before Ellie could express her gratitude, her father pulled her close to him and held her. Shocked by his gesture, she struggled for something to say. "Will I be having dinner with you tonight?" she murmured, with her face against his shoulder and her arms wrapped around his waist.

"No, not tonight." He kissed the top of her head, the way he had when she was a child.

"Good-bye, Eloree." He broke the embrace and turned to walk away.

"Bye. I love you, Father," she called.

He waved without looking back and strode away. He must have read the list, knowing she longed for his affection. She wanted to run after him and hug him again. But why didn't he repeat the three simple words, *I love you?* Had he changed and heeded Dr. Shanks's advice, after all?

Half of her mind danced with excitement, but the other half was like a maze with no end, leaving a deafening hollowness in her heart. She knew there was more—so much more he didn't say.

A black sedan with heavily tinted windows pulled up and honked the horn. Ellie knew this was the cue to follow the driver. She turned on the radio and found a station with uplifting music as she followed the car to the outskirts of the city. After several miles, they turned onto a winding country road. The station faded in and out--she turned the radio off and sang the song she and Jesse had first sung in the cabin, *In the Midst.*

When she finished the entire song, she began to talk to God, *"Am I in the midst of a storm? I know You're with me now but I'm feeling uneasy. Jesus, Jesus."*

After several miles, she followed Pierre onto a lane leading up to, what appeared to be a large rustic house. The sign read *Meadow Laurel,* and she realized the laurel bushes growing all around were like those on Gabby Mountain. There were pastures with horses and a creek that ran under a small covered bridge. As Ellie got closer, she could tell it wasn't actually a house, but a lodge of some sort made of logs with spacious windows, a wide porch with wooden rocking chairs, and dormers reaching beyond the treetops. The pristine setting seemed inviting, yet something didn't feel right.

Pierre parked near the main walkway, and before Ellie could open her own door, he was by her side, insisting on escorting her. He hurried her along the stone walkway leading to the front door, then turned to go as Ellie was greeted by a young woman with long blonde hair and inviting blue eyes. "You must be Eloree. Nice to meet you, I'm Misty."

"Nice to meet you. I prefer to be called Ellie."

Misty lead the way into an office with a big wooden desk, piled high with papers and books. "Have a seat at this table. How about something to drink, maybe a bottle of water?"

"No, thank you." Ellie pulled out a chair. "Are you one of the music instructors?"

"No, I'm the nurse."

"*Nurse?*" Ellie's jaw dropped. "I'm here to tour a *music studio.*"

"I understand. Music is our primary focus, and we have a one of a kind studio. Our music therapist, Dr. Stephanie Morton, will be here in the morning."

Ellie stood. "*Therapist*? There's been a misunderstanding. I'm only interested in touring your music studio. Thanks for your time."

"Please, sit back down," Misty said, with the same calm demeanor as Dr. Shanks. "I'm finishing the review of your reports. I wasn't expecting you until later this afternoon."

"I don't know what's going on. What do you mean by my *reports*? What is this place?" Ellie cringed, pushing back her chair.

Misty leaned across the table, placing her hand on Ellie's arm. "We're here to help you get over your fears."

"What are you talking about?" Color drained from Ellie's face. "I didn't come here to discuss *reports* or *fears*. I came here to talk about *music*."

"I see you're upset. Obviously, you weren't told what to expect once you arrived at Meadow Laurel." Misty put the folder aside.

"I'd like to speak to my father. There's been a huge misunderstanding." Ellie started for the door. "I have to go now."

Misty stepped between her and the door. "Let's get to the bottom of this. After we review your reports, you'll see why your father chose Meadow Laurel."

Ellie's heart shriveled into a near state of shock, as Misty interpreted the reports. She understood all too well. Her father tricked her into coming here after arranging her admittance. He'd waited until Dr. Shanks left, knowing he wasn't going to follow her suggestions. It'd been Pierre's job to see she didn't back out or get lost on the way. Evil. Conniving. Wicked. How could he father treat her this way? She felt like Hansel and Gretel, led into the forest to die.

"What am I *really* here for?" Ellie forced herself to remain composed.

"Your father reports you were preparing to have major surgery, to remove a facial scar, when you suffered a grave trauma. Due to the traumatic experience, you're having trouble relating to your own identity. *Stockholm Syndrome*--you're wanting to change your name, the way you dress, and your diet."

"That's preposterous," Ellie shrieked through a painful tightness in her throat. "What's Stockholm Syndrome?"

"Stockholm Syndrome is when a victim develops strong emotional bonds with their captor and often takes on the same morals and values."

"I don't have this bizarre *syndrome*."

"Let's see, the reports show you became lost on a mountain during a tornado, were attacked by a wild animal, and held captive in a shack by an anti-government extremist who lives in a barn with a wild dog," Misty spoke in a feathery soft voice. "No wonder you're not ready to have a major surgery after going through all that. Did the police find your captor?"

Ellie mocked a laugh through clenched teeth. "That's pure nonsense. I wasn't held captive. A nice young man found me and took care of me in an old cabin. His dog, which is part wolf, saved my life at least three times." She told Misty about the life-changing events that happened on Gabby Mountain and went on to explain how Dr. Shanks developed a plan for therapy, which her father now disregarded.

"Thank you for hearing me out. I need to discuss this matter with my father." Ellie stood, slipping her Navè over her shoulder.

"I'm sorry, but your father feels the traumatic situation you faced was a setback, and he specifically stated you're to stay here until you agree to the surgery. He had your clothes and personal items delivered this morning. Everything's already in your room."

Ellie didn't believe what she was hearing. She pulled her phone from her pocket. "I'll call Father."

"Use my desk phone, no cell coverage here."

Ellie's hands trembled as she dialed her father's office. The receptionist stated he was in a meeting and couldn't be disturbed. She tried his cell—no answer.

"He's not answering. I need to call Dr. Shanks."

"Honey, your father left explicit orders you're not to have any contact with Dr. Susan Shanks, Jesse Woods, or his family." Misty closed the file. "I'm sorry. Perhaps Dr. Morton can shed new light on things when she comes in tomorrow."

Ellie felt all hope ebbing away. Once again Father had riddled her with rejection, abandonment, and bitterness. She buried her face in her hands and wept. How could this nightmare be happening? She couldn't even tell Jesse where she was? How would she meet him tomorrow?

~~~~~

Misty opened the door to Ellie's suite. "It's four-thirty now and dinner is at six, in the main dining hall. If there's anything else you need, let me know."

"Thank you," Ellie stammered, refusing to make eye contact.

"Juniper, your suitemate should be back within the hour. She'll introduce you to the other girls."
~~~~~

The room felt like a cavern adorned with modern decorations and inviting windows. At any other time, she might have appreciated the yellow and green whimsical patterned bedding and matching sofa, and the cheery yellow walls with paintings of wildflowers.

Ellie stared out the window at the landscape she'd found enticing before she knew this was another of her father's tactics to tuck her away. The mountains were a fortress. The shadows they cast in the late afternoon sun created dreadful, dark caverns. The trees, like soldiers, standing guard over their captives. Just when she thought she was too emotionally drained to even feel anger, she spotted her truck. She'd give anything to be allowed to drive it, far, far away from here. Away from Father.

Seeing the laurels beneath the window reminded her of the little red fox Jesse found in the box trap. She was like the vulnerable fox having been lured to this place. Surely, someone would rescue her the same way Jesse let the little fox go free. Her only chance was Dr. Morton and the hope she could make sense of this whole situation. Somehow, she would get out of here. If she could only talk to Jesse. What would he think if she couldn't show up tomorrow?

Crying would have been a relief, but there were no tears. She felt confused and drained both emotionally and physically. Not wanting to see the fading sun, she closed the blinds, then hurled her Navè onto the sofa.

The brown leather Bible Jesse gave her fell out. She stared at it, almost daring herself to pick it up. Gathering her wits, she sat down on the sofa and opened the Bible. Her eyes fell on Acts 16. There was a colored picture of an artist's rendering showing two men standing in the rubble and an angel hovering overhead. Jesse had made notes along the margin. *With prayer and praises, God will send earthquakes to break down your prison walls.*

"Okay God, why did You let father do this to me? I want out of here. Are You going to send an angel or an earthquake to get me out? I don't care which. I can't believe I'm talking to You this way, but I have no options. You're my only way out. You protected Jesse and me from the storm, so I know You can get me out of here. Please."

She wasn't sure if she'd been talking to herself, God, or both as she hugged the Bible to her chest. The quietness of the room soaked in as she tried to sort out the events since her father had returned. If only she could speak with Dr. Shanks. What had she meant when she told Father to stop the charade and tell Ellie the truth about Mother?

There was a knock at the door leading into the common sitting area of the suite. Ellie didn't want to see or talk to anyone, but she pulled herself together and opened the door.

"Hi, I'm Juniper," the girl said with a heavy northern accent.

"I'm Ellie."

They locked eyes in a staring match. Juniper had an earthy look with a knit beanie pulled over her ears, barely exposing strands of short brown hair. She wore a choker made of cords knotted with beads. Birkenstock sandals were barely visible beneath faded, baggy jeans, topped with an over-sized, brown cotton sweater. She was a few inches taller than Ellie, and her body was round compared to Ellie's slender frame.

"Is this your first visit to Meadow Laurel?"

Ellie nodded. No words would come.

"You'll love it here. I'll show you around and introduce you to the other girls," Juniper offered, tapping her foot on the floor.

"I won't be here very long," Ellie mumbled, with a disparaging look. "I plan to leave as soon as I meet with Dr. Morton in the morning."

Juniper looked puzzled. "As difficult as it is to get into Meadow Laurel, I can't imagine wanting to leave so soon."

"There's been a misunderstanding. I'm not supposed to be here."

"Since you're here, you don't want to miss dinner. Friday nights are *exquisite.* Seafood and a chocolate buffet. This evening's featured musician will be Jodi Thiele on the piano."

"Thank you, but I'd rather have quiet time."

"Sure, I'll ask room service to deliver a tray to your room." She turned to go.

"No, thank you. I'm tired."

"If you change your mind, the dining room's down this hallway and to the right. Can't miss it." Juniper pointed.

Ellie leaned against the door, not sure what to do next. She ambled back to the sofa and plopped down, staring blankly toward the window. The setting sun left the room dark enough to switch the lights on, but she didn't bother--wishing she could hide in the darkness. She wanted to hate her father, but from somewhere in her soul, the word *hate* didn't ring true. For the first time in years, she'd told him she loved him, without the gesture being a formality. How could she ever forgive him?

Again, she opened the Bible to Acts 16. Even though the

verses seemed wordy, she remembered Jesse telling about Paul and Silas. She read on, realizing they'd been severely beaten for what they believed before they were thrown into prison.

"Father's punishing me for what I believe," she whispered, then strained her eyes to see the handwritten note at the bottom of the page. *Can you forgive someone who has intentionally made you miserable? Paul and Silas did. God expects you to do it, too. Tell your adversaries you love them. It heaps coals of fire on their head.*

Ellie's mind replayed the events of the day. She put the Bible aside and went to the window, catching a glimpse of the last rays of light over the treetops. Did this mean she had to be willing to forgive Father before she could get out of here?

~~~~~

When Juniper returned from dinner, she knocked on Ellie's door and stuck her head in. "Sorry if you're resting, but I brought you a pitcher of herbal tea."

"Thank you, but I'm not thirsty." Ellie didn't want to invite her in.

"You've got to try *this* tea," Juniper coaxed.

Ellie's eyes adjusted to the light coming from the adjoining sitting room. The room was surprisingly quaint, replicating a log cabin. Unlike her room, the furnishings and décor were rustic. In one corner stood a stone fireplace with a mantel and clock, like the cabin on Gabby Mountain. White, lacy curtains hung above the wide windows, and matching doilies draped over wooden shelves. A patchwork quilt draped over the arm of a rocking chair.

"Unique room, isn't it?" Juniper said. "I like the rustic country look, don't you?"

Ellie nodded, taking a seat at a small round table.

"Where are you from?" Juniper pouring two glasses of tea.

"All over. Currently Asheville." Ellie knew her tone sounded short. "You?"

"New York City, but I love it here in the mountains. Wish I could stay." Juniper smiled, taking a seat across from Ellie.

"At this place?"

Juniper laughed. "That would be grand, but my family could never afford for me to live here, year round, even if Dr. Morton took permanent residents. Besides, the waiting list is too long."

"Waiting list?" Ellie curled her lip.
~~~~~

"You mean you weren't on a waiting list?" Juniper looked skeptical. "The wait's at least a year out, unless you're an emergency case, meaning somebody famous."

"Do you mean you *actually* want to be here?"

"Of course." Juniper pulled her knees to her chin. "My grandparents paid to send me. Music helps me get my head on straight if you know what I mean."

"Music?" Ellie questioned. "If you like music, then why come here?"

Juniper shrugged half-heartedly. "This is a music retreat."

"Music retreat? Are you here to refine your musical abilities?" Ellie took a sip of tea, staring at Juniper out of the corner of her eye.

"Some girls want to improve their musical abilities, but most come for the music therapy. Everything offered here has something to do with music," Juniper stirred another packet of sugar into her tea. "Dr. Morton uses music to move people out of their comfort zone and help them deal with whatever they may be facing. Take me for example--I'm a college drop out. Why go to college when that's not what I want to do?"

"What do you want to do?" Ellie was glad to keep the conversation directed away from herself.

"My grandparents are hoping I'll change my mind by the time I leave Meadow Laurel, but I'm going to hike the entire Appalachian Trail, by myself, from Georgia to Maine." Her wide, toothy grin made her almond-shaped eyes squint almost shut.

"Have you ever been alone in the mountains?"

"No, that's why I want to do it. I can write books, do documentaries, be interviewed on television, and have speaking engagements. I'll be famous."

"What about storms and wild animals?" Ellie's voice wavered.

Juniper threw out her hands. "You sound like my grandmother."

For an instant, Ellie thought about telling her what a horrible idea this was but decided against it. "How many people are here?" she asked, changing the subject.

"You make number ten. Dr. Morton doesn't accept more than ten girls at one time. She likes to keep it low-key, homey like if you know what I mean. This way, we all get to know each other, and make the most of our experience."

"Do most girls actually like being here?" Ellie studied Juniper's face.

"Sure. Most girls come here to deal with unresolved

issues, but some come to get away from it all for a while." Juniper kicked her sandals off with a thud. "Being here is like being at summer camp, only much classier."

Ellie wanted to ask more questions about Dr. Morton, but before she could speak, Juniper began again. "My stay will be over in six more weeks. How long is yours?"

"I don't know. The arrangements were made for me."

"I doubt you'll want to leave early once you get into the routine." Juniper shrugged. "I take it you're not happy about being here."

Shaking her head, Ellie tried to hold back tears. "Thank you for the tea," she whispered and fled back to her room. She flung herself onto the bed and cried with her head burrowed in the pillows.

She awoke sometime later and went into the bathroom. The clock on the vanity showed 6:00 a.m. Not believing she'd fallen asleep, she splashed her face with warm water and weighed her options. She'd see Dr. Morton--her only hope to get out of here and meet Jesse.

~~~~~

An hour later, she felt refreshed after showering, styling her hair, and applying makeup and concealer to create a flawless complexion. Then she rummaged in the closet for something to wear. Father had sent plenty of clothes. Silk. Linen. Tailored. Imported. Designer. One-of-a-kind.

She vowed not to wear those clothes to meet Jesse as she shut the closet door and reached for the suitcase with the clothes from Judy Ann's. There was only one clean outfit left, a pair of dark denim jeans, a green plaid shirt with pearl snaps, and a white tank to create the perfect layered look. Standing in front of the three-way mirror, she admired her new outfit. "Jesse will like this outfit, and this ruby necklace matches perfectly," she whispered aloud, stroking the heavy red stone hanging against her chest. Now, to meet Dr. Morton and be on her way to see Jesse.
~~~~~

ꙮ 20 ꙮ

Without You

Ellie slung the Navè over her shoulder and walked along the hallway leading back toward the office where she had met with Misty. The walls were lined with pictures of musical instruments and plaques with motivational verses. No matter how long the wait, she wanted the first opportunity to state her case and leave. The quietness gave her a chance to clear her mind and rehearse what to say.

Rounding the corner, Ellie saw the words *Dr. Stephanie Morton* on a door along with a portrait of a young woman with shoulder length, brown hair. Ellie studied her face, knowing she'd be at the mercy of this lady with warm hazel eyes and wide friendly smile.

"Good morning. You're up and about mighty early on a Saturday morning."

Ellie wheeled, standing face to face with the woman in the portrait. "Are you Dr. Morton?"

"Yes, and you must be Eloree." She smiled, speaking in a soft voice, "I'm sorry I wasn't here when you arrived yesterday. I wasn't expecting you until Monday."

"I go by Ellie. There's a misunderstanding." Ellie stiffened her spine.

"Then let's discuss it over breakfast." Dr. Morton led the way toward the dining room.

Assuming it'd be no use to protest the idea of breakfast, Ellie followed Dr. Morton. The clock above the coffee bar showed 8:10--she had until 10:00 to find her way to the Biltmore House.

"It's such a pretty morning. Let's sit out on the screened porch. It's private. The other girls won't be up for at least another hour. Have you toured the grounds and had a chance to see everything we offer?"

"No, Ma'am. Since I won't be staying, there's no need." Ellie hung her Navè on the back of the chair.

Before Dr. Morton could respond, a server arrived with a tray of pastries and juice. Ellie resisted the urge to state her case and demand to leave. Instead, she sipped a tall glass of orange juice and nibbled a pastry as Dr. Morton made small talk about daily happenings at Meadow Laurel.

"Any questions?" Dr. Morton asked.

"Yes, Ma'am. My father misunderstood when he arranged for my stay here. I don't want to be a part of a residency. Even though Meadow Laurel must be a wonderful place, I need to discuss this further with him."

Dr. Morton's smile faded to a tiny curved line. "I see where you're coming from."

"I need to leave. I have to be somewhere by 10:00." Ellie squirmed in her seat.

"Your father says because of the horrific ordeal you've been through--you're anxious about the cranial surgery. And it can't be postponed."

"Ma'am, I don't want to have the surgery. Father needs help, not me. The scar doesn't bother me as much as it does him." Ellie felt herself losing ground.

"I understand your frustration. And if your father agrees, you're free to go." Dr. Morton reached across the table to pat Ellie's hand.

Ellie rose from the table. "Let's call him."

Dr. Morton led the way back to the office. Ellie didn't bother to sit but stood on the other side of the desk, her heart racing as Dr. Morton dialed the number, but there was no answer. She tried another number, and it went to voicemail. "Senator Evan, this is Dr. Morton. Please call at your earliest convenience."

Ellie sank into an armchair, feeling as if she might faint as she held her head in her hands, desperate for an action plan. How could she heap coals of fire on his head? Then, she remembered the call Jenna received from her father. "Call back. I want his voice mail." An accordion stretched between her heart and stomach.

Dr. Morton looked puzzled as she dialed the number and handed the phone to Ellie. "Hi *Dad*, it's me, *Ellie*. Just called to say *I love you*."

Ellie felt her insides tremble. This was exactly what Jenna would've said, only her dad wasn't the enemy. What now? Dad not Father--Ellie not Eloree--Was he brave enough to say he loved her? How would he vindicate this?

"So, what now?" Ellie felt anger rising, yet she hoped Dr. Morton would allow her to leave.

"Each time I've spoken with your father, he's been adamant you participate in this program. I can't give you permission to leave without his consent." Dr. Morton leaned toward Ellie. "I'll try to understand your point of view if you'll share it with me. There has to be a common ground for this matter."

"Common ground?" "Ellie flailed her hands. "Father doesn't know *common ground.* It's *his* way or *no* way. Misty shared those reports with me. I know what he told you about the ordeal in the storm. He made Jesse out to be a criminal. That was the most misconstrued story I've ever heard. I should know. I'm the one who lived it, not Father."

"I need to hear *your* side of this story, and I'm a good listener."

Ellie poured her heart out, recounting the events of the storm on Gabby Mountain and her interactions with Jesse. Dr. Morton listened, seldom interrupting with a question or comment. At last, Ellie came to a stopping place. "It's almost ten o'clock, and Jesse will be waiting for me at the Biltmore House. He doesn't know where I am. He'll be worried sick."

"I see where you're coming from, and I'm so sorry things turned out this way. But your father left a letter for you. He said to give it to you if you tried to leave."

Dr. Morton handed the legal-sized envelope to Ellie and stepped into the hallway.

Ellie opened the envelope and pulled out a typewritten letter on her father's office letterhead. As she began to read, tears streamed down her cheeks and dropped onto the formally written words--*Upon your twenty-first birthday, you will receive an endowment from your mother's estate. However, should you choose to prove yourself incapable before that date, I will hold and control these funds until you are deemed mentally stable. Furthermore, should you attempt to leave Meadow Laurel or refuse treatments of any kind, I am to be notified immediately. Respectfully, Walton Andrew Evan.*

Ellie flung her Navè onto the floor and collapsed beside it, drawing her knees to her chest, she buried her face and cried. Defeat riddled her mind. The was the worst case. More than the money, she wanted freedom. And freedom was a world away. No defense, only defeat.

Dr. Morton knelt beside her. "I'm here for you." She placed a tissue in Ellie's hand.

Ellie raised her head and wiped her eyes. “Look at this. Holding Mama’s money hostage.”

“I see you’re upset.” Dr. Morton sat cross-legged beside Ellie.

“He’s a thief and a coward, just like Andrew Jackson. Why can’t he say this to my face?” Ellie wadded up the letter and hurled it across the room. “He has no *respect*.”

“How can I help you work through this?”

“I need paper.” Ellie reached in her Navè for a pen. “If he won’t answer the phone, I’ll write him a letter.”

Dr. Morton handed a clipboard to Ellie. “Writing is a terrific way to gather your thoughts.”

Ellie bit her lip, fighting back more tears. “He needs to know what’s on my mind.”

“We have a bonfire every evening. The girls bring things they’ve written or sketched that they don’t want anyone else to see and toss them in the fire. Hurts and fears literally go up in smoke.” Dr. Morton turned back to her desk.

“Not this time,” Ellie snapped. “I will mail it to him.”

Taking a deep breath, she wrote *Dear Father*--then marked out *Father,* changing it to *Dad.* She pushed the pen across the paper, never minding her penmanship, marking out words, and ignoring spelling and grammar.

Five pages later her hand cramped, but her heart felt lighter. She ended with *Respectfully, Eloree Elise Evan*—then struck through it and wrote *Your loving daughter, Ellie.* She took the pages off the clipboard and folded them. “May I have an envelope and stamps?”

Dr. Morton looked up from the computer. “Sure you want to mail this without reading it later?”

“If I read it later, I might cop out and never mail it. Dad needs to know *his* child doesn’t take things sitting down. I’ve become a fighter like him.” Ellie tapped her fingers on Dr. Morton’s desk. “Except I fight fair. I’m not a cheater.”

As Dr. Morton turned to find the envelope, Ellie noticed a large picture of a football stadium and the band in center field. The caption read *University of Tennessee, Pride of the Southland Marching Band.* A smaller picture to the side showed a younger Dr. Morton wearing an orange band uniform and holding a flute. “I take it you went to the University of Tennessee.”

“Sure did.”

“My friends, Jenna and Cindi, are going there in the fall. They invited Dr. Shanks and me to visit.” Ellie’s voice trailed.

“*Dr. Shanks*? As in *Dr. Susan Shanks*, the world-renowned behavioral psychologist?"

"Yes." Ellie hoped her connection with Dr. Shanks would shed a new light on the situation. "She was with me until yesterday. Father wanted her to stay longer, but she had speaking engagements she couldn't cancel. She offered to take me with her, but he wouldn't allow it."

"This is strange. Why are there no reports from Dr. Shanks in your records?" Dr. Morton opened a thick file.

"I doubt you'll find anything. When I came here yesterday, Misty told me there were no reports from Dr. Shanks in my file."

"This is absurd. I mean, if you've been under the care of Dr. Shanks, I need to see those files. How could something that significant be left out? I see all kinds of reports from previous therapists, going back as far as the accident. The latest reports are from Dr. Link, but those discuss your physical needs, the injuries from the storm, and the proposed surgery." Dr. Morton continued sifting through the documents. "Wait, here's something."

Ellie's heart leaped. Maybe this was the key to leaving.

Dr. Morton looked up. "It says you're to have no contact with Dr. Shanks. That doesn't make sense."

Shifting her weight from one foot to the other, Ellie began, "Dr. Shanks's reports say I should have a normal life, make decisions on my own, not be under surveillance by bodyguards. She also recommended I be allowed to see Jesse Woods. Father seemed to agree, but now he's changed his mind."

Dr. Morton stood and closed the file, cramming it in a drawer. "I understand better now. Your father doesn't want to relinquish control of you."

"Exactly. I have Dr. Shanks's number in my phone. We can call her." Ellie reached for her phone.

"I'd love to speak with her, but without your father signing a release of information, I won't be allowed to."

"I can sign for it."

"I'm sorry, but the way he has the papers drawn up, your signature wouldn't matter."

Dr. Morton came around the desk and touched her arm. "Let's go back down to the dining hall. It's time for brunch, and you can meet the other girls."

"If it's all the same to you, I'd rather not be around the other girls. Hopefully, Father will call back, and you can explain to him." Ellie followed her to the door.

"I'll try to sort it out when he calls. Since you don't want to go to the dining hall, maybe you'd like to spend some time in one of our music galleries. Come with me."

Ellie walked beside Dr. Morton to a long hallway with doors along the side. The name of a wildflower and an instrument adorned each door. "I understand you're quite an accomplished pianist," Dr. Morton commented. "Looks like Magnolia Piano Gallery is available if you'd like to spend some time in here."

"Thank you." Ellie stepped into the room and closed the door behind her. Music had always been her escape mechanism, but now her mind was only on Jesse. Wide windows flanked the outside wall, and she lost track of time as she stared toward the farthest mountaintops, knowing Jesse would go back there—not knowing why she didn't meet him. The sadness and emptiness left her numb. Tears pooled in her eyes, leaving the mountaintops a blur until she blinked and felt hot wetness stream down her cheeks and drip onto her neck.

"Get a grip, Eloree Elise," she said aloud and ran her hands through her hair. "You'll figure out a way to get out of here by this afternoon."

Then, she turned her attention back to the contents of the room. Tidy shelves lined one portion of the back wall. She studied the music titles. Oldies. Gospel. Movie Themes. Broadway. Nothing seemed right, so she sat at the piano and began to play *In the Midst*. As her fingers captured every note and chord, she thought about first learning the song in the cabin with Jesse and the way he'd used the words to tell her about God. She closed her eyes and played the song over and over making up her own renditions. Loud, soft, bold, rhythmic.

She sang with all her might--so engrossed in the song, she didn't hear the door open or realize she had an audience. Hearing clapping, she spun around on the piano stool. There stood Juniper and three other girls. "Sorry to barge in. We couldn't resist."

Ellie grinned sheepishly. "I don't mind." She reached to close the lid on the keyboard. "I tend to get caught up in that song."

"Don't be so modest. You make the piano walk and talk. Meet my very talented suitemate. Ellie, meet the Kessler sisters." Juniper waved her hand.

Before Ellie could utter a sound, one of the tall girls with long, blond hair stepped forward. "Is Southern Gospel your forte?" the girl quipped, hands on her hips.

"No, I wouldn't say it is." Ellie clung to the side of the piano with one hand.

The girl stepped closer, with each arm around another girl. "We're the Kesslers. I'm sure you've seen us on TV."

Ellie swallowed hard. "Yes, I suppose I may have seen you on TV," she eluded, trying to cover the fact she had no idea who the three were.

"We're the sisters of the Kessler Family Gospel Singers. I'm Faith. This is Hope and the little one's Charity. Yes, we're triplets even though Charity doesn't look like Hope and me." Faith stared hard at Ellie.

"Nice to meet you." Ellie felt shaky.

"We sing with our parents. I'm the piano player in the group. Hope and I sing lead, and Charity plays the guitar. We've performed all over the United States, including Alaska and Hawaii--not to mention the UK and Canada," Faith went on, her piercing blue eyes challenging Ellie.

Juniper came to Ellie's rescue. "Come on Kesslers. We broke Dr. Morton's privacy rule." She scolded, herding them out the door.

Ellie leaned against the piano, not sure what to make of the Kessler sisters and the way Faith acted as though she didn't like her.

The door opened again. "*Ps-s-t.* It's me, Juniper. May I come in?"

Ellie nodded, even though Juniper was already in the room. "I'm sorry. When Faith heard you playing and singing, she went bonkers. I thought she liked it but turns out she's jealous of you. She won't act like that in front of Dr. Morton."

"Why would she be jealous of me? I don't play on TV or all over the world."

"Yeah, but you're awesome. Let me fill you in on these three. Faith and Hope tend to leave Charity out. I think they've grown up treating Charity like a kid sister, and she lets them get away with it."

"That's unfair."

"I know, but Faith orders the other two around like she's their mother. Her excuse is because Charity got lost at the state fair when she was a kid, so she can't be left alone."

"What about Hope?"

"She's a lot nicer when she's not around Faith. Hope's engaged to, Ronald, a guy who rides motorcycles and races cars. Faith badgers her every time she puts on her engagement ring calling her *Gear-head.*"

Ellie shook her head, puzzled with the whole affair.

"The triplets have been traveling around in a bus, singing gospel music their entire lives. They talk about God and Jesus like they know them personally." Juniper made a mocking face. "If

Hope gets married--she'll leave the group and travel on the racing circuit with Ronald. She doesn't want to let her family down, but she loves Ronald. Faith wants to become a big-time singer, and if Hope leaves, she's afraid it won't happen." Juniper went on.

"What are they doing *here*?"

"Taking a sabbatical. They travel three hundred days a year and have no free time. They have no life. This is a vacation for them. Could you imagine living on a bus with your parents? I'd be worse off than Faith." Juniper laughed and stuck her tongue out.

"I'll play more quietly if I'm ever in here again."

"Oh no, you won't. When you're in here, whatever you do is your business. We really weren't allowed to barge in on you." Juniper reached for the door.

Ellie followed Juniper back along the hallway. Dr. Morton came toward them and stopped to tell Ellie she hadn't heard from her father yet. Not knowing what else to do, Ellie followed Juniper outside where a volleyball game was getting underway. Ellie opted against playing and sat down on a bench beside Charity.

"You play the piano well."

"Thank you, Charity."

"I don't like to play ball of any kind. Do you?"

"No, I've never been the athletic type." Ellie squinted into the sun.

"Me neither, but I do like horses."

"Me, too."

"Want to walk down to the stable?" Charity invited.

Ellie nodded and the two set out down the hill where several horses grazed.

"Do you know how to ride?"

"Yes," Ellie mumbled, her thoughts drifting back to Jesse and his horses.

"I've never ridden a horse. I'm afraid of them."

"Why?" Ellie kicked a stick.

"I'm afraid of lots of things. I'm never by myself. I have a horrible fear of being alone, and I faint at the sight of blood. My parents sent us here hoping I'll get over my fears, Hope won't get married and leave us, and Faith will stop being so bossy. How about you?"

"This was my father's idea. I'd rather be someplace else." Ellie reached across the fence, taking hold of the halter of a white horse. "Let Charity pet you."

Charity stepped closer. "Will it bite me? A horse bit Faith

once."

"No, just rub right here between her ears, like this." Ellie held the halter with one hand and guided Charity's hand with the other.

Ellie was losing hope her father would call Dr. Morton or any resolution about her leaving would be reached. Even though she wasn't in the mood for small talk, having Charity's company helped pass the time. For the next half hour, they meandered around the stables. Charity chattered nonstop, but Ellie's mind reeled with any hope of leaving.

ꙮ21ꙮ

Tattered Memories

"**H**ere come Dr. Morton and Juniper." Charity pointed.

"You left this in my office." Dr. Morton handed the Navè to Ellie. "Juniper, you and Charity go around to the back fence and see if the dogwoods are blooming while I speak to Ellie."

Ellie's heart raced, hoping the time had come to leave.

"I got a voicemail from one of your father's assistants. It seems he's gone out of town and can't be reached for several days."

"This makes no sense. With all the technology in the world, why can he not be reached?" Ellie gritted her teeth.

Dr. Morton shook her head. "I'm sorry. I wish I could give you the answer. All I can do is encourage you to unwind and make the best of your stay."

"This is so hard. Especially since I had to stand Jesse up." Ellie pulled her ruby necklace from under her shirt.

"What a ruby." Dr. Morton leaned closer.

Ellie rubbed her finger across the stone. "I found it on the trail when I was with Jesse."

"Don't you think I should put it in the safe?" Dr. Morton tilted her head to get a closer look.

"No. It means too much to me."

"Whatever you say but I know quite a bit about gems. Digging in the dirt is my hobby." Dr. Morton rested her hand on the fence.

"You should meet my brother, Terrance. He's an archeologist and travels all over the world."

"Do you hear from him often, Ellie?"

"Not as often as I'd like. Mainly holidays and birthdays," Ellie answered as Juniper and Charity rounded the corner.

"I'm going for a hike up to the top of the ridge. Anybody

want to come with me?" Juniper pointed.

Dr. Morton shrugged her shoulders. "You might want to go, Ellie. The view's spectacular from up there. Charity's never been either."

"Come on, Ellie. I'll go if you go." Charity grabbed Ellie's arm.

The trail led through the meadow and wound up the hill toward the top of the ridge. Ellie became lost in her own thoughts, and Juniper spoke nonstop about plans for her trek along the Appalachian Trail. The path led into a grove of trees and along a rocky face. The buildings below faded into matchboxes boxes, and the fences stood like rows of toothpicks.

"Are you okay?" Ellie turned to Charity as the trail narrowed.

"I don't know," she whispered. "It's a long way up here."

"We're nearly to the top," Juniper called as she climbed over a large boulder.

"Let's join hands to steady ourselves on these rocks." Ellie remembered the comfort Jesse's hand brought her and reached for Charity's small, clammy hand.

The trail became steeper, with low hanging limbs and moss-covered rocks jutting onto the path. They stopped to catch their breath, swatting gnats that swarmed in their faces.

"Whoo-hoo. We're here." Juniper shouted when they reached the clearing at the top of the ridge. "Look at that view. It goes on forever. I'll have this view every day on the Appalachian Trail."

Ellie wished she was alone or even better, with Jesse. The view wasn't as spectacular as Gabby Mountain, but the layers of blue and purple mountains brought back vivid memories of Jesse and Mohan.

"What's that pinging noise?" Juniper motioned toward Ellie's Navè.

"My phone. I have a voicemail. There must be cell service up here." Ellie grabbed the phone and held it close to her ear. "Hey Ellie, this is Jesse. Hope nothing's wrong that you didn't come. Give me a call. Bye."

"Fourteen missed calls, all from Jesse." Ellie grimaced as she dialed his number.

The phone went to voicemail. "Jesse, this is Ellie. I'm sorry I couldn't meet you. Father tricked me into coming to a place--"

Ellie sat down and put her head on her knees. She felt dizzy and everything was spinning out of control.

Juniper put her hand on Ellie's shoulder. "What's wrong?"

"The battery went dead on my phone, and I didn't get to finish the message."

"That's a tough break." Juniper picked up a pebble and tossed it toward a clump of bushes.

"I want to go back. I don't like it up here." Charity's voice quivered.

"That's ridiculous, Charity," Juniper snapped. "We hiked all the way up here, and all you want to do is go back."

Charity's eyes were wide, and Ellie put her arm around her thin shoulders. "Juniper, you stay as long as you want to. Charity and I will start on back."

"I'd love to stay up here by myself, but I have to take care of you two," Juniper scoffed and bounded down the trail ahead.

"Why does Juniper act like this?" Ellie asked as she and Charity started back down the steep, rocky trail.

Charity shook her head. "She's usually nice, but she has diabetes. When her blood sugar gets too low, she's hateful."

Ellie and Charity grabbed hands to steady themselves. Ellie couldn't believe she was scaling down a trail and helping someone else—the way Jesse helped her. But her thoughts were shattered by a bloodcurdling scream up ahead. "Juniper, we're coming," Ellie yelled, dragging Charity with her, grabbing laurel branches to steady herself.

When they reached Juniper, she lay on the trail, blood oozing from her right leg. "Help me," she screamed. "My leg's broken."

Ellie glanced at Charity. She was as white as a ghost with her hand over her mouth. She knew Juniper couldn't walk back and she couldn't leave her with Charity to go for help. The only option was for Charity to go. "Juniper, listen to me," Ellie snapped. "I need you to calm down. The calmer you are--the less your leg'll bleed. I'll stay with you, and Charity'll get help."

Charity shook her head and cried, "I can't. I'm afraid."

"Charity, you *can*. Follow the trail. Once you get out of the trees, keep going down the mountain. It'll only take you a few minutes to make it back. Quicker than it took us to hike up here."

"I can't go by myself," Charity blubbered, covering her face with her hands.

"Yes, you can. I'm counting on you. Juniper's counting on you. Show your sisters you're strong. Prove yourself."

"What will I say?" Charity gasped, between sobs.

"Here are the keys to my four-wheel drive truck," Ellie reached into her *Navè*. "Give them to Dr. Morton. She can drive the truck to the edge of the clearing. Then, I'll whistle through my fist, like this." Ellie paused and gave the resounding whistle Jesse taught her. "That way, Dr. Morton will know which trail we're on."

Charity wailed, *"Jesus, Jesus, Jesus,"* as she disappeared among the trees.

Ellie turned her attention back to Juniper's wounded leg. Her stomach felt squeamish as she eyed the blood-soaked gash. But she had to get the bleeding stopped. Remembering how Jesse had stripped his undershirt to make a bandage for Mohan's side, she stood and flung her shirt off, pulling the white tank over her head.

"What are you doing getting undressed? I'm bleeding."

"Calm down, Juniper. I'll use my tank top for a bandage to slow the bleeding." Ellie forcing herself to stay level-headed.

Her fingers struggled with the buttons as she put the plaid shirt back on. Grabbing the Navè, she unraveled a cord, the same way she had to help Jesse bandage Mohan.

Juniper grimaced as Ellie held the shirt in place over the wound and secured the cord.

"Last Saturday, I was bleeding on a mountain. I remember what it's like. Stay calm." Ellie applied pressure to the makeshift bandage.

Juniper became eerily quiet--her face pale, dripping with sweat, and her breathing shallow. Ellie grabbed her face. "Juniper, speak to me."

"*S-g-r...c-n-d-e...*" Juniper moaned.

"Are you saying sugar? Candy?"

Juniper's eyes rolled. "*Di--a--bet—ic ...*"

Ellie dug in her Navè, and her hand hit the jar of jelly Jesse's grandmother gave her. She unscrewed the rim and used a pen to pry off the seal. Holding Juniper's head at an angle, she scooped the sticky purple jelly into her mouth. After several swallows, Juniper's breathing steadied, and color came back into her face. Ellie continued to cradle her upper body in her lap, reassuring her Dr. Morton would be there soon.

Ellie saw the truck come up the hillside. When the engine stopped, she cupped her trembling fists and blew a long, low whistle. The truck's horn blew, and she whistled again and again until Dr. Morton and Misty found them on the trail.

"I hope I did the right thing. I tried to stop the bleeding."

"You did the right thing." Misty donned rubber gloves, and when she unwrapped the makeshift bandage. "A bad cut on the bone causes a lot of blood loss. Did she faint?" Misty wanted to know.

"Nearly, but I had a jar of jelly in my Navè. When she told me she needed sugar, I scooped it into her mouth."

"That's a miracle. An injury can trigger a diabetic's insulin," Dr. Morton said.

Dr. Morton and Misty wrapped their arms around Juniper and half carried her to the truck. Ellie sat up front with Dr. Morton while Misty tended Juniper in the back.

The other girls swarmed around Misty and Ellie, asking for details. Faith stood rigid with her arms wrapped around Charity like a rag doll. As Ellie started to walk away, Faith blurted, "What do you mean, forcing my sister to run off the mountain by herself? Don't you know that scared her?"

Ellie wheeled on one foot and stared back at her. "Your sister is a very strong and courageous woman. She's as tough as a pine knot, and she stands her own ground."

Hope stepped up. "Stop, Faith. You don't need to stand guard over Charity. She did what was right and came through fine."

"Great. I guess you two don't need me then. Go on. Get married to *Gearhead*. See if I care." Faith stomped away.

Hope turned to Ellie. "I apologize for the way Faith's acting. It has nothing to do with you."

Ellie was at a loss for words. She had enough problems of her own, much less someone else's. Not the Kessler's. Not Juniper's. More than ever, she wanted to run away. *Run where?* For now, the seclusion of her suite would have to do.

The afternoon sun filled the suite with a golden glow, but Ellie's mind was a blur of everything that had happened. The last twenty-four hours of her life had been like a bad movie in slow motion. Drained emotionally and physically, she sank onto the sofa and slipped her boots off. She was like all the Kesslers—weak and scared like Charity. Longing to be with that special someone, like Hope and feeling pressure, like Faith.

Ellie dozed until a light knock at the door awakened her. She traipsed to the door, finding Charity on the other side. "May I come in?" she asked in a whisper.

"Sure." Ellie rubbed her eyes. "I look like a mess. I fell asleep on the sofa."

"I wanted to talk to you before supper." Charity stepped into the room.

The word *supper* burned in Ellie's heart. Jesse would be having *supper*, not *dinner*.

"Is everything okay? You look a little sad." Charity clasped her hands in front of her.

"I'm fine. It's been a trying day, and I have a lot on my mind." Ellie patted the sofa for Charity to sit beside her.

Charity twirled a strand of hair around her finger. "I wanted you to know I'm all right. I was scared to death up on that mountain, and I thought I was going to faint when I saw the blood. But I didn't. When you told me to walk back by myself, I didn't think I could. But I did."

Ellie patted her arm. "You did great."

"Did you actually mean those things you said about me being a strong woman and tougher than a pine knot?" Charity squinted, grabbing another strand of hair.

"Sure, I meant it."

"Thanks for saying those things. Nobody's ever said that to me before. They say I'm little and weak, and Faith and Hope are big and strong." She mocked in a singsong voice. "I hate being called a little girl when I'm as old as they are."

Ellie sat straighter. "After you left, she nearly passed out. Luckily, I had a jar of jelly in my Navè and was able to get it in her mouth."

"That's not luck. I bet you don't always carry jelly in your bag." Charity's eyes grew wide. "That's the hand of God. He sends ministering angels when we need them, and He used you as an angel for Juniper."

Ellie listened, not quite sure what to make of Charity's revelation.

"Is that a Martin?" Charity gasped, pointing toward Ellie's guitar. "Play it."

"I just got it and I don't know the first thing about playing the guitar. Go ahead. You can play it."

Charity stroked the neck and strummed the strings. Ellie was enthralled at the melody coming from six strings and ten tiny fingers.

"Wow, Charity. That's a beautiful tune. Sing along."

Charity looked up. "I can't sing. Faith and Hope won't let me. They say I throw them off-key, so I stay in the background."

"I'm sure you have a lovely voice."

Charity continued strumming. "I'll make a deal with you. You teach me how to sing and I'll teach you *everything* I know about playing the guitar."

"There's a deal I'll gladly take you up on." Ellie patted her shoulder.

Misty's voice came over the intercom. "Ladies, it's time for Fireside. Bring a jacket. See you at the pavilion in fifteen minutes."

Charity started for the door. "Come on. Fireside is great. I'll be playing guitar tonight."

"I'd love to hear you play, but I really don't feel up to socializing. Besides, I want to change clothes, but I don't have any clean outfits."

"Bring all your dirty clothes, and I'll show you where to drop them off. They'll be delivered back to your room later. Please, come I really want you to," Charity said, with a playful pout.

"You win." Ellie smiled down at her.

Charity led the way through the garden to a pavilion overlooking a small lake. Most of the girls were already seated on the benches around the fire pit. Faith and Hope had saved a seat for Charity. She attempted to follow Ellie and sit someplace else, but Faith grabbed her arm.

The tables were laden with hamburger fixings and pitchers of tea and lemonade. The crackling fire and aroma of meat cooking reminded her of the smells in the cabin. Jesse was somewhere beyond the mountains she saw in the distance, and she hadn't even been able to get a complete message to him.

She closed her eyes, trying to visualize his face. Her thoughts were interrupted by the sounds of a guitar. Charity sat on a stool in front of the group--her hands moving along the frets and plucking the strings the same way Jesse had. And the reflection of the fire on the guitar brought back more memories of Jesse playing by the fireplace in the cabin.

As the event wound down, Misty asked each girl if anyone had something to share. Ellie passed, hoping to go as unnoticed as possible. When it was Hope's turn, she stood and held out her left hand. "I've made up my mind. I'm marrying Ronald, and I won't be pulling this ring off again. I'm sorry Faith and Charity. I don't want to betray my family, but my heart will die if I can't be with the man I love."

The silence was deafening, with only the sound of the crackling embers. Ellie wondered how Hope gathered so much courage. Closing her eyes, she rubbed the ruby that dangled on her chest. Would she be strong enough to walk away from Father?

When Ellie got back to her suite, Juniper was propped up on the sofa in the sitting area, reading a book.

"Hey," Ellie whispered, trying not to startle her. "Glad you're okay."

Juniper crossed her arms over her chest. "Thanks to you, I didn't have to be hospitalized."

“For a cut on your leg?”

“Not only am I diabetic, I’m a free bleeder. If you hadn’t slowed the blood loss, I could have gone into shock.”

“Whoa, God was looking out for you.”

“What? You sound like the Kesslers. I don’t go for all that God stuff.” Juniper frowned.

“You don’t believe in God?”

As the conversation went on, Juniper told Ellie she had no reason to believe in God. There were too many bad things happening to good people. And she saw no reason to accept any of it.

“I haven’t been to church since I was a child. But I can tell you what I learned during my ordeal.”

“What ordeal?” Juniper snapped, adjusting the pillow under her leg.

Ellie pulled a chair closer and told Juniper her story. She began with the bitterness she felt from losing her mother in the accident, how she didn’t think about God. She elaborated about being on Gabby Mountain with Jesse, how God spared their lives, and the details of each time she came close to being killed. She explained how hopeless she felt while under the bed and the peace that came over her when she asked God into her life.

“Wow, Ellie. We’ve been talking for two hours. I thought you didn’t know much about God. Sounds like you know a lot more than you give yourself credit for.”

“Sorry if I’ve talked your ear off. I miss having Dr. Shanks and Jesse to talk to. For the past week, I’ve been very passionate about God in my life. I know He’s real and He’ll make a way for me to leave here.”

“Why is leaving a problem? You’re almost twenty-one, aren’t you?”

“Yes, but Father won’t-” Ellie stopped.

꧁22꧂

Without You

Ellie woke the next morning to Dr. Morton's voice on the intercom. "Good morning, ladies. Brunch is now being served. Gathering will begin in one hour in the Laurel Dome."

Ellie had no idea what Gathering was, but she intended to participate in the events, then leave on her birthday. The thought of this mammoth step shook her insides. "If Hope can do it, so can I," she told her reflection the bathroom mirror. "You're a strong, courageous woman who's tougher than a pine knot."

Realizing Juniper had already gone, Ellie scurried to the dining hall to find her. "Hey Juniper, are you feeling okay this morning? I thought you might sleep in."

"Oh, not me. Not on a morning we have Gathering. I'll prop my leg up and keep the ice pack handy. You're coming, too, aren't you?"

"Promise you won't tell the others what I shared with you last night."

"You mean about your plans to leave?" Juniper reached for her juice glass.

Ellie glanced over her shoulder. "Do the other girls know who my father is?"

"Yes, and it doesn't matter to them."

Juniper showed her to the Laurel Dome, and they found seats on the back row. Ellie took in the splendor of the dome-shaped room. Even the ceiling was glass with a magnificent view overlooking a garden of laurels, beyond the rolling meadow with grazing horses--into the purplish mountains.

As the girls filed in, Faith played the piano. From the look on her face, Ellie could tell she was upset. Even though she played beautifully, sadness resonated with each note. Hope and Charity sat on the front row with their eyes fixed on Faith.

Dr. Morton stepped to the front, acknowledging Faith as the featured musician. Faith sat as if she'd been programmed and had an audience of ten thousand, instead of ten girls. Her eyes were fixed straight ahead, looking over the tops of everyone's heads, her torso swaying, as her hands rambled over the keyboard.

"Faith's losing it," Juniper whispered. "She was like this when they first got here. She plays like she's trying to mutilate the piano."

Faith played louder and faster as if the piano was out of control until she slumped across the keyboard. "I can't do it anymore."

Ellie watched as Dr. Morton and Misty wrapped their arms around Faith and escorted her from the room. She recalled taking her own frustrations out on the piano to the point she wanted to pick it up and throw it like an angry child with a toy. Then, she watched as Charity slipped her arm around Hope's shoulders. Like Ellie, Charity was now the strong, confident one, not a weak, little girl.

Dr. Morton returned and took a seat at the piano. As she played, the dismal tone lifted and some of the girls sang along. After three songs, Dr. Morton stood and addressed the group. "Ladies, we all go through trying situations in your lives. Sometimes we understand, other times we have to accept the circumstances we're in, trusting God to see us through. For those who brought Bibles, please turn to Ecclesiastes 3. Here, Solomon reflects on life in the form of a beautiful poem comparing opposite events."

Ellie hung onto each word Dr. Morton read. Hearing the words read aloud by someone else was like rain on a withering plant. Soon it would be her time to leave.

Dr. Morton finished and closed the Bible. "Let us pray. Dear Heavenly Father, You know the perfect timing for all things in our lives. Help these girls to submit themselves to You and by Your grace be led. In Jesus' name, Amen."

The stillness of the room became saturated with the melody of the piano as Dr. Morton began to play and sing a song using the words from the Bible verses. Ellie took in every word, wishing the song would never end.

When Dr. Morton finished, she addressed the group, "Ladies, lunch will be served at noon. I encourage you to take this time to reflect, either alone or with a friend. I'll be in my office this afternoon for individual sessions, so please come see me."

Ellie dashed to Dr. Morton. "I love the verses you read, and the song was magnificent. I'd love a copy of the song."

"Glad you enjoyed it. That is one of my favorite scriptures, and you'll find the song *Turn, Turn, Turn,* by the Byrds, in the 1960's sheet music in the Magnolia Gallery. It was written by Pete Seager," Dr. Morton said.

"Hey Ellie," Juniper called. "Is it okay if I go with you to the Magnolia Gallery? I bet you'll play that song really well."

"Sure."

"Hard to believe it's a 60's song. Dr. Morton's version sure didn't sound that old," Juniper commented, as they made their way down the corridor that led to the galleries.

Once inside the gallery, Juniper positioned herself on the floor, stretching her leg out with her back leaned against the wall.

"Do you play an instrument, Juniper?" Ellie thumbed through a stack of sheet music.

"No, I'm a listener, but I'd like to learn. Can you teach me?"

"If I was going to be here long enough, I would." Ellie propped the yellowing sheets above the keyboard.

"When are you leaving?"

"Not sure, but this song will help me get my plans together." Ellie's hands waltzed across the keys, bringing the melody to life. "Come on Juniper. Sing along with me. *And a time to every purpose under heaven...*"

After singing the chorus again, Ellie paused, realizing Juniper wasn't singing. "Don't you like this song?"

"Ellie, the song's fine, but I need to talk to you."

"About what?" Ellie stopped playing.

"Do you really believe there's a heaven?" Juniper sounded serious.

Ellie moved onto the floor and sat facing her. "Yes, I believe in heaven."

"I've thought about the things you told me about God. Hearing it from you sort of made sense, but I'm still confused."

"I'm not a Bible scholar." Ellie drew in a long breath.

"I don't know where to start to become a Christian."

"Maybe you could talk to Dr. Morton or the Kesslers."

"I don't want to talk to anyone but you." Juniper stared at the floor.

Ellie drew her knees to her chest. "You could start by telling God you believe He and Jesus are real. Ask Him to forgive your sins and tell Him you'll praise Him forever. That's pretty much how it happened with me."

"It can't be that simple." Juniper shook her head. "I mean people go to church for years to learn about God. How did you learn all this in a cabin in the middle of a storm?"

Before Ellie could answer, Dr. Morton's voice came over the intercom. "Girls, please make your way to the dining hall. Sunday dinner will be served in ten minutes."

Juniper grabbed Ellie's hand. "Promise you'll give me your phone number so we can talk, even after you leave."

"I promise." Ellie extended a hand, helping Juniper to her feet.

"Thanks." Juniper grimaced, gripping Ellie's shoulder to steady herself. "Sunday dinner, which is really lunch, is always fried chicken."

"Why fried chicken?" Ellie asked as they started toward the dining room.

"It's a Southern tradition. Dr. Morton's all about trying new things, but she likes traditional things, too. We all sit together at one table, and Dr. Morton and Misty sit with us. It's like having an old-fashioned family dinner at Grandma's house, where we pass the bowls and talk."

By the time they made their way into the dining hall, most of the others were already there, but Juniper and Ellie found seats together. The round table was covered with a red and white checked tablecloth and twelve place settings. In the middle of the table were platters piled with golden brown fried chicken and biscuits, surrounded by bowls of vegetables. The smells reminded Ellie of the meal Jesse's grandmother prepared the day Gustave forced them to leave.

Ellie went through the formalities of the meal, but her mind was beyond the mountaintops, visible from where she sat. This was probably what Jesse was having for lunch today, seated around the table with his family. Would he give up on her?

After lunch, Ellie and Juniper relaxed on the front porch. Juniper settled into a rocking chair--her leg propped up, reading a book. Ellie perched on the wooden porch swing facing the driveway leading back to the main road. From where she sat, she eyed her truck, lost in the thought of driving away.

The screen door swung open, screeching on its hinges. Juniper looked up from the book and Ellie halted the swing. "We're leaving. Daddy and Mama are coming for us," Charity announced, leaning her suitcase against the railing.

Juniper shrugged. "I'll miss you, girls."

"I'll miss you, too." Charity sat beside Ellie on the swing. "Let's stay in touch. Ellie, have you ever thought about getting a job with a Southern gospel group?"

The seriousness in Charity's voice echoed in Ellie's head. "No, I haven't considered becoming a full-time musician."

"You could join us when you're finished here and take Hope's place on the keyboard. As well as you play, you could learn all our songs in no time." Charity handed a CD to Ellie. "Here's our latest album. Daddy and Mama wrote all the songs. Listen to them and see what you think about joining us."

"Like running away and joining the circus." Juniper almost laughed, stopping short when Ellie shot a scolding look her way.

"Here's our contact information." Charity pointed to the back of the CD case.

Ellie patted Charity's hand. "I'm flattered you'd consider making an offer to me. I have some things to take care of right now, but you never know. I might take you up on it."

Charity jumped up from the swing. "Mom and Dad are here! Oh, how I missed them." With a leap, she scampered down the steps and bolted across the lawn to a brightly painted van--covered with images of each girl, their parents, and the words *Kessler Family Gospel Singers*. A tall man, bearing the resemblance of Faith and Hope, ran to meet Charity and swung her off the ground as she wrapped her arms around his neck. The passenger door opened and a dark-haired woman, a striking older image of Charity, stepped out. Charity let go of her father and embraced her mother.

"That's freaky," Juniper commented, observing the trio.

"What do you mean?" Ellie stopped the squeaking swing.

"See how much Charity looks like her mom? I'm glad I don't look like my mom. Do you look like your mother?" Juniper frowned, wrinkling her nose.

Ellie's voice dropped. "Yes, I look exactly like my mother did at my age."

"I bet your father finds that hard to bear--with you losing her and all. Do you think he tries to control you to keep you from looking differently than her?" Juniper speculated.

"Why would you say that?" Ellie's face tightened.

"Makes sense to me. You said he tells you how to wear your hair and how to dress. What else could it be? I'm just saying--" Juniper cut herself short as the Kesslers stepped onto the porch.

"Mom, Dad, meet Juniper and Ellie." Charity rocked back on her heels.

"Nice to meet you, Mr. and Mrs. Kessler." Juniper smiled up at them and Ellie nodded.

"Ellie's the girl we prayed for who was lost out in that awful storm." Charity waved her hand. "This is Juniper. She's the one who fell and got hurt up on the mountain yesterday. Ellie took care of her while I ran back for help."

"I'm proud of you, Darling." Her mom kissed the top of her head.

"I didn't faint when I saw the blood either." Charity covered her mouth with one hand.

"We love you, Honey. Sounds like you've had a better time than your sisters have. Where are they?" Mr. Kessler looked toward the door.

"Dad, Mom, wait. Before we go find Hope and Faith, I need to tell you something. Ellie can play the piano and sing *really* well. She'd do a wonderful job taking Hope's place. What do you think?" Charity beamed up at her dad.

"Yes, Sweetie, I'm sure this young lady's a fine musician. Let's all pray about it and see what the Lord would have us do." Mr. Kessler nodded, dismissing Charity's suggestion.

Mrs. Kessler extended her hands to both Ellie and Juniper. "Thank you for taking Charity under your wing. You're both so sweet," she said, with a lacy southern drawl.

"Mom and Dad." Hope burst onto the porch, lugging two suitcases.

With a round of hugs and laughs, the three embraced Hope. "Oh, beautiful daughter. We've got a wedding to plan." Mrs. Kessler took Hope's hand in hers, rubbing the engagement ring with her thumb.

"Yes, Mama. I've decided. Thanks for coming to get us early. Faith's taking it hard and I'm sorry," Hope's chin quivered.

"Now, now, a bride-to-be doesn't need to be crying over anything. We trust your judgment. All we asked you to do was come here and seek God for His perfect will in your life. If this is His answer, then we won't dispute it." Mr. Kessler closed his eyes, holding Hope to his chest. But Ellie saw tears in his eyes.

Tears rolled down Mrs. Kessler's cheeks. "You'll be a beautiful bride and a godly wife. We understand how you feel. We know Ronald loves you, but we do, too."

"Then is it okay if I stay here and let Ronald pick me up on the motorcycle?"

"Ask your daddy." Mrs. Kessler brought her hands to her heart.

"Hope, you're going to be Ronald's wife, and you'll now be covered by his prayers and protection. If he sees fit for you to ride that motorcycle with him--I don't have a right to interfere. Ronald and you will have to seek God's protection on your own. I'll always be your daddy and I'll always love you, but I won't tell you what you can and can't do."

"Thank you, Daddy. I'll wait for Ronald. I haven't seen him in over two weeks," Hope said as the Kesslers made their way into the main hallway, leaving Juniper and Ellie alone on the porch.

Ellie wondered if the Kesslers always treated their daughters with this much respect—hug and say *I love you.*

Before Ellie could begin to digest the scene that had played out before her eyes, Mr. and Mrs. Kessler came back out with their arms around Faith--her head was down and still crying. Charity paused to say final farewells to Ellie and Juniper as her parents escorted Faith to the van. Mrs. Kessler climbed into the back with Faith. Charity hopped into the front passenger seat.

Mr. Kessler came back for the suitcases. On his last trip, he addressed Ellie and Juniper. "I appreciate the love and kindness you've shown my girls. God knows every little thing you've said or done—He'll bless you."

He offered a handshake, first to Juniper and then Ellie. Before either could speak, he addressed Ellie. "Charity says you're about the best piano player she's ever heard. Are you considering a start in gospel music?"

Ellie sat up straighter. "No, Sir. I don't think so. I have some important decisions to make, and I'm not sure what my next step will be."

"Then let the Lord lead you. Remember Philippians 4:13. You can do all things through Christ. Where He guides, He provides." An instant smile flashed across his face. Then, he waved without looking back and half-ran across the lawn to the waiting van.

Hope stepped onto the porch as the van inched its way out of sight. Her face was red and swollen, and she clung to a wad of tissues in her hand, like a child with a security blanket. "Bye Daddy, Mama, Faith, Charity--I love you," she called--then sat on the top step. She hugged her knees to her chest and rocked back and forth like she was dancing to the tune of her diminishing sobs.

Juniper leaned over and whispered, "Misty's having an interpretive dance session down by the lake. Want to go watch?"

Ellie shook her head and pointed in Hope's direction. "I think I'll stay here."

Juniper shrugged and turned back to her book.

After a few minutes, Ellie moved the step beside Hope. "Do you want to be alone or do you want company?"

"Please stay with me. I'm not used to being without my

sisters and my parents. They're the best family ever." Hope sniffed, wiping her nose. "I don't want Ronald to see I've been crying so hard."

"When will he be here?"

"Not for another hour. This will be the longest hour of my life. Daddy wouldn't let me ride on the back of Ronald's motorcycle before. This will be the first time, and I may be scared."

"You can do all things through Christ who gives you strength." Ellie put her hand on Hope's shoulder.

"You've been talking to my dad. Philippians 4:13 is one of his favorite verses." Hope raked her hands through the strands of blonde hair that fell across her face. "You're right, I can do all things through Christ. But getting to this point and making the decision to get married is the hardest thing I've ever done. I couldn't have done it without my faith in God."

For the next hour, Ellie sat on the step with Hope. Juniper pretended to read the book, but Ellie knew she took in every word Hope shared about how great God had been in her life. She told about meeting Ronald, how they fell in love, and she knew from the beginning he was the right one for her. Sometimes she laughed--other times she cried, sharing the loneliness she felt while on the road with her family while Ronald was in another state for weeks at a time. She went on about the anguish her family felt when she told them she intended to travel with Ronald on the racing circuit.

"What will that be like?" Ellie asked.

Hope leaned against the porch railing. "I don't really know. NASCAR will be a new adventure for both of us. I want to be there for him when he comes across the finish line, whether he comes in first or last."

"Congratulations. I'm sure you'll be very happy." Ellie's fingers traced the leather cord holding the ruby.

"I'm doing all the talking. How about you? Do you have a boyfriend?" Hope peered through the curtain of blond tresses falling over her shoulder.

Ellie grasped for a suitable answer. "I don't know if you could call him an official boyfriend, but there's someone I'm interested in. But I don't have a supportive family like you. My father forbids me to see him."

"I'm sorry. I know how you must feel. At first, Daddy didn't want me to see Ronald, either. He said I'd raise a bunch of grease monkeys instead of saints of God if I married Ronald. He thought I should marry someone in the gospel music business."

"What did you do?"

"Mama came to my rescue. She said God can use grease monkeys for saints just the same as musicians." Hope put her hands over her eyes and laughed.

"I'm glad your mom saw things your way."

Hope stretched her legs out in front of her. "Yep, I'm Daddy's little girl, but Mama's my best friend. I don't know what girls do without their mamas."

Hope's words sent a searing sword through Ellie's soul. What if her mother was here to defend her?

"Daddy wanted Faith to fall in love with our drummer. Mama told him God is the one who chooses who we fall in love with--it's nobody else's business. That's how it is with Ronald and me. From the first time I met him, I couldn't get him off my mind. I don't think I can live if I can't be with him. We may not be rich, but we'll be together even if we live in a travel trailer on the racing circuit."

As Hope rambled on, Ellie's mind reeled out of control. Was she in love with Jesse? Like Hope—money didn't matter to her. She'd live in the cabin on Gabby Mountain if she could be with Jesse.

"That's him" Hope stuffed the tissues into her pockets. As the roar of a motorcycle drew nearer, she jumped to her feet and Ellie stood beside her. "I've waited a long time for this day. I guess that's why my name's Hope. I never gave up *hope* we'd be together."

Hope bounded down the steps and ran toward the motorcycle. Like a perfectly choreographed scene, she threw herself into Ronald's arms. He swooped her off the ground and her arms clung around his neck. He held her for a long time and Ellie could tell their embrace had locked with a kiss. He placed a helmet on her head, and she looked up at him as he secured the straps. He held a jacket for her and she slipped her arms in. Hope climbed on the back with him and waved as they disappeared down the same tree-shaded lane that led her family away.

Ellie knew she had to have the same hope and courage to step beyond the obstacles standing in her way of leaving. Just a few more days and she'd be going down that same lane.

~~~~~

"May I come in?" Ellie peered in the open door of Dr. Morton's office.

Dr. Morton motioned for Ellie to follow her to a sitting
~~~~~

area in the corner of the room. “This has been an unusual day. Tomorrow, we’ll be back to our regular routine. Besides a couple of mishaps, what do you think of Meadow Laurel?”

“Remarkable.” Ellie gave the expected answer, her emotions rearing to break loose like a racehorse.

“Glad you think so, Ellie. But you seem a bit tense.”

Ellie bit the insides of her lips, attempting to remain composed. “Dr. Morton, my situation’s different from the other girls.”

“I understand, but what have you gleaned in the short time you’ve been here?”

Ellie rubbed her sweating palms on the knees of her jeans. “I’m glad I wrote the letter to Father. Did you mail it?”

“Yes. Are you expecting him to call when he receives it?”

“Probably not.”

“How do you feel when your father doesn’t contact you?”

Ellie closed her eyes, knowing the discussion had to come up sooner or later. “I’ve become complacent about it. He sent me to boarding school after the accident. I was only eight. He’s always had contact with my caregivers--not necessarily with me.”

For over an hour, they talked—Ellie finding comfort in Dr. Morton’s easy-going approach. As the conversation continued, Ellie divulged more than she intended, especially when the conversation turned to Jesse, the storm, and the panther.

“While you’re here, make the most of the situation.”

“Everything here reminds me of Jesse and Gabby Mountain. I miss him and can’t stop thinking of him.”

“I’m sorry but your father left strict orders.” Dr. Morton’s voice trailed.

Ellie’s nostrils flared. “And he’s wrong. He won’t admit it or back down like other men. Do you know how I felt watching everything that happened with the Kesslers today?”

“How did you feel?”

“My whole life was being played out before me. I saw how kind and understanding their parents are. Seeing their mom reminded me how much I miss *my* mother. I know my circumstances would be different if she was here to defend me.”

“So many things ran through my mind while I sat with Hope--how her dad opposed her dating Ronald--the way her mom stood up for her. Her dad once said mean, hurtful things, but he apologized and admitted he was wrong. She made her own decision, and her family still supports her.”

“I see.” Dr. Morton nodded.

Ellie stared out the window. “I want to make my own

decisions without interference from Father. I want this to be my time and my season."

She turned back to Dr. Morton. "I want Jesse to take me away, the same way Ronald came for Hope."

"I understand." Dr. Morton rested her fingertips under her chin. "Find a quiet place--write what you're feeling. It'll be good therapy."

With notepad and pen, Ellie strolled through the laurel garden to the lake. Seated on a large rock, a few feet from the water's edge, she hugged her knees to her chest. The afternoon sun cast shimmering ribbons on the gentle waves. The breeze rippled through the budding leaves of the flowering trees, and the smell of wet earth brought back memories of crawling through the mud with Jesse. She laughed aloud, recalling how muddy she'd been--how Jesse hadn't minded how she looked.

The sun sank behind the tallest trees as Ellie started back toward the main building for dinner. She paused at the edge of the laurel garden and read the words she'd written aloud to herself--then folded the paper and stuffed it in her pocket.

~~~~~

Ellie went to the dining hall and took a seat between Dr. Morton and Juniper. "Hey, I saw you down by the lake. Is everything okay?" Juniper dipped her spoon into a steaming mug of broccoli cheddar soup.

"Needed quiet time." Ellie picked up the sandwich from the side of her plate--ham and cheese--another reminder of Jesse.

Dr. Morton leaned toward Ellie. "How did your writing go?"

"I started out writing a letter to Jesse, but it seems more like a poem."

"Like to share?" Dr. Morton lifted her brows.

"Share?" Ellie took a long sip of sweet tea. "I don't mind you seeing what I wrote, but I doubt it's anything to create a song from. Random thoughts. Nothing cohesive."

"Never underestimate. Beautiful arrangements start with one word."

Ellie sighed. "If you can arrange a song from this, I'll be pleasantly surprised."

"Let's meet in the Magnolia Room at 7:00. At least, I can hear you play the piano. I've heard nothing but rave reviews about how well you play."

Shortly before 7:00, Ellie arrived at the Magnolia Room.
~~~~~

While waiting for Dr. Morton, she played *In the Midst*, closing her eyes as her hands glided through the familiar chords. She looked up as Dr. Morton stepped beside her.

"You really play well. I don't think I've ever heard that song."

"Jesse sang it to me in the cabin--his mom wrote it."

"I love the stories behind songs. Sometimes words come at you and when put to music, they make perfect sense."

Ellie and Dr. Morton combed through the words scribbled on the folded paper. "Your song comes straight from your heart, but I'll give suggestions."

Together they created the melody line and determined the chord progression. Even in its earliest form, the song reflected her deepest thoughts. How she closed her eyes and thought of him as they walked hand in hand--the laughter, thoughts, and dreams they shared. How the thought of him was like a shelter from a storm.

"You've created a masterpiece. What's the title?"

"*Thinking of You.*" Ellie rubbed her hand against her heart.

"Will you play it for the girls?"

"I'd have to practice."

"How about Friday--your birthday." Dr. Morton gave a crisp nod.

A chill ran along Ellie's heartstrings. Should she tell Dr. Morton she had no intention of being here on Friday?

⅏23⅏

Escape

As the week wore on, Ellie practiced *Thinking of You*--believing she'd play it for Jesse—let the words show her heart's desire and not hide her feelings.

And she planned to leave. Would Juniper tell? Would Dr. Morton or Misty try to stop her? Above all, she had to decide what to do about her father and her fear he'd put her in a mental institute.

On Thursday morning, Misty called Ellie into her office. "Your father asked me to check the wound on your forehead. He's concerned it may leave a scar."

"What? Father called?"

Misty nodded. "Early this morning."

"Did he want to speak with me?"

"No, he said not to disturb you."

Ellie studied Misty's face, but her pleasant expression revealed nothing. "Did he mention any plans?"

"He said he'd be back in town this afternoon and will call you at 2:00."

Ellie felt as helpless as a leaf in the wind. She sat on a nearby couch and tried to get hold of her emotions. She'd meant every word she wrote in the letter, but would she be able to stand up to him?

Misty sat beside her. "Aren't you glad he called?"

"He confuses me--I want to hate him. Ecclesiastes even says there's a time to love and a time to hate."

"Oh Ellie, the Bible doesn't give you the right to hate--especially your father. The word *hate* shouldn't be taken in the absolute sense. You may hate what he's done--how he makes you feel, but it's not okay to hate another person." Misty's eyes locked on Ellie's.

"Then what should I do? He sends me away--one boarding school or facility after another. He's never been a part of my life." Ellie paused to wipe a tear. "He's only the man with the money and political power with no regard for how I feel or what I want. He doesn't even know who I am."

"God can intervene in this situation. He parted the Red Sea, and His people walked across on dry land. He can do miracles for you." Misty handed Ellie a tissue.

Ellie fumbled for the right words, "I need God to intervene, but I don't even go to church."

"Going to a church building is great, but God proved long ago He's not confined to a building. He'll be with you no matter where you are or what you're going through."

"What do I have to do to get a miracle from God?"

Misty leaned closer. "Forgiving your father would be a good place to start."

"I don't know if I can. He's done so much to hurt me." Ellie twisted the tissue around her hand.

"Forgiving someone doesn't mean you agree with them or what they did was okay. Your forgiveness releases you from the burden and allows God to work in both the other person's life and yours. Every time you think about something he's done to hurt you say, '*I choose to forgive my father*'."

"That simple?" Ellie's lips parted.

"Simple, though not always easy. Sometimes we have to say it through clenched teeth." Misty sighed. "Only God can right the wrongs. Exodus 14:14 says God will fight for you while you keep silent. All your battles belong to the Lord."

Ellie drew a deep breath. "There's a song I like to sing with the words *in my sorrows and trials Lord, oh be with me. In the midst of it all, I can hear You call.* Do you suppose it applies here?"

"I'm sure it does. Try to think of things that bring happiness, like a favorite song or memory."

Ellie left Misty's office—her mind a blur. During the morning activities, she rehearsed in her mind what to say to her father—but how forceful could she be?

After lunch, she was alone in the sitting area of the suite when Juniper came in. "What's eating at you? You've been acting kind of weird today."

Ellie moved over, making room for Juniper on the sofa beside her. "It's my father. He's coming back and will call me at 2:00. I've got one hour to decide if I'm going to speak with him."

"You're not about to scram, are you?"

"I wish, but I'm not twenty-one *yet*."

"But you will be in less than twenty-four hours."

"You're not going to tell anyone, are you?"

"Your secret's safe with me." Juniper propped her leg between them on the sofa.

"Maybe he's calling to say you can go free." Juniper made a laughing sound in her throat.

"He'd never say that." Ellie pinched the bridge of her nose and squinted.

"Beat him at his own game then," Juniper scoffed.

"You don't know my father. No one beats him at anything. I'm afraid he'll come for me before I get a chance to leave."

"The way I see it, if you refuse to take his call, he'll definitely come looking for you. Might as well outsmart him."

Ellie drew in her bottom lip. "How can I do that? He controls my every move."

"Want my advice--give him all the right answers. Tell him you love being here, and you want to stay forever. That way, he'll leave you here long enough to get away."

"Get away--that makes me sound like a criminal. I'd be double-dealing if I said I like it here, and he would know it." Ellie's shoulders slumped.

"Come on, Ellie. I'm not kidding. You won't be lying if you tell him how nice Dr. Morton and Misty are. Mention the beautiful grounds and your brilliant friend from New York City. That's all the truth."

Ellie sat straighter. "Juniper, you're a genius--worth a try."

"You got cell service up on the mountain. Are you going to hike up there and call your boyfriend?"

Ellie held out her palms. "I can't. My phone's dead and I can't find the charger."

"Too bad." Juniper grimaced, shifting her leg. "By the way, what are you going to do after you visit Jesse?"

"At first, I'll stay in a hotel in Franklin--then get an apartment."

"If things don't work out, I've got a grand scheme."

"What now?" Ellie leaned forward--elbows on her knees.

"Hear me out. My mom lives in Canada, and we can live with her. No one will come looking for you north of the border."

"Juniper, you're a comic. My father's a U.S. Senator—he'd find me."

"You have a car. We both have money. I'll leave with you and we can drive to California. Then, to New York City. Travel all over. Never slow down. We could write a book--make a movie. We'd be famous." Juniper flailed her arms.

"Right after I go on the road with the Kesslers. It's nice to have friends who want to take care of me."

The lively conversation continued with giggles and *what ifs*. For now, she had to make sure her father didn't come before her birthday.

Ellie waited in Misty's office. When the phone rang, she handed it to Ellie. "Hello, Father, I trust your trip went well."

"How have you been, Eloree?"

"Very well, thank you. This facility is beautiful, and Dr. Morton and Misty do a superb job with the music. I'm relating to them very well, and I have a new friend from New York City. Perhaps we can visit her next time we're there."

"I'm pleased you're doing well. Something's come up and I have to leave the country. I'll try to spend your birthday with you, but if not, I'll send a car for you when I return."

"I certainly don't mind staying here longer," Ellie tried to sound like her usual self.

"Very well, I trust you'll have a happy birthday. I've instructed Dr. Morton and her staff to throw a fine party for you if I'm not back in time."

"Thank you, Father. I appreciate your call."

The call was over--no *I love you* or a simple *goodbye*.

Ellie's face flushed, and her heart pounded in her temples. "Father's allowing me to stay here longer."

"Of course you'll be staying." Misty tucked a pen behind her ear. "You have a six-month reservation with the option to add additional six-month increments--up to two years. You'll be coming back here between surgeries."

Ellie rushed out the door and ran down the corridor to her suite. She locked the door and flung herself across the bed. Her mind was a blur of questions and her stomach ached.

Seconds seemed like hours--the veil of fear and anxiety threatened to smother her. She reached for the Bible, but the words on the pages looked like a jigsaw puzzle, except one verse circled with blue ink. *Jeremiah 29:11 For I know the plans I have for you...plans to prosper you and not to harm you...plans to give you hope and a future...*

She closed the Bible and pounded it with her fist. "God, how can this be Your plans for me? Father has no intentions except to harm me—no hope for my future. Why? Do something?" she raged.

A knock came at the door. Ellie ignored it, hoping whoever

it was would go away. The knock became louder, followed by a familiar voice. “Ellie, this is Dr. Morton. Are you okay?”

Ellie cracked the door. “I was resting.”

“May I come in?”

Ellie stepped aside even though she didn’t want to see anyone, not even Dr. Morton.

“Did the conversation with your father upset you?” Dr. Morton followed Ellie to the sofa.

“Somewhat. He told me he’ll be out of town on my birthday, and you’ll be throwing a party for me. I don’t want you to go to any trouble. Really, it’s just another day.” Ellie looked away.

“No, it’s not just another day.” Dr. Morton reached for her hand. “But I have something to ask.”

“Okay?” Ellie scratched her temple.

“We have a series of concerts in the Laurel Dome. I’d like you to be the featured performer at our next concert.”

“I can’t.” Ellie scrounged for words. “I haven’t had time to prepare or rehearse.”

“Before you give a definite answer, let me explain. You’re a confident and talented musician. I have no doubt you could be prepared in two weeks. You may invite family and friends as your honored guests.”

“I’m flattered you’d ask, but I don’t like to be the center of attention.”

“I understand, but this’ll be a smaller group than most of the gala events you’ve attended and less formal. You can wear whatever you like--even blue jeans depending on the theme you choose. As the featured performer, you choose the menu for the evening, which includes dinner for each guest.”

“I can’t make a commitment, right now.” Ellie dropped her gaze toward the floor.

Dr. Morton stood. “I’m sorry. I shouldn’t have sprung this on you so soon after speaking with your father. Promise me you’ll give it ample thought.”

“I will.” Ellie hoped the conversation was over.

“Besides, your father will be quite honored to have you perform. When Misty spoke with him this morning, she told him we were planning to approach you with the idea. He wholeheartedly agreed.” Dr. Morton beamed--seemingly pleased to include Ellie’s father in the decision.

When she left, Ellie leaned against the door, knowing there was little time to make plans. She sagged to the floor, pulling her knees to her chest. She had to come up with a plan that wouldn't fail—and she had to do it *soon*.

~~~~~

After another restless night, Ellie awoke at 6:00 on the morning of her birthday. She turned on a lamp instead of the overhead light and tiptoed about the room. She knew the doors were on an automatic locking system, and an alarm would sound if she attempted to leave before 7:00. Then she intended to steal away unnoticed, and no one would miss her until breakfast at 9:00. With a two-hour lead, she'd be in Franklin before anyone realized she was gone.

Her pulse pounded like hammers in her ears, and her clammy fingers trembled as she unlatched her bulky suitcase. She looked around, stunned--her laundry was gone. All her clothes were in the laundry bag, and housekeeping wouldn't return them until later in the morning. She'd have to wear the same clothes she wore the day before or relent to wearing one of the stuffy outfits in the closet.

She slid the suitcase back into the closet, opting to slip out the door with only an over-stuffed Navè and guitar case. Dressed and ready to go, she sat on the foot of the bed and listened as rain pelted the windowpanes, followed by claps of thunder that rattled the windows, and flashing bolts of lightning. Wind whipped through the trees--every sense in her body reacting in double time.

Before going to bed the night before, Ellie had written a note to Juniper, asking her not to tell anyone she had left unless they asked. And she was to give no details, only stating that Ellie would be in touch.

At 7:00, she slipped the note under Juniper's door. The storm had not let up but had intensified. Ellie peered out the window into the grayness of the morning and saw hail hitting the handrails of the porch. The tension in her stomach grew, but she had to go, *now*.

It'd be quite a chore to get out the door without making any noise. But with the overstuffed Navè on her shoulder and the guitar case in one hand, she opened the door, looking both ways down the corridor. With no sign of anyone else, she tiptoed through the commons area to the front door. The doorknob wouldn't turn. Her heart ripped. She grabbed it again, and this time it turned. Hidden in the shadows of the porch, she peered through the grayness of the dawn--no time to rethink this. She put her head down and ran through the torrent toward her truck.
~~~~~

The pouring rain and mud-soaked her clothes and boots. She ran harder, pushing against the wind--ignoring the hail that stung her face. As she fumbled to unlock the truck door, she saw headlights coming up the driveway. She crouched in front of the truck--out of sight. The rain and hail hitting the hood were deafening. She was too petrified to think. Her knees cramped, but not nearly as hard as the earthquake inside her. Water dripped into her eyes as she squinted to see where the car had gone. When the lights were no longer visible, she determined it had gone to the barn. Half-crawling, she managed to get the driver's door open.

She pushed sopping wet hair out of her face and felt a twinge of relief as the engine started, and the windshield wipers battled the downpour.

She wasn't exactly sure how to get back to Asheville. She drove down the winding country road, hoping she was going the right way. She clung to the wheel--eyes fixed on the road, like a robot. The windshield fogged up, and the defroster sent a blast of frigid air in her face. Cold. Wet. Scared. She couldn't go back now and drove on through the blinding rain.

She had no idea how slow she was going until an eighteen-wheeler passed on the left, jolting her truck with a deluge of water. Panic gripped her as she hung onto the wheel, not even seeing the road in front of her.

Mile after mile, semi-trucks and cars passed her. She didn't care. This was the right thing to do--that's all that mattered. The steady beat of the windshield wipers was her ally as the dirty water from passing vehicles hit the windshield. She turned the radio on. Static jumped from the speakers until finally, a station came through loud and clear.

"Good morning, listeners. Thank you for tuning in to Pillars of Power. Our message today is for all the young people who are facing milestones in their lives. This time of year, many of you are making major changes in your lives--graduating, planning careers, or getting married."

Ellie turned the volume up and hung on every word. It was as though the D.J. addressed her directly. He went on to say parents often think they know what's best for their grown children when they should let go and let God take charge of the direction of their lives. He spoke of the importance of faith and how Peter had to keep his eyes on Christ in order to walk on the water.

"Isaiah 40:29 says He gives strength to the weary and increases the power of the weak. Oftentimes, when we are facing a difficulty, it's easy to become weary, and trying to sort things out by our own strength can be exhausting. But we weren't meant to figure everything out. We were meant to trust and call on Jesus. Let Him be the hero of our story. Do you need power to stand in the midst of a storm? Call on your heavenly Father and He will hear you. Open your heart by faith and receive His strength and might. No matter what's going on in your life today, God is greater than any obstacle you may be facing. Let Him empower you to live in victory all the days of your life. This edition of Pillars of Power has been brought to you by Dr. Evan Butcher at Trinity Chiropractic."

The words sunk deep into Ellie's spirit and she felt more composed, especially since the rain tapered off. A sign up ahead read *Franklin 20 miles*. Before she breathed a sigh of relief, a chime rang--a light flashed on the dash--gas.

She pulled into the next store and parked at the gas pump-- having no idea how to pump her own fuel. She read the instructions at the pump and swiped her card. An error message came up. She grabbed her wallet, went into the store, and got in line.

The smell of coffee and freshly baked biscuits filled the air. Her stomach gnawed--from hunger, along with nerves. She reached for a bottle of orange juice from an ice-filled tub.

Then, her eyes fell on a jar with a picture of a little boy and a note--*Donations Pray for Jason in his fight against ALL.* Ellie had never seen anything like this—but she saw a few coins in the jar?

A tall man with dark hair and a beard stepped behind her. She cut her eyes at him. "Good morning." He smiled down at her.

She didn't answer--thinking he might recognize her.

"Excuse me." He reached around her and dropped a bill into the jar. "I can't stand to see those jars empty."

Ellie reached into her wallet and took out her last three dollars, dropping it into the jar.

She was next in line and put the orange juice on the counter.

"Will this be all?" the lady at the register asked.

"No, I'd like a biscuit and to purchase gasoline."

"Okay. What pump are you on?"

Ellie stared at her, not knowing the answer.

"Honey, what're you driving?"

"The blue truck."

"Do you want to pay in here or at the pump?" The lady asked.

"Here, please." Ellie handed her a card. The lady swiped it

and pushed some buttons on the register.

"Says the card's declined."

"Try this one," Ellie stammered, choking on her own breath.

"This one's no good either." The lady handed it back.

The sinking feeling threatened to suffocate her as she handed out three more cards--none worked.

The dark-haired man behind her stepped up. "This'll work." He put a one-hundred-dollar bill on the counter.

"No, I can't let you do that. I'm sure I have more cash." Ellie raked through her wallet, coming up with a sparse handful of change.

The man ignored her. "We'll take a sausage biscuit, orange juice, and a fill up for the blue truck. I'll take the rest of it in diesel on pump eight."

Ellie tried to hold back tears. Her voice quivered, "No, I can't let you--"

"Listen, Honey. I have a daughter about your same age. Sometimes she gets in predicaments--happens to everybody sooner or later. I'll bet your daddy would help her out, wouldn't he?"

Ellie couldn't speak as the man walked to her truck and pumped the fuel. The smell of the gasoline, coupled with the rush of emotions. She needed to pinch herself to see if this was really happening. "Sir, if you'll give me your information, I'll have my father reimburse you as soon as possible."

"No, I want to bless you. God has blessed me and my family."

"I'm grateful, but ..."

The man took her hand. "Honey, I'm going to pray for you. Whatever's troubling you is nothing in the sight of God. Trust Him." He opened the door for her. "Drive safe and be blessed."

Ellie reached for her seatbelt and turned the ignition. There was a peck on the window. The man smiled at her again. She opened the window. "Sir, I can never thank you enough. Please let me make arrangements to repay you."

"No, no. Here's twenty dollars. A young girl doesn't need to be out on the road without a little money."

"Only if you agree to let my father re-pay you. You've already generously bought my gasoline and breakfast."

"Your heavenly father will repay me, but your earthly father owes me nothing." He waved and stepped away.

Ellie watched as he made his way to his own truck. The

sign on the door read *Southern Professional Painting, David Jenkins, Robbinsville, NC.* Ellie waved to him as she pulled away. She knew who he was—he had no idea who she was. Yet God had come to her rescue.

꧁24꧂

Then

The sun broke through the lingering clouds as Ellie pulled up to Gabby Mountain Stables. She ran through the entry climbing partway up the ladder to the barn loft. "Jesse. It's me, Ellie," she yelled.

She ran to the corner of the barn and climbed onto the fence, looking for any sign of him in the pasture. Again, she yelled--the echo of her voice resounded, with only the horses appearing to notice. Nanta stopped grazing and trotted to the fence.

"Well, little girl. We've met before. Wish you could tell me where Jesse is." Ellie stroked the horse's neck. "Nanta, without you none of this would've happened."

She pulled a wad of grass and held it for Nanta to nibble from her hand. Nanta trotted away leaving Ellie alone with her thoughts. She heard the roar of the river in the distance, the birds' chirping, and the sounds of a horse's occasional stomp. She climbed the fence and started toward Saja and her babies on the far side of the pasture--but stopped when she heard a vehicle coming up the steep, winding road. She made out what appeared to be a tow truck--then watched as it backed up to her truck, and a burly man hooked a chain to the back of her truck.

She bolted across the pasture and climbed the fence. "Stop," she screamed—out of breath.

"This truck's been reported stolen."

"There's a huge misunderstanding." Ellie gasped. "That's *my* truck. It's *not* stolen."

The man pulled a yellow slip of paper out of his pocket. "Says a blue Ford Explorer Sport Trac 4x4, belonging to Senator Walton Evan, was reported stolen from Asheville early this morning. Suspect probably traveling to Gabby Mountain Stables."

Ellie's mouth fell open. Her father would stop at nothing.

The man lifted his hat and scratched his head. "Doing what I'm told. I guess Senator Evan wants this truck back awful bad."

"I'm getting my things." Ellie reached for the truck door.

"I'm not supposed to let you take anything out."

Ellie clutched the door handle. "That's *my* bag and *my* guitar. Please."

"Well, since it's Senator Evan's truck, go ahead." He turned his head, spitting a stream of tobacco across the gravel.

Ellie flung the door open and grabbed her Navè along with the guitar case and phone. Tears might come later, but for now, she felt like a book with no cover—the pages being ripped out.

Clinging to the Navè and guitar case, she watched as the tow truck's motor grew louder--and like a monster's hand, it hoisted her Sport Trac onto its back. Her little blue truck looked as helpless as she felt.

The man climbed into the cab of the tow truck. "I'm sorry, Miss. A man's got to do his job."

"Will you be talking to Senator Evan?" She stepped in his direction.

"No, I doubt it." The man leaned out the window.

"If you do, tell him he no longer has a daughter--I never want to see him again."

The man's mouth curved on one corner. "Looks like that old dog's got more than one enemy. I'll tell him if I see him."

Stunned, Ellie walked into the entry and sat on a bale of hay--her face in her hands. The cool damp spring breeze tousled her hair, strands clinging to her face in the tears. Feeling empty and overcome with uncertainty, she leaned against the wall as cold tears trickled down her neck. What now? No money. No truck. Nothing but a guitar she couldn't play and the clothes on her back.

Gr-howl... Mohan bounded into the entry, stopping short of knocking her off the hay bale. He darted through the entry--Ellie behind him. Then, she saw Jesse riding Tauga across the pasture, and she ran toward him.

"Ellie," Jesse called, and like a scene in a movie, he dismounted, swooped her off the ground with her arms locked around his neck. "I'm glad to see you."

"Me, too." She buried her face in his shoulder.

"We could be in a heap of trouble." He took her hand as they started toward the stable. "Anybody with you?"

"No, I drove my truck, but Father had it towed a few minutes ago."

"That's what I heard. I was working up on the ridge and heard a rig down here--got here as fast as I could. I've been worried sick. Did you get my message?

"Not for several hours. I tried to call you back, and while I was leaving a message, my phone died."

Jesse looked straight into her eyes. "Couldn't you have borrowed a phone?"

"No, Father tricked me into going to a facility where there was no cell phone service. Because of him, the staff wouldn't allow me to use their phone to call you. The next day I hiked up a mountain and got reception--until my phone died."

"What about Dr. Shanks?" Jesse furrowed his brow.

"She left the day after we came here."

"Does your dad know where you are?"

"I'm sure he does." She followed him toward the tack room. "I would've called you this morning, but my phone is still dead. I don't have a charger. Do you have one I can use?"

"Sure, in my office."

Ellie saw the distressing look on his face when he turned to lead Tauga into a stall. And her heart raced as he held the door to his office for her.

"Is this where everyone stayed during the storm?" She tried to keep the conversation alive.

"Yep." He turned to wash his hands in the sink. "I'll fix us some sandwiches. I haven't had dinner, have you?"

"Thanks. I'll freshen up." Ellie called as she stepped into the bathroom.

She patted her face with cool water and ran her fingers through her hair. She looked like a mess--hair disheveled, eyes red, make-up worn off—yet she knew her appearance wasn't what concerned him.

When she returned, he motioned for her to take a seat at a small wooden table--set with two paper plates, each with a ham and cheese sandwich, a bag of chips, and a can of Coke. He bowed his head and asked a blessing. Ellie didn't close her eyes but stared at him, praying Jesse wouldn't be angry with her, and pleading for God to help him understand.

Ellie took a sip of Coke and cleared her throat. She hardly ate, giving detailed accounts of every situation since she last saw him.

Jesse took a bite of the sandwich—then stopped chewing and stared at her. "I got a visit from the sheriff when I got back home from the Biltmore House." He pulled a folded envelope from his shirt pocket. "Did you have any idea I was going to get this?"

Ellie fumbled as she unfolded an envelope from her father's office. A check written to Jesse in the amount of ten thousand dollars fell out. She read aloud, "Enclosed is a contribution for your efforts in securing Eloree Evan's safety during the recent ordeal. Any further contact with Miss Evan must be submitted to Senator Evan's office in writing. Otherwise, all contact, including phone calls, text messages, and personal confrontations involving you or your family will be considered harassment and will be addressed in a court of law."

"I'm sorry. I never wanted to cause trouble for you. I'll leave if you want me to." Her voice quivered, as she stared at him.

"That's just it. I don't want you to leave."

Ellie's stare was intense. "I'm sorry--please try to understand."

"How do you think I felt when I went back up Gabby and came across everything that reminded me of you? Your clothes, the gloves you left on the rock at the top of the mountain, and the Mason jar by the spring. Mohan even went in the old barn and came back out with my hat that had your bloodstains on it. You may as well have written your name all over Gabby Mountain. This letter didn't get you out of my head."

"I do know how you felt. I have your Bible and this ruby as constant reminders." She pulled the stone from under her shirt.

"I can't fight what this letter says. Your father has the political power. I'm nothing in his eyes."

Ellie searched for words to combat the battle in her heart. "I'll tell Father I came here of my own accord, and I'll take full responsibility. Besides, the man I met at the gas station said he would pray for me, and whatever I'm going through is nothing God can't handle. Then, on the radio, I heard Philippians 4:13 I can do all things... "

Jesse broke in, "...through Christ who strengthens me. I know all those things are true, but we can't take on your father alone. David had to hear from God before he slung the stone at Goliath."

He reached across the table and took her hand, rubbing her knuckles with his thumb. "Go ahead and plug your phone up here. They've done lots of work on the cell towers since the storm, and we've got better service in the last few days. I can even use mine here in the office now. I guess Gustave's the last feller who had to climb in the barn loft to use one." Jesse half-chuckled as he got up from the table.

"Don't worry about Gustave." Ellie reached for the charger. "He's gone to visit his own family."

"Is there someone else coming for you?" Jesse's deep brown eyes widened.

"If they do--I'll refuse to leave. I'm twenty-one now, and I'll make my own decisions."

"I hope your plan works." Jesse shook his head. "Reckon if he's going to try to put me under the jail, I better hurry and get my work done."

"You're teasing." She forced a weak smile.

"Yeah--I do have some things I need to get done around the stable. You stay in here and charge your phone. Then we'll head to town and celebrate your birthday, *Cousin Ellie Mae.*"

~~~~~~

When Jesse came back, Ellie dashed toward him. "You'll never guess. My brother, Terrance, called to wish me a happy birthday."

"Did your dad put him up to it?"

"No, Father practically ostracized Terrance years ago--I used to wish they'd reconcile, but he doesn't cater to Father's demands."

"Did you tell him where you are?"

"Yes, and he didn't even know about the storm. But he said if we have any trouble, *whatsoever,* out of Father, I'm to contact him *immediately.*"

"How can your brother help if he doesn't talk to your dad?" Jesse scratched his head.

"Apparently they've spoken recently. Terrance says Father will be back in Asheville by Monday."

"Then what?" Jesse leaned against the wall.

"Terrance's coming to North Carolina when he finishes in New York and will have a long overdue talk with Father—and see me. He says Father's nonsense is getting ready to come to an end."

"What did Terrance say about the letter?"

"He said we should forget about it--just Father's typical scare tactic. It's not a legal document even though the sheriff delivered it."

Jesse stared at her. "Is Terrance okay with you being here?"
~~~~~~

"Yes, he said to tell you he appreciates you taking me in." Ellie paused. "Don't worry, Jesse. Terrance's on my side and always has been. Father's tried to keep us apart, but Terrance always finds a way to get in touch with me. Now that I'm twenty-one, he says he won't let Father force me to have the surgeries or send me to another facility."

"I don't know about all this, and I sure don't want to get mixed up in your family's personal business." Jesse scuffed his boot heel against the floor.

Ellie looked into his questioning brown eyes. "For the first time in my life, I'm convinced Father can't coerce me. Yes, he took away the truck, but his money is not what makes me happy."

"What does make you happy?" Jesse laid his arm around her shoulders.

Ellie tilted her head from side to side. "Celebrating my birthday with you."

~~~~~

"Well, Cousin Ellie Mae, you're now in downtown Franklin." Jesse pulled the truck into a parking space in front of the bank.

Ellie could tell the downtown probably hadn't changed much in several years. The storefronts reminded her of a quaint village with antique shops and art galleries.

"I need to go to the bank--then buy clothes."

Jesse opened the door for her. "Just like Jenna and Cindi—always needing a new outfit."

"I have to buy clothes." Her smile lessened to a straight line. "I didn't take time to wait for my laundry this morning. I only have what I'm wearing."

He held her hand as she slid off the seat and onto the sidewalk. "Let me buy you some clothes for your birthday."

Ellie stepped in front of him as they entered the bank. "No, I can't let you do that. I'm sure I can get money at this bank."

Jesse stayed back as Ellie conversed with the teller, but each account had been frozen. Finally, she turned and shoved her wallet back into the Navè.

"I'm appalled Father actually blocked *all* my accounts," Ellie held her head down as they left the bank.

"Don't let this spoil your birthday. I've got cash."

"Here I am like a beggar." She brushed away the tears that crept down her cheeks. "I've never been penniless before."

"There's no use for you to feel that way."
~~~~~

"That's easy for you to say. Your father's never treated you like this. My father's a villain."

"Let's get your mind off everything and buy something special for your birthday. It won't be a surprise since you're with me, but you can pick it out."

The bell above the door jingled as they walked into a quaint jewelry store. A middle-aged man behind the counter peered over wire-rimmed glasses. "Good to see you, Jesse."

"Hey, Doyle." Jesse nudged Ellie forward. "This is my friend, Ellie."

"Nice to meet you," Ellie said in a low tone, hardly making eye contact.

"I hear you two had quite an ordeal during that storm."

"Yeah, I don't know if I could've made it off Gabby Mountain in one piece without this young lady helping me."

Ellie smiled up at Jesse, hoping any mention of the storm would be dropped. She braced herself, assuming her father's name would come up, but Doyle continued the conversation, asking Jesse how all his family was doing. "I haven't seen your grandma in a while. Tell her I'm coming to see her soon."

"I'll sure tell her, but we'd like to look at some chains for necklaces. We need something pretty that'll be sturdy enough to hold this." Jesse pointed to the ruby.

Ellie blushed as she slipped the leather cord over her head and handed it to Jesse. He placed it on the counter, and Doyle brought out an assortment of chains.

Jesse nudged her elbow. "Which do you like best, Ellie? Yellow gold or white gold?"

Ellie rocked back on her heels. "I prefer white gold."

"Let's see how this one does." Doyle slid the ruby onto a glittering chain.

"What do you think?" Jesse held it up.

Ellie smiled. "It's perfect."

She held her hair up and Jesse placed it around her neck. "Beautiful," he whispered, leaning near her ear as he fastened the clasp.

"Thank you." Their eyes held for a lingering moment that spoke a thousand words without uttering a sound.

~~~~~

Jesse waited on a bench outside Callahan's Department Store and handed Ellie three one-hundred-dollar bills, and she took it, only after vowing to pay him back. "You don't need to
~~~~~

worry about paying me back," he told her. "It's a custom in our family for the ladies to go shopping on their birthdays."

After an hour, Ellie carried two bags from the store. "Thanks again, Jesse. I got jeans and tops for horseback riding. And I couldn't resist an adorable blue dress with matching sandals."

Jesse opened the truck door on Ellie's side. "You'll need a Sunday dress for church—it's homecoming"

Ellie shot a sidelong glance. "Meaning?"

He started the engine. "The day goes something like this. We go to the cemetery before services start and decorate the graves with flowers. Then, we go back to the church and listen to preaching. After that, we have dinner on the ground. Then, we go back in the church and listen to singing for a couple of hours."

"You'll have to tell me what to do. I haven't been to church since the accident. Mama used to take me as a child, but I don't remember much about it."

He squeezed her hand. "You'll be fine, just fine."

~~~~~

The next stop was Butcher's Steak House. Jesse gave his name to the host, and they joined the crowd of people waiting to be seated. From all the laughing and talking, it seemed everyone in Franklin knew each other. But Ellie stayed close to Jesse--hoping no one would recognize her, especially as Senator Evan's daughter. The very thought made her stomach quake.

"Ellie—Ellie." She looked around in astonishment as Hope Kessler barged through the crowd--Ronald by her side.

"Hope." Ellie's mouth fell open.

Amid the flurry of introductions and surprises, it turned out Ronald was Jesse's cousin. But Hope rambled--filling Ellie in on her plans to leave for Talladega. Ellie nodded in agreement--avoiding telling Hope what she'd done since they last talked.

When it was time for Jesse and Ellie to be seated, they invited Ronald and Hope to join them. Jesse took Ellie's hand as they wound among people laughing and talking. She wasn't used to brightly lit restaurants, with noise and commotion, and peanut hulls on the floor.

"Are you okay?" Jesse slid onto the bench beside her.

"Yes," she half-lied, feeling overwhelmed and claustrophobic.

Jesse and Ronald reached for the menus propped along the edge of the table, held up by an assortment of sauce bottles.
~~~~~

Jesse handed one to Ellie. “Order whatever you want. It’s your birthday, and we’re here to celebrate.”

Ellie relaxed as she became more engrossed listening to the conversation between Jesse and Ronald. For a fleeting moment, she felt like a different person--carefree and excited. And when Hope ordered a petite sirloin with a side salad and baked potato--Ellie ordered the same.

Before the steaks arrived at the table, Ronald asked the blessing. Ronald prayed almost the same blessing Jesse always did--then added another sentence, “God, thank you for bringing Hope back to me, and we ask your blessings on her family. Amen.”

A tear leaked from Hope’s eye and Ronald kissed her cheek. “I love you, Darling.”

“I love you, too.” Ellie watched as Hope rested her head on his shoulder, then said nothing for several minutes. Ellie knew she must be thinking about the decision she’d made. But Hope’s decision wasn’t like hers. Hope would still see her family. And Ellie knew her father might never want to see her again for rebelling against him. And even though she’d told herself it didn’t matter—inside she knew it did.

Ellie and Hope excused themselves from the table and went to the bathroom. As they washed their hands at the long sink Hope leaned closer to the mirror, dabbing smudges of mascara. “Crying always messes up my makeup. I think I’m doing okay then more tears come.”

Ellie’s eyes met Hope’s in the mirror. “I understand.”

Hope turned to her. “I know. There are no secrets with Juniper. That’s why I didn’t ask you what you were doing here. Juniper let it slip that you were going to leave Meadow Laurel and come to Franklin.”

“I trusted Juniper.” Ellie leaned against the wall, taking several deep breaths to regain her wits. “I didn’t even tell Dr. Morton.”

“Dr. Morton and Misty are great.” Hope ran her hands through her hair. “They didn’t tell me what to do but helped me find the courage to make the decision on my own.”

“How are your sisters?”

“Faith’s still taking it hard. Ronald and I eloped, so my family wouldn’t have to deal with a big wedding.”

“How’s Charity?”

“Better than ever, thanks to you. She was like a little bird, too afraid to fly until you pushed her out of the nest. We all have to be pushed out of the nest sooner or later.” Hope stepped aside for a lady to use the sink.

"For crying out loud," the lady shrieked. "You're one of the Kesslers. Which one are you?"

"Hope." She donned the same instant smile as her parents.

The lady grabbed Hope's hand. "You are even more beautiful in person than you are on television. My grandma has been awful sick. Would you pray for her?"

Hope nodded as the lady rambled on about her grandma's ailments. Ellie noticed Hope never appeared to be annoyed with the lady's ongoing chatter and seemed to be listening to every word.

As they started back to the booth, Hope explained, "The Kesslers are always on stage. Because we sing *about* God--people think we know something about Him they don't."

"How do you handle always being recognized?"

"Always smile." Hope flashed the instant smile, as they slid back into their places at the table.

Shortly after their steaks arrived, the lady from the bathroom appeared at their table with an elderly woman by her side. "Mamaw, this is one of the Kessler girls. She's going to pray for you."

The older woman extended a limp hand to Hope. "Thank you, Honey. I appreciate the prayers of your family." Before Hope could respond, the older woman turned to Ellie. "Are you Senator Evan's daughter?"

"Yes, Ma'am."

"You're a pretty girl. I'm glad you didn't get hurt bad in that storm."

"Thank you, Ma'am." Ellie smiled.

When the lady and the old woman had gone, Ronald leaned across the table. "Cousin Jesse, looks like we got ourselves a couple of celebrities. I remember how we used to tease you, saying you'd have to find a girlfriend up on Gabby Mountain."

"Now, let's see. You've been trying to get Hope since you were a kid. What took *you* so long?" Jesse shot a silly grin toward Ronald.

"Is that true?" Ellie laughed.

Hope and Ronald looked at each other and nodded. "It's true. I've been in love with Hope since I was three. My dad was their bus driver, and he took me on road trips. Hope sat and stared at me the whole time. That's why she's still *googly-eyed.*" He laughed, making a face at Hope.

"Stop it, Ronald. You're a nut." Hope playfully punched at

him. "Seriously, he's the only boyfriend I've ever had, and I'm his only girlfriend."

As the meal wound down, a troupe of servers marched through the restaurant singing 'Happy Birthday' and clapping. Ellie sat in disbelief when they stopped at their table with an enormous slice of chocolate cake and four forks.

"Go ahead, birthday girl. Make a wish and blow out the candle." Jesse chuckled.

With a sense of calm and ease, Ellie whiffed the candle out. She'd never been served a dish meant for four people to share. Timidly, she picked up one of the forks and scooped a dollop of frosting. The others followed until nothing, but fudge crumbs were left on the plate.

Jesse winked and gave her an easy nod--an ordinary birthday--one more step on the path to her new life.

ꕤ25ꕤ

Peace

The setting sun gave way to a purplish-gray night sky as Jesse turned up the tree-lined drive to his parents' house. The surreal feeling of everything that had happened in only one day left Ellie with a mix of emotions. "Are you sure your parents don't mind me staying with them? I intended to get a hotel room," her voice wavered as they made their way toward the front of the house.

"I'm sure--don't give it another thought. They understand the situation, and you can stay as long as you'd like." Jesse slipped his arm around her shoulders as they neared the front door. "I'm glad you're here. I missed you."

"I missed you, too." She looked up at him.

Jesse opened the door and Ellie walked in first. Her eyes adjusted to the brightly lit living room--filled with a brown leather sectional, family photos hung on the white walls, and a newspaper strewn beside a recliner. The lingering fragrance of potpourri and the ticking of a grandfather clock in the corner added to the hominess.

"Ellie, it's good to see you again." Jesse's dad shook her hand, placing his other hand on her shoulder.

"Nice to see you as well," Ellie stammered, looking into his face. He was tall, with friendly brown eyes like Jesse and dark hair like Jenna.

"Have a seat." He settled onto one end of the sofa, propping his sock-clad feet onto an ottoman. "I checked the weather--looks like it's going to be a good day for Jonathan and you to work in the Christmas trees tomorrow."

Jesse's mom dashed into the room, leaving an empty laundry basket beside the door. She hugged Ellie. "It's so good to see you. Can I get you something to drink?"

"No, thank you." Ellie felt quite self-conscious as she and Jesse walked to the couch.

"How about you, Jesse?"

"No, thanks. We went to Butcher's for Ellie's birthday. You'll never guess who we ate with--Ronald and his new bride."

"How about that." Dave pointed to the newspaper. "There's a full-page article about him in today's paper. Rookies, like him, cause quite a stir in NASCAR."

As the small talk turned to Ronald and Hope, the uneasiness of being Jesse's parents' houseguest hovered over Ellie. She wondered what they really thought and if they'd ask questions—she didn't want to answer.

"I never thought they'd marry. Last I heard, her daddy was dead set against it," Jesse's mom said.

"They actually eloped and Ronald's pretty pumped about going to Talladega." Jesse leaned back--brushing Ellie's arm. "Funny thing is Ellie and Hope had already met."

"We met at a music enrichment retreat." Ellie forced a smile.

"That must be quite a place. I can't imagine the Kesslers trying to improve their music. And Ellie, you're the most phenomenal pianist I've ever heard." Jesse's mom winked at her.

"Thank you." Ellie felt her ears turn red.

She tossed her short blonde hair. "Jesse says you'd like to teach piano and voice. You can start with me. I've always wanted to take formal lessons."

"I'd love to. That's a beautiful baby grand." Ellie tilted her head in the direction of the piano. "Jesse tells me you play quite well, and I love the song *In the Midst* that you wrote."

Darlene glanced toward Jesse. "That little tune has been with us in the midst of many storms, hasn't it, son?" She rambled on about the song, telling how Jesse and Jenna sang it in church and how people's lives were touched by hearing it.

Even though Jesse's parents welcomed her--Ellie knew they had to be somewhat uneasy with the situation. And she pondered whether she should say anything or wait until they asked.

Jesse's dad broke the ice. "Ellie, make yourself at home. Darlene and I know you've been through a lot--we're here to help you."

"And you're welcome to stay as long as you'd like." Ellie heard the sincerity in Darlene's voice.

"Thank you." Ellie swallowed hard, gathering her thoughts. "I'm sure you're wondering about my father. I haven't heard from him, but I did speak with Terrance, my brother. He's coming to North Carolina in a few days and intends to address my situation with Father."

Tears pooled in the corners of Ellie's eyes. Jesse took her hand. "It's okay, Ellie. You're going to be all right with us."

Jesse's dad leaned forward, resting his elbows on his knees. "Ellie, I know your dad's opinionated. We got to know each other *pretty* well the night of the storm, and there's one thing I do know about him. He loves you."

"Then why does he treat me like this?" Ellie's voice drowned in the sob she tried to hold back. "The last time I saw him, I told him I loved him--he ignored me."

A blanket of silence fell on the room. Finally, Dave spoke again, "Ellie, our family's been praying for you and your dad since the day you came to Gabby Mountain. God changes people and circumstances. Nothing is too big for Him."

"That's basically what David Jenkins, the man who bought my gas, said as well. I wanted to believe him, but then Father had my truck towed. Why is God allowing all this to happen to me?"

"Isaiah 55:8 says my thoughts are not your thoughts, neither are your ways my ways. We don't always understand what God's doing, but He's working on our behalf. Don't worry. If your dad comes here, I'll speak with him."

"He won't listen to anyone." Ellie's voice quivered. "I thought he listened to Dr. Shanks—but he didn't."

"I believe he'll listen to me. We earned a mutual respect during the storm. Sometimes men need to talk, daddy to daddy."

"Let's have a family devotional--the way we used to when the kids were all at home." Darlene moved next to Ellie and held her hand.

"How about Ecclesiastes 3?" Jesse reached for a guitar, beside the piano.

Dave opened the Bible and read the verses, as Jesse strummed *In the Midst*. Ellie closed her eyes and relished the words that mingled with the melody of the guitar. When Dave finished the passage, Darlene softly sang, "*In the midst of it all, I can hear you call...*"

Ellie joined in, then Jesse and Dave - singing the familiar tune. After the last verse, the four stood in a circle and held hands. "Let's pray." Dave bowed his head, "Heavenly Father, we praise You. We're thankful You know Ellie's needs. Give her courage to stand in the midst of it all and show her who she is in You. Lead her in Your will and remind her You're always with her. We thank You for bringing total peace and restoration to every circumstance in her life. In Jesus' holy name, Amen."

For a long, peaceful moment, the three wrapped their arms around Ellie and held her.

"What are your plans for tomorrow?" Darlene asked. "I'm going to Asheville. Want to come with me?"

"Thank you, but I'd rather stay here." Ellie glanced at Jesse.

"Mom, Ellie can go with Jonathan and me."

"She'll be bored watching you two work in the Christmas trees."

"If Ellie gets bored, she can talk to Mohan." Jesse grinned. "I better scoot along. Ma doesn't like me to come in too late when I stay with her. I'll see you bright and early in the morning, Ellie."

Darlene showed Ellie to a bedroom down the hall. "I see Jesse brought your things into Cindi's room. You'll be comfortable in here, and you have your own bathroom."

"Originally, I planned to get a hotel room, but Jesse insisted I stay with you. Are you sure Cindi won't mind me using her room?"

"Not at all. Cindi's my laidback child and keeps her room neat and orderly. Jenna's room always looks like a cyclone came through, but she seems to like it that way." Darlene fluffed the pillows and turned back the covers.

"When do you expect Jenna and Cindi home?"

Darlene took in a deep breath. "Not for a while. Dave and I are empty nesters. Jesse stays in his office at the stable or with Ma most of the time."

"I hope I'm not imposing. Thank you for allowing me to stay with you."

Darlene wrapped her arms around Ellie, the same way Dr. Shanks and Dr. Morton had. "You're precious and I'm glad you're with us."

"Thank you," Ellie said, as Darlene left the room.

UNC memorabilia, along with photographs, adorned the walls. Ellie strolled around the room, viewing athletic awards, academic honors, and pictures of family vacations. She wondered what it would be like to be part of a family like this.

Later, as she lay in bed, she prayed, "*God, You brought Cindi into this family and made a way for her. You've shown me how a dad should be. Please make my dad like the Kesslers'-accepting of changes. Make him like David Jenkins---understanding and giving. And make him like Dave--kind and considerate.*"

~~~~~

At sunrise the next morning, Jesse drove his old blue truck to the Christmas tree patch on Gabby Mountain. Ellie sat in the middle of the bench seat between Jonathan and him. As the truck lunged over rocks and ruts she held on to the dash--constantly sliding against Jesse. Each time she caught his eye, he flashed a smile. "Sorry, the ride's so rough, Ellie. This road nearly washed away during the storm. I'll work on it soon as I get caught up with the Christmas trees."

Jonathan shook his head. "With the patch of young trees getting wiped out by the storm, the Christmas trees won't be taking as long this year."

"I'm not worried about it. These trees are a whole lot of work for a little profit." Jesse stopped a few hundred feet from the cabin. "We'll have to walk the rest of the way. I cut a path through the mess of tree limbs, but this is as far as the truck can go."

"It's okay. I don't mind going to the Christmas tree patch with you." Ellie shrugged half-heartedly.

"Stay in the cabin while it's chilly. We've got to spray this patch, and I don't want you to be around the chemicals. I'll walk you on to the cabin, and Jonathan can get the spray ready."

Jesse took Ellie's hand as once again, he led her through downed tree branches and around rocks. "I'm glad you're leaving Mohan with me," Ellie said, as they stepped up on the porch. "I'm not sure I'm up to being alone today."

Jesse held the door open for her. "Mohan's not healed enough to turn him loose. You'll be good company for one another."

"Are you concerned he'll meet up with another panther?" Ellie's eyes grew wide.

"No, I haven't seen any tracks, and Mohan hasn't been acting spooked." Jesse knelt in front of the fireplace and lit a fire.

"I'm happy to be back on Gabby Mountain. Dr. Shanks recommended I come back here to gain closure."

"Are you going to be okay in here with just Mohan?"

"Yes, he's come to my aid more than once." Ellie stroked the dog's back.

"If you're sure about this, I'll get on out there with Jonathan. Stay in here with the door shut. You can see the Christmas tree patch from the kitchen window. If you need me, open the window and whistle through your fist"

"We'll be fine won't we, Wahya?" Ellie brushed her cheek against Mohan's head.
~~~~~

"I'll be back to check on you two in a little while." Jesse winked at Ellie as the door closed behind him.

She pulled a rocking chair closer to the fire and Mohan curled on the rug beside her. "You always do a fantastic job rescuing me, but today—I'll stay out of harm's way."

As the morning wore on, Ellie rocked, watching the flames lick at the logs until they became smoldering embers—soothed by the peaceful serenity. She tried to push the looming dilemma of her father out of her mind. The only way he could get to her—up here on the mountain—would be by helicopter. And since he owned a helicopter and would stop at nothing—she realized he might try it. But she wouldn't let that happen. If she heard a helicopter, she'd take Mohan and hid in the brush—like a fawn or red fox.

Her eye caught a glimpse of something brown on the mantle. *Her journal.* She jumped up from the rocking chair and opened it. The words that had poured from her heart hit like a log thrown on the fire. Jesse had no doubt found it and put it on the mantel. Had he read--*princess, handsome cowboy prince, happily ever after... fall in* love? Ellie struggled to breathe as she thumbed through the pages.

The hinge on the door rattled. "Hey, you two. Is Mohan keeping you good company?"

"*Err ... Yes.*"

"Is everything okay? You look upset." Jesse stepped closer.

"I... found... my... journal."

Jesse didn't say anything but blushed beet red and looked away as he rubbed Mohan's head.

"Did you read it?" She lowered her chin to her chest and peered up at him.

The moment hung in the air like heavy smoke. "Yes, and there's nothing in that book I don't feel, too." Their eyes locked.

"Jesse, bring me a bottle of water," Jonathan called from the porch.

"I've got to go now, but we'll be back for dinner in about an hour." Jesse touched her arm as he turned to go.

But she stood speechless and rigid.

For the rest of the morning, Ellie sat at the kitchen table, gazing out the window, watching Jesse as he worked. This was the first time such a feeling had come over her - an elation leaving her stomach dancing to the rhythm of her throbbing heart. She closed her eyes, rehearsing Jesse's words- *there's nothing in that book-- I don't feel, too.*

~~~~~

After lunch, Ellie went with Jesse and Jonathan to the Christmas tree patch near the top of the mountain. As he and Jonathan worked in the trees, Ellie and Mohan strolled to the big rock where she sat with Jesse the morning after the storm. She sat on the rock and hugged her knees to her chest. Mohan lazily stretched out in the warm sun, and she savored the peaceful stillness, the rumble of the river in the distance, and birds fluttering through the budding trees.

As the afternoon wore on, her mind rambled, and she wondered what life had been like for others who sat on this same rock. The legacy of Jesse's ancestors--Daisy Marie--who married the rich young man from Savannah and lived a refined life. Ruth and Naomi--who came to Gabby Mountain as seemingly destitute strangers who secretly had gold. The Cherokee--forced from their own land by *her* ancestor, Andrew Jackson.

Jesse climbed up the bank to where Ellie sat. "I hope you and Mohan are not too bored."

"Not at all. Quite the opposite. I was thinking about all your ancestors who sat on this very rock and gazed out over these same mountains."

He propped beside her. "I think about things like that, too. It leaves a lot to the imagination, doesn't it?"

"I have some words swirling around in my head. *Learning how to live in peaceful harmony ... helping those along the way ... that's how God wants us to be...*"

"Sounds like a song. Keep working on it, and we'll be finished in another hour. We want to get home in time to see the race."

"Race?" Ellie peered up at him, shielding her eyes from the sun.

"Ronald's racing at Talladega tonight, and it'll be on TV."

"Isn't racing really dangerous?"

"Of course, but what's bigger--fear or faith?" Jesse called over his shoulder as he started back toward the Christmas tree patch.

The question hovered in Ellie's mind. Aliyah faced the fears of going to Africa with faith. Hope faced her fears, with faith. And Ellie determined when she had to face Father again--her faith would be bigger than her fears.
~~~~~

ଛ26ଓ

Secluded Glade

"Well, Ellie are you ready to get off Gabby Mountain?" Jesse grinned, as Ellie climbed into the truck for the trek back to the stable.

"I love being up here--I understand why people like to ride horses and hike up here."

"All that'll be a thing of the past for a while." Jesse slid behind the wheel. "I've got a lot of work to do around the stables."

"What keeps you so busy?"

"Jesse is one of the busiest guys in this county. Between boarding and training horses, he barely has time to ride his own. Not to mention, he travels all over western North Carolina shoeing horses." Jonathan slid in beside Ellie and pulled the door shut. "You still thinking about hiring somebody to help you train all the high dollar horses you've got lined up?"

"Been giving it some serious thought." Jesse shifted the truck into gear. "How are you at training horses, Cousin Ellie Mae?"

"Are you kidding?" Ellie shrugged with a giggle. "I've never trained a horse."

"No, I'm not kidding. I need to hire somebody who understands horses, can talk to them when they get skittish, and sing to calm them down. It'd be mighty helpful if they liked to ride, too."

"When do I interview?" Ellie drummed her foot against the floor.

"How about as soon as we get to the stables? We'll see how well you do with a grooming brush. Little Elise hasn't had a good brushing all day, and that little sorrel filly needs some extra special attention from her namesake--Miss Eloree Elise."

"Be careful, Ellie. Jesse's trying to sugarcoat the deal. He'll con you into mucking stalls."

"Now Ellie, don't listen to Cousin Jonathan. He doesn't think cleaning stalls is much fun, but you might think it's a grand job."

Jesse winked at her and squeezed her hand.

~~~~~

While Jesse and Jonathan bustled about the stables, fed the horses and stalled them for the night, Ellie brushed Saja and the babies.

Jesse walked in and found Ellie with her head resting on Elise's neck. "Now, that'd make a pretty picture." He hooked his thumb through a belt loop. "Her coat's about the color of your hair. Nothing's prettier than a sorrel filly and her caretaker."

"I take that as a compliment."

"Meant to be one. Sorry, I had to work in the trees all day, but this was the only time Jonathan could help me."

"No need to apologize. I'm not going anywhere."

"I wish I could've taken off and spent the day with you. We'll ride Nanta and Tauga up to the falls after church tomorrow."

"I'd like that." Ellie frowned, pushing hair from her face.

"You okay?"

"I'm trying not to worry about what Father may do."

"I'm sorry you're going through all this, but I'm really glad you're here." Jesse took her hand, and they started out of the stable, across the gravel road to Ma's house. "Let's go see what Ma's fixed for supper. I'm getting hungry, aren't you?"

"Are you sure Ma doesn't mind us dropping in like this?"

Jesse laughed. "Of course, she doesn't mind. I practically live with her, and Jonathan's staying for a few days. Ma's always got plenty cooked and expecting somebody to eat it. If I was guessing, I'd say she's got cinnamon apples fixed for one particular little buddy of mine."

"Look here." Jesse pointed to a chicken potpie on the stove, along with cinnamon apples, and a note saying Ma had gone to a neighbor's house.

Jonathan found the race on TV, while Jesse filled plates, along with glasses of milk, and carried them to the living room. Ellie surveyed the scene and smiled to herself. Here she was with Jesse, eating in front of the TV—the way she had with Dr. Shanks.

"Ronald doesn't have a very good pole position. It'll be a miracle if he can pull a win out of this one," Jonathan said, as the
~~~~~

race got underway.

"Miracles happen every day. We've got to think positive. Right, Ellie Mae?" Jesse propped an ankle on his knee.

Miracles ... Ellie's mind wandered as she stared at the cars whizzing across the screen. Was it a *miracle* she and Jesse survived the storm? Was it a *miracle* she got away from Meadow Laurel before Father came?

Each time an announcer mentioned Ronald's name, Jesse and Jonathan yelled and Ellie clapped, not used to this kind of excitement. Throughout the entire race, Ronald's number 56 car zipped between other cars--passed some and barely missed others.

Ma came in and sat on the couch beside Ellie. "Are you *young'uns* watching Ronald race?"

"Yeah, Ma, and if Ronald keeps this up, he'll be cruising into victory lane in about fifteen more laps." Jonathan pointed out Ronald's car.

After a few minutes, Ma got up. "I can't stand to watch this. That boy knows better than to drive a car like a *Sputnik*."

"Don't worry, Ma. You know he's been training for this race since he was a kid."

"Maybe so, but it still scares me. I can't watch it. I'm going to feed the ducks."

"Have faith, Ma." Jesse patted her arm. "You know the power of life and death is in the tongue. Better speak life over your own kinfolks."

"Whoa--did you see him pass number 30?" Jonathan shouted. "Come on Ronald, don't let off now."

Jesse grasped Ellie's hand. "Go--go!" he yelled, as the number 30 car ran neck in neck with Ronald. "Look Ellie--Ronald's pulling ahead. Whoever gets across the finish line first wins."

Jesse pulled Ellie to her feet just seconds before Ronald soared over the finish line, only feet ahead of the other car. Victory lap--checkered flag. Ellie joined in the whoops and hoorays. Jesse lifted her off the floor in a flurry of thrills.

Then Ellie stepped closer to the TV and watched as Ronald climbed out of the car and embraced Hope amid the spectacle of cameras and reporters. The reporters crowded around them with a sea of microphones. Ronald spoke, giving details of the race, but concluded saying none of this would be possible without God.

~~~~~
~~~~~

On the way to Jesse's parents' house, Ellie asked, "Do you think it was a miracle Ronald won?"

"I reckon so. He's a rookie and this was his first big race. Even getting to race at Talladega is a miracle for a rookie."

"He mentioned God. How do people get a miracle from God?"

"The Bible says He will give you the desires of your heart and this has always been the desire of Ronald's heart. God gives miracles every day we don't even think about. But we just tend to dwell on the big miracles like Ronald winning his first NASCAR race."

"Do you think I'll get a miracle where Father's concerned?" Ellie asked as Jesse stopped in the driveway.

He crooked one arm over the steering wheel and took Ellie's hand with the other. "Some things are open-ended, and God doesn't always reveal His perfect plan until the exact moment we need it. Just like when the fellow bought gas for you. God didn't leave you stranded on the side of the road. He put you in the right place--at the right time for your need to be met. Faith is when you believe He'll meet your needs again."

"Do you think it was God's plan for me to leave Meadow Laurel and come here?"

Jesse squeezed her hand. "I'm sort of selfish--I want you here. But do you have peace with it?"

"Yes, but I still worry. It's like being a little pig and knowing the wolf's out there. But not knowing when or how he'll blow my house down."

"But God knows, and He's already arranged the solution."

Ellie looked away as tears trickled down her cheeks. "I wish I was courageous like Ronald, but instead I'm scared like Ma."

"Look, Ellie. Sometimes it's hard to recognize God's plan when you're in the midst of it. Let's take this situation one day at a time. Nothing's going to happen tomorrow. With it being homecoming, we're going to be at church most of the day. Then, we'll head out on Nanta and Tauga. Let's see what God does."

"I know you're right, but...," her voice trailed.

Jesse put his arm around her shoulders. "You are courageous like Ronald. Even though he had to come from behind, he didn't give up. I'm sure he wasn't thinking about where he *started* but where he was *going*. If he'd quit, he wouldn't have won. A miracle win is still a victory."

"I've never won anything. I wanted to train for the

Olympic Equestrian team. But Father only allowed me to ride with them one time."

"Then see yourself in victory lane. That's where God sees you. For right now, I better let you get on inside. It's past 11:00." He opened the door. "Dad and I have to get to church pretty early in the morning to help get everything set up. You come on later with Mama and Ma."

Ellie took a step and turned. "How can I ever thank you and your family?"

"Just being here is more than enough thanks." Jesse waved with a grin as he walked away.

Ellie's heart froze—for an instant, she was the luckiest girl in the world.

~~~~~

By ten the next morning, Ellie was perched in the backseat of Darlene's car—a box of flowers on the seat beside her and a hefty banana pudding cradled on her lap. She half-listened as Ma and Darlene discussed who had died since last year's homecoming and which cousins would attend today.

As they drove past the small, white church, Ellie spotted Jesse outside with a group of men. He waved but Darlene went on until they reached the cemetery. The thought of walking among the graves tied a knot in her stomach. She wanted to ask Darlene if she could wait in the car, but decided against it, knowing she and Ma needed help carrying the boxes of silk flowers.

Darlene handed Ellie a white wicker basket filled with silk roses. "If you see a grave without any flowers put one of these on it. It breaks my heart to see a grave without flowers."

"Does everyone always put out flowers on the same day?" Ellie asked as they started along the path leading toward the cemetery.

"It's a tradition to show respect for those who've gone on before us," Darlene added, kneeling to place a bunch of pink silk roses on a grave. "This is my grandmother's grave. I never met her, but I know I'll see her in heaven. It's nice to think about her today."

"Some of the people buried here don't have family close enough to come and put flowers on their graves." Ma squinted into the bright morning sun. "Even though I'm ninety years old, I still put flowers on my mama and daddy's graves. I couldn't stand it if I thought they wouldn't have any flowers."

Mama ... Mama ...where was her grave? Would anyone put
~~~~~

flowers on it? Ellie blinked back tears.

Ma and Darlene stopped to talk with a group of women, and Ellie was glad to be by herself. As she stooped to place a silk rose on the small grave, she heard a familiar voice, “Ellie.”

Ellie stood as Adrianna almost knocked her off her feet with a giggling hug. “I never expected to see you here. Who are you with?”

“Darlene.” Ellie pointed. “The lady in the pink dress.”

Adrianna brought her hand up to shade her face. “That’s Darlene Woods--Nana’s cousin.”

“I didn’t expect to see anyone I knew, today. Where’s Aliyah?” Ellie shifted the basket.

“She left for Nigeria earlier than we expected, and Aunt Sheila went with her. I’m here with Nanna.”

“I’m sure you’ll be excited to see them.”

“Yeah, they’re flying back today, and we’re picking them up at the airport this afternoon. We leave for Myrtle Beach next weekend.” Adrianna locked her arm through Ellie’s.

“Sounds like fun,” Ellie commented as they strolled to another grave.

“You should go with us. Nanna’s got a house rented for a whole week. We’ll have a blast riding every roller coaster on the Grand Strand.”

Ellie didn’t answer but stared at the ground.

“You do like roller coasters, don’t you?” Adrianna tilted her head to one side--silver bangle earrings resting against her cheek.

“Not really. I had a terrible experience on a roller coaster when I was a child. Thanks for inviting me anyway.”

Adrianna walked with Ellie through the cemetery, chattering about all the people who had come into Happy Hair Fashions and her plans for the summer.

When they arrived back at the church, Adrianna and Ellie helped Darlene and Ma carry the cooler and boxes filled with dishes. “Ma and I can finish up here. Ellie, you and Adrianna go help Sarah carry her things.”

With Sarah’s picnic boxes on the table beside Darlene’s, Adrianna and Ellie headed for the bathroom. As they stood at the sink washing their hands, Adrianna peered out the window. “See the three-story house up on the ridge? Well, my uncle’s building it for some rich dude. When I get rich, I’m going to build a big house in Myrtle Beach.”

“That’ll be nice.”

“Where’s your big house?” Adrianna ran her hands

through her hair.

Ellie waited before she answered. “I don’t have a big house.”

Adrianna’s jaw dropped. “Nanna says your daddy’s rich.”

“He is--I’m not.” Ellie wadded a paper towel and hurled it toward the garbage can.

“That doesn’t make sense. If your daddy’s rich, you should be rich, too.”

Ellie forced a wane smile. “Come on, Adrianna. Let’s go.”

~~~~~

Fried chicken, sweet potato casserole, green beans, and countless other delicacies and desserts filled the tables. Jesse and Ellie mounded their plates and sat in folding chairs along with his family. As kinfolks came by, Jesse introduced Ellie. Most simply said ‘hello’ and went on their way, but a few stopped to ponder--going as far as asking questions about the storm. Jesse handled the comments and, Ellie looked away, relieved no one mentioned her father.

After lunch, Jesse showed Ellie to a pew a few rows from the front. The music started before Darlene and Ma joined her. She kept her eyes on Jesse--his head was down as he strummed along with the piano and singers.

For another hour, the singing continued. One of the men leading the singing asked if anyone else had a song they felt led to share.

A girl, about Ellie’s age, stepped to the piano. “Pray for me,” she said. “This is my first time playing in church, and with God’s help I’ll play *Amazing Grace*.”

The congregation stood, took red hymnals from the backs of the pews, and sang along as the girl played. No one seemed to notice she hit the wrong keys or the timing was off. But as she finished, they clapped—several older men calling *Amen*. Maybe this is what it’d be like if Ellie accepted Dr. Morton’s invitation to lead a concert at Meadow Laurel.

~~~~~

By late afternoon, Jesse and Ellie began the trek to Bridal Veil Falls. Jesse assured her they’d stay on the path to the base of the falls—not go near the trailhead where she fell. Jesse and Tauga led the way--Ellie and Nanta followed close behind. As they rode across the pasture toward the river, the sound of the water pouring over the rocks grew louder and triggered a mix of emotions inside Ellie's head.

The trail narrowed, and Ellie got a glimpse of the falls. The sun glistened on sheets of water cascading over the rocks, creating the illusion of a bride's veil. Jesse dismounted and tied the horses to a sapling--then extended his elbow. "Mademoiselle Ellie, may I escort you to one of the most majestic places in this kingdom?"

"I'd be honored, Sir Jesse." She slipped her hand into the crook of his arm, and they walked to the river's edge.

"I thought you'd like to see the falls with the late afternoon sun shining on them." Jesse motioned Ellie to sit on a dry rock a few yards away from the river.

"It's beautiful." Ellie drew her knees to her chest.

"You okay?"

"Not really. This has been an unusual day."

"How's that?"

"First of all, going to the cemetery made me think about Mama. I want Father to tell me is where she's buried. I've never been to her grave, and I don't even know if anyone puts flowers on it." Ellie's chin quivered.

Jesse placed his arm around her shoulders. "I can't imagine how you must feel."

"That's not all." Ellie rubbed her hand along the edge of the rock. "Adrianna invited me to go to Myrtle Beach with her family. Father owns at least two resorts there. Other families go there to have fun but not mine."

"Do you want to go with Adrianna?"

"No, she's going to ride roller coasters. I had a horrible experience on a roller coaster and I never want to ride another one."

Jesse threw a stick into the swirling water. "What happened?"

"Father sent me to boarding school soon after the accident. All the kids went to an amusement park and got on a roller coaster. I'll never forget the feeling of being totally out of control. When it stopped, I was too frightened to get off or even say anything. Before I knew what was going on, it started up again. Just thinking about it petrifies me."

"Ellie, you don't have to ride another roller coaster. We all have things we're afraid of, and God doesn't want us to be controlled by fear."

"I'm overreacting, but everything's beginning to overwhelm me." She rested her head on his shoulder.

“I’m sorry. Is there anything I can do?”

“Thank you for understanding. I feel like one of those rocks jutting up--constantly bombarded by water.”

After a long silence, Jesse said, “I see what you mean. We have to be steadfast like the rocks when the problems of life come against us. We don’t always have the answer--but God does.”

“I have no way of knowing what Father will do next. I need an answer *now*.”

“Look up there.” Jesse pointed. “That’s an eagle. Wow, I haven’t seen one in years. Isaiah 40:31 says to wait on the Lord and He will renew your strength. You’ll mount up with wings as eagles, run, and not be weary, walk, and not faint.”

“I don’t know--.” Ellie lowered her head.

“Maybe the eagle’s God’s sign for you to be patient and wait for Him to give you strength to face whatever comes.”

27

Yesterday's Gone

The next morning Darlene dropped Ellie off at the stable on her way to work. She advised her to wear Cindi's old overalls, a flannel shirt, and to take a change of clothes. "Working at the stable can be mighty dirty work," she teased. "You might as well take these galoshes to wear over your good boots. If things get too messy, just hightail it to Ma's house. She's always glad to have company."

"I don't want to be treated like company. I'll help Jesse at the stables."

"You're the prettiest stable hand we've ever had around here. By the way, I love the ponytails on each side." Darlene laughed.

"Thanks." Ellie bounced out of the car. "Do I look like Ellie Mae Clampett?"

"Even cuter. I've got to run. See you this afternoon."

Ellie strode into the entry as Jesse came around the corner, carrying a bale of hay. "Well, look at you. If I didn't know better, I'd say you came to work expecting to muck a few stalls."

"I'm ready. What do you want me to do first, Boss?" She shoved her hands into the pockets of the overalls.

Jesse shook his head. "If you're sure you're up to this kind of work, put your bag in my office. Then, put the galoshes on. Start by grooming Saja and brushing the babies."

"This is my first job, you know. Are you going to teach me how to train a horse?"

"Sure am. Next week, Makayla, one of Jenna's friends, is bringing her Thoroughbred for us to train. Now that's a high dollar horse. He's in the same bloodline as Secretariat."

"What will I do with him?"

"Same thing you'll be doing with all the others. Around

here, we treat all horses--." Jesse stopped, turning his attention toward the road. "Who in the world just drove up?"

Ellie took a few steps and peered closer. "That's my truck that was towed." She grabbed Jesse's arm.

"Terrance," she called when he stepped out of the truck.

Seeing Ellie and Jesse in the entry of the stables, Terrance waved and motioned for his passenger to get out.

"Who's the lady with him?"

"Dr. Morton," Ellie gasped, too stunned to say anything more as the two came closer.

"Hey, birthday girl. Aren't you glad to see your brother? I came all the way from New York City to get a hug from my twenty-one-year-old sister." He placed his arm around her shoulder--extending the other hand toward Jesse. "Terrance Evan, Eloree's brother."

"Jesse Woods."

Dr. Morton stepped forward. "Hi, Ellie. Hope you don't mind that I came along." She turned to Jesse, "You must be Jesse. Ellie's told me so much about you. I'm Stephanie Morton."

"Pleased to meet you, Dr. Morton." Jesse nodded, accepting her handshake.

"I don't want to go back to Meadow Laurel." Ellie stared hard at Dr. Morton.

"I'm not here to ask you to come back. Of course, you're welcome to, but I understand the situation you were in."

"Somebody tell me what's going on. How do you two know each other? Where's Father?" Ellie felt herself losing control as she wiped her sweaty palms on the legs of the overalls.

"No need for alarm." Terrance stepped back, "Remember when I called you on your birthday, and I told you we'd get things straightened out with Father?"

"Yes, but he's not here. What's he going to do?" Ellie gulped, taking a seat on a hay bale.

Terrance sat beside her and took her hand. "Father's had a change of heart. Hasn't he, Stephanie?"

Dr. Morton nodded. "Your father and Terrance met with me for several hours yesterday. We made great progress."

"How?" Ellie's mouth tightened into a line.

"I managed to leave New York sooner than expected, and Dad met me at Meadow Laurel. Dr. Morton compared her findings to those of Dr. Shanks."

"What's Father going to do to me? Is he going to deceive me into going into another facility? Disown me? Force me to have surgery?" Her eyes darted from Terrance to Dr. Morton.

Dr. Morton patted her hand. "I understand why you're asking these questions, but none of those things are going to happen."

"That's right, Ellie. A lot's happened since you left Meadow Laurel. In fact, a lot has happened since the storm." Terrance turned to Jesse. "I understand the two of you went through quite an ordeal. Thank you, I appreciate all you and your family have done for my sister."

Jesse nodded. "Ellie's a courageous girl."

"Yes, *she is*," Terrance agreed.

"Enough small talk, Terrance. What's going on? I don't understand, and this is making me nervous." Her voice rose.

"Ellie, I need you to think about something before you answer. Dad has some things to discuss with you, but he doesn't quite know how to go about reaching out to you. That's why Stephanie and I came on ahead. I wanted to speak with you before Dad gets here to let you know things are getting ready to change in our family."

"What? He's coming here?"

"Yes, he and Captain Jim will be here by helicopter within the hour."

Ellie closed her eyes and took a deep breath. "Why do you keep referring to Father as *Dad*?"

Terrance's smile widened. "It was on your wish list. He's agreed to be called *Dad*."

"You don't know him as well as I do," Ellie scoffed, clenching her teeth.

"Let's think about this from a realistic standpoint." Terrance cleared his throat. "Granted, he's made mistakes, but he's willing to make amends with both of us."

Ellie stared at her feet, with the toes of the galoshes digging into the dirt.

Dr. Morton intervened. "Ellie, your dad realizes the treatments he's sought for you haven't worked. Since the storm, you've been vocal in letting him know where you stand."

"He hasn't listened to anything I've said--or Dr. Shanks. He pretended to go along with her—then ignored it all. I can't trust him." Ellie clenched her fists.

A sly grin crossed Terrance's face. "Aw, but you're mistaken. You showed him you're every bit as savvy as he is. He wasn't ready to find out that his little girl is a chip off the old block. It worked, didn't it Stephanie?"

"Yes, Ellie. Your brother's right. Your father was quite taken aback by your list. Then, the letter you wrote to him--" Dr.

Morton's smile became a tight line.

"He realized he'd lost you when you didn't come back or even call for help." Terrance paused. "Everything won't change overnight, but we have to start somewhere."

"What about my endowment? If it means going back to him—*he-can-have-it*," Ellie sneered. "But he can't own me."

"It automatically transferred to an account in your name, *only*. All you have to do is sign, agreeing to claim it."

"I hear the helicopter coming now. Should Captain Jim land or turn and go back to Asheville?"

Ellie held her breath, narrowing her eyes to fight the tears streaming onto her cheeks. "Land ..." she whispered.

The four stepped outside as the helicopter set down a few hundred feet from the stable. As her father walked toward the group, Ellie's heart pounded like a waterfall on jutting rocks. Terrance and Dr. Morton went to meet him, talking briefly before making their way to where Ellie and Jesse waited.

Ellie looked up at Jesse, her face pale. "I'm scared of this roller coaster."

Jesse squeezed her hand. "Terrance and Dr. Morton seem to think everything's going to be okay. Give it a chance."

"Father's devious. Promise you'll stay by my side."

"I promise." Jesse let go of her hand as the trio approached.

"Good morning, Eloree. Jesse." Her Father's glaring gaze went from her toes to her head. "I see you've been keeping yourself occupied."

Ellie stood speechless and Jesse nodded. "Good morning, Senator."

"Well, Eloree--your brother and Dr. Morton have told you I have some matters to discuss with you." He stepped closer to Ellie. "I've reinstated all your accounts and am returning your vehicle, so finances will no longer be an issue."

Ellie stepped back and crossed her arms.

"I've discussed your present situation with Dr. Morton and her staff. They compared their recent evaluations with those of Dr. Shanks, and I've decided you're to stay in the Franklin area. I'll make arrangements to purchase a condo for you, along with a music studio."

Ellie stared at him. "That won't be necessary."

He looked at her from the corner of his eye. "I don't understand. I thought you wanted a music studio, and you need a place to live."

"I've changed my mind."

"See how obstinate she is. She's been determined to defy me ever since the storm." Her father's nostrils flared. "This conversation will have to wait for another time. She's in no mindset to listen to anything I have to say."

"Dad, drop the professional tone." Terrance stepped in his direction. "Ellie's been through so much deception and disappointment. Speak to her like she's your child. You owe her an apology."

Her father turned his back as if he might walk away. After a long silence, he turned to Ellie. "Very well. I apologize, but I've always done what I deemed best for you, even though your brother sorely disagrees."

"Dr. Morton and I came here with you to make things right and answer the questions Ellie has. We had our discussions yesterday. Today is about *your* daughter and *my* sister. If we're ever going to be a family, we need to reconcile--*now*."

Ellie couldn't believe what was happening. Would Terrance and her father have harsh words? Would Dr. Morton keep the peace?

Finally, Dr. Morton spoke up. "From discussions I've had with Ellie, she'd like explanations about your demands that are out of the ordinary for a girl her age. For example--the way she's been expected to dress and wear her hair."

"Dad, do you choose to speak with Ellie about these issues?" Terrance's voice was unusually calm. "She has every right to know."

Again, her father stepped back from the group, his gaze fixed on the helicopter. "I should go check in with Captain Jim."

Terrance put his hand on his dad's shoulder. "This is no time for you to leave."

"Then tell your sister what you may."

Terrance began, "Ellie, as you've grown up, you look more and more like Mom. Dad has tried to preserve her memory by having you dress the way a lady her age would dress and keep your hair long, the way Mom always wore hers. I know that may be hard for you to understand, but controlling you was his way of coping, even though it wasn't fair to you."

"This makes no sense. Why does he insist I have the facial surgery, even though I don't want it?" She collected strength to speak, with tears streaming down her cheeks.

Her father looked from Terrance to Dr. Morton and back to her. "I've never allowed the accident to be discussed because it's been the hardest thing I've ever had to deal with. What happened to your mother was bad enough, but the scar on your face is a constant reminder of what *I* did to you," he paused. "Terrance, Eloree--I was driving the car the night of the accident. Not your mother. The accident was my fault. I walked away physically unscathed, but--."

"I always thought so." Terrance interrupted. "Mom never drove when you were in the car. It made no sense to me when the newspapers said she was driving, and a drunk driver caused the accident."

"I'm sorry. I thought it best to leave well enough alone, but I've had to deal with the guilt all these years. I was the drunk driver. Had I divulged the information, my political career would have been over."

Terrance clenched his jaw as his father turned to walk away. "No, come back here, Father. If you don't face Ellie, I'll tell her everything myself. She deserves to know where Mother is."

"Where Mother is?" Ellie gasped, her emotions running rampant. She stood in shock, clinging to Jesse's arm. Dr. Morton took Ellie's hand and guided her to a bale of hay. Ellie sat numbly. Jesse put his hand on her shoulder.

"Ellie, everything is going to be okay. I'm here for you," Dr. Morton said.

Terrance turned to face his father. "Sir, do you tell her, or do I?"

Her father sat on a bale of hay facing her as he leaned forward, elbows on his knees. "Eloree, I've considered telling you, but the time was never right. For instance, I planned to have this talk with you on Easter at the mountain home with Dr. Shanks, but of course, the storm came, and our circumstances changed. She felt the Easter holiday was an appropriate time to address the situation since the accident happened on Easter. Again, I was planning to divulge this information to you on your twenty-first birthday, but of course, those plans didn't work out either." He stopped, looked to Terrance--then back to Ellie. He lowered his head.

Terrance placed his hand on his father's back. "Ellie, Mother was injured very, very badly in the accident. You and I were told she was gone. I later figured out she was alive, but Father felt there was no reason to tell you. He and I have disagreed about this for years."

Ellie gasped, her hand flew to her mouth--not able to utter a sound.

Her father began again, "You were very young and had accepted the fact she wasn't coming back. She's been in a coma for the past thirteen-."

"How could you?" Ellie's shriek interrupted scoffing first at her father, then Terrance.

"The doctors always say she could go at any moment. I wanted to spare you the agony of having to lose her twice."

Silence enveloped the group for moments that felt like an eternity. Without saying another word, Ellie stood, grabbed Jesse's hand, and darted into Saja's stall. She grabbed a grooming brush, feverishly raking it across Saja's back. Jesse stepped closer and placed his hand on the brush. "Ellie, Saja can wait."

She laid her head against Saja's back. "They're lying to me. None of this is true."

"It's okay, Ellie. I'm right here." He placed his hand on her shoulder. "Let's sit down over here."

Jesse led her to a wooden bench where they sat in absolute silence. He slipped his arm around her shoulders--her head on his shoulder. "I feel like I'm the little girl stuck on the roller coaster," she breathed, after several minutes. "I close my eyes and I see the broken chocolate bunny and the crushed purple bow on the Easter basket. I screamed for Mama, but she didn't answer. I heard sirens and saw bright lights, but I couldn't see Mama."

"I'm sorry." He stroked her shoulder with his fingertips.

Tears soaked into Jesse's shirt as Ellie sobbed her heart out.

The stable door opened. "May Terrance and I come in?" She heard Dr. Morton's voice.

"Yes, but not Father," Ellie breathed.

Dr. Morton knelt beside Ellie. "Honey, you can take all the time you need, but I'm here for ..." Her words were interrupted as Mohan sidled through the open stall door, finding his way to Ellie and thrusting his head into her lap.

"Do you want me to shoo him out?" Jesse asked.

"No, I need him here," she whispered, focusing on her hand as she rubbed the dog's ears.

"I understand your frustration, but there's more to be said. Will you let me explain?" Terrance moved to the bench beside her.

"I feel so confused already. I'm not sure I can bear to hear any more."

"Ellie, let's see what Terrance has to say," Jesse suggested.

"When Father disappears, and you don't hear from him for days--he goes to see Mom. He spends lots of time with her--even though she doesn't even know he's there."

"What do you mean?"

"Even though she's in a coma, Father's never given up hope one day she'll wake up and we'll all be fine. He's done everything in his power to provide for her and spend time with her, but he can't control her circumstances. On the other hand, he's neglected you, leaving your care to others. That's why he's so controlling of you."

"It's not fair. Father and you get to spend time with her and I don't." She jumped up—hands on her hips.

"I've never agreed with his decision, but this was his way of protecting you from the pain of having to see Mom this way."

"I want to see her. Where is she?"

"Father has a house in Myrtle Beach that's set up as a hospital with a staff of doctors and nurses who care for her around the clock."

"Myrtle Beach?"

"Mom always loved the beach. Father thought she'd be more likely to wake up if she was near the ocean."

Ellie leaned her head against the wall and closed her eyes. "I don't think I can live another day if I don't get to see her. Take me there."

"How long will it take you to get ready?"

"All I have to do is change. I want Jesse and Dr. Morton to come, too."

"Yes, Ellie I'll go with you," Jesse said. "I need to get changed, too."

"Capt. Jim is waiting. With Dad at the helm as First Officer, we should get there in about an hour and a half," Terrance wrapped his arms around her. "I love you, little sister, and I've waited all these years to tell you."

"I love you too, but why didn't you tell me sooner?" she murmured--her face burrowed against his shoulder.

"I've wanted to a million times, but if I had gone against Father's wishes to that extent, he would've made life even harder for us by keeping me totally away from you. The way things were, I at least got to see you."

Ellie saw her father seated on the bale of hay--his head down. "Is Dad praying?"

"I don't know. He turned bitter toward God when Mom didn't wake up after the accident. He seems to think he can bargain with God. Hopefully, getting all this out in the open will help him have peace with the situation." Terrance held her tighter. "Let's try not be too hard on him."

"I need peace, too," Ellie moaned, gripping his shirtsleeves in her clenched hands.

Terrance prayed, “God, I ask You to give my sister peace that passes all understanding. Help her heart to see things as true and pure. To think on this as a good report and give You praise in the midst of it all.”

ꕥ28ꕥ

Living with a Broken Heart

The helicopter trip seemed an eternity to Ellie. The hum of the engines mingled with the thoughts whirling around in her head. She was glad her dad was in the cockpit with Capt. Jim--she wasn't ready to face him. Usually, she enjoyed helicopter trips, but today she stared idly out the window, engulfed in her own thoughts.

Jesse clasped both of his hands around her smaller one, and each time she glanced at him, he smiled. There was little he could say or do except be by her side. Finally, Ellie turned to him. "Jesse, I'm sorry. I don't mean to be ignoring you. I'm trying to sort through this and I feel frozen in time."

"It's okay. I'm glad I'm here with you."

Ellie dug through her Navè, coming up with an iPod and headphones. "Terrance, Dr. Morton, I need to listen to music. It helps me clear my head."

"That's understandable." Terrance raised the top of a cooler compartment and offered bottles of water.

Ellie took a bottle, but barely sipped it--instead, she rested her head against the back of the seat and stared ahead. Even with the earbuds, she heard Terrance and Dr. Morton making small talk with Jesse, commenting about the horses and the impact of the storm. Her mind wandered, clouded with layers of questions. Her hand dabbed at first one eye, and then the other as tears forced their way down her cheeks.

"Mind if I sit by you?" Terrance moved next to Ellie.

Ellie removed the earphones and turned the iPod off. "I'm okay. I was just listening to one of Patrick Lee Hebert's songs, *Living with a Broken Heart*. That's me, Terrance. I've been living with a broken heart ever since the accident."

"I know. I've lived with a broken heart, too."

Ellie stared at him, her brow drawn tight. "You don't seem upset. You're acting as if nothing happened."

He placed his arm around her shoulders. "I see where you're coming from. But I've wrestled with this for thirteen years--wanting nothing more than to tell you. For that reason, I'm grateful for this day. It doesn't matter if we spend the day laughing or crying. Eventually, we'll get the peace we need to be a family again."

"How does this make you feel, Ellie?" Dr. Morton asked with her usual smile and soft voice.

Ellie's eyes tightened, and she stared back at her. She'd come to trust and respect Dr. Morton—more like a friend than a doctor. "I'm having a tough time pinpointing anything but fear."

"Fear's a natural reaction to things we haven't experienced yet. But fear isn't always a terrible thing. Sometimes conquering fear means having a deeper understanding of what we're facing."

Jesse reached for Ellie's hand. "Ellie, you and I made it through some fearful situations we had no control over. Do you remember how we called on the name of Jesus when the storm hit the cabin? There was nothing else either of us could do, but He brought us through. Little did we know He was preparing us to face something more."

Terrance leaned around Ellie and extended his hand to Jesse. Their hands were almost in her lap, and she fixed her eyes on their clenched fingers as their knuckles turned white. Neither said anything at first, and Ellie saw tears well up in Terrance's eyes.

"Thank you. What more can I say to the man who saved my sister's life? Who would've ever imagined she'd be caught out in a storm or come face to face with a wild animal? I'll always be grateful to you." Terrance released his grip of Jesse's hand.

"I know you're proud of Ellie--you have every right to be. She's tougher than a pine knot, as country folk say." Jesse flashed a boyish grin.

Ellie cut her eyes at him. "Do you really mean that, or do you just say it to try and make me laugh?"

"I mean it." Jesse leaned forward. "Even with a cut on your head and a sprained ankle, you were a trooper getting off the mountain. Little did we know we'd both be faced with the panther. I should never have left you alone, even for one minute, but God had it all in control. He knew how every second would play out--right down to the instant I pulled the trigger. That was God's hand on us. He proved to both of us He's bigger than any of our fears."

"As horrifying as the experience was, it set you on the road to recovery in other areas of your life." Dr. Morton placed her hand on Ellie's arm. "Even though the fears you may be feeling today are different in some respects--dealing with them can open avenues for more healing."

"Terrance, are you ever afraid?" Ellie asked with an anxious tone.

"Of course--everyone is." He sat straighter. "I was riddled with fear after the accident. That's when Dad and I began to have major disagreements."

"Disagreements about me, right?"

"Not entirely. Even though I was eighteen, I wasn't very grown up when the accident happened. Suddenly, all my plans for the future didn't mean much anymore."

"You went away to college." Ellie pursed her lips as if she didn't quite understand.

"What a mess. From the time I first left for boarding school at eleven, until the accident, Dad had my future all mapped out. I would go to the military academy, serve in the Air Force as he had, then step into the political arena. After the accident, I couldn't do things his way."

Ellie's crossed her arms. "I get angry when he says unkind things about you. He's so unfair."

"Now, now." Terrance propped on the edge of the seat. "We don't need any more contention. Today's the day we lay it all aside and move forward. We can't change the past--so let it go."

"That sounds simple, but how do you let something go that's been so painful?"

Dr. Morton cleared her throat. "We have to realize God's the only one who can fix things in our lives--even though we try to fix them ourselves. Instead of reacting on impulse--we say, 'God, I give this to You. You take care of it for me.' And each time you're tempted to pick it back up, give it back to Him."

"Are you saying we don't have to confront Father with all the things that have happened in the past?"

Dr. Morton shook her head. "You don't have to bring up everything. Forgiveness is the key to moving forward--bring peace and harmony, to make us stronger. The grudges we hold hurt us much more than the other person."

"Father's done so many hurtful things not only to Terrance and me but to others as well. Jesse's family saw this during the storm." Ellie's eyes widened as she peered up at Jesse.

"Those are his issues, not yours." Jesse shook his head.

"When somebody's hurting--they hurt other people."

"That would be Dad, but he tries to control situations and people with power and money." Terrance's face tightened.

"He always told me he never gave you money because you defied him--and if I ever did it, he'd do the same to me." Ellie drew in her bottom lip.

"I didn't need his money. The family fortune was Mom's, to begin with, and she gave me an endowment on my eighteenth birthday. Dad couldn't take it away from me or control me with it."

"Why did I have to be twenty-one to get my endowment?"

"Father had yours changed after the accident. But I already had mine."

"I see." Ellie's stare lingered on Terrance's face. "What did you do with yours?"

"For a couple of years, I did whatever I wanted and dared him to stop me. He wanted me to stay out of the media, not drawing any negative attention to spoil his political agenda. Finally, I decided to stay in the UK and I met a group of Christian friends, enrolled in college, and studied archeology."

"Father didn't want you to become an archeologist, did he?"

"No, but I had to do what was best for me. I realize Dad didn't exactly get to plan his life--volunteering for the Air Force and going to Vietnam right out of high school. He became a military helicopter pilot, and helicopters are his passion. Digging for ancient ruins is mine and music is yours. We can't become what someone else wants us to be."

Ellie thought for a few moments. "Why did he volunteer to go to war?"

Terrance shifted his gaze and drew a deep breath. "He won't talk about his past, and I know he still harbors bitterness for the way he grew up. His mother left him with his uncle when he was about ten. He had to work on a dairy farm, and his uncle was hard on him. His mom came to visit on his eighteenth birthday. He hadn't seen her in years and she had another son. The bitterness and anger got the best of him, and he joined the military."

"That would've been heartbreaking. Did he ever see his mom or his brother again?" Ellie brought her hand to her throat.

"His mom died while he was in Vietnam. And Dad doesn't have much contact with any of his family. Now that things are getting out in the open with you--he'll see things differently."

"Maybe this's another reason he's so controlling of me. I

simply want to make decisions on my own and be an ordinary person."

"Well young lady, you certainly blew him away. He thought he would always control you to the extent you'd never turn away from him. That's why he didn't push you to go to college. He was afraid you'd turn out rebellious like me." Terrance chuckled. "He sure didn't know what to make of the fact you decided to become your own person. Why--you've even found God."

Ellie smiled at his light-hearted attempt to make her laugh. "Do you suppose Dad will ever find God?"

"I'm going to speak on faith and say he will. It may not be due to anything you or I say or do, but he listens to Capt. Jim and he's a devout Christian."

"How does Father act around Mom?"

"I think you'll be pleasantly surprised. He usually avoids being there when I visit. But when he's near Mom, he unwinds and relaxes. He has an office in her house, but he spends most of the time by her side even if he's on the phone."

Ellie absent-mindedly tapped her foot against the floor. "Tell me about Mom. There's so much I've either forgotten or never knew about her."

Terrance rubbed the back of his neck. "She was a teenager when she and dad met. Her father was in the oil business, and Dad was his personal pilot. They got married when she was eighteen, and Dad is ten years older than her. They had me when she was twenty and you when she was thirty."

"How did her parents feel about her marrying so young?"

"At first, they opposed it, and from what I understand it caused quite a stir. Her family was rather involved in New Orleans social circles--Mom a debutante, the belle of every ball."

"What does she look like now?"

Terrance stared out the window as if searching for the right words. "Mom is beautiful, as always. She simply looks like she's asleep."

"What about her hair?"

"Long and wavy--auburn like yours, with a few strands of gray. Dad won't allow it cut, thinking she'll wake up and be upset her hair is different." He shook his head.

"Does she know when you speak to her?" Ellie pressed her lips together.

"The doctors don't know the full extent of what people actually sense when they're in a coma, but I speak to her as if she can hear."

"How should I act when we get there?"

He pulled her close to him. "Any way you want to. This trip is for you. If you don't want to say or do anything, you don't have to."

Ellie sat in silence and rubbed the arm of her seat with her fingertips. "Will Father be upset with me if I say or do the wrong thing?"

"No, and don't worry about his reaction. There's no right or wrong thing to say or do. We discussed this at length, didn't we Dr. Morton?"

"Your dad understands it's normal if you have mixed feelings. It's taking pressure off him to get everything out in the open with you." Dr. Morton smiled.

"Tell me what to expect."

"Mom has the best care. Capt. Jim's wife, Kathy, oversees everything." T cleared his throat. "Mom and Dad were planning to build this beach house before the accident, so he had it built to her specifications, adjusting for the medical amenities she'd need."

"What does the house look like?" Ellie asked.

"The house is pink, Mom's favorite color, trimmed in white and mint green. It's three stories, lots of windows with ocean views, patios and verandas on all sides."

"What's in the house? I mean if she's never gained consciousness what does she need besides medical stuff?" Ellie shrugged.

"Understand--Dad's been in denial about Mom's condition. He convinced himself she'd wake up one day, and everything would be the same as it was before the accident. When you first enter the house, you are in a grand ballroom of sorts, for entertaining. There sits Mom's Steinway. He has the staff play it, thinking if she hears her own piano--she'll wake up."

"The same Steinway that was at our estate in Huntington?" Ellie grasped his arm.

"The same one. And he took other things from Huntington, including your books, toys, and pictures."

"What? All those things that disappeared after the accident are with Mom." Ellie clutched her arms to her chest.

"Yes, I'm making you aware of this now--I don't want you to be alarmed when you walk in and see your things, as well as Mom's." Terrance forced a smile. "But right now, we better get buckled and ready to land. We're nearly there."

The short walk from the landing pad to the beach house seemed like miles. A brisk ocean breeze flung Ellie's hair into her face and seemed to be pushing her with each step she took. She felt unsteady--not sure what to expect or how the moments might unfold. Terrance tucked her hand into the crook of his arm as if escorting her to a grand ball--her father stepped to her other side. Were they trying to protect her or force her to move forward? As they approached the entrance, she looked over her shoulder, knowing Jesse and Dr. Morton were close by. Would the numbness go away? Would she be able to speak? What would she say?

When they stepped into the foyer, Kathy, Capt. Jim's wife greeted them. "Good morning. You must be Eloree." She smiled, her dark blue eyes locked on Ellie's. "You look so much like your mother."

"Good morning," Ellie whispered, not sure if a sound came out. Terrance made the introductions--then led the way to a sitting area. Everything looked as Terrance described--portraits, artwork and, décor—all familiar to Ellie. She sat on a sofa with Terrance by her side, taking it all in.

"Please let us know if you need anything. There'll be refreshments and a buffet in the dining room throughout the day."

"Thank you, Kathy. I'll show everyone around the house."

"Where's Father?" Ellie stood on trembling legs.

"He's gone on into Mrs. Evan's room." Kathy smiled.

"Terrance, why's it taking so long for me to get to see Mom?" Ellie steadied herself, with one hand on the back of the chair.

"You can see her when you're ready. No one's pushing you or holding you back--it's up to you."

"I want to go now."

"Okay, Mom's room is over this way." Terrance took her arm.

As they stepped toward the hallway, Ellie glanced over her shoulder and stopped. "I want Jesse and Dr. Morton to come."

Jesse and Dr. Morton followed a few paces behind. Terrance tried to make small talk, but Ellie remained rigidly quiet. Until they stopped at the doorway of a spacious, impeccably decorated room. It was exactly as Ellie remembered her mother's bedroom before the accident, with fresh flowers, the lingering smell of Mama's perfume, the hand-painted family portrait.

Father looked up, with a pleasant smile. "Come in. We've been waiting for you, Eloree. Say good morning to your mother."

Ellie had no words. All she could do was cling to

Terrance's arm and stare. The burning lump in her throat expanded into her whole being. Her temples pounded, her knees felt like rubber, and her stomach quaked. The beautiful woman sleeping on the bed was her mother. A pink bow, matching her lacy gown, held her long auburn tresses in a side ponytail. The slippers on her feet resembled ballet slippers. A simple, gold wedding band adorned her slender finger, and a diamond pendant lay against her chest. Though frail and small, it seemed she should open her eyes or say something.

"Do you want to go on in?" Terrance asked.

Ellie shook her head. "Not yet."

"Tell me when you're ready." Terrance motioned to a floral print couch.

Jesse sat beside Ellie and took her hand. Dr. Morton placed a hand on Ellie's shoulder. Ellie drew in her bottom lip and as she watched Terrance. "Good morning, Mom. You're looking beautiful as always." He kissed her cheek--then held his cheek against hers. "We have visitors today. Eloree's here and she's brought two friends. We're looking forward to spending the day with you here at the beach."

Their father proceeded to open the blinds, giving way to a full view of the ocean, allowing the brightness to fill the room. "Eloree, is there anything you'd like to say?" Her father's tone was unusually calm and inviting.

Ellie closed her eyes and shook her head, not sure if she would ever have the courage to take another step closer to the bedside. She had no words to say to her father—mother--or anyone. She couldn't think, and the silence was her ally. The world stopped spinning, but she felt caught in a perpetual vacuum.

She realized Jesse was whispering something and leaned closer. "Jesus, Jesus."

Her mind reeled--like being under the bed during the storm when all they could do was call on the name of Jesus.

Her father took a seat in a wing chair on the other side of her mother's bed. He pulled a book from the bedside stand as if busying himself. Terrance came back and knelt in front of Ellie. "Remember, this day is all about you and your feelings. Nothing has to happen until you're ready."

"When will Father leave the room?"

"We can ask him to leave any time--if you want him to."

"I want to speak with her alone."

"Alone? Are you sure?"

"Yes." Ellie sat straighter.

"All right then. We'll all step out, but if it's okay, I'll be right outside the door."

When the others left, Ellie inched closer and took a seat on a brocade side chair by the bed. A Bible lay on a stand nearby and Ellie turned to the dedication page. *To my loving wife—Dalaina Delle DuPree Evan on your twenty-first birthday. Forever yours, Walton.* Blue crayon marks littered the page—Ellie remembered making the marks--instead of being angry, her mother had said it was *added love.*

She put the Bible back on the shelf--stroked her mom's hand and tried to remember the last time they'd touched. Her fingertips grazed the ends of her mother's hair. Ellie didn't say anything or even cry. She wasn't sure what she felt, but emotions came from all angles—though none made sense, except the faint peace that seemed to be growing stronger with each passing minute.

Ellie leaned closer. "Hey, Mama. It's me, Eloree. I know you remember me, even though you're asleep. I want you to wake up today, but if you can't, I understand. There's so much I want to tell you." She reminisced through the events of her childhood, brought up things she remembered from her few short years with her mother, added details of places she'd traveled and things she'd done. Tears streamed down her cheeks, dripping onto the side of the bed.

"Oh Mama, I'm trying to make it all sound like I've had a wonderful life, but I haven't. I've missed you so much, and Father didn't tell me where you were. It's not my fault I haven't been with you. You wouldn't have wanted it this way if you could've spoken. He's been unfair to you and me. I'll forgive him--I hope you can, too. Today, we begin our new life. Dad, Terrance, you, and I are together again--a family."

꧁29꧂

Soul Search

As the hour passed, Ellie knew Terrance waited outside the door.

She motioned to him. "Look what I found on Mom's bookshelf. *Althea Spineeta with Curls in Her Hair.*" She clutched the book to her chest. "This was my favorite book, and Mom read it to me every day. She said I'd be able to read to her one day. Today, I did."

Terrance placed his hand on Ellie's shoulder. "I'm glad you found the book. Are you okay?"

"I suppose." She closed her eyes.

"It's time for Mom's therapy. She'll be tied up for about two hours. Let's go check on the others and get some lunch."

The five sat around the ornate table, but Ellie had little to say. She moved shrimp and fresh strawberries around on her plate but paid little attention to the conversation between the others. As the meal ended, Terrance turned to her. "Would you like a grand tour of the house?"

She thought for a long moment. "First I need to clear my head. Do you suppose Jesse and I could go for a walk on the beach?"

"Sounds like a perfect idea," Terrance answered. "Dr. Stephanie, could I interest you in a walk along the beach? Let's meet back here in an hour and regroup."

Jesse and Ellie slipped off their shoes, rolled up their jeans, and walked across the sand to the water's edge. "Let's go up the beach this way." Ellie pointed. "I don't want to follow Terrance and Dr. Morton."

Jesse took her hand as they started up the shoreline. "I'm proud of you."

She hugged his arm and rested her head on his shoulder

as tears streamed down her cheeks--followed by gentle sobs. The ocean breeze raked her hair across her face--the sounds of the surf and gulls mingled in her head. Finally, she spoke. “Seems like I cry all the time, but I’ll get through this. I know I will. It’ll just take some time, that’s all.”

“I’m glad I’m here with you.” He stopped and wrapped his arms around her.

“I need this time with you, away from the others.”

For the rest of the hour, they walked along the beach, mostly in silence with only the cry of the seagulls, the roaring tide, and the wind on their faces. Ellie had come to appreciate the way Jesse willingly held her, allowed her to cry, not forcing her to talk or trying to find solutions.

~~~~~

Once they returned, Terrance and Father showed Ellie through the house. Dr. Morton and Jesse were invited along. As they passed through hallways flanked with portraits and memorabilia of her mother’s life, Ellie asked questions and stared at the items to get a glimpse into her mother’s past. She’d been a beauty queen, preparing to enter the Miss Louisiana pageant, when she met Ellie’s dad. Pictures of their wedding made her father smile as he reflected on the grandeur of the event.

In another room, Ellie saw equestrian trophies. “What’s all this?”

“Dalaina loved spending time at the stables. Nothing made her happier than caring for the horses alongside the stable hands—getting them ready to show.” Her father pointed out. “Over here are awards she won for growing roses. Couldn’t keep her from always trying to do the gardener’s job. She loved to dig in the dirt.”

As the tour ended, they returned to the area her father referred to as the Grand Ball Room. Ellie’s eyes fixed on the Steinway. “Would you like to play your mother’s piano?” her father asked as the group was seated.

Ellie stared at the piano, remembering how her mother played it and held her on her lap--allowing her to pound the keys. “I’d like to play, but I’ll wait for Mom.” She took a seat beside Jesse.

“I’ll check on Dalaina.” Her father excused himself from the group.

A member of the staff accompanied him back to the ballroom, pushing her mother in a reclining wheelchair. Dressed
~~~~~

in a yellow gown, and her long auburn hair fell in ringlets about her shoulders--her facial features accented with touches of makeup and pink lipstick. Her hands were folded in her lap as if waiting for the concert to begin.

Ellie stared for the longest time before she stepped to the piano. As she began to play, she looked at her mother and said, "Mama, the name of this beautiful song is *Living with a Broken Heart*." She held back tears as her fingers glided across the keyboard. The melody simple, the playing tender, but the notes sounded alive and hovered around her head as she played. Such sadness and loss. The heartbreaking sound. She swayed slightly as each melody was answered by another. As she lifted her hands from the piano, a tear escaped, falling to the keys.

When the number was finished, Ellie looked at her mom. "Mom, this has become one of my favorite songs. Few people have ever heard me play it, but it makes me happy to play it for you. This song brings hope and encouragement to me when I'm feeling down. I know you'll like it, and I hope you can hear the words I sing."

The sounds of the magnificent instrument echoed throughout the house, as members of the staff stopped what they were doing and congregated in the hallways. Chorus after chorus and verse after verse, Ellie belted the words to *In the Midst*. The more she played, the more intriguing each stanza became.

Again, she looked at her beautiful, silent mother. Her father held her mother's hand, his arm propped beside her shoulders. "Mom, this song is my surprise for you. You chose it for your wedding, so many years ago and as part of my name. I love this song, too, and only dream I'll play it as splendidly as you." Ellie closed her eyes and her hands flowed across the keys, as *Fur Elise* came to life.

Ellie stood--her audience mesmerized by the magnitude of the performance. But she rushed to her mother's side, knelt. "Mama, did you hear me?" Ellie waited for any sign of consciousness. But Her mother's frail body remained unmoved.

"Dalaina, I'm so glad you were here for Eloree's concert this afternoon. She certainly has your touch." Her father stroked her mother's hair.

Ellie continued to stare into her mother's expressionless face. Maybe in one more minute, she would move or answer.

"Your mother and I are very proud of you, Eloree. We've never heard a more moving performance." Her father reached his hand toward hers.

Ellie couldn't hold back her own tears as she clutched his

hand. "She may not have heard me, but you did, and I love you, Dad."

"I love you, too." He moved to Ellie's side. Their arms locked in an embrace. He kissed her cheek. "You're the most remarkable daughter a father could ever have."

"Thank you," she breathed, feeling a rush of emotions that brought a smile to her face.

He let go and followed the attendants as they wheeled Ellie's mother away. Terrance stepped to Ellie's side along with Dr. Morton and Jesse. "You gave it your all, little sister."

"Beautiful, Ellie. Simply beautiful," Dr. Morton wiped tears from her own cheek.

Ellie reached for Jesse and burrowed her head against his shoulder. With no words spoken--he wrapped his arms around her shoulders, and they clung to each other.

~~~~~

As the afternoon wore on, Dr. Morton and Jesse sat on the veranda, leaving Ellie alone with Terrance and her dad. They gathered around her mother's bed--the first time the four had been together as a family in thirteen years. The moment seemed dreamlike to Ellie, and when Kathy came to arrange for the next session of her mother's care, they moved to their father's study.

For the first time, Ellie didn't feel overwhelmed by intimidation as she and Terrance faced their father.

"Eloree, I assume this's been an overwhelming day for you," he began as if this was going to become a one-sided lecture. Then, he cleared his throat and softened his tone. "Today, I'm going to share my plans with the two of you. I'm not seeking re-election. Instead, I'll live here permanently--be close when Dalaina needs me."

"What does this mean for Ellie?" Terrance looked first at his father and then Ellie.

"Eloree, what would you like? You're welcome to live here with your mother and me. Now that you're twenty-one, you're an integral stakeholder in the family businesses and finances."

Ellie's heart raced in her chest. "With all due respect, Sir, I have little interest in business and finance. I might see things differently at some point, but please excuse me from those responsibilities."

"Very well, would you like to live here?"

Ellie closed her eyes, searching for the right words. Terrance placed his hand over hers. "No one's putting pressure on
~~~~~

you."

"In light of everything, I'd prefer to visit here often, yet not make this my permanent home. This house is a perfect place for Mom—it brings back memories." She stopped, knowing from experience--to never say too much at one time.

Terrance cut his eyes at her and winked.

"You see, Jesse's family has an old cabin on the mountain with quite a collection of heirlooms." She went on, "When they spend time there, they reconnect with their heritage. It gives them a place of *Penial*."

"*Penial*?" Terrance almost laughed. "You mean a place for a personal encounter with God like Jacob in the Old Testament?"

She nodded and slid closer to the edge of her seat. "I'm pleased all these heirlooms from our family are here. I need this to be a special place where I come, but I don't want to live here."

"Would you like a condo? Or a music studio?" her father peered over the rim of his glasses.

Ellie shook her head. "Not right now. I've never lived alone, and I'm not ready to. As for a music studio, I don't want to be tied down to the point I can't visit Mother and you often."

"That's noble, but where do you want to live?"

Ellie looked at the floor before meeting his stare. "With Jesse's family," she answered, in a hushed tone.

She felt her father studying her--his fingertips pressed together in front of his face. "Terrance and I need to discuss this." His jaw twitched.

"No more secrets, Dad." Terrance moved closer to Ellie and put his arm around her shoulders.

Her father walked to the window and turned his back. Ellie felt like a hot brick smashed in her stomach. She started to stand, but Terrance motioned for her to stay.

"If you have something to say—say it to Ellie's face,"

"Now that everything's out in the open, I hoped she'd have higher expectations for herself than to shovel horse manure." Her father lifted a brow—as though he meant to be amusing.

Ellie flinched. "Don't speak as though I'm not in the room—I'm not a little girl."

"Dad. Ellie." Terrance held up both hands. "I remember Mom loved caring for the horses--and digging alongside the gardener-- taking care of her own flowers."

"You'll soon tire of living among commoners." Her father unbuttoned his cuffs and rolled up his sleeves.

"Come on, Dad. You know the story of Miss Dalaina Delle

DuPree, the beautiful New Orleans debutante who fell in love with Capt. Walton Andrew Evan, the Vietnam War hero." Terrance lowered his voice and stepped closer to their father. "I think Jesse is a class act, and I admire the way he treats Ellie like a lady."

"He should treat her well. I sent him a ten-thousand-dollar reward."

"Jesse still has the check and doesn't intend to cash it." Ellie stepped closer and met her father's eyes. "His family's not driven by money."

"Then find happiness." Her father placed his arms around her and pulled her close.

She wrapped her arms around his waist and clung to him—her head against his chest. She didn't need to pull away or fear he'd desert her ever again. "I love you, Daddy."

"I love you, too. But I have one request. Your mother and I need to call you Eloree. To the rest of the world, you can be Ellie—but to us, you'll always be Eloree. And promise you'll visit often and bring all your friends."

"Sure Dad." She kissed his cheek and smiled up at him.

"And to answer one more of your questions—I do love God." He placed his forehead against hers. "I've lived a miserable thirteen years. I've reeled in bitterness and hated myself. Will you both forgive me and give me another chance to be a godly father?"

Terrance stepped beside Ellie and placed one arm around her shoulders and the other around his father's. She leaned against her brother as she watched tears stream down her father's face.

~~~~~

As the day ended, Ellie sat by her mother's bedside as her father led the group in prayer. "Heavenly Father, I'm thankful for Your amazing grace and abundant peace. God, it's our desire to walk with Dalaina here on earth, but we know we'll walk with her one day in heaven. In Jesus name, Amen."

Ellie didn't want the moment to end. She sang *Amazing Grace* and the others joined in. She ended with the refrain *Praise God, Praise God* taking both her parents' hands in hers.
~~~~~

30

Peace

Ellie stared at her reflection in the mirror. This was the day of her concert at *Meadow Laurel*, and the events of the past few weeks replayed in her mind. Life had changed, bringing closure to the issues with her father and the family secrets. Most of all, she felt content with what she had learned about God and the freedom to be the person He created her to become.

Knowing her mother was alive, even though she couldn't respond, gave Ellie peace and contentment. She visited her mother at least once a week, and each visit became a little easier than the last. In between, she visited Meadow Laurel. Time spent with Dr. Morton, Misty, Juniper, and the other girls brought a sense of belonging--a circle of friends, bonded by the love of music.

Ellie often spoke of her mother to Dr. Morton and Misty. Like Dr. Shanks had assumed the role of a mother in Ellie's life after the storm, now Dr. Morton became like a sister in the aftermath of finding out about her mother. Visits with her were simple, not in-depth therapeutic sessions riddled with medical jargon, but long talks and walks in the garden.

As Ellie shared her feelings with Dr. Morton, she realized how healing music had always been in her life, especially the songs she played and sang for her mother. For this reason, she accepted the invitation to host a concert at Meadow Laurel, sharing songs dearest to her heart. Preparing for the concert had already been great therapy.

~~~~~

The guests would arrive in less than an hour, and she was
~~~~~

applying the finishing touches to her hair and makeup. Judy Ann helped her choose the right outfit--a simple dress made of ivory lace with a jewel neckline, making the ruby necklace the perfect accessory. Lacy ruffles accented the raglan sleeves and, the full skirt draped gracefully over the edge of the piano stool when Ellie was seated--falling just below her knees when she stood. From having been on stage before, she knew it was the perfect dress for this concert.

The fifty seats in the Laurel Dome would be filled with those Ellie invited--along with the girls residing at Meadow Laurel. Jesse helped her finish writing the song she started while on Gabby Mountain, naming it Peaceful Harmony.

~~~~~

Spending time with Jesse had become a way of life. Ellie loved working around the stables, tossing hay with a pitchfork and caring for the horses. She hadn't told Jesse about the song *Thinking of You* she'd written about her feelings toward him during her stay at Meadow Laurel. She was waiting until the time was right, and tonight's concert would be the perfect moment.

~~~~~

Ellie was pleased Terrance had arranged to spend time with her before returning to Europe. One Sunday, he and Dr. Morton came to Gabby Mountain, attended church with Jesse and her--then rode horses to the cabin. Terrance and Jesse seemed like old friends, but Ellie hoped he and Dr. Morton would become more than friends.

When Ellie spoke of the way their father had deceived them, Terrance gave her brotherly advice. "God gives the gift of grace, so we can show forgiveness to others. We now choose to forgive Dad instead of being forced to respect him."

Terrance and Dr. Morton suggested Ellie stay in close contact with her father, visiting often and leaving messages if he didn't answer the phone. At first, she found herself half-expecting him to revert to the way things had always been--but with each visit, she became more at ease. And, they laughed when he reminisced about things that happened when she was a child.

Hearing a familiar knock, she pulled on red cowboy boots and stepped to the door. Jesse tipped his black felt cowboy hat. "Miss Ellie, you sure do look pretty. It's my pleasure to be your escort for the evening."

"You look mighty nice yourself, Mr. Jesse." She giggled, as they started down the hallway. He extended his arm, and she slipped her hand into the crook of his elbow. "It's quite an honor to have such a handsome escort. I love your smoke colored shirt, jeans, and cowboy boots."

"Well, *ole'* cowboys like me *ain't* used to such fancy *gatherins*," he teased, with a slow, exaggerated drawl as if they were actors in an old movie.

Ellie giggled, again. "We'll be fine once we get on stage. I'm excited to see Patrick Lee Hebert even though it makes me jittery to think about performing with him in the audience."

"He'll be proud of you."

"I know he will be, but I've never performed numbers I wrote myself. I'm so glad you and I are doing *Gabby Mountain* and *Amazing Grace* together."

"Your songs are close to my heart." Jesse stepped aside, holding the door for Ellie. "Just think, you started *Peaceful Harmony* sitting on a rock on Gabby Mountain."

"It started there, but you helped me finish it. The song belongs to you as much as me. Don't forget--we also wrote *Gabby Mountain* while sitting on the porch of the cabin, watching the sunset."

"Songs are special and so are people. Here come some special people." Jesse waved as his parents came down the hallway, followed by Jenna, Cindi, Ma, and a number of his aunts, uncles, and cousins.

Jesse and Ellie stood near the entrance of the dining room, welcoming each guest. Dr. Link and Judy Ann arrived, followed by Dr. Shanks. Ellie was elated to see her again. "Dr. Shanks, promise you'll come to Gabby Mountain soon."

"When I finish my speaking engagements, I'll be coming to visit you. I've yet to see the cabin on Gabby Mountain."

Adrianna led the group from Happy Hair Fashions, delighted to have Aliyah and Aunt Sheila back on American soil. And Jesse was pleased to see Aiden, and they made quick plans to get together.

Terrance rounded the corner, and Ellie recognized the man with him. "Jesse, this is David Jenkins, the gentleman who helped me out at the gas station." Amid handshakes and how-do-you-do's--Ellie gathered Terrance had contacted him through an online business site, arranging for him and his family to attend.

Ellie peeled her eyes, watching her father walk down the corridor wearing his traditional black suit with a striped tie. But unlike times before, he smiled--happy to be in the company of the man and woman with him. The man was tall with dark hair--he and the woman wore jeans, with embroidered western shirts, and cowboy boots.

Jesse leaned toward Ellie. "Is this some famous country music singer?"

"No, that's Uncle Royce and Aunt Azelia." Ellie waved, as they strolled down the hallway. "Now, my family's here, as well."

Jesse stepped aside as they greeted Ellie with hugs and well wishes.

"Eloree, introduce your Uncle Royce and Aunt Azelia to your beau," her father suggested.

Ellie's eyes sparkled as she made the introduction. "This is Jesse, a horseman from Gabby Mountain. Jesse, meet Aunt Azelia and Uncle Royce—horse ranchers from Texas."

As they stepped away, Jesse asked, "The same uncle who breeds horses for the Olympic Equestrian Team?"

"Yes, and I can't wait for you two to get acquainted."

"I can learn a lot from a fellow like him—and a pretty cowgirl like you." Jesse winked.

Ellie tossed her head. "You're flattering me."

When the others had gone into the dining room, Ellie grabbed Terrance. "Why didn't you tell me they were coming?"

"I knew you'd be thrilled to see them, but I wasn't sure they'd make it and didn't want to dash your hopes. They're staying in Franklin for a few days. Aunt Azelia wants to attend a gem show. Think you can show them around?" Terrance chuckled. "Hey, the guy who just came in the door looks like Ronald Woods, the NASCAR driver."

"Yes, it's Hope and Ronald." Ellie clapped, bringing her hands to her mouth. In a bout of hugs and congratulations, Jesse managed to introduce Terrance and Ronald.

~~~~~

Ellie smiled to herself as she surveyed the group—laughing, talking, mingling. Then, Dr. Morton stepped beside her. "Are you pleased with the way things are turning out?"

"I couldn't be happier, and I'm glad we decided to serve a buffet instead of a sit-down dinner. And our theme, *Peaceful Harmony,* couldn't be more fitting."

"I'm pleased, too. Looks like everyone's here now. You two go visit with them." Dr. Morton waved her hand. "By the way, who's the girl chatting with the lady by the chocolate fountain?"

"That's Adrianna, from Happy Hair Fashions, and Aunt
~~~~~

Azelia. Can't say which one wears the most jewelry, but it looks like they hit it off." Ellie laughed as she and Jesse stepped on into the dining room.

~~~~~

By 7:00, the guests finished dinner and took their seats in the Laurel Dome for the concert. The sinking afternoon sun filtering through the laurel bushes illuminated the room with a welcoming glow.

Ellie and Jesse waited offstage. Ellie's heart surged, and she took a deep breath, slowly releasing it. Jesse put his hand on her shoulder. "Nervous?"

"Yes, and this isn't my first concert or the largest audience, but these are all people I care about. That makes it more special than ever. What if I get emotional?"

Jesse leaned toward her ear. "It'll be great--no matter what happens. All you've got to do is show them how much you love them with your songs."

Dr. Morton took the stage. "Good evening and welcome to the Laurel Dome. I'd like to thank each of you for attending our performance this evening. Miss Eloree Elise Evan will present *Peaceful Harmony*, a collection dear to her heart. As highlighted in your program, some of the selections were written by Miss Evan, demonstrating how God's love brings peace and harmony. This collection will blend past masterpieces--including Beethoven's *Fur Elise,* the old hymn *Amazing Grace,* along with contemporary pieces, and Miss Evan's rendition of bluegrass in *Gabby Mountain*. Without further ado, I present Miss Eloree Elise Evan."

As the applause welcomed Ellie to the stage, she gracefully strolled to the piano, settling into her realm. She and the instrument became one--her fingers danced across the keys bringing *Fur Elise* to life. For an instant, she thought of her mother as her playing brought forth the splendor of Beethoven.

When the applause quieted, Ellie spoke, "I'd like to recognize my friend and mentor Patrick Lee Hebert. His compositions of *Teary* and *Living with a Broken Heart* depict times in our lives when we overcome obstacles," she said. The audience listened with unexplained apprehension. The notes went higher with simple bursts. As the song drifted away, the people began to clap.

Moving to the next number--she paused, playing softly as she spoke, "Mrs. Darlene Woods wrote this song. I've been moved
~~~~~

by *In the Midst.*" Ellie sang, changing keys to accentuate the message of each verse. *Show me who I am, Lord ... In my sorrows and trials ... In life's raging storms ... In my joys and praises ... In my journey every day ... In the midst of it all, I can hear You call ...*

After the last chorus, she transitioned into *Amazing Grace*. Jesse stepped onto the stage, accompanying with the guitar, as he and Ellie sang the Cherokee version of the beloved hymn. They continued playing together, and Ellie invited the audience to sing along. She played with all her heart as the fifty voices blended in unison.

Then, Ellie switched to a bluegrass version, flowing into the melody of *Gabby Mountain*. "This song is for all who call Gabby Mountain home." As they brought the lyrics and melody to life, as the audience clapped along.

As the piece ended, they began playing softly. "And now, I'd like to welcome *Meadow Laurel*'s dance instructor, Misty, to join me for *Peaceful Harmony*." Ellie's voice flowed along with Misty's graceful movements, reflecting the legacy and journey of those gone before. "*Learning how to live in peaceful harmony ... helping those along the way, that's how God wants us to be ...*" As the last refrain ended, the audience rose to their feet with thundering applause.

Jesse stepped backstage and reached for a dozen long-stemmed roses to present to Ellie. Dr. Morton touched his arm. "Wait. Ellie has one more song that's not on the program. You can present her with the roses after this song."

Without explanation Ellie began to sing, her hands gliding across the keys. "*I'm thinking of you ... whether you're near or far away ... you're in my heart always ... I see us on the mountain ... we're walking hand in hand ...*"

Jesse crossed the stage as she finished the final chorus. It took a moment for the audience to realize she'd finished. Again, they were on their feet, with resounding applause.

Ellie stood, her eyes locked with Jesse's as he placed the roses in her arms. "I love you," he said.

"And I love you."

Epilogue

"Mama, tell me a bedtime story," Tiffani begged.

"It's getting late, and I know a little girl who has a big day tomorrow." Ellie smoothed the patchwork quilt over her daughter.

"Will Aunt Stephanie and Uncle Terrance be here before we leave for church?" Tiffani pushed ringlets of auburn hair off her face.

"I hope so, Sweetie. They're flying in with Grandpa Walton, in the morning." Ellie sat on the edge of the bed and took her daughter's hand. "You're such a big girl."

"I'll be seven tomorrow." Tiffani flashed a toothy grin.

Jesse stuck his head in the door. "Who else is having a birthday tomorrow?"

Tiffani bounded out of bed, charging into Jesse's arms. "Daddy, it's your birthday," she squealed as he spun her around and playfully flung her onto the bed.

Ellie stood beside Jesse, wrapping her arms around his waist. "How are we ever going to get her to settle down and go to sleep?"

"I'll tell a bedtime story." Jesse pulled a chair beside the bed.

Winking at Ellie, he leaned closer to their daughter. "Once upon a time, there was a beautiful princess, named Tiffani Dalaina, whose mommy was Princess Eloree Elise."

"And she met you, Daddy." Tiffani giggled. "*You* were her prince, and she was beautiful."

"That's right, and you look just like her."

Tiffani's eyes grew wide. "And she looks like her mama, who's in heaven. She's so special I'm named after her."

Jesse reached for Ellie as tears filled her eyes.

"Don't cry, Mama. I'll sing to you. *Show me who I am Lord ... Oh, be with me ... In the midst of it all - I can hear You call.*"

What readers are saying:

This book showcases the beautiful Appalachian mountain range. And the highland people I grew up with. The characters feel like people I know. The story is entertaining while still making you consider your beliefs, your own hang-ups, and challenges in a new light. Debra Jenkins is a new voice to watch. The story is refreshing, uplifting and very well constructed. ~ Lisa

I loved this book and could hardly put it down. The author's descriptions are so vivid, it made me want to visit Gabby Mountain, go buy a *Navè* bag, and meditate to the sounds of the beautiful music she wrote about. The book is not only filled with adventure, but also lots of wisdom. I loved the themes of forgiveness and redemption. I think anyone would enjoy this book and benefit from the positive message. This is definitely the best book I have read in many years, and I highly recommend it for both entertainment and inspiration. ~ Scotty

I thoroughly enjoyed this book. I felt like I 'flowed' through it. I saw it played out in my head. But the story is all of ours. God finds us broken and afraid; and slowly, lovingly begins to mold the pieces together purifying us, healing us as He does! ~ Renee

This is a wonderful book which shares a great story of family, friends, and God's great love. It is written so that the ending has a surprise. Recommend for all. ~ Judy

Awesome read! Shows how God can help us through life's problems! The description of the area and the characters made me feel as if I was there! ~Glenda

This was one of the best books I have ever read. It was very well written, and I could picture myself there in the mountains. Very uplifting to read a book that reminds us of God's presence in everything. I hope the author writes another book soon.
~ Barbara